Fanning the Flames

The Women of *Beowulf*
Book Two

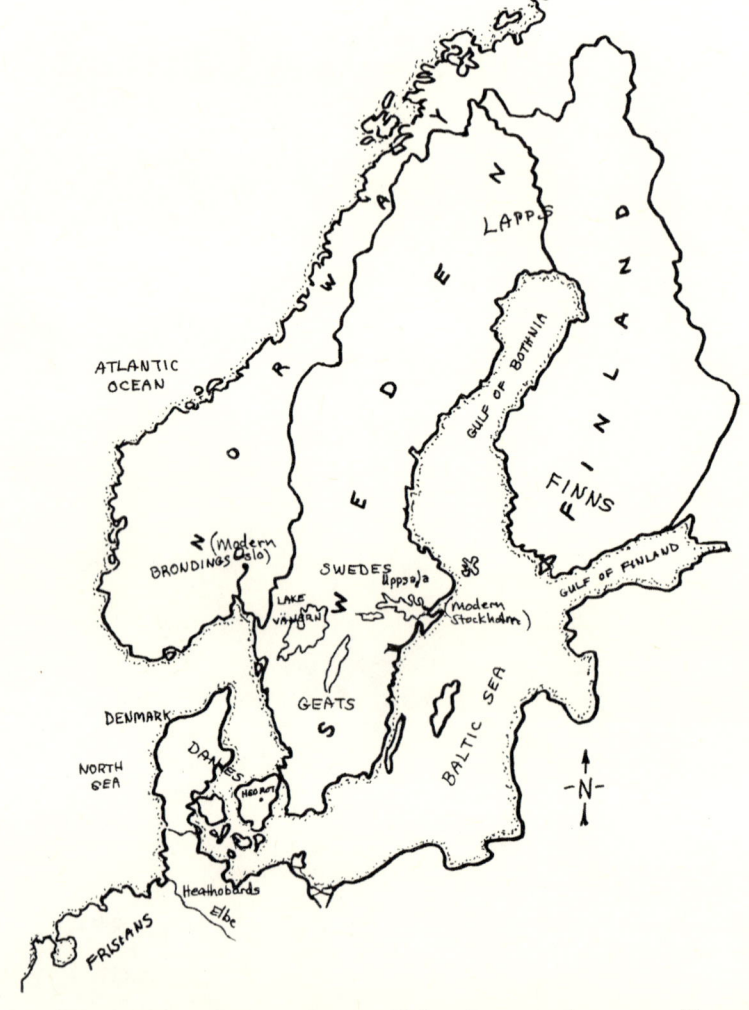

Tribal locations in the time of Beowulf placed on a modern map of Scandinavia *(from Osborn 1983 after Klaeber, emended 1993).*

Fanning the Flames

The Women of *Beowulf*
Book Two

Donnita L. Rogers

Baqwyn Books

Tempe, Arizona
2014

Published by Bagwyn Books, an imprint of the Arizona Center for Medieval and Renaissance Studies (ACMRS), Tempe, Arizona.

© 2014 Donnita L. Rogers
All Rights Reserved.

For Don, who always listens.

Contents

Chapter 1	A Rocky Welcome	1
Chapter 2	Lost in Frisia	17
Chapter 3	Blood Bond	33
Chapter 4	Hrethelskeep	51
Chapter 5	Neighbors and Ghosts	69
Chapter 6	Clearing the Way	83
Chapter 7	Face to Face	99
Chapter 8	Missing	113
Chapter 9	Invitations	129
Chapter 10	Circle of Stone	141
Chapter 11	Catching the Pizzle	157
Chapter 12	Child of Ingeld	171
Chapter 13	Rings and Riddles	189
Chapter 14	A Winter's Journey	203
Chapter 15	Uppsala	219
Chapter 16	Putting to Rest	239
Chapter 17	Battle on the Ice	253
Chapter 18	Return to Eaglesgard	271
Chapter 19	Hammer of Death	291
Chapter 20	Breath of the Dragon	319
Chapter 21	Facing the Future	339

Acknowledgments

For continued inspiration, information and professional advice, I thank Marijane Osborn, *Beowulf* translator and scholar at University of California, Davis.

I also owe a debt of gratitude to retired schoolmaster Jan Ekborg of Bohuslän, Sweden, who shared his home with me and personally took me to visit relevant historical sites.

My thanks to Louisiana Quaker friend Marty Vidrine for the loan of personal materials on Finnish history and culture.

My thanks also to Dr. Rolf Engel of Arden Hills, Minnesota, for sharing his medical expertise and obstetrical textbooks.

To Barbara Henwood in the computer lab at Northfield Senior Center, Northfield, Minnesota, and to Carl Henry of Northfield, my thanks for assistance in matters electronic.

To the reference librarians at St. Olaf College, Northfield, Minnesota, my thanks for guiding me to needed research materials.

My thanks to Cassie Warholm-Wohlenhaus, archivist at the American Swedish Institute in Minneapolis, Minnesota, for research assistance.

I am grateful for permission from Oxford University Press to use 32 lines of "Aino's Lament" from *The Kalevala* translated by Bosley (1999)

To all my former students at Kingwood High School in Kingwood, Texas, my gratitude for your enthusiastic embrace of *Beowulf*, a timeless classic.

Finally, my ongoing gratitude to my partner, editor and sometimes co-author, Don, whose discerning ear and timely suggestions have saved me from error and given impetus to my work. Thank you for your love and patience.

A Note on Translations

For passages in the novel quoted or paraphrased from *Beowulf* I have drawn upon three translations: that of Seamus Heaney (Farrar, Straus & Giroux, NY 2000), Marijane Osborn (University of California Press, Berkeley and Los Angeles 1983) and Burton Raffel (New American Library, NY 1963).

Guide to Pronunciation

DANES

Aeschere	= ASH-heruh
Freawaru	= FRAY-uh-WAH-roo
	(Initial H before R is sounded)
Hrethric	= HRETH-rick
Hrothgar	= HROTH-gar
Hrothmund	= HROTH-mund
Hrothulf	= HROTH-ulf
Unferth	= UN-ferth
Wulfgar	= WOLF-gar
Wealtheow	= WAY-ul-THAY-oh

GEATS

Beowulf	= BAY-oh-wolf
Ecgtheow	= EDGE-thay-oh
Hygelac	= HIG-uh-lack
Hygd	= HIG
Hrethel	= HRETH-ull

SWEDES

Ongentheow	= On-GEN-thay-oh
Othere	= OH-ther
Onela	= Oh-NAY-luh
Eanmund	= EN-mund
Eadgils	= ED-gils

Illustrations

Note: Illustrations are copies of pictures from ancient artifacts, drawn by the author

Ch. 1 Cargo ship (reconstructed) from Skuldelev, Denmark, in the Viking Ship Museum, Roskilde
Ch. 2 Helmeted head of a warrior found in Sigtuna, Sweden
Ch. 3 Harp-lyre (reconstructed) from ship burial in Sutton Hoo, England c. 600 A.D.
Ch. 4 Royal bed from a ship burial in Norway
Ch. 5 Whalebone board from Norway used to smooth or pleat dresses with a glass ball as an iron
Ch. 6 Bronze keys to Viking-age storage chests, worn on a belt by the mistress of the farm, from Rogaland, Norway
Ch. 7 Decoration on a rune stone from Lund, in Skåne, Sweden, c. 1000A.D.
Ch. 8 Bronze age lur horn found at Tellerup on Funen, Denmark
Ch. 9 Gold bracteates, ornamentation based on Roman-inspired medallions or decorated with a representation of Odin. 5th–6th century A.D.
Ch. 10 Icelandic pendant of a Norse woman, 14th century
Ch. 11 Fighting stallions. Detail from a picture stone, Hablingko, Götland, Sweden c. 500 A.D.
Ch. 12 Tiny bronze fertility figure. Late Bronze age, possibly representing Freyja. Raised hand suggests goddess driving a chariot
Ch. 13 Mask on a gravestone dedicated to a man who fell "when kings fought"
Ch. 14 Design from a picture stone found in Uppsala, Sweden, c. 700 A.D.
Ch. 15 Swedish tapestry depicting the gods Odin, Thor and Freyr, 12th century
Ch. 16 Bronze amulet representing a priest of the cult of Odin, c. 800 A.D.
Ch. 17 Great iron battle axe inlaid with silver wire from Mammen, Jutland, Denmark
Ch. 18 Detail of a carving on a wagon in the Oseberg ship burial
Ch. 19 Charm from Iceland depicting Thor gripping his hammer, 11th century
Ch. 20 Dragon head belt end mount of bronze gilt, found at Vendel, Uppland, Sweden, c. 600 A.D.
Ch. 21 Mervalla stone in Södermanland, Sweden, commemorating a fallen warrior

GENEALOGIES

1. THE ROYAL HOUSE OF THE GEATS

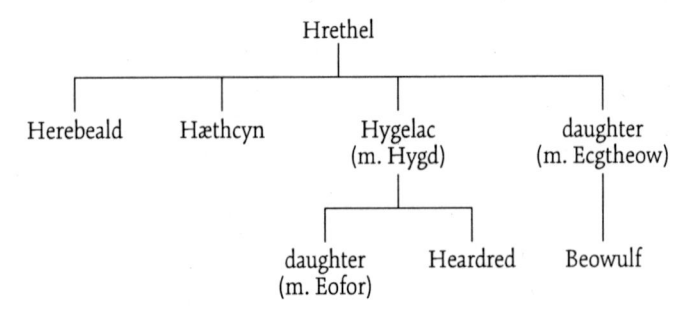

Hrethel
- Herebeald
- Hæthcyn
- Hygelac (m. Hygd)
  - daughter (m. Eofor)
  - Heardred
- daughter (m. Ecgtheow)
  - Beowulf

2. THE ROYAL HOUSE OF THE DANES (SCYLDINGS)

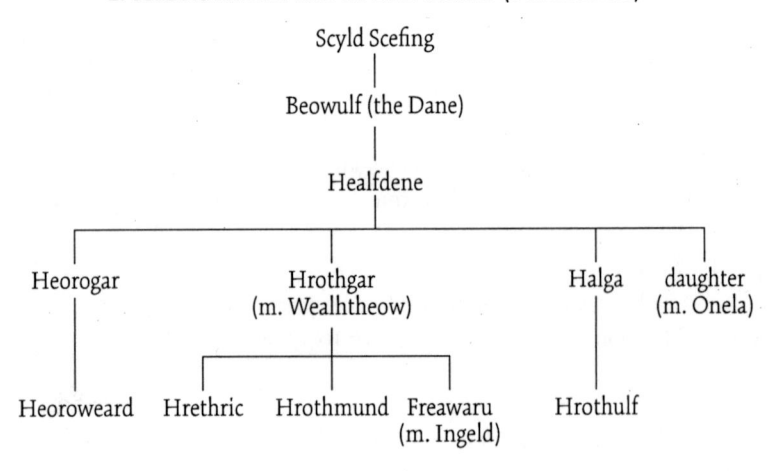

Scyld Scefing
- Beowulf (the Dane)
  - Healfdene
    - Heorogar
      - Heoroweard
    - Hrothgar (m. Wealhtheow)
      - Hrethric
      - Hrothmund
      - Freawaru (m. Ingeld)
    - Halga
      - Hrothulf
    - daughter (m. Onela)

3. THE ROYAL HOUSE OF THE SWEDES (SCYLFINGS)

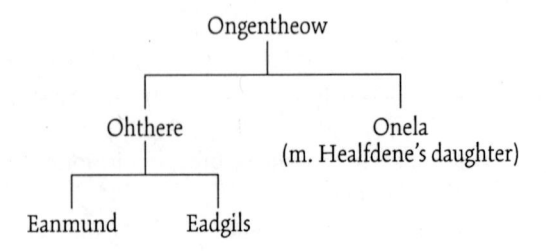

Ongentheow
- Ohthere
  - Eanmund
  - Eadgils
- Onela (m. Healfdene's daughter)

Chapter One
A Rocky Welcome

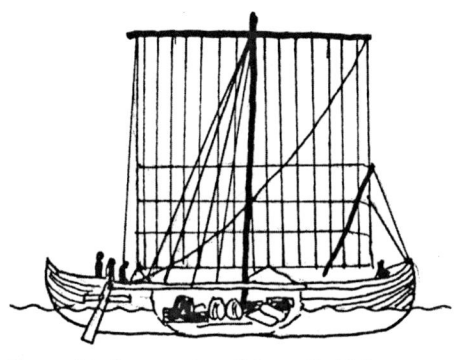

Cargo ship (reconstructed) from Skuldelev, Denmark, in the Viking Ship Museum, Roskilde.

Strong winds whipped at the sail and stung my face as I opened my eyes from an uneasy slumber. Curled in the ship's stern on a packet of sealskins, I'd been lulled to sleep by the motion of the waves. Now I sat up, yawned, and stretched. My shawl felt damp with salt spray. High above me the sun had disappeared, obscured by clouds in a darkening sky.

"Awake, are you? Seems I'm the only one who can't sleep."

Ana's face came into focus beside me. She gestured toward the other women, nodding where they sat: Ragnhild, Ingeborg, and Estrid perched on chests, Brita leaning against a grain sack with her mouth open, snoring too lightly to be heard above the wind and waves.

Our men, however, were upright and alert: Wulfgar in the bow keeping lookout, Thorkel at the tiller, Olaf, Gorm and Saxe handling the sheets for the sail. Each wore a look of grim satisfaction, with good reason. Had we not escaped with our lives and left Hrothulf lying senseless back in Heorot? Unless...

"Ana, have we been pursued? Any sign of another ship?"

She shook her head with certainty. "No, I think we're safe — at last."

"Perhaps."

Despite a lingering mixture of fear and doubt, my heart momentarily rose within me, light as the gulls spiraling about the mast. Unfortunately so did a wave of nausea. I grabbed for the ship's rail and gripped it tightly until the feeling subsided. Ana laid her hand on my shoulder.

"Freaw, is it . . . ?"

I smiled weakly and nodded reassurance. The baby? Yes, no doubt the baby, Ingeld's baby. Suddenly his dying face rose before me, my husband's once-handsome face so ruined by fire and sword. *Not now. I can't think of him now. Now we must find a new homeland!* Resolutely I pulled my shawl closer about me.

"Wulfgar!" I shouted to make myself heard. "Can we reach Beowulf's kingdom before nightfall?"

"No, my lady. Against this wind it will be another day's sail, by my reckoning. The coast ahead is treacherous, with reefs and submerged rocks along the shore, but we'll land soon and make camp for the night."

Wulfgar's profile against the lowering clouds matched the face carved on the prow of our ship: squinting eyes, a sharp beak of a nose and fierce whiskers.

We are in good hands with Wulfgar. He served my father faithfully, and now serves me as leader of our small band — at least for now. Soon I will take charge — when we reach Geatland and set up our own court.

As if divining my thoughts, Wulfgar turned, but only to shout orders.

"Sail down! Oars out and row for the shore!"

Olaf dropped the heavy woolen sail with its bold red stripes, then sprang to join Gorm and Saxe at the oar holes. My women, muttering and yawning, shook themselves awake and took their places beside the men. They put their shoulders to the work, pulling on the oars with backs straining. Brita smiled, as if enjoying the task. Perhaps she was recalling that long-ago trip to Moon Cliff when she and I had been companions, just two young girls on an adventure instead of mistress and slave.

Ana and I stood, peering toward shore, eager to set our cold feet on dry land. My old delight in being on board a ship had fled, replaced by a heaviness devoid of feeling. *What is wrong with me? Sailing used to feel like flying!*

As we rounded a rocky headland, the pungent scent of evergreens filled my nostrils. I breathed in deeply, glad for its invigorating effect. *I will need all my strength and fortitude in the days ahead.*

In fading light we made landfall with difficulty, our craft creaking and sliding around huge boulders that stuck up like whales in the swirling surf. Making light of the slippery footing, the younger men waded ashore first to tie ropes to the nearest trees. Then they waded back with these lines to guide the rest of us. By the time we had all reached the rocky beach, we were wet to the skin and trembling with cold.

"Get a fire going, lads, so our women can cook up something hot!"

Wulfgar was grinning as if enjoying a great adventure.

"Tents first," I shot back, "so we women can get into dry clothes. Food later."

Much later, huddled around a smoking fire with hot food in our bellies, we took stock of our situation.

"Nothing but rocks and trees," observed Ana. "Do people really live in such country?" She was wrapped in so many shawls she looked like a bale of cargo.

"They do," said Thorkel. He poked at the fire with a long stick, causing a glowing log to fall and sending up sparks that briefly illuminated the faces in the circle.

"My uncle had a small farm in a valley where he'd cleared out the rocks to plant rye and barley. Most of the time, though, he fished or hunted s-s-s-seals."

"Was he part of Beowulf's settlement, or rather, Hygelac's?"

Wulfgar's steady voice woke me to my own concerns. Before Thorkel could answer, I rose from my place of honor at the head of the circle and addressed the group.

"What do we know of this Hygelac? Did Beowulf talk about him during his stay at Heorot?"

Saxe stopped picking his teeth and snorted. "Among our men he talked of little else. 'Hygelac did this, Hygelac said that' — it was the name most on his lips."

"It is fitting that a thane should give honor to his lord," said Wulfgar quietly, leaning toward the fire. "As I remember, Beowulf asked that his weapons and armor be sent back to Hygelac should he not survive the fight with the Grendel monster."

As if in approval, the fire flamed higher. Now Olaf, seated next to Wulfgar, rose, his face working strangely. He pulled off his cap and twisted it as he spoke.

"I remember Beowulf telling King Hrothgar"—here he paused as if choking back a sob—"telling the king that if the Danes were ever attacked, he'd come to our aid with a thousand armed Geats, a thousand warriors! I wonder..." his voice trailed off as he sank back down, this time beside me.

"You wonder if Hygelac's forces number so many," concluded Wulfgar gravely. "I have wondered about that myself." I touched Olaf's shoulder briefly and nodded in recognition of our shared sorrow. There had been little time for mourning since my father's passing. In the flickering firelight Olaf's face looked as young as... Hrethric's. Another pang of loss assailed me, but I pushed it aside. This was no time to give way to grief. I turned toward our circle.

"Wulfgar, what do you know of the Geats?"

He rose, cleared his throat and turned to face me.

"My lady, they have a reputation for fierce fighting. I have heard that in earlier times in their feud with the Swedes, Hygelac and his men killed the Swedish king Ongentheow, a famous warrior." He paused and turned toward the couple sitting close together near the fire. "Thorkel, you spoke earlier of that feud. Tell us what you know."

Thorkel took his arm from Ragnhild's waist and got to his feet.

"I was just a boy when the S-S-Swedes attacked the Geats at Sorrowhill. That started the feud, it did. I heard my father, Thorstein, tell of it many a time. He later took part in a r-r-raid where the Geats kidnapped Gudfrid, Ongentheow's wife. Of course the Swedes s-s-struck back. In the battle at Ravenswood Ongentheow was k-k-killed, but so was Hathcyn, Hygelac's brother. That's how Hygelac came to be k-k-king of the Geats."

I was astonished to hear such a long speech from Thorkel. Then I remembered something he'd told me earlier.

"Thorkel, what happened to your father?"

"He was cut down defending Hathcyn, my lady. He d-d-died beside his king."

We were all silent for a long moment. I motioned Thorkel to sit down, then turned to Wulfgar.

"What bearing does this talk of Swedes and Geats have on our situation? My question is, will we be welcomed at Hygelac's court? We do not know what position Beowulf holds there, though his uncle is the king."

Wulfgar took some time before answering. Each face in the circle reflected my concern.

"My lady, if the feud continues, Hygelac will always need warriors to swell his forces. Though we be few . . ." here he looked around the circle, "we are stalwart thanes who should find a welcome with the Geats. As for you and your women . . ." he paused again, "that may depend on Hygelac's queen."

"Hygelac's queen? What queen? I've heard of no queen! Have any of the rest of you?"

I searched the faces around me. Someone coughed on the other side of the fire. Hesitantly Gorm rose to his feet and spoke in a low voice.

"My lady, I did hear Beowulf speak of a queen. 'Hygd' was her name, I think. He said she was famous for her beauty and generosity, a true queen."

"Thank you for your words, Gorm; you may sit down."

Inwardly I wondered: *if this Hygd is such a famous beauty, why have we not heard of her?* Out loud I said, "If this Hygd is famous for her generosity, that should bode well for us. But we do not come as beggars."

With these words I felt for the key to my strong box, hanging beneath my tunic, and clutched it firmly.

"Does anyone else have something to say? What about you women?"

Ana responded first, her voice somewhat muffled by the layers wrapped around her.

"The Geats can't be worse than those Heathobards! We were all glad to leave Ingeld's hall!"

At the mention of Ingeld I drew in a breath and held it, then slowly let go as I heard someone else speaking. Ingeborg? Yes, Ingeborg. It was getting very dark beyond the small circle of firelight.

". . . and we all remember Beowulf as a great-hearted man who put others before himself. After all the riches King Hrothgar piled on him, he'll surely give us a royal welcome — if he's still alive."

"Alive? Of course he's alive!" I laughed out loud. "Who could kill Beowulf? Not even the Grendel could do that!"

Then a memory suddenly surfaced. I seemed to hear Unferth's voice declaring that he saw blood on the golden collar Mother and I had given to Beowulf. I shivered in recall.

"Freawaru, my lady, are you ill?" Ana's voice was filled with concern. "It's time we got you under cover. This damp, cold night air isn't good for any of us! We don't want to straggle in to this Hygelac's court tomorrow bringing sickness with us!"

"Tomorrow? Wulfgar, is that possible?" I turned to the figure still standing just beyond the firelight.

"It depends on the wind, but it is possible. Tonight we post a watch guard. In the morning we'll leave at first light."

We all rose and crunched over the stony beach to our tents, leaving Wulfgar to extinguish the fire. Once inside, Ana, Brita, and I settled down together, glad of each other's warmth.

Next morning a light fog hung over the water. At first blink I could not see our ship, but was relieved to find the mooring lines still taut as they vanished in the mist. A hasty meal of bread and cheese had to suffice, as our wood was too wet for another fire. Once again we waded in icy water, but less of it this time with the tide going out. Brita slipped on the boarding plank and would have fallen, but Saxe caught her arm and hauled her aboard. Wulfgar and Thorkel helped me over the side, leaving the other women to fend for themselves. Though our craft was a *knorr*, a trading ship with wide deck and low sides, it was still difficult to board from the water.

"Once I set my feet on dry land again, I'm never going to leave it!" declared Estrid, wringing out the hem of her apron.

Ingeborg busied herself arranging a cushion of furs for my comfort, while complaining that her own backside was "raw as a dog's bone" from sitting on wooden chests. Ana and Ragnhild laughed, and Brita joined them, but I only smiled. My women: they would be a great solace to me in this new land.

As we sailed further and further north along the grey, rocky coast of Beowulf's homeland, it grew colder and colder. It was early spring, but the wind felt as bitter as midwinter back in Heorot. Heorot . . . Would I ever see it again? With a rush the events of the past days engulfed me. I bit my lip in anguish and turned away from my companions. Ana, close at my side, reached up to touch my cheek.

"Let them flow, Freawaru, release your grief, here in the ship where you are safe among your own people. When we reach Geatland we must show strength, but now you can release your sorrow."

Grasping her hand I nodded, letting pent-up tears flood down my face, salty rivulets hot against my cold, red cheeks. Then I clenched my fists and sobbed aloud as Ana held me, shielding me with her cloak.

Father ... gone. My two brothers ... gone. All because of my heartless husband's need for revenge. Yes, Ingeld got his revenge. Heorot lies in ashes, Hrothulf has seized father's throne and poisoned my dear, innocent brothers to eliminate his rivals ... Gone ... gone ... all gone, even Ingeld himself who did not survive his wounds.

I wrapped my arms tight around my body and shivered.

Will my world always be filled with loss and anguish? The Geats are feuding with the Swedes. Are we escaping one cycle of vengeance only to plunge into another?

I don't know how long I lay in this darkness of mind. Ana sometimes pressed water to my lips and I drank, but I turned away when the others took food at midday.

My knees ache, my back aches, my hands and feet are numb and my heart is empty; can I be more miserable? Suddenly Mother's face rose up before me. *Oh, Mother, why did you desert me? Why did you stay behind? Surely the living are owed as much as the dead! I need you! Your Freaw needs you!*

"A ship! A ship dead ahead!"

"Freaw? Freawaru? Wake, my lady. A ship is coming!"

Ana was standing over me, pointing straight ahead. North? It could not be our enemy. Could it be Beowulf's men, come to meet us? We would soon know, for the ship was fast approaching, parallel to our port side.

"It's a longboat," shouted Saxe from his post as lookout.

"With fourteen oars," added Olaf, peering ahead, one hand on the sheets.

"Let the sail go slack," ordered Wulfgar from the tiller, "but be ready to catch the wind if they try to attack."

Attack? Surprise and consternation spread across the faces of my women. Then my eyes made out the figure carved on the ship's prow: a dragon head.

"Wait!" I cried. "That could be Beowulf's ship, the one he sailed to Heorot."

But the man at the helm looked nothing like Beowulf. He was short and stocky, fur-clad, with the reddest beard I had ever seen.

"Perhaps we should show ourselves," whimpered Brita, pulling at my sleeve. "If they see women aboard they'll know we are not a raiding party."

"What if *they* are the raiding party?" I protested, but hastily drew myself erect and wiped the tears from my face.

Now the redbeard shouted something indistinguishable to his men, who rowed backward to slow their approach, then pulled in their oars. Wulfgar stepped to the side of the ship, his hand on his sword hilt, and waited.

With a jolt that almost threw us off our feet, the two ships met side on side, wood groaning on wood. We held our breaths. Would the strangers reach for their swords and shields?

No. Instead, they grabbed the sides of our craft and held fast as their leader, the redbeard, made his way forward. I did not recognize a single man.

"Identify yourselves," bellowed the redbeard. "Who is your master and where are you headed?"

Wulfgar replied with authority, as if standing at home in his own mead hall.

"I am Wulfgar, son of Wulfstan. We are Hrothgar's men, headed for Geatland and Beowulf, he who serves Hygelac."

The redbeard grunted and looked around, taking in our cargo and crew.

"Not all men, I see. Who might you be?"

He was staring past Wulfgar, straight at me. The other women drew back as I stepped forward.

"I am Freawaru, daughter of King Hrothgar and Queen Wealtheow. Who are you and who do you serve?" I stared back with all the confidence I could command.

The redbeard threw back his head and laughed admiringly.

"Lucky for you we are Hygelac's men, out to welcome him back from a raid ... my lady." He bobbed his head. "If you're headed for Eaglesgard you'll need to follow us. The rocks and skerries of Wedermark are treacherous. My name," he added, "is Ragnar, son of Ragnfast."

"I shall call you 'Redbeard'," I said, smiling graciously. Then a sudden image came to me, and my smile grew broader. "I see that you are not only a stout warrior but also a master woodcarver. That is your work on the prow, is it not?"

The man's mouth fell open.

"By the gods, how do you know this?"

"By the gods, indeed. I see many things that others do not." I let this sink in before continuing. "We welcome your offer of escort. We will be pleased to see our friend Beowulf again."

Redbeard now resumed his blunt manner.

"Oh, you won't see him soon. Beowulf went raiding with Hygelac. They always fight together. But Queen Hygd will show you the hospitality of Eaglesgard."

He turned to his men.

"Back to your oars, lads. We are bringing home a prize!" He flashed a grin at me, as if to say 'two can play at this game.'

Redbeard was certainly right about the treacherous approach to Hygelac's hall. Sailing alone was impossible among the rocks and shifting winds, so our crew once again took up oars as well. We closely followed the Geat's longboat through the twisting maze. Higher and higher rose the rocks, some covered with heather or juniper, but most bare. This was a forbidding country. Would we find a welcome here?

It was almost dark, with heavy clouds obscuring a weak sun, when a wind-borne shout from the Geat's boat came to us.

"Eaglesgard! Look up!"

Our eyes had been focused on the water, anxious for our ship's safety in the rocky passage, but now we looked up. Above us loomed an immense wall of rock, dark and cold as death. Had Beowulf actually come to us from this strange land?

In the fading light at first I could see no place for a landing, but we followed our guides faithfully, and shortly found a narrow harbor at the foot of the cliff. Redbeard's men ran their boat up onto the stony beach, then jumped out to secure it with iron rings set into the rock, as did our men.

Geatland. At last. I felt both relief and apprehension.

Once helped out of the ship, we women shook ourselves and kneaded cramped muscles. Our men picked up their weapons; we women took our small personal chests. I was careful to select the chest with my treasures — our future. Although our cloaks hung stiff with salt spray, the wind had abated, and the feel of the stony ground under our feet was reassuring.

Suddenly a ray of sunlight emerged from beneath the heavy cloud bank and shone full on the cliff face. Dazzling pinks and purples were reflected, flecked with glints of light. I gasped, surprised by its beauty.

"A good omen, my lady?" It was Brita beside me.

"Perhaps. We shall see."

The moment passed.

From high above us a horn sounded and sounded again, resounding off the rocky cliff.

"That is our coast guard announcing your arrival," said Redbeard. "Erik!" he shouted at a young man who looked too small for the shield he carried. "You have nimble legs. Run ahead to tell the queen that we have royal guests. Ketil!" This time he spoke to an older man with an immense gray beard. "Light a torch for the ladies and lead their way." Now he turned to me. "My lady, leave what you can't carry with you." To Wulfgar he said, "Your ship is safe here. Follow me."

Without hesitation Redbeard turned and seemed to disappear directly into the cliff face, his men right behind him. For a moment Wulfgar and I looked at each other.

"Proceed," I said.

"We follow!" shouted Wulfgar at the backs of the receeding Geats. He and the rest of our men fell in behind us women.

The steep path up to Eaglesgard was challenging, even with Ketil's torch wavering ahead of us. The path was dark and our exhaustion great, but there was no alternative. To reach our new home we must climb.

Let there be a welcome for us at the end of this ordeal, I breathed silently, then added, *Freaw, be strong. Remember who — and what — you are.*

As we climbed I could hear Ana puffing behind me. Ketil must have heard her too, as he called back reassuringly.

"Almost at the top, good women. Hot food and a warm fire await you. Our queen knows how to welcome weary travelers."

The queen, Yes, Hygd. Soon we will be able to judge her for ourselves.

Fanning the Flames

Even in the darkness the size of Eaglesgard was impressive. Not as big as Heorot, certainly, but a large mead hall nonetheless, stretching along the cliff's edge with its back to the sea. As Ketil led us to the entrance, I noted with approval its placement on the south side, away from the wind.

Silhouetted in the doorway, Redbeard motioned us inside.

"Food is coming, and good strong ale. Warm yourselves by the fire — here you, hurry with that basin!" He spoke sharply to a gangly lad bearing water and a hand cloth, then turned back to us. "When you have refreshed yourselves, Queen Hygd will attend you. She will no doubt ask the reason for your visit."

Redbeard's tone was cordial, but our men did not immediately put down their weapons.

"Wulfgar," I said, drawing him to my side. "For tonight we are protected by the laws of hospitality. We are guests. Lay aside your weapons, but keep them close at hand, as Beowulf did when in Heorot."

He nodded, and so directed the men. Olaf seemed especially relieved to add his shield to those of the others. I caught his eye and smiled.

"Rest yourself, Olaf. All may yet be well."

Where had I heard that before? A voice in my head repeated the phrase. Unferth? Yes, Unferth, my old rune master back in Heorot. How would he assess our present situation? Other words came back to me: *"Each of us is a warrior, Freaw, though we carry no sword or shield."* Yes, and a warrior must be mindful of his — or her — surroundings at all times. I glanced around me.

In the light of the hearth fire I saw that the mead hall was almost empty. A few thanes gathered at one end of a long corner table appeared to be playing a gambling game, for they laughed and cursed good-naturedly, seeming to ignore our presence. All looked to be graybeards.

Now I thought about the men I'd seen in Redbeard's ship; they had been either very young or advanced in years, no doubt left behind to maintain Eaglesgard while Hygelac's athelings went raiding with him. Surely our men could defend us, if need be, against such striplings and graybeards!

Near the double throne at the far end of the hearth sat an old man on a low stool, softly running his fingers over the strings of a lap harp. He stood up as we trooped in and sank down on the nearest benches, stripping off our heavy cloaks. He nodded respectfully.

"Welcome to Eaglesgard, strangers." His voice was surprisingly strong. "While you eat and drink, I will ease your weariness with a lay, a song of my own devising." He cleared his throat and began to sing in a high, steady voice.

> Come and open up your
> Ear and heed this hearing!
> Broadly, brightly, Odin's
> Brew is outward spewing.
> Mead of mug of Bragi
> Makes our night much lighter.
> Cling to class! Your song-caves
> Close...

At this point three serving maids hurried in with hot broth and hunks of venison. The smell of the roasted meat made my mouth water, and I suddenly realized how empty my belly felt.

Befitting my rank, I was offered the basin of water first, then it was passed down through our group, with Gorm getting it last. He poured the dirty water over his head and shook like a dog, splattering some of us.

"Here now, watch your manners," said Wulfgar sharply. "We don't want these Geats to think we are barbarians!"

Redbeard laughed at this, then left the hall. His men had disappeared earlier, perhaps scattering to their own homes.

In a moment we were all tearing into our food like hungry animals, washing it down with strong, hot broth and even stronger ale — which went immediately to my head.

"Freawaru, my lady, you look flushed. Are you ill?"

Ana had paused, both hands holding a bowl of broth, and studied my face across the table.

"No, no, it's just..."

Suddenly I turned and doubled over, vomiting everything I had just eaten. My women jumped up in alarm, but the men continued chewing, no doubt familiar with such scenes.

"Brita, get that cloth at the end of the table and help your mistress!" cried Ana.

It did not take long for me to empty the contents of my stomach, and when I had washed my face with fresh water hurriedly brought in, I felt much better.

"I'm sure it's only the strain of the voyage, too much ale, and not eating all day," observed Ana to the other women, though she nodded knowingly at me as she sponged the front of my tunic. "We'll all feel better tomorrow."

All this time the harper had been chanting in a sing-song voice, though I had paid little heed to his words. Now, however, a phrase caught my ear and I listened with full attention.

Wise was the woman
She fain would use wisdom.
She saw what well meant
All they said in secret.
From her heart it was hid
What help she might render . . .

Hygd! She may arrive at any moment! We must prepare!
"Ana, hand me my chest."

She hastened to do my bidding, but looked at me quizzically.

"Women, smoothe your hair and garments. We must put on a good face for Beowulf's queen."

From the box she brought me I lifted out my crown, fitted with the three jewels Ingeld had given me on our wedding day. Ana helped me place it securely on my head. Hardly had we adjusted ourselves and assumed a more regal posture, than a voice from the doorway announced:

"Queen Hygd."

The harper ceased his song and the men in the corner fell silent. As we rose, all eyes turned to follow the figure that entered, slowly, purposefully. She was not alone. At her side, tugging at her hand, strode a young boy — about Hrothmund's age, I judged. He seemed more eager than she to view these newcomers.

As she came more fully into the hearth light, I caught the glint of gold from her wrists and throat. *She too has adorned herself. We are alike in that,* I thought.

Hygd wore a cream-colored gown under a soft gray tunic. Her golden hair was pulled up in a top-knot, but fell in ringlets over her shoulders.

Her face was pale, as if she seldom saw the sun. Gray eyes flecked with gold stared at us evenly, but a trace of a smile played about her lips.

She is certainly older than I, yet not so old as Mother.

Hygd stopped a few paces from our group and raised her right palm in greeting.

"Welcome, Danes, people of Hrothgar. Welcome, Freawaru. We have heard of you. This," she added, allowing the squirming boy at her side to come forward, "is my son, Herdred. We welcome you to Eaglesgard."

"Have you seen my father?" the boy burst out. "We were expecting my father and his men, but you came instead. We . . ."

"That will do, Herdred. These folk are our guests." Hygd admonished her son gently, fondling his hair. Clearly he was the darling of her heart.

Now it was my turn. Holding my head high, I advanced and made a slight bow. "Queen Hygd. We accept your hospitality with thanks. In answer to the invitation once given us by Beowulf, my people and I have come to seek a home among your people."

Her eyes widened in surprise, but she answered graciously.

"Beowulf is not with us at present. When he returns, we will speak of this matter. Tonight you may enjoy the comforts of our hall."

She turned to beckon the same serving maids, now laden with blankets and furs.

"Take your rest in peace. Hygelac's hall is safe from any attack," she said proudly. "Hygelac himself should soon return . . . his absence has been . . . overlong," she added as if to herself, and her face darkened.

Redbeard advanced from the shadows to clear the hall for our repose.

"My lady," he said to Hygd, pausing. "Be advised: this woman has more power than she shows." He smiled at me in acknowledgment. "She has the gift of *sight*."

"Really? How do you know this, Ragnar?"

"She told me that I was a woodcarver at our very first meeting!" he said emphatically.

"Oh." Hygd turned her attention back to me. "What say you to this, Freawaru? Are you a seeress?" Her tone was light, her expression quizzical.

"Yes," I answered simply.

Herdred's eyes opened wide and he looked up to Hygd. "Mother, may I ask a question now?"

She nodded in acquiescence.

Fanning the Flames

"Does 'seeress' mean you can see into the future?" Without waiting for an answer, he plunged ahead. "Can you tell me if Father is bringing me a real sword?"

I laughed. "That was two questions. As to the first, my answer is 'sometimes.' To your second question . . ." I paused, waiting for an image to form in my mind. "Yes, you will be getting a sword, but not from your father."

Herdred opened his mouth as if to ask another question, but Hygd pressed a finger on his lips, her expression thoughtful. A shadow passed over her face.

"Come, Herdred, we'll leave our guests for now. You can question them further in the morning." Hygd laughed then, and turned to us almost apologetically. "My son is always most curious about strangers. I hope he won't trouble you overmuch."

"We will be delighted to answer his questions," I replied. "My little brother at home . . ." Suddenly my eyes filled with tears and I could not speak.

"Is all well in Heorot?" asked Hygd kindly.

So, the news of Hrothgar's death and Hrothulf's takeover have not yet reached the Geats. How much should I reveal? Yet the whole story must come out eventually.

"No, it is not, but that too can wait for morning."

I bowed again and Hygd nodded, taking Herdred's hand to go. As she left the hall, she turned and spoke once more.

"I hope all is well with Ingeld."

Then she was gone. Redbeard followed her out of the hall. Now it was my turn to be astonished.

What does she know of Ingeld? What has she heard about me? Did Beowulf speak of me upon his return to Eaglesgard?

My mind was racing with questions, but fatigue now overcame me. With trembling legs I sank down on the nearest bench. Wulfgar approached.

"Boldly done, my lady," he chuckled. "Beowulf's invitation did not contain the same words you used, but you stated our purpose clearly. Now we must wait for the return of Hygelac and Beowulf."

We did not have long to wait.

Chapter Two
Lost in Frisia

Helmeted head of a warrior found in Sigtuna, Sweden.

Sunlight was streaming through the smoke-hole when a crew of serving women cautiously entered the mead hall. They carried a big pot of steaming porridge, armfuls of soapstone bowls, and brands to light the torches on the walls. I yawned. Could it be morning already? I did not feel rested. I felt... what? Not nausea, exactly, but a sense of unease, as of impending doom.

There was little time to dwell on this feeling, for Hygd's son, Herdred, had slipped in with the servants and planted himself beside my bench, waiting impatiently for me to rise. A shock of curly blonde hair framed his round face. I noticed that he had gray eyes, like his mother.

"Where's your leader?" he asked peremptorily. "I looked for him, but he's not inside."

"Wulfgar? He must have gone back down to our ship," I replied, then added, "I, however, am the leader of our group."

Herdred looked at me with surprise, then amusement, and finally disdain.

"A woman can be the leader at home — like my mother," he declared, "but men are the leaders at sea — like my father. He's off fighting the Frisians." His eyes sparkled with delight. "You were wrong last night. My father promised to bring me a sword. Right now I have only the wooden one that Beowulf made for me."

"Beowulf? Is he a friend of yours?" I asked casually, rising and shaking out my sleeping robe.

"Oh, yes! Beowulf is teaching me how to use a sword and shield. And he lets me sail with him sometimes. My father and Beowulf are like brothers. Everyone says so. My father . . ."

"So here you are!" An exasperated female voice sounded from the doorway. A heavy-set woman with a flushed face bustled in, wiping her hands on her apron.

"Beg pardon, my lady. This young man hadn't ought to be disturbing you this early. Queen Hygd wouldn't like it. Oh, beg pardon again. My name is Signe and this boy has been my charge for all his eight years."

She bobbed a curtsey with a grimace, as if it hurt her knees.

Signe looked to be about the age of Willa, my former nurse when . . . when she was killed by the Grendel. Willa . . . another painful memory caught me short. I must have frowned, for Signe bobbed again.

"It's my fault if he's offended, my lady. Beg pardon." Her red cheeks grew even redder.

"It's all right, Signe. My own brothers at home were always full of questions." I gulped down the lump in my throat. "After we have taken our breakfast there will be time for talking."

I smiled at Herdred's eager face; he smiled back with a boyish grin.

All around me my women were rising, and other folk were now entering the mead hall, people of all ages, come to partake of the morning meal. Signe hustled Herdred off to one of the tables near the throne. I directed Ana and the others in folding our bedding and putting it aside. Just then Wulfgar and our men entered, carrying some of our ship's cargo — primarily chests of clothes and bedding.

Well done, Wulfgar. We've slept in our clothes for so many nights, a change will be welcome!

Another voice, masculine this time, announced, "Queen Hygd."

I was surprised to see the queen joining her people for a meal in the absence of her husband. Back home in Heorot, Mother always ate with her women, only joining Father in the mead hall on formal, special occasions. I wondered: are *we* a special occasion? We certainly should be!

After satisfying our hunger on platters of herring and bowls of thick, rich porridge (much tastier that the gruel served at Wolfhaus, I thought), our group was summoned to the head table.

Queen Hygd sat on one of the throne chairs, costumed differently this morning. She wore a soft blue gown under a white kirtle trimmed with bands of embroidered flowers. Her brooches gleamed with jeweled insets, and she wore golden circlets on both wrists. If it was her aim to make a strong impression, she was succeeding. Her beauty was undeniable.

"A fair morning to our guests. You slept well?"

She smiled at us all, but directed her question at me.

"Yes, my lady," I lied politely. "We thank you again for your hospitality."

"It is time I met your followers," said Hygd.

"And I yours," I responded.

Taking no notice of my response, Hygd waved her hand at those seated nearby.

"Friends, make room for our guests."

Several people obediently moved down to make space for us to sit. I remained standing, however, to introduce my women before they took seats.

"This is Ana, my boon companion." Ana made a slow curtsey.

"My women: Ingeborg, Ragnhild, and Estrid." Each bowed in turn.

"My servant, Brita." Brita faltered as she bowed low.

"And your men?" Hygd gestured to the silent figures still standing politely to one side.

"Of course. Wulfgar leads our men." Wulfgar stepped forward solemnly and briefly bowed his head.

"This is Thorkel, who once lived among the Geats and fought against their enemies."

Thorkel acknowledged my statement with a nod of the head.

"And these young thanes complete our band: Olaf, Gorm, and Saxe." Each smiled respectfully and nodded his head.

Hydg surveyed us in silence for a moment.

"You are few in number to make such a journey from the land of the Danes," she observed. "Last night you spoke of trouble in Hrothgar's court. What news do you bring us?"

The time had come. I took a deep breath, lifted my chin and faced the queen squarely.

"Evil news, Queen Hygd. My father no longer lives. King Hrothgar died after defeating the Heathobards at Heorot. His two sons are also dead — killed by a usurping traitor, Hrothgar's nephew Hrothulf." My voice was even.

Murmurs of surprise rippled through the mead hall. Hygd's eyes widened as she absorbed this information. Then she spoke, thoughtfully.

"The Heathobards — were you not allied to their leader, Ingeld?"

I nodded, my eyes locked on hers.

"What was his fate in the battle at Heorot?"

"He too is dead, my lady. He did not survive his wounds." My voice betrayed no emotion.

"Ah, I see." She paused. "It is as Beowulf foresaw. The marriage peace did not hold. Now your husband and your kinsmen are all gone. You are alone."

"No, not entirely alone, as you can see!" I retorted. "And we have the means to set up our own hall, here in your country, if we can reach an agreement."

Hygd stared at me, her face blank.

"That will be for Hygelac to decide. He will be here soon — with Beowulf. They should be returning . . . today." Almost to herself she added, "Fortunately Hygelac's nephew is true to him. They are boon companions, inseparable."

Hygelac's nephew? Oh, she means Beowulf. Can Hygd be comparing Beowulf to Hrothulf? The idea shocked me.

As we held each other's gaze, a dark vision entered my mind: the golden torque, the great necklace Mother presented to Beowulf at Heorot. I saw it . . . covered with blood. Shivering, I shook my head.

Hygd's voice rose a pitch. "You doubt me? You shall see for yourself when they stand here side by side in this mead hall!"

"No, my lady, I do not doubt you." A troubling thought struck me. "Tell me, please. Did Beowulf bring back from Heorot a great golden collar? It was a gift to him from my mother, Queen Wealtheow."

Hygd nodded, her face strangely flushed.

"Yes, he did, but he presented it to me, his queen, along with three handsome horses on which we oft ride out together."

I smiled in relief.

"I am glad to hear that the necklace is safe in your keeping, for I fear there may be ill omens attached to it."

"Omens? What omens? What do you mean?" Hygd had risen from her throne in agitation, eyes flashing.

Just at that moment a horn sounded and sounded again — from the direction of the harbor. Hygd's face cleared instantly.

"Hygelac! Home at last! Now you will see the king of the Geats — wearing my golden collar! Yes," she added at my look of concern, "he wore it as a talisman, for luck in battle."

She turned, searching the hall.

"Ragnar! Take charge here while I go to greet my lord!'

My heart sank. The vision had been clear. I feared Hygd's joy would be short-lived. And Herdred... what of Herdred?

The mead hall emptied quickly, leaving only Ragnar, our band, and a few serving women inside.

"Wulfgar, what do you advise? Follow, or wait here?"

"I think it best to wait here in the mead hall, my lady, but let us move to one side."

"Yes, good council. We do not want to intrude on the Geats' homecoming — if there is one."

As we waited quietly, sitting on benches along the outer wall, Redbeard paced back and forth at the entrance. He clearly wished he could join those hurrying down to the harbor; we could hear joyful shouts and the sound of running feet outside the wall.

"Hygelac left with three ships," offered Redbeard, "so it will take some time to unload the booty." Even at a distance we could see the broad smile of anticipation on his face.

"Is your king a generous giver of gold rings?" inquired Wulfgar.

"What's that question about? Have you heard otherwise?" Redbeard stalked over to our group, a questioning look on his face.

"I know your King Hrothgar liked to boast about his riches — sending all that loot back with Beowulf! Trying to impress us, I wager. You Danes should know that we Geats have treasures of our own — and now Hygelac is returning with more!" He thumped his chest proudly.

But Hygelac did not return.

"Beowulf?"

Redbeard sounded uncertain and amazed as he stared out the door. Then he turned to our group.

"Lord Beowulf," he announced with certainty.

A lone figure had appeared in the doorway, blocking the light with its great bulk. It hesitated and momentarily swayed, then almost staggered into the mead hall.

Can this be Beowulf? Is this the same man I met in Heorot?

He was dripping wet and his chain-mail battle shirt hung in shreds, as if savaged from all sides. He wore no helmet; long locks fell in wet strands beside his swollen, ashen face and red-rimmed eyes. Grief and exhaustion were etched into his features. He looked like a great beast cast up by the sea.

I caught my breath, stricken at the sight of this man, so different in appearance from the man who had once saved my life — saved all our lives, long ago in Heorot.

Beowulf made it as far as the king's chair, but collapsed at its base. Redbeard rushed forward to help him to his feet. Head down, Beowulf grasped the arm of the throne. Then he threw back his head and howled.

The sound chilled my blood, for I had heard such a howl before — from my father the king. When his aethelings were smashed and devoured by the Grendel monster, Father had given vent to the same unbearable agony. I covered my ears, shuddering in pain and terror. What had happened? Where was Hygelac?

Hygd entered next, supported by weeping women. Her face was drained of color, her unseeing eyes staring straight ahead. She took no notice of our group as she let herself be led to the throne chair. There she sank beside Beowulf, whose howl still echoed in the chamber.

We stood frozen, in the grip of a dark force that had entered the hall with Beowulf. Where were the other men? Where was Hygelac?

Now other folk began to slip inside, by ones and twos, some feeling their way toward tables and benches as if blind. I saw Signe, her arm around Herdred, who appeared more puzzled than grieving. He looked about, shaking his head.

Beowulf rose and walked slowly toward Herdred, took the boy's hand, and led him to the empty throne chair. When he spoke his voice was barely audible despite the heavy silence.

"Take your throne, my liege," he said tenderly to Herdred.

The boy hesitated, looking up with questioning eyes. Beowulf, turning to the assembly, spoke now in a solemn, measured tone.

"King Hygelac is dead. Herdred is king."

"No!" cried Herdred, springing back from the chair. "No! It can't be so! Father is bringing me a sword, Father is . . . No, no, oh no!" He shook his head vehemently. His face worked strangely, as if torn between laughter and tears. "Father!" he cried, then his words dissolved in great, hiccupping sobs.

Hygd put up her hand toward Beowulf, who helped her rise and seated her beside the empty throne, which Herdred steadfastly refused to occupy.

"Beowulf?" she began, her voice weak as she lifted her face to his. "Herdred is just a child, he's a little boy. We need a warrior to defend us against our enemies. We need you, Beowulf. Only you can take Hygelac's place."

Only you can take Hygelac's place? Does Hygd fully understand what she is saying?

Beowulf knelt before her. "I would obey you in anything but this, my queen. Herdred is the rightful heir." He paused. "I could not save Hygelac, my king." His voice was bitter. "But I did save . . . this!"

He stood up, pulled something from beneath his byrnie and held it aloft.

"Behold the golden torque! It did not go to the Frankish king, for I crushed Dayraven in my arms, crushed him until his bone-house burst and red blood frothed from his mouth!"

I shuddered in revulsion at the savagery in Beowulf's voice. Never had I seen anyone look so cruel. Yet, who could blame him? Beowulf was now bowing before Hygd, offering her the great collar. She took it with both hands and laid it in her lap.

Hygelac's talisman, his battle charm . . .

"And for Herdred," Beowulf was speaking again, reaching for the sheath on his right hip. "For Herdred, this!" He drew a great sword, its hilt encrusted with gold and garnets, and held it aloft for all to see. "This is the sword that killed his father. May he one day wield it to avenge that death!"

Herdred looked up, wide-eyed. "Give it to me!" he cried, leaping to his feet. "Give me my sword!"

He tried to lift it as Beowulf had done, but managed only to hold it waist-high. Suddenly he stopped, stock-still, and raised his head, looking around the hall.

"Freawaru? Where is Freawaru? She was right about the sword!" His face filled with wonder.

Now Beowulf froze. "Freawaru? Hrothgar's daughter? Why do you speak of her?"

His face softened and, following Herdred's gaze, he too began searching the faces in the mead hall.

"My lord Beowulf that can wait!" Hygd's voice sliced the air like a blade. "We must gather our council members, we must choose a course of action with those who are left... how many are left?" her voice faltered.

"Only a handful," he replied grimly. "They were to follow when they had repaired their ship. I swam home alone."

Swam? Alone? From Frisia? Surely even Beowulf could not accomplish such a feat — yet here he stands before us!

Now Hygd seemed to return to herself. She straightened and placed her hand on Herdred's back.

"Ragnar, clear the hall of all but our aethelings! Have food and drink sent in for Beowulf!" Her voice was strong. "Signe, take Herdred out with you, and — here are the keys — stow this collar in my chest." She picked up the heavy torque as if it were a venomous snake.

At Herdred's protest, Beowulf lifted his hand. "Let the boy stay. He should hear the story of how brave Hygelac met his death."

Now his gaze fell on our group, standing motionless in the shadows. I shielded my face, unwilling to reveal my presence just yet.

"Who are these folk? They look familiar..." Then he was striding forward, arms outstretched. "Wulfgar! Head of Hrothgar's hall-guard! What brings you to Eaglesgard?" His face cleared momentarily. He looked almost like the Beowulf I had once known. "You have women with you? Why have you brought these women?"

Wulfgar stepped aside and my women parted to reveal my person. Beowulf's eyes widened in stunned surprise.

"Can it be... Freawaru? I heard your name spoken, but I could not credit the possibility..." He stared at me as if at a vision.

"It is I, Lord Beowulf," I said quietly, looking into his eyes.

"Yes, but... you were promised to Ingeld, the Heathobard!"

"That is true, but Ingeld is dead, my lord. So is King Hrothgar... dead. We understand your grief, my lord, for we have brought our own."

Fanning the Flames

Beowulf took a step back. "There is much to be told here, but now is not the time." He turned back to the queen, "You have offered hospitality to these guests?"

"Of course, my lord Beowulf," she answered — coldly, I thought. "They arrived yesterday, when we were expecting you... and... Hygelac." Her voice broke and she covered her face with her hands.

Beowulf looked at us uncertainly, then strode back to her side. He placed his huge hands on her shoulders.

"Queen Hygd, Hygelac died a warrior's death. We will mourn him as befits a king... though we have no body for a funeral pyre..." His voice trailed off, and he seemed at a loss for any further words of comfort.

The entrance of serving women with food and drink broke the spell that held us all in our places. Hygd wiped her eyes and pulled herself erect.

"Come." Hygd spoke firmly. "Sit and eat, my lord. Having swum all the way from the Rhineland, you must be both exhausted and ravenous." She forced a smile at his nod. "I myself will pour the mead cup." Suiting action to words, she picked up a heavy silver pitcher.

Beowulf stripped off the remnants of his mail shirt, wincing as bits of metal caught his flesh, and lowered himself onto a bench.

"I will be grateful for food and rest, my lady, but after meat we must plan a course of action. Wulfgar!" He called across the room. "Bring your people to join us! Let us renew our friendship on this day of sorrow. Let Danes and Geats together mourn the death of Hygelac."

Herdred, at his mother's bidding, brought the towel and basin to Beowulf to refresh himself. As he wiped his face, I noted bruises under his eyes, and swollen cheeks. Approaching Queen Hygd, I spoke gently.

"My lady, I have herbs with me that would make a fine poultice for Beowulf's face."

"Oh?" She grimaced. "Are you now a healer as well as seeress? Wait!" Her eyes narrowed. "That collar... the evil omens... You knew it carried some sort of curse — yet you gave it to Beowulf — who gave it to me — and now it has brought about the death of my husband! Was that your intent? To destroy us?" Her eyes now blazed with rage and suspicion.

"No, my lady, you mistake me! Please, calm yourself!"

I held my ground as she advanced with lifted arm as if to strike — to be met with a strong grip, for Beowulf had risen from his seat to intervene.

"Hygd, stay your hand! You are not yourself! Freawaru is not at fault here. Hygelac chose to wear the collar, Hygelac chose to attack the

Frisians — a fatal mistake . . ." He halted, as if regretting his words, then started again.

"There is much I do not know, Hygd, but I know that death comes to us all. Do not blame Freawaru for the ways of Wyrd. Hygelac's fate was not in her control."

"Perhaps." Hygd glowered at me before turning to Beowulf. "Did you know that this woman is a seeress? Did you know that? She can see into the future. She could have foreseen what would happen to Hygelac!" She almost spat these words.

Now everyone was looking at me, uncertainty in their eyes, accusations forming on their lips. I held up both hands for silence.

"Queen Hygd, I could not prevent the death of my own husband, Ingeld. I could not prevent the death of my father, nor that of my two young brothers. I could not prevent the death of your husband, Hygelac. I have no power to control the future. I do see faint images, brief visions, but their meaning is often unclear. As Freyja is my witness — Freyja — goddess of love and death — that is the truth."

Silence — broken by the tremulous voice of Herdred.

"Freawaru, you told me my new sword would not come from Father."

"Yes," I nodded, "I knew that much, for in my vision it was held by Beowulf."

I looked beseechingly at Beowulf, who frowned in confusion. Unexpectedly, Ragnar Redbeard came to my rescue.

"Begging your pardon, Queen Hygd, but it seems to me that having a seeress in Eaglesgard could be good — give us an advantage over our enemies, who now include the Franks and Frisians."

Silence again. To my surprise, Ana now stepped forward and spoke with quiet authority.

"Queen Hygd, I have known Freawaru all her life. She was born with the mark of Freyja, and has learned to use her powers wisely. She . . ."

"Enough!" Hygd interrupted, raising her hand. "We will consider all that has been said in council. This is a hard time for us all," she admitted. "This is not the moment for decisions. Beowulf . . ." She managed a smile in his direction. "Please begin your repast. We have been inconsiderate to delay you."

She poured a stream of golden mead into a drinking horn and handed it to him. As we watched, he drained it.

Before Beowulf turned to his food — herring and porridge from our morning meal and chunks of venison no doubt left over from last night — he called for the harper.

"Jesper! Where are you? Give us a song to lift our hearts!"

"Here, my lord."

The man who had entertained us last night appeared at Beowulf's elbow.

"What would you like to hear? Perhaps 'The Battle of Ravenswood'?"

"A good choice." Beowulf turned to our group, now seated at a nearby table. "Have you heard it?"

"No, my lord," answered Wulfgar, "but we know of the battle and of the Geats' victory over Ongentheow and the Swedes."

"Yes!" A look of satisfaction spread over Beowulf's face. "Begin, Jesper!"

Jesper plucked his harp and let the notes die away.

Remember Ravenswood, the Swedish slaughter
Of Hathcyn, Hrethel's son, our king
Who boldly launched attack upon Ongentheow
Fierce fighter who returned the foray.
Old and terrible, he felled our sea-king, saved
His own aged wife, Onla and Ohtere's mother.
Hard on the heels of Geatish warriors
He drove them desperate into Ravenswood
Where all night through he shouted threats.
But at first light relief arrived. Hygelac's horn
Revived their spirits, raised their swords.
Then blood ran everywhere in murderous feuding.

As Jesper paused to drink and wet his throat, I leaned toward Ana and whispered, "I wonder what became of Ongentheow's wife? Did she escape the battle?"

Ana shrugged.

Jesper looked around to see if he had our attention, then struck the strings a sharp blow that set my teeth on edge. His voice took on a harsher tone.

Ongentheow pulled back to higher ground, his fortress
Ringed with earth wall, faced with Hygelac's

Pride and prowess in the open field.
But Hygelac swooped on Swedes at bay,
Destroyed the camp, exposed the king
To Efor's hands, and Wulf his brother
Who struck a blow that split the helmet.
Ongentheow's gray hairs ran with blood.
He parried back, a harder stroke
Repaid Wulf's blow, split Wulf's helmet
Sent him reeling, grevious wounded.
To brother's aid now Efor the brave
Raised high his sword, smashed through the shield,
Laid low Ongentheow, king of Swedes.

Here Jesper paused again and smiled as jubilant shouts erupted among the Geats. I was feeling slightly nauseous at the images conveyed in the song, but determined to quell my unease. Would this bloody battle story never end? I shut my eyes and shut my ears, so did not hear all that followed.

Stripped iron mail-coat, sword and helmet
Took to Hygelac...
Now king he promised noble treasures
Gave homesteads, hides, and hoarded rings
... to Wulf and to Efor
His only daughter as a wife.

I opened my eyes when the singing stopped, replaced by shouts and laughter. It seemed that, just as in Heorot, men were cheered by songs of battle victory.

"Ragnar, reward our harper with a handful of silver! Well done, Jesper!" Beowulf was almost smiling. Then his face turned grim.

"Even Ongentheow's mail shirt did not save Hygelac in Frisia," he observed. "He should have worn the one I brought back from Hrothgar. Ah, Hygelac..."

I heard these words indistinctly, for I was thinking about the final line in the song: 'his only daughter as a wife.' Hygd and Hygelac must have a daughter as well as a son ... I wondered where she might be, but knew it would be unwise to question Hygd today. Despite her earlier

Fanning the Flames

anger, I hoped we might come to a friendlier footing, we two women who had lost our husbands.

"... like his brother Hathcyn? Yes, Thorstein, both were proud and often rash, rushing to battle."

Beowulf was speaking to a stout warrior with a braided mustache seated across from him. Gold gleamed on several stubby fingers. Did this mean he had killed a man to earn each ring?

"My lord Beowulf," said Thorstein, "the matter of the kingship should be settled soon. Our *athelings* — those who stayed at Eaglesgard when Hygelac went to Frisia — have assembled." He gestured to a group of men, a dozen or so, who had entered during the harper's song. "Should we wait for the return of your companions, or take counsel now?"

Beowulf looked at Hygd, then back at Thorstein.

"Let's give them . . . one more day," he said. "During that time we need to build a funeral pyre for Hygelac and mourn him as befits a king." He paused, looking around. "And we will honor all those who fell with Hygelac, those who died in Frisia," he concluded. "What say you?"

Thorstein turned to the other warriors seated in the hall. Slowly, each nodded in agreement.

Beowulf bowed to Hygd and nodded to the assembly. "If you will excuse me? I have not slept for many days."

He turned and strode out of the mead hall. Hygd rose silently and left without a word, accompanied by her women. Everyone else began to stir and stretch.

I feel as if I've been confined here; I've not even seen daylight except through the smoke-hole. It would be good to be out of doors!

I glanced around the room. Herdred had claimed a table in the center of the hall where he was surrounded by a group of warriors, all examining his new sword. Herdred seemed to show little emotion at the loss of his father. I wondered if the death had not yet become real to him. He called to one of them.

"See, Ingvar, there on the edge — there's a piece missing."

Ingvar bent to examine the blade.

"Yes, but barely a nick. You'd best take it down to Oskar. He'll smooth it out for you."

Herdred saw me looking at him and beckoned me over. The men backed away at my approach, eyeing me with curiosity.

"Frea...waru — I mean, my lady Frea...waru — will you come with me? Oskar is our blacksmith. He can fix anything!"

Redbeard, who had approached at my side, turned and winked at me.

"Right you are, young master Herdred," he boomed. "May I join you? I would be honored to carry the sword. I have the sheath right here."

Herdred hesitated, his face clouding.

"Oh, well, yes you may... but I have questions to ask Frea... lady Frea...waru."

"You may call me Freaw," I told him, smiling. "My brothers always called me that."

"Thank you... Freaw." The boy raised a face still stained with tears, but his eyes were clear.

"Herdred, may my Danish friends come with us? None of us has yet seen anything of your settlement beyond this grand hall. We arrived at night, as you may remember?"

"Oh, yes, of course. Ragnar, you be their guide. I want to talk to... Freaw."

And so we set off.

It was a shock to emerge from the dark interior of the mead hall into dazzling sunlight. A brilliant blue sky stretched above us. I took a deep breath, filling my lungs with the pure air.

"Is it always this windy?" I heard Ana asking Redbeard. Her eyes were watering.

"Windy?" He looked surprised. "This is nothing. The great gales come in winter, straight off the sea. You've arrived at a good time with summer almost upon us."

My women were pulling their shawls about them, but I felt exhilarated.

A fresh wind — a fresh start — let it blow away the sorrows of the past.

I did not see then all the sorrows to come.

The settlement at Eaglesgard looked nothing like my former home at Heorot. Instead of rows of longhouses lined up along a central pathway, the structures here took advantage of level areas dotted randomly among the rocky hills. From the mead hall winding paths took off in many directions.

Fanning the Flames

I looked back at the hall and saw Redbeard pointing out something to my group. Following his raised finger, my eyes were drawn to the crossed arms of the roof supports — but these were no ordinary timbers. They had been carved into wings, magnificent wings, eagle wings.

"Your work again, Redbeard?" I called out.

"Yes, my lady." He might have had more to say, but Herdred was tugging impatiently at my hand.

"This way, Freaw. Oskar's smithy is this way."

Herdred led the group as we climbed, with Redbeard at the rear carrying the sword. As we passed a longhouse, faces often appeared in the doorway: sometimes children to gawk at us strangers, sometimes a woman in apron and kerchief who gave us a brief nod before returning to her duties.

Their hair may be whiter and their faces redder then those of us Danes, but these people look friendly and almost familiar.

Despite his earlier desire to question me, Herdred had fallen strangely silent. At the edge of the settlement we stopped before a shed-like structure open at one end. Inside stood a powerfully muscled man in a leather apron, his face grimy, his eyes red-rimmed. He was feeding chunks of wood into a stone oven.

"Oskar! Here is my new sword! There's a piece missing."

Herdred reached for the sheath being removed from Redbeard's shoulder. He pulled at the heavy sword, then backed away to remove it completely.

Oskar straightened, wiped his hands on his apron, and came forward.

"My lord Herdred." Oskar bent his head to the boy. "I am honored. Leave the sword with me for a day, and I will return it to you ready for battle!"

His tone was serious, and Herdred answered just as seriously, a dark scowl on his brow.

"I'll avenge my father's death, Oskar, I will!"

"Aye, my lord, I have no doubt of it."

Suddenly Herdred turned to me, his tone beseeching.

"Freaw, lady Freaw, you see the future. Tell me. Where is my father now?"

His question took me by surprise, as it did the others.

"Poor lad," murmured Ragnhild.

I stared at Herdred's anxious face, sensing his great need for reassurance.

"I know not . . ." I began, then smiled in relief as the image came to me, brief but clear. "Yet I see my father, King Hrothgar, feasting in Valhalla among a host of champions. He is raising his glass to a newcomer, a warrior who wears on his middle finger a gold and silver ring entwined with serpents."

Oskar and Redbeard gasped. Herdred beamed.

"My father! His favorite ring! Oh, thank you Freaw, thank you."

He buried his face in my bosom as I knelt to embrace him. Then he straightened and spoke proudly.

"One day I will join him there!"

That night at the evening meal my words were repeated in many mouths. Heads turned as we made our way to a table. Hygd herself came to greet me and thank me for sharing my vision with her son.

Chapter Three
Blood Bond

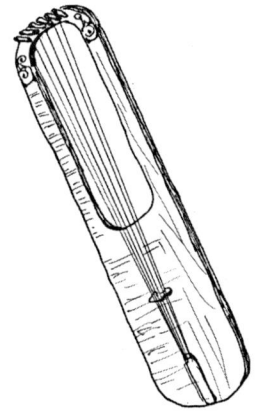

Harp-lyre (reconstructed) from ship burial in Sutton Hoo, England c. 600 A.D.

The next morning I awoke to the cry of gulls and the thin, high shriek of eagles. For a moment I did not know where I was. Yawning, I looked about and recognized the timbered interior of Eaglesgard. Our men were already up and gone. Of course. They would be helping construct the funeral pyre for Hygelac.

"My lady?" Ana hovered near my bench. "Hygd sent over water and a kettle so we can bathe and change clothes — about time, I'd say! Apparently the men will be gone for a good while, gathering and stacking timbers, so we'll have the hall to ourselves."

In fact Brita was already pouring water from wooden pails into a large cauldron on the hearth. Ingeborg and Estrid were sorting through their chests for fresh undergarments, and Ragnhild had begun stripping off her apron.

"What do you think, Lady Freawaru? Should we dress in our best for this funeral today?" Ana looked and sounded cross this morning.

"What's wrong, Ana? Don't you feel well?" I rose and stretched.

"No, I don't! And now there's to be no morning meal. We're all supposed to fast until after the burning!" She was almost snorting with disapproval.

"Perhaps that is the custom here," I answered. "We must learn what is expected. Ah, here is someone who may help us!"

Signe was bustling in with an armful of towels.

"Beg pardon, my lady, those wenches forget half their duties! But everyone's unsettled this morning, with the burning and the banquet to prepare and all."

"Banquet?" Ana's face brightened.

"Of course! After the mourning is over everyone will need to be fed!"

"How long does the mourning take?" asked Ana.

"Hard to say. It could last all day — but not everyone needs to stay," she added, seeing Ana's face fall. "King Hygelac's *athelings* will stay with the pyre until it burns down to ashes. Lord Beowulf will probably be the last to leave. He was so close to Hygelac — they were like brothers, those two." She shook her head sadly.

"Does everyone wear their best attire?" Ana asked.

"Oh yes, it's the king, after all! Now I'll leave you to your bath."

By the time we had all bathed and dressed, even Ana was feeling more cheerful. I selected the white pleated gown and blue woolen overdress that I'd worn at my wedding. As I fastened the straps with oval brooches, I felt a distinct kick in my belly. Ingeld's baby. How long would I be able to disguise my condition?

We walked out into another dazzling day. The planked path creaked beneath our feet as we looked about, unsure which direction to take. The air here seemed clearer, brighter than back home. The wind had a clean scent, free of the fishy odor that clung to Heorot's shoreline. Heorot, my one-time home. I thought of the swans in Heorot's harbor, the swans that flew with me in dreams...

We are so high here, so far above the sea. I could be a swan, rising on strong white wings to soar above the rocky hills...

I lifted my arms — and almost ran into Ana, walking in front of me.

"My lady?" She turned in surprise.

"Sorry, Ana. I was . . . somewhere else."

People streamed down the various paths that led to the mead hall. Big families seemed to be common, for I saw groups with six, seven, even eight blonde-haired children. Most were barefoot, dressed in simple tunics of grey and brown; most looked healthy and well-fed.

Several women were weeping, making no effort to hide their tears. I wondered: wives — mothers — of men who fell with Hygelac? Some carried bits of battle gear or pieces of clothing. One had tucked a game board under her arm and her hand clutched a bag of tokens.

Oskar stood out among the crowd with his broad shoulders and great head of gray hair. He nodded soberly in our direction, but did not speak. Most of the men were dressed in working clothes, but some wore cloaks clearly reserved for special occasions, as they showed little signs of wear. All passed us by, continuing toward a distant promontory, well above the sea.

Hygelac's *athelings* had built a platform of timbers on a rocky headland within sight of the mead hall, but distant enough to let off-shore breezes carry away the smoke. Freshly-felled trees formed the great square framework, high as a man's waist. More seasoned wood was stacked inside, splashed with seal oil.

Without a body to burn, the council had decided to sacrifice Hygelac's battle horse and three of his dogs. Later, gold arm-rings and wargear would be added to the pyre, and whatever else the sorrowing survivors had brought to honor their dead.

As we approached the platform, a flash of golden light blinded me momentarily. Shading my eyes, I discovered the source: Hygd. Hygd, dressed in a gown of shimmering silk, her blonde hair down, falling to her waist. Her arms gleamed with spirals of gold, a circlet of gold graced her brow, and on her neck — the golden torque.

My throat constricted. *How can she bear to wear it? Perhaps she intends to add it to the funeral pyre?*

Herdred stood slightly apart from his mother, head held high, as if ready to assume his father's place. He was dressed in a blue tunic and wore no gold, but at his side he carried his wooden sword.

Hygd and Herdred stepped back from the platform as the animals were led up to it. The rest of the settlement's folk stood quietly, forming a half-circle facing the platform. Our group stood to one side.

The killing of animals was so painful to me that I could barely watch the slaughter. Memories of our horse sacrifice at Heorot came sharply to mind, our futile attempt to seek aid against the Grendel monster. Only Beowulf had been able to destroy that evil. Now, here he stood beside Hygelac's war horse — a handsome roan with flowing mane. I gasped as he drew a knife across its throat. Blood spurted in a great arc as the animal shuddered and sank to its knees.

Other men took two of Hygelac's hunting dogs, gray elkhounds with pointed ears and tails that curved above their backs, and put them to the sword. The third dog sacrificed reminded me of a bear with its bulky body and dark, shaggy coat. All were slain and cast on the pyre to honor their master.

I wondered: would some unfortunate slave be butchered to join them? Ingeld's men had wanted such a companion for their king, but I had overruled them. Then his own mother, impelled by grief, had slain herself. Her body joined that of her son on the funeral pyre at Wulfhaus.

I drew a deep breath and told myself, *All that is over. We're in Geatland now. Yet... death continues, as it ever must.*

Apprehensively I looked in Hygd's direction. Was she feeling any impulse to join her husband in death? Apparently not. She stood quietly between two of her women. Her eyes were fixed on Beowulf. *Beowulf and Hygd...* Something, some whisper of warning, flickered at the back of my brain.

Beowulf lit the pyre with a torch handed to him by Redbeard. As flames leapt up and greasy smoke began to billow, Beowulf drew his dagger and cut a fistful of his long blond hair. Casting it into the flames, he groaned aloud.

"A part of me goes with you, my liege. Forgive me. Forgive me. I could not save you."

Then Herdred approached Beowulf and motioned to be lifted, brought close to the flames. Beowulf picked him up and held him forward in his great hands. Herdred raised his sword — the plaything of a child — and cried out with all the force of his eight years:

"Father, as I am now a man, you shall be avenged!"

He flung the sword into the flames.

As Beowulf put him down, the boy's frame trembled and his face was bathed in tears, but he walked back to his mother's side with great dignity.

As we stood beside the mounting flames, our faces hot with heat, I heard an echo from the past: our harper in Heorot singing of the

Finnsburg Feud and the resulting funeral pyre. I closed my eyes to hear it better:

> *Logs roared, wounds split, skulls melted,*
> *Blood bubbled forth as fire drank flesh and bones...*

Then I heard a different voice singing—it was Jesper, chanting words of praise for Hygelac.

> *... our king, protector, giver of rings,*
> *Our Hygelac, battle-hardy, fallen in Frisia...*

At these words a keening wail arose among the queen's women, an eerie wail that penetrated my very marrow. I opened my eyes and saw Queen Hygd standing rigid, right hand on the torque, head thrown back as she let her grief erupt into the air. I found myself in the grip of sorrow, releasing sounds from deep within me. To the rising storm of grief I added my own losses: husband, father, brothers. All the women were keening now as we joined our voices, wailing in a sisterhood of sorrow.

Now individual names were raised: "Hjalmar... Kasper... Erland... Torstein..." The litany of names spiraled higher, higher in a moan that grew into a shrieking climax. Some women fell to the ground, overcome. Others remained standing with arms upraised, blinded with tears. Beowulf's men stood guard lest anyone throw herself on the pyre as a further sacrifice.

The strong smell of burning hair and animal flesh had made me nauseous, and I withdrew for a time, stepping back from the heat until I could recover. All through that morning Beowulf, Hygd, Herdred and their people kept watch, watching as the last remnants that had belonged to their king—husband—uncle—father—brother—son—curled up in smoke and disappeared into the sky.

Embers were still glowing when the deep note of a horn sounded, drawing all eyes toward the sea. A ship? A ship! Perhaps survivors of the Frisian raid? It must be! Joyful shouts broke the silence. Beowulf lifted his head as if waking from a reverie. Thorstein ordered a cluster of young thanes to hurry down the cliff-path. I noticed Gorm and Saxe among them. We waited under the noonday sun, hopeful for good news in the midst of sorrow.

The men who appeared one by one, at the top of the path, looked beaten and exhausted, but at least they were alive.

"Lars! Leif! Aksel!"

As Beowulf reached out to these men, I recognized their faces. I'd seen them in Beowulf's band when he came to Heorot. So, once again they had survived.

"And the rest . . . ?" Beowulf asked.

"Unloading the ship. Twelve in all—but we managed. How did you get back?"

The speaker was staring at Beowulf in wonder.

"I swam," he said simply. "Aksel, were you pursued?" Beowulf's face darkened.

"No. The Franks and Frisians were busy burning our other ships when we slipped away. We thought you were dead!"

Aksel gripped Beowulf's shoulder, then gave him a hearty slap on the back.

"Thank the gods!"

Now other men appeared, accompanied by the young thanes laden with battle gear. They stopped near the edge of the pyre and dropped the booty on the ground: a number of swords and spears, two helmets, and a dozen shields. Then with a clatter Gorm and Saxe emptied out a fur robe containing plates, pitchers, jewelry . . .

What is this? Did Hygelac lose his life for such household nothings???

Beowulf must have been thinking similar thoughts.

"Throw it all on the fire!" he ordered. "Such loot was dearly bought, a poor exchange for the life of Hygelac!"

He took up a wooden shield, fiercely broke it in two and tossed it on the embers.

"Too dearly bought," he groaned.

Hygd still wore the golden necklace. She made no move to cast it on the pyre.

The funeral feast was a feast indeed. Eaglesgard was crammed with mourners, chiefly men, hungry and thirsty. Jugs of ale on each table were quickly emptied into wooden cups, as bowls and platters of food streamed in, carried by an army of servants: smoked eel, pickled herring, reindeer, venison, fresh herring, cod, roast duck, and herring again, salted this time. Great rounds of flatbread in woven baskets big as kettles found ready takers. Root crops and fruit were not yet in season, but we lacked for little else. One dish which I could not identify was revealed to be deer tongue—considered a delicacy.

"Here, my lady. Try it with this sauce of lingonberries. You won't find anything finer—'red gold' we call it."

The speaker at my elbow was a girl younger than Brita. By her shabby dress she appeared to be a slave, yet she spoke with ease. I had noted earlier the lack of formality at Eaglesgard, but was not prepared for such familiarity.

"What is your name, girl?" I asked stiffly.

"Runa, my lady. Deer tongue is well suited to a woman with child," she added.

Taken aback, I paused. *Runa, you had best keep your eyes—and your tongue—to yourself!*

"Thank you," I smiled.

She smiled in response and carried her sauce bowl to the next table.

"Ana," I whispered to my companion, "ask some of Hygd's women about that girl . . . She sees . . ." Then it struck me: *She sees what others do not. This girl could be useful.*

At Heorot on a high feast day the king and court would be served first, but here the throne and head table still sat empty. We had almost finished our meal when Redbeard's voice rang out from the doorway.

"The King's Council, Lord Beowulf, Queen Hygd, and . . . King Herdred!!!"

Cups and crockery clattered on the boards, benches scraped the floor as everyone rose. Then . . . silence. All seemed shocked. Now the murmurs began. "King Herdred?" "Not Beowulf?"

They had dressed Herdred in what must have been his father's cloak of fine red wool trimmed with bands of gold. It hung down to his feet. On his head he wore a circlet of gold much like Hygd's. He marched straight to the throne and climbed up on the high seat, pushing back the folds of the heavy cloak. His small hands gripped the arms, curved like eagle's claws. When he turned to the hall, his face was grave, his lips set in a firm line.

Where is the little boy I met just three days ago?

After seating Hygd in the adjoining throne, Thorstein planted himself to her right. Beowulf stood to the left of Herdred and raised his hand for silence.

"People of Eaglesgard, people of the Wedermark! The council has reached a decision. As the rightful heir of Hygelac, Herdred is now king. All hail King Herdred!"

Some mouths opened automatically to repeat the hail, but several hesitated. At this juncture Hygd nodded toward the door, where serving girls entered bearing pitchers of mead. Soon every cup was filled to the brim. Beowulf raised his goblet in a formal toast. "All hail King Herdred!" repeated Beowulf forcefully.

"All hail King Herdred!" came back the echo as cups were hoisted and drained.

Once again Beowulf spoke.

"I was urged to take the kingship, but I could not accept. I could not place myself between Hygelac and his son. In your presence, people of Eaglesgard, I take my oath to serve King Herdred, to aid and protect him, to be his man so long as I have life. All hail!"

"Hail," shouted the voices, more enthusiastically this time.

So Beowulf will be regent, mentor and advisor to the young king. It seems a sensible choice to me.

Apparently satisfied that all was now in order, Hygd and Herdred took their places at the head table, where fresh platters of food were quickly served. I noticed that Hygd took little, but Herdred ate eagerly. I was glad to see that his boy's appetite had not been affected by his new station.

When those at the head table had finished their meal, Beowulf approached us. Redbeard signaled for the others in the hall to leave. When they had gone, Beowulf spoke.

"King Herdred and Queen Hygd bid you stay, to discuss the matter of your ... your future here in Wedermark," he concluded.

"Very good, my lord." I smiled and rose, motioning for my people to join me for this council meeting, one on which our futures hung. We settled ourselves at the next table.

After some hesitation, Beowulf began.

"Queen Hygd tells me that you came to Eaglesgard in response to my invitation — given at Heorot years ago?"

"Yes, my lord, though you named Hrethric in that invitation. Hrethric is now dead, as are his brother Hrothmund and King Hrothgar himself. Heorot was burned to the ground by Ingeld, my late husband. Hrothgar's men are now ruled by Hrothulf, my traitorous cousin. So you see, Lord Beowulf, there is no home for me in Denmark."

"Stay with us, Freaw! I . . . we will need your seeing!"

All eyes turned toward Herdred, now standing beside his throne.

"It's true — she does, Beowulf! She saw Father in Valhalla! And she knew you were bringing me the sword!"

Now all eyes turned toward me. Beowulf spoke quietly.

"What do *you* see in your future, Lady Freawaru?"

I let a space of silence hang in the air before giving my answer.

"It would please me to make a home among the people of the Wedermark, Lord Beowulf. We have the means to set up a household here, and my men are ready to join your forces should you require their service."

Beowulf absorbed my words in silence. His forehead wrinkled in thought. Then his eyes brightened.

"You may be the solution to one of my own problems, Lady Freawaru. My hall — which lies a half day's ride from Eaglesgard — has long lacked a gracious lady to sit in the head chair, to present the mead cup to worthy champions. It has been dark and cheerless since my grandfather's death, and after it came to me there was little improvement. A sadness seems to hang over that hall. Perhaps . . . perhaps if you would consent to take up residence there . . . all that might change?"

His face showed mixed emotions, as if he were struggling with himself, but his eyes were beseeching. Something in his gaze held me fast, drawing me in. I almost felt dizzy, standing on a precipice. Taking a deep breath, I drew back from the edge.

"Perhaps." I echoed gravely, bowing to him. "I will carefully consider your most generous offer."

My response was measured, but inside my heart beat faster.

"Lord Beowulf, give me a day to make my answer. I must consult with my people."

"As you wish."

Beowulf bowed as our meeting ended.

At midday I found a moment to dismiss my women and pull my rune-bag from its chest. Should we accept Beowulf's offer? I was strongly inclined to do so, but wanted confirmation. I needed to consult the runes.

Slipping out of the mead hall, I made my way to the promontory where Hygelac's funeral rites had take place. For a time I stood motionless facing south — the direction of Heorot. Inhaling the sea breeze, I strove to clear my mind of recent events, to be fully present to this moment, this place. On a bare stretch of rock facing the sea, I knelt and pulled a white cloth from the bag. After spreading it out, I closed my eyes and offered up an invocation to Odin, giver of the runes. "God of the unknown, be present to me now. Reveal what is hidden. At issue is a home for us Danes."

Still with eyes shut, I reached into the fur pouch. My fingers met and closed on a rune-stick. I drew it out, laid it on the cloth, and opened my eyes. Ehwaz. Rune of forward movement. I had my answer.

Later that afternoon another formal oath-taking took place, in a location known only to those thanes and *athelings* who attended. Wulfgar, with my permission, was one of them, as were the rest of our men. That night Olaf described the scene to me.

"We followed Hygelac's — I mean Herdred's men—to a stone circle deep in the forest. In the center of a clearing stood the oath-stone. Not much to look at," he shrugged, "just a weathered stone with a rounded top. Each man had to kneel and place his hand on the stone and swear loyalty to Herdred. Then Herdred gave each of us a gold ring."

Olaf spread his left hand wide to display his new treasure.

I thought to jest with him.

"So, now you are Herdred's man, you won't be supporting Freawaru anymore?"

"Oh no, my lady!" His face showed immediate distress. "I'll have to fight for Herdred if it comes to that, but you'll always be first in my . . . thoughts." He trailed off, blushing.

"Thank you, Olaf. I value your . . . honesty."

The Geats, now Herdred's men, assembled in Eaglesgard the next morning to hear details about the Frisian raid and take counsel for their own future. Wulfgar and I were asked to attend, and I also brought Ana with me. After Hygd and Herdred were seated, no time was spent on formalities. A tall aetheling stood and asked the question on every mind.

"Beowulf, how did Hygelac meet his end? Tell us what happened."

Beowulf took some time before answering. Then he smiled as if recalling happier times.

"You all know how Hygelac chafed at the bonds of winter, how eager for the spring that he might launch a raiding party and set off for adventure."

Nodding heads. Rueful smiles.

"When his blood was up, Hygelac was not to be denied. He would go unprovoked to Frisia, to 'the fat Frisians' as he called them, 'ripe for raiding.' As his lieutenant I was bound to join him. He relied on my strength to match his own brave heart."

Here Beowulf paused, looking down. Then he raised his head.

"Einar, I will tell you, tell you all, the whole story."

Each Geatish warrior leaned forward in anticipation, as did we Danes.

"You all know that in every battle my place was at the front. When we landed on the Frisian shore I advanced ahead of Hygelac. At first the attack went well. I had taken thirty trophies when a horn sounded behind me. It was Hygelac, surrounded by a horde of Franks. What had begun as a raid now turned into a battle."

Beowulf looked away, as if hearing that horn again.

"Hygelac had no chance. He fell to the blade of their standard-bearer, the brave and noble Dayraven. By the time I could reach Hygelac's body the Frank was already stripping his corpse, removing the golden collar to carry it back to his own king. But that did not happen!"

Beowulf raised both fists in the air.

"I seized Dayraven in my arms and crushed the life from him!"

Now he called for ale, and downed a cup before resuming his story.

"Our men were badly outnumbered. The river tribes had joined together — the Hugas, the Hetwares — river jackals who looted corpses as they floated down the Rhine. We killed as many as we could on our retreat to the ship. I held off the jackals while our few survivors loaded booty and set sail. I swam home alone, to return the torque to Hygd."

He bowed in Hygd's direction, then shook his head.

"After that encounter the Franks will be our friends no more. No more trading on those shores. No more Frankish blades for our warriors or Frankish glass for our womenfolk!"

Einar broke the silence that followed.

"Should we expect an immediate reprisal?"

Beowulf considered his answer.

"No, I think not, for their losses were great. It will take them time to rebuild their force. But we too lost many men."

Here he stopped and looked at Wulfgar.

"Wulfgar, you and your men are welcome additions to our corps — since you have a mind to join us?"

Wulfgar stood and made a slight bow. "We do, Lord Beowulf. We have taken the oath."

Beowulf nodded in satisfaction.

"Now, to our royal Danish guest, who has waited patiently for a hearing."

He smiled openly at me.

"Lady Freawaru. It is your turn. Please tell us of Hrothgar and the events at Heorot."

I rose, bowed toward Hygd and Herdred, then opened my word-hoard, carefully selecting those words which would best suit my story yet reveal only what I wanted others to know.

"As you know, Lord Beowulf, when you came to Heorot I was betrothed to Ingeld of the Heathobards. Our marriage took place at Heorot the second winter after you killed the Grendel."

Here there were grunts and nods of approval among the men—I assumed in approval of Beowulf's feat rather than my marriage.

"With a small band of my people, we journeyed by boat and horseback with Ingeld and his men to his hall among the Heathobards, on the River Elbe. For the first winter we lived together peacefully. Then an old warrior, Starcartherus by name, arrived at Wulfhaus. He stirred up old resentments against the Danes and incited Ingeld to take revenge against my father, who had killed Ingeld's father long ago."

Here I paused, remembering that terrible night when Starcartherus had called Ingeld a coward and me a whore. I chose not to repeat those words in this company.

Beowulf was frowning; he had a question.

"Did not Ingeld swear to keep the peace between Danes and Heathobards as part of the marriage contract?"

"Yes, my lord, he did — but he broke his word."

I waited for cries of indignation, but heard none. Beowulf merely looked thoughtful.

"Ah, I see. A conflict of loyalties. A hard choice."

"What do you mean? What choice?" My anger was rising.

"A choice between avenging his father's death, and keeping his vow to you — conflicting duties. He could not do both."

What is this? Beowulf almost sounds sorry for Ingeld. Where is his sympathy for me?

"He paid for his choice with his life!" I flared.

"Yes, that is often the price," observed Beowulf, still in that maddeningly calm tone of voice. "But tell us," he continued, "what happened at Heorot? How did Ingeld take his revenge?"

I swallowed my anger to reply.

"That spring he and his men left Wulfhaus. They left during the night, so we Danes would be unaware of their departure. They were gone for many days. We waited, in suspense, fearful of the outcome — for we knew they had gone to Heorot."

I had to stop, suddenly reliving the agony of that suspense. Beowulf handed me a goblet of wine, concern on his face.

So he does care about me! But ... I am carrying Ingeld's baby ...

"Lady Freawaru? Can you continue?" His voice was gentle.

"Yes, Lord Beowulf, I can continue."

Looking around at the faces before me, I saw concern — and curiosity.

You are a king's daughter, Freawaru, a queen's daughter. You are a warrior ...

I lifted my head proudly.

"When the Heathobards attacked Heorot, they found a welcome party ready for them!" I smiled grimly.

"With burning brands the Heathobards attacked the hall, hoping to trap Hrothgar and his men inside and burn them alive!"

Knowing nods among the men. Yes, this was a well-known tactic.

"But my father and his men were not inside Heorot; they lay in wait outside. They had set a trap for the invaders!"

More vigorous shaking of heads. *Why, they are enjoying my story! Perhaps that's how I should think of it—as a story!*

"Inside Heorot, inside the mead hall ..." I paused, "... waited Queen Wealtheow, my mother! Beside her stood our harper, singing loudly as if entertaining at a feast. When the hall timbers caught fire, my mother emerged dressed in white like a Valkyrie."

Wonder and surprise shone on the faces of my listeners.

"Yes! Like a Valkyrie! The Heathobards were momentarily stunned, long enough for father and his men to surround them!"

"And Ingeld? Where was Ingeld?" asked Beowulf.

"Leading the Heathobards. Queen Wealtheow threw fire in his face. Blinded, he ran straight into the sword of Hrothgar, my father."

Cries and shouts erupted among the Geats. Beowulf lifted his hand, but it was Hygd who spoke.

"So your father killed your husband?"

I turned toward her chair and saw her staring at me in horror.

"Almost." *It's a story, Freawaru. You are telling a story.* "Almost. Ingeld still lived when his men — those who survived — brought him back to Wulfhaus. He died there ... three days later."

"So, Hrothgar had the victory."

This time it was Beowulf who spoke.

"Victory?" I pondered this. "For the moment, yes. The Heathobards were driven off, but they did succeed in burning father's mead hall. Heorot lies in ashes."

Beowulf shook his head sadly.

"That shining hall — a beacon for every warrior seeking fame and glory. Gone ..." he looked at me again. "... and Hrothgar?"

"Gone too. When I returned to Heorot with my small band of loyal Danes, we found Hrothgar lying on his deathbed. We gave him a royal burial, a ship burial, set aflame at sea."

Exclamations of surprise greeted this information.

"By Thor, I wish I'd been there to see such a thing" declared Einar. "A full ship burial!"

"I've only heard of it in ancient lays," added Thorstein.

Their reactions pleased me. I was comforted by their recognition of the great honor given to King Hrothgar, my father.

"Who had the honor of setting Hrothgar's funeral ship ablaze?" asked Beowulf.

"Ah." I frowned. "The flaming arrow was shot by Hrothulf, Hrothgar's nephew, but he proved to be a traitor! He poisoned my two brothers and took the throne for himself!"

My eyes flooded with angry tears, but I blinked them back.

"By the gods! This is news indeed! Hrothulf rules at Heorot?" Thorstein looked incredulous.

"Yes, Hrothulf rules at Heorot," I echoed bitterly.

"And what of Queen Wealtheow, your lady mother? Does she live?" Beowulf asked.

"She lives and she remains in Heorot. She would not leave her sons to lie unmourned. I will never see her again."

Now I could no longer hold back my tears.

Hygd's voice cut through my pain. "I have lost my husband, but you have lost every member of your family! Hear me, Lady Freawaru. You have now found friends among the Geats. We will be sisters, you and I; we will be family."

Surprised by the warmth in her tone and the smile on her lips, I hesitated.

Can I trust what she is saying? Can her invitation be genuine?

Hygd held up her jeweled hand and slid a gold circle from one of her fingers.

"Take this ring, Lady Freawaru, as a bond of friendship."

She held it out toward me in the palm of her hand.

Responding with my heart, I involuntarily did the same. Removing a ring from my left hand, I extended it toward Hygd.

Beowulf stepped forward and drew out his dagger.

"A bond of blood?" He looked at each of us in turn.

"Yes," we answered.

While Beowulf held the knife, Hygd and I each touched a finger to the blade. When blood sprang forth, we pressed our finger tips together. Then we exchanged rings, slipping them over our reddened fingers. Tears streaming down our faces, we bowed to one another and to King Herdred.

"Hail the union of Geats and Danes! Hail the bond between Hygd and Freawaru!" Beowulf's voice boomed out.

"Hail! Hail!"

I recognized Herdred's boyish shout among the cheering voices. Then Hygd spoke again.

"Sister Freawaru, we hope you will accept the offer of Beowulf's hall as your residence. And you may choose from my own servants to fill out the number needed for your new household."

Runa. Ask for Runa.

"Thank you, Queen Hygd . . . Sister Hygd. I do accept your generous offer and the generous offer of Beowulf. Thank you both for your friendship and hospitality. From henceforth we Danes and Geats will be as one."

More cheers and shouts, but I had begun to feel faint, and staggered slightly. Beowulf immediately came to my side. He took my arm and led me to the table where my companions sat, beaming. As Beowulf stepped away, Wulfgar murmured.

"Well done again, Lady Freawaru." He was grinning like a boy.

"Thank the gods," whispered Ana. "You've won her over!"

Apparently I had.

Later that night, still feeling slightly queasy from the smoke and smells inside the mead hall, I slipped outside for a lungful of fresh air. Ketil, acting as hall guard, gave me a questioning smile.

"A fine night, my lady."

"Yes." I nodded.

I looked up at the cloudless sky; a pale half moon hung above us, partially lighting the darkness. I lifted my chin, inhaled the coolness, and licked my lips, savoring the tang of sea-salt spray blown from the cliff edge. Ahh...

"That's Aurvandil's Toe*," said Ketil, gesturing toward the sky.

"Aurvandil's Toe? Is that a star?" I asked in surprise.

"Yes, my lady. Don't you know the story?"

At the shake of my head Ketil launched enthusiastically into an explanation.

"It seems Thor was carrying Aurvandil on his back in a basket out of Jotunheimar, but one of Aurvandil's toes stuck out of the basket. Thor saw that it had frozen, so he broke if off and cast it into the sky!"

Ketil chuckled to himself, closed his eyes and yawned. I was about to ask for more detail when something else caught my attention.

Wait! What's this? A serpent, long and black, flying like a bat across the moon's face.

"Ketil, look to the moon. Do you see that creature?"

"I see only the moon," he said, squinting.

The creature had by now disappeared. I thought it had wings...and a barbed tail.

"I saw...a kind of serpent. Ketil, I swear it."

"A serpent, my lady, a sky-serpent? Do you mean...a dragon?"

At the last word his voice fell.

"Have you never seen one before above Eaglesgard?"

---

* This may refer to the pole star, or to the planet Venus, or to the toe of the constellation Orion.

"Never, although... they were spoken of long ago in my father's time. Perhaps you saw a cloud passing, my lady."

"A cloud? Perhaps." I considered this for a moment, knowing it was not so. "Ketil, what lies to the north of Eaglesgard?"

"That's an area of high heathland, seldom visited. We have no reason to go there."

"I see. Thank you Ketil, and a good night to you." I nodded my head as he opened the heavy door for me to step back inside.

No informing image came to me that night, nor in the nights to follow, but I could not escape the thought that Denmark might not be the only country to harbor monsters.

Chapter Four
Hrethelskeep

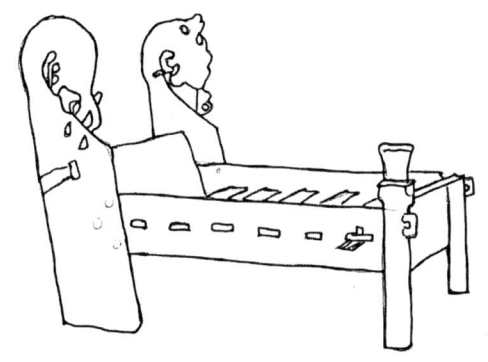

Royal bed from a ship burial in Norway.

"Horses. We'll need horses—and wagons to carry our goods." Wulfgar gestured toward the stack of travel and sea chests in one corner of the mead hall.

"Yes," I said, "I have thought of that. I've already asked Beowulf to speak to the kinfolk of those killed in Frisia. If they have any carts and horses they are willing to sell, I'll pay a good price."

It was late evening as we sat around the mead hall hearth, laying plans for our future. A handful of Geats were stationed inside and out as hall guards, but everyone else had retired for the night. The crackle and hiss of the fire and its warmth on my face sent a wave of contentment through me. I looked around at my companions. We were all assured of a home now: Beowulf's home. As if listening to my thoughts, Ana spoke.

"What does Beowulf call his hall? I've not heard it mentioned."

"He told me it was named for his grandfather," I answered. "It is called 'Hrethelskeep'."

"Hrethelskeep? By the gods that's a mouthful! These Geats like long names."

Saxe laughed and nudged Gorm in the ribs. "Maybe we should change *our* names."

"That won't be required," I observed drily. "I hope you men were more serious when taking that oath of loyalty to Herdred."

Saxe made a face. "Herdred is a fine lad, but we all know that Beowulf is the real leader here — and any man would be proud to serve him."

The other men nodded in agreement. Now Ragnhild voiced a concern of my own: "What about Hygd's offer of servants? How many will we need to set up our household at.... Hrethelskeep?"

"I think it will be best to visit the hall before we make such decisions," I said. "After we see what arrangements already exist, we can better judge what we will need."

I looked across the hearth at the faces of my women. Ana caught my gaze.

"I, for one, will be glad to leave this hall," she said, yawning and stretching, "though we've been treated well enough," she added hastily. "I hope Beowulf's hall is not so drafty as this one. The wind comes right through the walls — especially at night — have you noticed?"

In confirmation of her complaint, the fire suddenly blazed up as if puffed by a bellows.

"Don't worry, Ana, we'll find a warm place for you to sleep at Hrethelskeep," I reassured my old friend. "Perhaps we will weave new tapestries to adorn the walls — and keep out drafts. Right now we should all get some sleep. Tomorrow we have much to do."

As I rose, yawning, Brita hurried to my side, ready to help should I need her.

"My lady?" She spoke in a low voice. "What will be my place in this new...hall?"

I knew what she meant, but I had not yet made up my mind about her status. By circumstance Brita was a slave, yet during our long association she had come to seem more like — what? A friend? Hmmm...a freewoman...?

Should I free Brita? If I do, how would the other women react?

"You will help me with the baby, Brita, just as you wanted. But remember: no one is to know of its presence just yet — no one outside our group."

She nodded, apparently satisfied for the moment.

The next morning brought as fine a spring day as one could wish. Breezes from inland carried the fresh scent of herbs and other growing things. A brilliant sun shone in a cloudless sky. It was a day to be up and out of doors — a day for action! As I turned back from the door of the mead hall, Beowulf sought me out.

"Lady Freawaru, I have good news." He gave me a broad smile. "Ragnar — or as you call him, 'Redbeard' — has found thirteen families who are willing to sell one of their horses, and three wagons are also available. That should provide a mount for each of your people, with enough extra horses to pull the wagons."

I did a quick mental calculation.

"Thank you, Lord Beowulf, but does that not leave us one horse short? We'll have two horses left to pull three wagons."

"No, my lady." His smile broadened. "Queen Hygd has something else to bestow upon you. Here she comes with the gift."

Beowulf beamed with approval as Hygd entered the mead hall, followed by Herdred leading a large dun-colored horse with a dark stripe running from its forelock to the tip of its tail. I recognized it immediately.

"Why, that's Burningfax! He was one of my favorites in father's herd!"

"Yes," Beowulf grinned, "he was a gift to me from King Hrothgar. I gave him to Hygd, and now she gives him to you."

Hygd took the reins from Herdred and turned toward me.

"This horse is very high-spirited, sister Freawaru. I hope you can handle him. He is not so strong as Skinfaxi, but he's strong enough."

Is that a challenge I see in her eyes?

"Thank you, Queen Hygd. If I remember the old story correctly, Skinfaxi had to pull the cart of the sun. Burningfax will only have to carry me, so I should be able to manage him."

Delighted with this unexpected gift, I impulsively embraced Hygd, then quickly gave a bow. "Thank you again, my sister. Someday I shall repay your generosity."

Neither of us could have guessed how that payment would be made.

As I rose to my feet, a dark vision suddenly replaced the light: Hygd lying on a bed of blood writhing in agony, her mouth open but making no sound. I swayed and thrust out my arms to steady myself. Herdred rushed forward to take my elbow. He looked up anxiously.

"What is it, Freaw? Are you alright? Did you see something?"

"I'm not sure... I saw... a woman... perhaps in childbirth?"

"Giving birth? Surely a good omen!" Hygd herself spoke, eyeing me curiously.

"Perhaps."

I straightened and leaned forward to rub my cheek against the soft muzzle of Burningfax. He lifted his head, ears twitching, and gazed at me with deep brown eyes. Breathing in his animal smell, I stroked the muscles of his strong neck.

"Hello, old friend. Remember me?"

Burningfax gave a soft whinny in answer. He snorted and shook his mane, then nosed at my fingers as if snuffling for the apples I used to feed him — back in Heorot.

Ah, Burningfax, Heorot, home. Strange: both of us have left our homeland, only to be reunited here. Finding you again must be a good omen.

I put the recent bloody vision behind me and looked around at the earnest faces gazing back.

"Beowulf, how soon can we visit Hrethelskeep?" I asked cheerfully.

"Today, if you like." He seemed pleased by my eagerness."I will take you there myself, accompanied by Queen Hygd and King Herdred, for they too are curious to see Hrethelskeep, which seldom has visitors. Redbeard and Thorstein can take charge here for a few days while we are away."

He looked at Hygd and Herdred, who nodded assent.

"Then I shall ride Burningfax this very day!"

I patted my new, old friend and handed the reins back to Herdred with a smile.

It was midday by the time the necessary purchases were completed and we were ready to ride. My coffers of silver were somewhat depleted, but I still had gold enough to finance our future.

Beowulf had mounted a fine black stallion named Frostmane, another of my father's gifts. Hygd and Herdred rode matching grays. Burningfax and I completed the royal party.

Hygd chose three of her servants to ride on the horses pulling our wagons. To my surprise, Runa was one of them. So, was she not a thrall after all? I should have known from the length of her long, black hair, glossy as a raven's wing. Thralls were usually required to keep their hair cut short, though at Heorot my mother had allowed our female slaves to let their hair grow out after the initial cropping. The resulting good will and cooperation were well worth it, she always said.

Dear Mother, always so wise. Are you still alive? By Freyja, I hope so.

Brita hung back when it came time to mount the shaggy fjord-horse allotted to her.

"Oh, my lady," she gasped. "I've never ridden a horse in all my life! Couldn't I ride in one of the wagons instead?"

Perplexed, I paused, but Runa stepped forward with a solution.

"She can ride in my wagon, lady Freawaru. We can tie her horse to the back."

In response to Brita's beseeching look, I agreed.

"All right, but Brita, that horse will become your charge once we reach Hrethelskeep. You will be responsible for its care and feeding."

"Thank you, my lady." Brita bowed to me and smiled shyly at Runa as she climbed nimbly atop the chests in Runa's wagon.

"Everybody ready?" shouted Beowulf. "Let's be off while the sun is high. Stay close. Don't lose sight of the horse in front of you, as the path divides in places. The trail gets narrow in the forest and there are a few rocky slopes to negotiate, but unless there were rock falls during the winter the way should be open."

Rock falls? Are we climbing into those distant mountains? Has Beowulf been absent from his hall all winter, not to know what conditions lie ahead?

"Don't worry." Herdred drew his horse near mine, handling it as expertly as a grown man. "All our horses are hard-hooved and sure-footed. This will be a fine adventure!"

That's what your father thought about the Frisian raid. By Freyja, I pray this adventure turns out much better!

We set off at a brisk pace, with Wulfgar and my men at the rear. Any anxiety I felt soon melted in the warm sunshine, as we headed for our new home. The clatter of horses' hooves and the creak of wagons made a kind of music in my ears. By the time Eaglesgard disappeared from sight, the flat and rocky headland of the Wedermark had given way to birch groves and mossy banks, for we followed the course of a rushing river. Göta Alv, Beowulf called it. The trail sometimes ran close enough for a glimpse of its sparkling water, seen through the new young leaves of the rustling birches.

Hygd and I must have presented a colorful spectacle. Hygd's blonde hair flowed over a cloak of dark wool, while my golden cloak set off the red-gold of my hair.

Two sorrowing widows, ready for adventure!

I giggled inwardly. We were no more grown up than Herdred!

It felt good to be on a horse again. I had no difficulty controlling Burningfax, who obediently followed the horse in front of him, Herdred's gray. Riding astride was difficult in my long dress and apron, which I had bunched up in front of me, exposing my legs up to the thigh, but my cloak covered them. The warm flanks of Burningfax rubbed my skin where it was not protected by the saddle cloth, and the stirrups were too big for my feet to fit securely, so I was grateful for my mount's good behavior.

I wonder what Beowulf's hall will be like — more grand than Eaglesgard?

Ana had heard from one of Hygd's women that Hygelac had given Beowulf many hydes of land when Beowulf returned from Heorot — further rewards for his deeds of valor. He must be a respected landowner as well as a valiant warrior.

We climbed gradually, riding higher and higher, past trickling waterfalls released from the snow-melt of winter, then up onto rocky slopes (just as Beowulf had described them), then down again into green valleys that smelled of spring. Up, down. Up, down, over and around.

Overhead the sun felt almost hot. In open stretches I threw back my hood, but there were other stretches where the sun did not penetrate the dense stands of fir and pine, where snow lay at the base of the trees. In such somber passages I pulled my cloak more closely about me.

Finally, just when my backside was feeling numb from so many unaccustomed hours in the saddle, we emerged into a broad valley. High on its gently sloping sides I saw white dots — no doubt sheep grazing on the new green grass. In the distance wavering plumes of smoke marked the site of longhouses, and—at last—a large structure. The sound of a horn echoed through the valley.

This must be Hrethelskeep, Beowulf's village.

My heart rose in anticipation. Burningfax seemed to recognize our destination and picked up his pace. Beowulf urged his own horse into a trot and we followed suit, the four of us together. I reveled in the prospect of our journey's end.

As we drew near the outbuildings, clustered in a line at the base of the slopes, I noted signs of neglect: missing planks in side walls, breaks

Fanning the Flames

in the wattle fencing. This did not match my image of Beowulf as a prosperous landowner. And where were his people? Surely they would be eager to welcome their lord? As if divining my thoughts, Beowulf slowed his horse and shouted over his shoulder to Hygd, Herdred, and me.

"We come on short notice, so some lapses of hospitality may be expected. Fear not. All will be amended."

I glanced at Hygd; she raised her eyebrows and shrugged, but her face wore a smile.

"Sister Freawaru, I think our presence here will be much needed!"

Herdred rode ahead to join Beowulf as we trotted into the settlement, so Hygd and I now rode side by side. Faces began to appear in doorways, recognition lighting their features. From one longhouse a young boy, barely old enough to walk, toddled out into the path, almost under the hooves of our horses. We pulled on the reins, causing our horses to stop abruptly, while the boy's mother snatched him out of harm's way.

"Have a care, lad, or you won't grow up to become one of my thanes!"

"Lord Beowulf, welcome home! We have missed your presence," shouted the mother as we rode on past. I wondered again how long Beowulf had been absent from his hall.

In a short time we reached the largest building, clearly the mead hall. Two fellows in ragged clothes with collar chains around their sallow necks emerged from the hall, mouths agape at our appearance.

"Here, you thralls — where is Sigfast, the *atheling* who's supposed to be in charge here?" Beowulf demanded, coming to a halt.

"Sigfast? Dead, I think," said one.

"There was much sickness during the winter," added the other.

Are they simple-minded? To speak so discourteously to their lord?

I wondered how Beowulf would react to their lack of manners, but he seemed more concerned about the possible death of this Sigfast.

"Not Sigfast," he cried, "not another dear comrade!"

Just then a tall, ruddy man strode out of the mead hall, clearly an atheling by his dress and demeanor.

"Lord Beowulf!" he boomed. "At last we see you!" He hurried forward as Beowulf dismounted, and the two men clasped shoulders.

"Magnus, what's this I hear of Sigfast's death? Is it true?"

"I'm sorry to say it is true, my lord. He died one bitter night when winter still gripped the valley — died of a fever, he did. We had to wait for a spring thaw to build the funeral pyre. But more of that later. Who have you brought with you? Ladies?" He smiled broadly, revealing missing teeth, as he nodded toward Hygd and me.

"Here, you louts," he shouted at the thralls, "help these ladies dismount!"

Both Hygd and I hastily slid off our horses to forestall any contact with these dirty fellows, but we handed them the reins.

"Magnus, this is our queen, Queen Hygd, Hygelac's wife. Have you never met her?"

Magnus immediately made a deep bow.

"Forgive me, Queen Hygd. I came to your wedding feast years ago, but have not seen you since that great event. And this young man . . . ?" He turned to Herdred, who had joined our group after giving instructions to the thralls about the care of his horse.

"This must be your son, for he looks just like Hygelac. Where . . . ?"

Our faces must have reflected our recent loss, for Magnus suddenly stopped and turned to Beowulf. "Does Hygelac live?"

"No," said Beowulf soberly. "Hygelac died in a raid against the Frisians, brought down by a Frankish blade. He feasts in Valhalla now."

Magnus absorbed this information in silence, then shook his head.

"A great loss, a great loss indeed. Who is now king?"

Beowulf called Herdred to his side. "This young man: Herdred, son of Hygelac. Until he comes of age I will be his advisor and protector. The council at Eaglesgard has so decided."

Magnus looked at Beowulf as if in doubt, but he bent his knee to Herdred and made his vow. "I will serve you, King Herdred, as my liege."

"Rise, Magnus. I welcome your service." Herdred spoke in a boyish treble, but with solemnity.

By now the rest of our group had arrived at the mead hall door. Wulfgar made his way to my side.

"Where shall I direct the wagons, Lady Freawaru?" he asked quietly.

Ignoring Wulfgar for the moment, Beowulf came to my side, took my hand, and led me forward.

"Magnus, this is the lady Freawaru, daughter of King Hrothgar of the Danes. At my invitation she has agreed to take up residence at Hrethelskeep. Is my grandfather's house still empty?"

Magnus bowed slightly, not hiding his surprise. "Yes, Lord Beowulf, it is. No one . . ." he paused, seeming to consider his words. "No one has entered it . . . since your departure."

Behind me I heard an intake of breath.

"Empty all winter? By the gods, there will be work for us all to get it ready!"

The outburst had come from Ana, who stood beside Wulfgar whacking travel dust and pine needles from her cloak.

"These are my people," I said drily, gesturing to the assemblage now surrounding us.

My women were easing themselves off their horses, no doubt as sore and stiff as myself. Brita scrambled down from her wagon perch to join them, leaving Runa at the reins. The rest of our men kept their mounts in the rear, looking about curiously at their new home — if home it was to be. Suddenly I had doubts.

"One moment." Beowulf held up his hand. "We've been told of sickness during the winter. Is there pestilence here, now?"

Magnus shook his head.

"Nay, my lord, we have lost many good folk, but only through accident, old age, and the usual sicknesses. We will need replacements to do the spring planting — you come in good time with fresh hands."

I heard Saxe, Olaf, and Gorm snorting behind me and knew that they saw themselves as warriors, not farmers, but clearly there was much to be done here to repair the ravages of death and a bitter winter.

"We will talk of this after we eat, Magnus. Send word to the women of the settlement to prepare a suitable feast for our guests."

"As you wish, Lord Beowulf." Magnus bowed and turned away.

After the departure of Magnus, Beowulf led Herdred, Hygd, and their retinue into the mead hall. I and my people followed. As my eyes adjusted to the dim interior, I saw that Beowulf's hall was almost as big as Eaglesgard, though clearly much older. The stamped dirt floor was cold beneath the thin leather of my boots, and the reek of burnt grease from the hearth pit filled my nostrils. The walls smelled of dampness and decay; the benches lining the walls were dark and worn.

"Welcome to Hrethelskeep, my friends," said Beowulf cheerfully. "Tonight we will eat and sleep in the mead hall. Tomorrow we will determine the suitability of other quarters for our Danish friends, and put all in order."

He sounded confident, but I did not think "putting all in order" could be done quickly or easily in this establishment. Too weary to ponder the issue, I settled myself on a bench and leaned back against the rough wall.

Brita hurried forward; she knelt to remove my boots and rub my feet, aching from the pressure of the stirrups. Removing my cloak, she folded it into a pillow and placed it behind me. Gratefully, I sank down on the cushioned space. I must have slipped into a doze, for when I opened my eyes a fire was blazing in the hearth and tantalizing aromas rose from cooking pots hung over the fire.

"My lady?"

Runa stood before me with a bowl of water and a towel. My eyes met hers.

"All will be well," she said, returning my gaze.

I sat up, surprised at these unexpected words.

"My old rune master used to tell me the same thing," I said, yawning.

"Was she right?" asked Runa.

"*She* was a *he*—but yes, he was usually right." I paused. "Why did you say *she*?"

"Because my rune master was a woman," answered Runa calmly.

I was just about to dip my hands in the water, but stopped.

"You know runes?"

"Yes," she said simply. "Here, use this towel; water is dripping on your clothes."

My eyes widened at this admonition, but I quelled a hasty retort.

She knows runes? From a female rune master?

"We will speak of this later," I said.

"As you wish, my lady."

She bowed and turned away.

Perhaps it was our hunger or perhaps it was the unexpected skill of the cooks at Hrethelskeep, but food that night had never tasted better to me: succulent pork turned on a spit and sweetened with the last of the stored apples, haunches of venison with lingonberry sauce, and bread—wonderful bread! This bread was new to me; baked flat and crisp on a metal griddle, it went perfectly with the good hard cheeses and herring in vinegar—all washed down with foaming cups of barley ale.

We ate ravenously; we ate until we fell asleep at our places—at least some of us. I heard Ana snoring with her head on the table before sleep overtook me, but I had managed to make my way back to my cushioned wall bench before collapsing there.

Fanning the Flames

Brita must have covered me with a sleeping robe, for when I awoke during the night to use the latrine, I was sweating, my hair clinging to my face. I sat up and turned my head slowly, hoping to clear away the fog of ale.

A sour smell throughout the room turned my stomach, and I rose hastily lest I add to the vomit on the mead hall floor. Moving slowly to the door, I nodded to the guard, lifted the bar and slipped outside.

Cool, damp air caressed my face and the wave of nausea subsided. Now, where was the latrine? Only a half moon hung in the night sky to guide me. Stepping cautiously, I felt my way along the outside walls, ducking under support posts. By the time I found the wattle fencing around the waste pit I was wide awake.

The latrine was already occupied. As I felt for the gate latch I saw a head that seemed to float above the top row of fencing. A gray head. A woman's head.

"Oh, excuse me, I..."

"Husband, husband, where are you? When do you come to my rescue?"

Was I hearing correctly? These desperate mutterings made no sense to me.

"May I help you, old mother?"

I opened the gate wide enough to see a gaunt form: an ancient woman. Her face was pale and bony, but her eyes blazed in the moonlight like coals of fire. She whirled toward me.

"Curse you," she hissed, "Curse you and all your kind!"

Shocked, I lifted a hand to ward off her curse—and found myself staring through my fingers into emptiness. No figure, no woman, nothing. Had I been dreaming? Slowly, I let myself into the enclosure and gingerly lowered myself onto the wooden frame provided. It was icy cold.

Next morning there were scattered groans and mutterings as we roused ourselves to greet the day—our first full day in our new home. Hygd looked as though she had barely slept, but Herdred was bright-eyed and full of energy. He went out with Beowulf and the other men while we women dressed—or merely smoothed out the clothes we'd slept in. Runa attended Hygd while Brita came to assist me.

"Good morrow, Lady Freawaru. Did you sleep well?" asked Brita.

"Yes—no—that is, I had a strange... dream."

"A dream?" called Hygd. "I'm glad someone could sleep. There must be bugs in these furs... I was tossing all night!"

Her complaint drew my full attention.

"Fleas? We'd better examine all the bedding! Brita, bring a torch from the wall!"

Brita helped me remove the furs on my bench, while Runa did the same for Hygd. We spread them on an empty table and parted the fine hairs with a comb to look closely for signs of infestation. After an extensive search we had found no trace of the dreaded bugs, but we did find something else when we returned the robes to their benches. Runa noticed it first.

"Look, Lady Freawaru." She pointed to the bench upon which Hygd had slept. "Those look like runes."

"Brita, bring the light here."

I bent over and ran my fingers slowly across the scarred surface.

"Why, you're right . . . these are not random scratches. See—they repeat: Nauthiz, Hagalaz . . ."

"And Isa," finished Runa.

"Yes, Isa," I confirmed, nodding in agreement. We exchanged knowing looks.

"What are you talking about?"

Hygd joined us, stepping in front of Runa and peering down at the lines on the wood.

"These are runes, runes of power," I answered gravely.

"What do they mean?" asked Hygd, wrinkling her brow.

"I fear they mean that someone wishes harm to the occupants of this hall—Beowulf must see this!"

"Good morning, ladies. Are you ready to tour the settlement? Lady Freawaru can now inspect her new home."

We all turned to the doorway, where Beowulf stood smiling.

"My lord, there is something here you need to see first—here, on this bench."

Hygd summoned Beowulf to her side and I pointed to the place on the bench. He bent to look, but seemed not to understand.

"A few scratches—no doubt carved by idle hands during some long-ago feast, for the marks are old. Why do they concern you?" He looked at us both in puzzlement.

"My lord," I exclaimed, "these are runes, runes of power!"

"Oh? Can you . . ." he paused. "Can you interpret their meaning, or should I send for our rune master?" He paused again. "Sigfast . . . was our rune master."

"I can read them," I answered. "Look." I placed my forefinger next to Nauthiz. "This first one with the crossed lines is 'Nauthiz,' a rune of binding, of constraint. It's meant to inflict pain and suffering. The next is called 'Hagalaz.' It brings about disorder and disruption. The third and last in the sequence is 'Isa' representing ice; it causes bondage, standstill. It puts a halt to all motion."

Beowulf looked at me quizzically.

"So, you think there is power in these . . . marks?"

"I do. These are runes of binding and destruction; they were designed to dismay and dishearten whoever dwells within these walls. I wonder . . ."

The signs of neglect and decay I had noticed upon our arrival now began to make sense, but I needed to know more. Now the questions tumbled out.

"Lord Beowulf, how long was Hrethelskeep a home for you? Did you ever feel that some dark force was at work here? Is there a reason you have been so long absent from your own hall?"

"Freawaru, really! How can you ask such things?" Hygd's voice forestalled any further questions. "You are making too much of these . . . scratches."

Beowulf's face had lost its smile.

"My grandfather died of sorrow in this place — but I do not wish to speak of that. As for my absence from Hrethelskeep, I have been serving Hygelac at Eaglesgard for the past winter." Now his tone became positively icy. "King Herdred and the men are waiting. Join us now, please."

Beowulf did not wait for us to gather our cloaks, but walked stiffly out of the mead hall. Hygd touched my arm.

"Sister Freawaru, you have upset our host!" Her tone was accusing.

"I know, and I am sorry for it, but this is a serious matter. Besides causing damage in the past, those runes could affect the future — of everyone here."

As we gathered our things and emerged into the light, I tried to shake off a feeling of dread, but I wondered: *what else may we find on our morning tour?*

Beowulf stood just outside the mead hall with Herdred, Magnus, and our men. As we approached, Herdred ran forward to greet me.

"Freaw, did you dream last night? I did!" Not waiting for my reply, he tumbled out his tale. "... and when I fought the dragon, I won! Do you think that is a good omen for my reign?"

I smiled at his eagerness. "Yes, my lord, I'm sure it is."

Now Beowulf approached and addressed me formally.

"Lady Freawaru, I thought you would want to see Hrethel's longhouse before making a decision about a place to live." His voice bore no trace of his earlier irritation.

"Yes. Thank you, Lord Beowulf. That is very thoughtful."

"I am glad to please you." He turned. "King Herdred, lead the way and I will bring the ladies. Magnus, while we are inspecting the longhouse, assemble the villagers in front of the mead hall to meet our guests."

"Yes, my lord."

Drawing Hygd and me to his side, Beowulf followed Herdred as we walked together to the longhouse nearest the mead hall.

"I think my sister Freawaru should be the first to enter." Hygd smiled at me.

"Well said, my queen." Beowulf nodded his approval.

As we reached the open door, Beowulf took my hand to help me across the raised sill. The feel of his warm, callused fingers on my skin sent a shiver of delight through my body. Drawing a quick breath, I turned to look up at his face. Our eyes met. His were dark pools whose depths I could not fathom. For a long moment we stood, locked in a wordless gaze. Beowulf freed himself first, with a slight laugh that sounded almost like a sob.

"Welcome to my boyhood home, Lady Freawaru. I hope it will become your home as well."

His voice was husky, but his face wore a smile. Smiling back, I stepped over the sill.

As we entered, I felt warmth radiating from the hearth. A fire burned brightly there, giving light to the large space. I looked about curiously.

So, this was Hrethel's longhouse and Beowulf's home. Not as fine as Heorot, but habitable — with a good cleaning.

Clearly the house had not been occupied for some time. Loops and strings of cobweb hung from the thatched roof. I shivered as one brushed my face. The oak timbers on walls and ceiling beams looked sound. Bare but sturdy oak benches lined the walls. With the addition of some furs and tapestries, it could be made comfortable. I ran my fingers slowly over the nearest bench. No runes, nothing amiss.

"Come, let me show you one of my grandfather's treasures."

Beaming, Beowulf led me to a partition at one end of the room. Behind it stood a massive bedstead, ornately carved. I leaned close to examine the design on its posts: dragons entwined in a linking pattern. Nothing sinister there.

Then I saw them, carved on a low stool beside the bed: three malevolent runes.

"Lord Beowulf, look! The same runes we found in the mead hall!"

"I know a way to eliminate their power!"

Beowulf picked up the stool, snapped off its legs, strode to the hearth and tossed the pieces on the fire.

"May that be an end to it!" he muttered.

Outside the longhouse Hygd had held back the rest of the group, but now they came in one by one, looking around curiously. No one appeared to notice the broken stool burning in the fire. Touching Beowulf's hand, I gestured toward the partition.

"Beowulf, was that Hrethel's bed?"

"Yes. He died in it."

"I see." But I did not yet see clearly enough. "Who else has slept there since your grandfather died?"

Beowulf shrugged.

"Many people — Hathcyn, Hygelac — I've slept in it myself. It is the only real bed in the village. I had planned to offer it to you, my honored guest, and this house to be your home." In a lower tone he added, "Do you fear that a curse lies upon it?"

I responded quietly. "Curses may be removed and overcome — once they have been discovered."

Raising my voice to be clearly heard by all the assembled company, I held out my hand. "Thank you, Lord Beowulf, for both bed and house. I accept your offer, generous gifts from a generous man."

He took my hand and lifted it to his lips. The hairs of his beard tickled my wrist, but I did not dare laugh. *This is a serious moment, Freawaru! You are making a commitment here — but to what? What exactly is Beowulf offering you? And what does Beowulf want for himself? Despite flashes of affection, he seems to hide his emotions. I cannot discern his true feelings.*

Sudden shouts from my people signaled their approval. Herdred was beaming, but the expression on Hygd's face was hard to read.

By the time we returned to the mead hall, Magnus had assembled all the people of the settlement to greet us. As they stood shyly in a half-circle, I looked them over. Hardy folk, used to hard work. Although somewhat taller and blonder those at Heorot, they would have fit in well with the folks back home.

Home. I must stop thinking of Heorot as home. Hrethelskeep is now my home.

Several women held their hands over stained aprons, which told me that they had probably prepared last night's feast — which still sat uneasily on my stomach. Most of the men wore work clothes, as if just called from daily chores.

Beowulf introduced King Herdred and Queen Hygd first. A few women made awkward bows; others bobbed their heads uncertainly. Clearly the inhabitants of Hrethelskeep did not often receive visits from the royal family!

One ancient woman startled at the sound of Beowulf's voice, but was held back by her companions. He took note of this, and after it was my turn to be presented, he called her to come forward.

"Gunilla, Gunilla, my dear old nurse, I rejoice to see you alive after this hard winter!"

He took her shoulders gently, as if afraid she might break. The old woman smiled a toothless smile and reached up a bony hand to touch his face.

"You've grown," she said.

During the good-natured laughter that ensued, Beowulf turned to me.

"Lady Freawaru, Gunilla can tell you the whole history of Hrethelskeep, for she has lived here since before my birth."

Gunilla peered at me from rheumy eyes.

"Who did you say this lady is, Lord Beowulf? And why is she here?"

Beowulf leaned over and spoke loudly.

"This is Lady Freawaru, a Danish princess, come to take charge of my hall."

Gunilla looked back and forth at us.

"Does that mean you are taking a wife — at long last?"

This time the laughter had a nervous edge and was quickly choked off. Beowulf seemed struck by the question. He paused for a long moment.

"No, Gunilla, no," he said, shaking his head. "Lady Freawaru is to live here in Hrethelskeep — she and her people — and will act as hostess in the mead hall in my absence, for I am to be guardian and guide to King Herdred at Eaglesgard."

Gunilla looked up questioningly.

"Not a wife? But . . ."

She was cut off when Beowulf lifted his head to address the whole group.

"Thank you, men and women of Hrethelskeep, for gathering here to welcome our guests. Now it is Lady Freawaru's turn to introduce her people." He nodded to me.

As I called out the names of my party, each person stepped forward.

"My women: Ana, Estrid, Ragnhild, Ingebord, and my servants, Brita — and Runa. Our men: Wulfgar, Thorkel, Gorm, Olaf, and Saxe."

I smiled broadly at the curious faces before me.

"Now, Lord Beowulf, may we learn the names of our new friends and neighbors?"

"Of course, my lady. Magnus, take charge."

Magnus proudly presented the villagers by family group, naming each man, wife, and child.

"This is Rolf and Thora; they live in the first longhouse past the mead hall. This is our blacksmith, Orm, his wife Ortrud and son Olaf. Gunilla you already know. This is Emund, Tove and their two daughters Ginnlaug and Gyrid . . ."

On it went, name after name. I tried to keep them straight in my head, but knew it would take time to learn the names and even more time to know the person behind each name.

The little boy who'd toddled into our path upon arrival was called 'Toke' — a chubby lad with dirty face and full, pouty lips. His arms hugged a scraggly dog, barely a pup. Toke reminded me strongly of my own little brother Hrothmund, whom I would never see again.

Toke suddenly spoke up. "I'm hungry!"

"So am I!" I declared gaily. "We have kept you all from your morning meal! Lord Beowulf, thank you for bringing us to Hrethelskeep, our new home."

"We are honored to have you here, my lady."

He bowed to me and signaled to Magnus.

As if suddenly released from attention, the group of villagers broke up amid laughter and conversation. As they scattered to their homes, I was happy to see several women look back at us and smile.

Chapter Five
Neighbors and Ghosts

Whalebone board from Norway used to smooth or pleat dresses with a glass ball as an iron.

During the morning meal Hygd and Beowulf sat across from Herdred and me, all of us enjoying the thick, hot gruel topped with cream.

"Cows here give rich milk!" declared Herdred, his mouth wreathed with white as he tipped his bowl to get the last creamy drop.

"Yes," affirmed Beowulf, "and it will taste even better once they're taken up to their summer pasture. I remember doing that as a boy, following the cowherd up into the mountains for a day of rock-rolling and loafing in the sun."

I stared at Beowulf in astonishment.

"Why do you look so surprised, Lady Freawaru? Can't you believe I was once a boy?"

"Of course, my lord. It's just that you seem so . . . so serious . . . most of the time."

Beowulf grimaced.

"Sober attention to duty is needed, but not all the time."

As he smiled I noticed drops of milk on his mustache.

"My grandfather used to chide me for my laziness. He said I'd never become a great warrior if I did not apply myself more strenuously."

I gazed at him in disbelief. There was so much I wanted to know about his childhood, but felt it too soon to ask more questions.

"Lord Beowulf," said Hygd. "Are we departing today or do you plan to stay longer?"

Beowulf turned to her in surprise, then looked back at me.

"If Lady Freawaru does not need our help to get settled, we can leave today, of course. I had thought..."

Herdred broke into the conversation.

"Don't leave yet! Freaw and I haven't even seen all the village — like those funny huts that seem to be growing out of the ground. What are they, Beowulf?"

"*Lord* Beowulf," his mother corrected him.

Beowulf laughed.

"It won't take long to complete our tour, including those huts you mentioned ... *King* Herdred. We can do that now, if everyone is finished?"

In assent we rose from our places, pushing back benches as a few took last gulps of the rich, thick gruel.

The huts which had caught Herdred's attention turned out to be workshops and storage buildings, sunk into the ground and topped with turf. The buildings which puzzled me were small, square wooden structures dotted along the river. A line of birch trees sheltered them, their new young leaves still tiny as a mouse ear.

"What are those, Lord Beowulf?" I asked as we drew near.

"Why, saunas. Didn't you have saunas at Heorot?"

"No. What are they used for?"

"Let me show you — come inside."

He pushed open the door of the nearest sauna. Wooden benches along the walls ringed a fire pit filled with large river rocks.

"It's a bath house," he explained. "The rocks are heated, then water is poured on top to create steam. A good sweat in a sauna takes away all the pains of battle — or whatever ails the body."

"Why are they located out here by the river, not closer to your longhouses?" I wondered aloud.

"Ah — that's the best part. After steaming and sweating we cool off with a roll in the snow or a dip in the river! As my grandfather Hrethel used to say, 'it puts hair on a man's chest'!"

I laughed, as did Hygd and Herdred, listening from outside the sauna.

"You'll like it, Freaw," declared Herdred confidently as I stepped out.

"Our women use the sauna for a birthing place as well," said Hygd, glancing at the slight bulge under my apron.

"Oh, sister Hygd, that reminds me," I said, steering the subject away from childbirth. "Would you leave Runa behind to help us get settled? We could use extra hands."

Hygd did not reply immediately, but by the time we'd walked back to the mead hall she had made her decision.

"Yes, Lady Freawaru. Runa may stay with you."

"Thank you, sister — and Lord Beowulf, I also have a request for you. Would you send us Redbeard for a few days to do some carving? I propose adding strong runes of protection to the door posts of both mead hall and long house."

Beowulf stroked his beard, then nodded.

"A good idea, and he can bring extra thralls to help with the spring planting. Magnus asked for reinforcements."

I reached out to touch his sleeve. This brief contact made my fingers tingle.

"Will you be coming to visit us soon yourself, Lord Beowulf?"

My question hung in the air as Beowulf looked first at Hygd, then at Herdred.

"That is as Wyrd decrees."

Later that morning after Herdred, Hygd, and Beowulf were gone, I sent Brita and Runa over to Hrethel's longhouse with buckets of water and lye soap to swab every surface in the building. Everyone else in our party got to work unloading the wagons packed with our goods: chests of linens and clothing, tapestries, woodenware, glassware, soapstone bowls, frying irons and other cooking pans, grinding querns, cauldrons, looms, sacks of wool and flax, precious packets of herbs and seeds, and the whalebone ironing board given to me by my mother.

At my waist hung the keys to the strongboxes that carried our wealth. I counted the boxes carefully as Saxe and Gorm lugged them into the longhouse, pretending to stagger under their weight... four, five, six — yes, all accounted for.

"Put them under my bed," I instructed.

"Lady Freaw," called Ana. "Where do you want the looms set up? Here, or in the weaving hut used by the other women?"

Wulfgar and Thorkel, carrying the separated wooden frames easily atop their shoulders, stood in the doorway awaiting direction.

"Here. Put them at the far end in the space once used for the animals — but don't set them up until Brita is finished cleaning in there!"

The clatter and bustle of moving into our new home filled me with joy. Our new home! It was becoming home with each armload that came through the door. I busied myself with unpacking and hanging the tapestries I'd woven as a girl, including the scene of the goddess Freyja receiving the Brisinga necklace that had so offended my mother-in-law. Poor Hrun. Had Freyja received Hrun into her hall after Hrun's death? I hung this tapestry high on the wall beside my high, carved bed.

Thorkel had finished assembling the loom he carried, and now came to my end of the house with a very serious expression on his face.

"Yes, Thorkel, what is it?"

"Lady Freawaru, you once p-p-promised a dowry to Ragnhild so that we might m-m-marry. Is that still your intention?"

"Why . . . of course, Thorkel. We have been so involved in Lord Beowulf's affairs that I've had no time to think about it. Do you... do you and Ragnhild wish to marry soon?"

A smile spread across Thorkel's face.

"We do, my lady, yes we do. W-w-we would not hurry you, but there is a space available in the village made vacant by one of the deaths this winter — in the house of Sigfast. His w-w-widow is willing to share her home in return for a small sum of silver and help with the animals."

My eyes widened in surprise.

"You've wasted no time, Thorkel!"

"That's not how we look at it," he said boldly, then reddened. "Beg pardon, Lady Freawaru, I meant no offense. We s-s-seek your blessing in this matter."

"And you shall have it. After we get settled here, we will arrange for your wedding. You can assure Sigfast's widow — what is her name? — that you and Ragnhild will soon join her."

"Her name is Sigrid, and thank you, my lady."

As Thorkel resumed work he began to whistle.

'Lady Freawaru, Lady Freawaru, where should we put this? Where would you like that?' My head buzzed with requests for my attention, but it was happy work. This was my first real chance to make all the decisions myself. At Wulfhaus, in Ingeld's village, the household setup and daily routine had already been established before I arrived.

Here in Hrethelskeep I can be my own mistress, no longer under Hrun's sharp eye.

"Lady Freaw, don't you think it would be better to store the linens further from the fire? — and stack the cauldrons closer?"

Ana's face appeared at my side. I sighed.

"Do as you judge best, Ana. Here — hold up the corner while I fasten this hide above the sleeping benches. We can't have you getting cold at night!"

Ana grinned appreciatively.

In the midst of the hubbub one of the village women appeared at the doorway, bearing gifts. A tall, rawboned woman, she looked to be about Ana's age, but with more vigor in her step. I searched my brain for her name.

"Thora, is it? Yes. Please come in."

Thora stepped over the threshold carrying a heavy covered kettle in one hand and a small packet of birch bark in the other. She held out the packet without ceremony.

"Salt, lady. I thought you could use it."

I took the packet cautiously, examining the folded layers of bark that formed the container. Not a grain of salt could leak out.

"How cleverly you've fashioned this!" I exclaimed with delight. "Thank you, Thora."

Thora shrugged her shoulders.

"Birch bark is useful for making many things. I've used it all my life. This" — she extended the kettle with a strong arm — "is lentil stew with a bit of chicken for your evening meal. Thought you might be too busy to cook right away."

She shrugged her shoulders again as if embarrassed.

Knowing the leanness of village stores at the end of winter, I was touched by this generosity.

"Thank you, Thora, thank you. I look forward to learning from you what foods can be grown here and how to prepare them. Do you have an herb garden?"

"Not yet, though I mean to plant one when the ground gets warmer."

"Here, Thora. Sit down on this bench while I put away the salt." I moved a stack of robes to make a place for her.

"Brita, take this kettle. Ana, please bring me my seed chest."

Our visitor settled herself carefully and looked around at the rapidly filling room.

"Good to see this house alive again. Dark and empty it's been for too long. Lord Beowulf..."

She broke off as I sat down beside her with the chest and inserted a tiny bronze key into the lock.

"Treasure, is it?" she asked.

"Of a kind. Look."

I opened the lid to display dozens of cloth seed bags and rolls of dried herbs. Selecting one, I handed it to her.

"Here, this is rosemary. It makes a good seasoning for chicken, and fish. Please take it in return for the stew. Later, if you like, we can plant an herb garden together."

Thora held the rosemary to her nose, sniffed, then sneezed. "Strong — but good." She smiled. "Thank you. Now I must get back to my own hearth."

As she rose to leave, a thought crossed my mind.

"Thora, wait. I have a question for you. I'd like to speak with Gunilla, Beowulf's old nurse. Can you tell me where she lives?"

A smile spread across Thora's plain face.

"That I can. She lives with Rolf and me. She's Rolf's mother, she is. You can visit her — us — any time. First longhouse past the mead hall."

She turned toward the door, then turned back.

"Beg pardon. I forgot my manners. I'm supposed to call you 'Lady Freawaru'?"

I noted the question in her voice.

"Yes, Thora, that would be most proper, but here in my own house you may call me 'Freaw.' Now, thank you for your visit and for your most generous gifts."

She shrugged her shoulders and made her exit.

"Lady Freaw, are you sure that was wise, not insisting on your title?" Ana's voice murmured at my side.

"You need to establish a position of authority here if you are to act in Beowulf's place."

I considered her words.

"You are probably right, Ana, but Thora seems a good sort, unlikely to take advantage of a familiarity."

"You don't know that, my lady. We don't know these people yet. It would be better to be on guard until we do."

I was about to protest when a woman's cry sounded from the far end of the longhouse, from the byre where the old animal stalls were being removed.

"What is it? What's wrong?"

Ana and I rushed to the dimly lit area. Saxe and Gorm stood looking curiously at Runa, who held up a long piece of twisted straw — or so it seemed.

"What is it, Runa? Why did you cry out?"

"It's this, my lady. I found it in one of the mangers."

She held out the object with thumb and forefinger for my inspection: a faded golden braid... of human hair.

We all stared at the curious object. My mind flashed back to the sacrifice of women's hair we had made long ago at Heorot, designed to ward off the Grendel monster.

Can this old braid have been meant as a sacrifice? What is it doing here?

Suddenly my happiness in our new home was clouded with doubt. First the runes, now this. What could it all mean?

"Throw the filthy thing in the fire!" cried Ana.

"No! Let me take it! Runa, fetch me a cloth from my chest in which to wrap it."

Apparently there are secrets in this house to be uncovered.

"Now, let's all get back to work."

Without a word Saxe and Gorm cheerfully resumed stacking slats from the stall partitions. I drew Ana and Runa aside and spoke softly.

"Do not speak of this to the others. Something is amiss here, but I don't know what. I need to find out more about the history of this place. Perhaps..."

"Old Gunilla, my lady?" suggested Runa.

"Yes, old Gunilla."

Again we exchanged knowing looks.

The very next morning I made a visit to Rolf, Thora, and Gunilla. Runa came with me to carry the now empty kettle, and I brought gifts: strips of woven ribbon to ornament the hem of a gown or tunic.

Soft, green grass, springy underfoot from recent showers, tempted me off the path. By the time we reached the longhouse my shoes were quite damp with dew. A tall figure receding on the path ahead told me that Rolf had already left for the fields. From inside I heard sounds of milking — probably Thora at her morning chores.

Gunilla came to the door. At first she did not seem to recognize me.

"Gunilla, it is Lady Freawaru — the lady Beowulf brought to live in Hrethel's house."

"Freaw — who?"

She put out a thin hand to touch my face. I realized she must be nearly blind.

"It's all right, mother." Thora's voice came from the byre. "Invite the lady in."

I took Gunilla's bony hand from my cheek and gently returned it to her side.

"Thank you, Thora," I called.

Runa and I stepped inside, squinting to adjust to the darkness. Only a small fire burned in the hearth, but we could feel warmth coming from the cow byre. The thumping of tails and low mooing sounds were pleasant to hear, but the smell of manure made my nose wrinkle.

Thora came toward us carrying two wooden pails, frothy with milk.

"Would you like a cup?"

"This is Lady Freawaru," piped Runa, setting down the kettle near the hearth.

"Yes, I know. Would you like a cup, Lady Freawaru?"

"Yes, if you will join me — Thora."

We smiled at each other. A compact had been made.

Thora had butter to churn, so after our cup of friendship was drunk she turned to her work. I dismissed Runa and drew Gunilla to the bench nearest the hearth. She groaned as she eased herself down. The winter must have been hard on her.

"Gunilla, Beowulf only had time to tell me a bit about the history of Hrethelskeep, but he said you could tell me more."

I took her hand and stroked the gnarled knuckles.

"That boy," she sighed. "So much sorrow in that family, so much darkness of mind."

She was silent for so long I thought she might have fallen asleep.

"Were you always his nurse?" I asked, patting her hand.

"Yes, I was." She roused and straightened. "His mother died when he was just a boy. I raised him until his grandfather sent for him to come to Hrethelskeep. I came with him — couldn't bear to part with the lad."

"What was he like — as a boy?"

"A bit slow... but strong. Good-hearted too. When he killed that pup he cried and cried."

She shook her head at the memory.

"Killed a dog? How?"

"Oh, he didn't mean to — just didn't know his own strength yet. Squeezed it too hard, he did. After that he was afraid to touch an animal for fear he'd hurt it."

He squeezed the life out of Hygelac's killer — crushed the man's bone house in his mighty arms.

I shivered. "How old was he when this happened?"

"Still just a boy, still trailing after his cousins like they were gods. He grew up quick after Herebeald died. Had to. Hrethel was too sunk in grief to look after him. Beowulf needed Gunilla then, he did, though he was too proud to admit it."

She nodded emphatically to herself.

"Please, not so fast. I don't understand. Who is Herebeald and how did he die?"

Gunilla lifted her head and stared straight ahead.

"Herebeald was one of Hrethel's boys — the oldest and his father's favorite. Hrethel's son and heir, he was — until that day his brother Hathcyn came running in looking pale as milk, and took us to where Herebeald lay gasping for life, an arrow in his throat."

I shuddered, envisioning the scene.

"How did it happen?"

"According to Hathcyn, all three boys were out with bows and arrows, shooting at squirrels for target practice. Hathcyn missed his aim and hit his brother."

"So Beowulf was there when it happened?"

"Yes, but he couldn't — or wouldn't — say a word. He didn't talk for days after that. He just nodded his head 'yes' when Hathcyn told his story."

We sat in silence as I mulled over this information.

"Tragic, tragic for everyone," I said. "One son kills another, and there can be no recompense, no suitable *wergild* for the life lost. But wait — where was Hygelac that day? Wasn't he also one of Hrethel's sons?"

Gunilla wrinkled her brow.

"I can't remember — but he became Beowulf's friend and comforter after that, yes he did. Those two did everything together as they got older." She paused. "Hathcyn died later fighting the Swedes. Now Hygelac is dead. All gone. One might wonder if there's a curse been laid on that family."

I sat bolt upright and dropped her hands.

"A curse? Gunilla, in the short time I've been in Hrethelskeep, I've found evidence of a curse — which must go back many years." I paused, considering. "Gunilla, do you know of anyone who lived in the village who had reason to hate the Geats?"

She shook her head slowly, then hesitated.

"Long ago there was a woman, a Swedish captive. She raged and fought like a wild thing when Hrethel's men first brought her in..."

Gunilla rubbed her eyes as if to clear her vision.

"Now... now I remember. After they stripped off her jewelry and cut her hair like a thrall's, her spirit seemed to be broken, but then she refused to eat. That was long ago..."

I froze. *A Swedish captive? They cut her hair?*

"Who was she, Gunilla? Do you remember her name?"

"Somebody's wife — Ongentheow's I think..." Gunilla squeezed her eyes tight with effort. "... and Gudfrid was her name."

Words sung by Jesper, the harper at Eaglesgard, came back to me.

...the Swedish king... Ongentheow old and terrible... saved his aged wife...

The long faded braid of hair locked in my chest, the ghostly old woman in the latrine — the connection was becoming clear. I closed my eyes and breathed deeply, hoping to summon a vision of the face I had seen that night. Slowly, slowly it came: blazing eyes, a gaunt face, and hair — cut short!

Opening my eyes I rose and turned to face the old woman before me.

"Gunilla, I honor you. I believe you have helped me discover the source of a great evil that has long cast its shadow over the house of Hrethel. And now, by Freyja, I may be able to counter the curse."

Gunilla peered at me in confusion.

"What evil, my lady?"

I took her pale, veined hands in mine and raised my voice.

"I think that the Swedish queen, Gudfrid, laid a curse on this place, on Hrethelskeep, a curse that caused — or contributed to — the darkness and death it has experienced."

"What can you do about it?"

I squeezed her hands gently.

"As for what I can do, with the aid of the goddess I will take steps which may lift the curse, and lay to rest the ghost of Gudfrid."

Thora had approached as we were talking, wiping her hands on her apron.

"Lady Freawaru," she said earnestly, her eyes shining, "I heard you speak of the goddess. It has been many a winter since the women of this village gathered to honor the goddess. Can you summon her? It would be a boon to us all."

"Yes, Thora, I can. I too have been long absent from the presence of the goddess. We will seek her wisdom together."

Now I released Gunilla's hand to take up Thora's, joining us in a circle — we three women of Hrethelskeep. I closed my eyes again.

Runes... and Runa. Both may help us in this search.

"Lady... Freawaru?"

Gunilla's croak broke the silence and brought me back to the moment.

"Yes, Gunilla?"

"Could we dance?"

Her question was so unexpected that I laughed out loud and we dropped hands.

"Dance? Why of course we can dance — and you can show us the steps."

Gunilla grinned from ear to ear, exposing great gaps in her teeth.

"When I was a girl we went into the birch forest to a special place. Beowulf's mother was alive then. Slim as a sapling birch, she was. She led us in the circle."

Gunilla looked through us as if seeing again that group of maidens dancing in the forest.

"Beowulf's mother? What was her name?" I asked, eager to know her.

"Hylde. Hrethel's only daughter."

"Hylde." I tasted the name on my tongue. "And you said she died in childbirth?"

"No, no, it was later, after her husband was banished for a killing and left her alone with the baby."

"Ah, yes," I nodded. "I know that part of the story. Beowulf's father, Ecgtheow, came to my father, Hrothgar, king of the Danes, to find a safe haven. Hrothgar paid the wergild that allowed Ecgtheow to return to his homeland."

Gunilla shook her head. "I know nothing of that, but I know his return was too late. Hylde died of sorrow. Not even little Beowulf could keep her from leaving us."

Gunilla says that Hylde died of sorrow for her lost husband. Beowulf told me that Hrethel died of sorrow for his lost son. Grief has taken a terrible toll in this family. I hope the loss of Hygelac will not lead to another disastrous death!

"Lady Freawaru, about the goddess. I can show you the place where we used to worship her," Thora's voice broke in.

"Oh? Yes, of course. That could be a first step."

"We can go there now, if you like. My morning chores are finished."

I looked around at the neatly kept interior: fresh straw on the floor, sleeping robes folded on the benches, something aromatic simmering in a kettle above the hearth.

"You are a good housekeeper, Thora! You must get up early!"

"That I do, my lady. Mother Gunilla helps me as she can, but I fear her dancing days are behind her."

Gunilla frowned at this. "That may be, but I still remember some of the chants we used at our rituals — chants you've likely never heard, Thora."

I laughed again at their friendly rivalry.

"Your memory is very useful, Gunilla! Now, Thora, tell me how far it is to this place. Can we walk there and back before the mid-morning meal? My own household will be waiting."

Thora eyed my clothes critically. "Yes, but you'll need a cloak . . . my lady. You could use one of mine . . ."

"Thank you, but there is no need. I relish the freshness of the morning. It is so . . . invigorating here! I feel like a colt let out to pasture!"

Thora smiled. "As you like, my lady. Gunilla . . ." She turned to her mother-in-law. "Watch the fire and stir the gruel while we're gone."

I did not know what to expect as Thora and I set out, heading away from the settlement but following the path of the river. Back home in Heorot my mother the queen had conducted our secret rituals at a small pond in the marshes, hidden from men's eyes. At Wulfhaus, my husband's home, we had worshipped in an oak grove. Where was Thora leading me?

By the time Thora stopped near a stand of birches, the village was out of sight.

"It should be somewhere near here."

She looked around thoughtfully, as if searching the ground for markers. Then, I saw them: low standing stones arranged in a rough circle. Some were half hidden by weeds, and . . .

"Look, Thora, nettles! Now I do wish I'd brought my cloak, so we could gather their new leaves to make a spring tonic!"

"Or nettle soup — Rolf has a taste for nettle soup. Here, we can use mine."

She removed her cloak and spread it on the ground. Soon we were busy plucking the prickly young leaves, using parts of our aprons to protect our hands.

"Is this place big enough to hold all the women of the village?" I asked, judging the space around us.

Thora paused in her picking. "There are twenty-one of us, my lady — no, twenty since Alfrida died last winter. Oh, and of course your household. That would make . . . twenty-five women?"

"Twenty-six if we count Runa — who may stay with me for some time," I responded. "Yes, I think we can all fit."

On the way back we carried the cloak of nettles folded between us. As we neared the edge of the settlement a young woman digging in a fenced-off plot of land hailed us.

"Good morrow! What do you have there?"

"Nettles," called Thora, "for soup and a tonic. And you're speaking to Lady Freawaru, Ginnlaug."

"Oh! Beg pardon, my lady."

Ginnlaug dropped her digging tool — a large piece of antler — and wiped sweat from her brow with a grimy hand.

"What's a ... tonic?" she asked, eyeing our bundle.

Thora snorted. "Medicine to get the blood moving after a long winter, my girl. But there is more important news: tell your mother we're going back to the stone circle soon. She'll know what I mean."

We swept on past, leaving Ginnlaug with her mouth agape. Thora turned to me and smiled.

"You are the tonic this place has been needing, Lady Freawaru!"

"Thank you, Thora. With the help of the goddess we may bring a new birth to Hrethelskeep."

Just at that moment the baby in my belly gave a small kick, as if to say, "Don't forget about me!"

Chapter Six
Clearing the Way

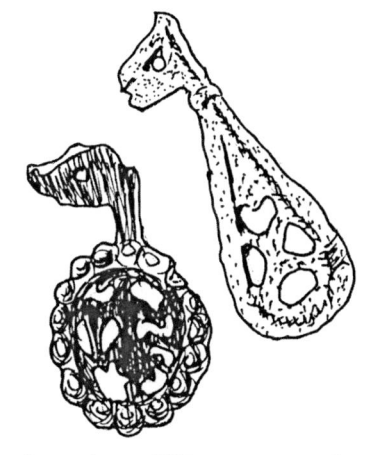

Bronze keys to Viking-age storage chests, worn on a belt by the mistress of the farm, from Rogaland, Norway.

When I returned to our longhouse I found everyone in my group assembled and waiting... for more than the morning meal. After we were all seated and Brita and Runa had served the bread and gruel, Wulfgar took the lead.

"Lady Freawaru, we need to establish our positions and duties in this new place, so that they are clear both to us and to the rest of the village."

"Quit right, Wulfgar," I responded. "Have you men already made some decisions about this?"

"Yes, my lady, we have. Thorkel here," he gestured to Thorkel seated close beside Ragnhild, "wants to take up farming again. The lads and I," he nodded at Saxe, Olaf and Gorm, busy cramming bread into their mouths, "we'll join Magnus in hunting to supplement the food supplies of the settlement."

I listened thoughtfully. It was understood that fishing would be left to thralls, as would be care of farm animals.

"Good choices, Wulfgar. Now, Ana," I turned toward the other end of the table. "What about my women? What are your wishes?"

Ana put down her bowl. "Thank you for asking, my lady. Ragnhild thinks she and Thorkel could work together: he producing honey and she brewing mead."

I glanced at the two of them across the table. "Ragnhild's skills I know well, but you, Thorkel — I didn't know you were a bee-keeper!"

He nodded, reddening.

"I used to h-h-help my uncle. The hives here have been neglected, but I'm s-s-sure we can bring them back — with your help, my lady."

"My help? I know nothing about bees," I countered.

"It's your words we'll need, my lady — charms, that is, charms to attract the bees and later to m-m-move the swarms."

"Charms? Perhaps. Now, what about the rest of you?"

At my nod Ana picked up the thread of her report.

"Estrid wants to tend the gardens and Ingeborg will keep us supplied with bread. Of course we'll all work at the weaving, which I will supervise. From what I've been told by Hygd's women, we'll need to lay up a stock of heavier clothing for the long winters ahead."

"I see." Below the table my hand strayed to my belly. "With such able companions there will be little left for me to do!"

"Oh no, my lady. We all know you are in charge here," asserted Ana. "In all things you will be our leader."

"Yes," I said, rising, "and as your leader I now announce two important events to be arranged this spring: a ritual to honor the goddess, and a wedding to unite Ragnhild and Thorkel."

Cheers and the pounding of mugs greeted this announcement. Ragnhild looked down at her bowl, but Thorkel laughed good-naturedly as Saxe and Gorm reached over to pummel his shoulders.

They do not need to know yet that I will also be wrestling with a curse and hopefully putting to rest a ghost from the past.

Runa, standing beside Brita, now spoke up. "Lady Freawaru, I could teach Brita how to milk so she could help with the dairy. And we're both good cooks — as you can tell from the gruel you're eating."

Indeed the gruel was good, almost as good as that we'd been served in the mead hall on our first morning in Hrethelskeep. Ours only lacked... cream.

"Wulfgar, Ana, what shall we do about acquiring cows? And pigs? Chickens? Sheep for wool? Can we buy these animals here in the village?"

This time Thorkel spoke up.

"It will take time, my lady. As you know, spring is the b-b-birthing season for lambs and calves. We'll purchase what we can, and slowly build up our herds and f-f-flocks. A few chicks and piglets may be available now — I'll ask S-S-Sigrid about it."

As a girl I had never paid much attention to the requirements of farming, taking for granted all that it provided. Even at Wulfhaus such details had been the concern of others.

Now I must learn all I can and take an active role in our enterprise. Perhaps I should ride out today on Burningfax to survey the area.

"Oh, Wulfgar, another question: who is in charge of the horses?"

"I am, my lady. Ours are pastured with those from the rest of the settlement — a small herd for a small place."

I looked at him sharply.

How long will Wulfgar be content to stay in this 'small place'? Without the excitement of raiding and plundering, without the joys of the mead hall to celebrate, how long can I keep any of my men?

A thought formed at the back of my mind.

"Wulfgar, you were the leader of my father's hall guard and a seasoned warrior. It will be essential that you assess the battle skills of the young men here and teach them what may be lacking. Since Beowulf has been away, his men may have lost their edge."

Wulfgar's eyes shone and a smile spread across his face.

"Right, my lady. I shall consider such training to be my primary duty! Saxe, Olaf, and Gorm can use their experience to help me. I've heard that those Swedes once attacked Hrethelskeep itself, and it could happen again — once they know that Hygelac is dead!"

Wulfgar sounded almost jubilant at the possibility. Inwardly I shuddered. No such idea had entered my head. I prayed only for a long period of peace in which to raise my child. A tiny kick from my womb doubled that prayer.

Later that morning Saxe brought up Burningfax for me. Beside him rode Magnus, astride a great horse blacker than night.

"What a fine animal!" I exclaimed as they came to a halt. "What is its name?"

"Nightsea," replied Magnus gruffly, his face like a thundercloud. Without dismounting he suddenly unlocked his word hoard.

"Lady Freawaru, you need to know that I have been in charge at Hrethelskeep since Sigfast died. I own ten hydes of land here, the largest holding of anyone in the village, and I've lived here all my life. Beowulf may have named you the hostess of his mead hall, but I am the chief in this village!"

I smiled and put my foot in the stirrup to mount Burningfax. "I'm very glad to hear that, Magnus. Now, will you join me in a ride? My ladies have all declined the opportunity!"

He grunted in surprise as I swung myself into the saddle and gave heel to my steed. Without looking back I headed west, toward Eaglesgard. Magnus, however, soon overtook me and pulled even with my horse.

"I'll show you my lands," he shouted, waving a hand toward the opposite direction.

"Agreed!" I shouted back.

It will be best to give this village chief the respect he desires, while maintaining my own position. Besides, I need to know the boundaries of Beowulf's holdings, now my responsibility.

We spent the rest of the morning touring the length and breadth of the valley. Magnus pointed out a few stone markers on the boundary of his land, but there was little else to separate one field from another. The soil in a few newly-turned plots looked dark and rich. It appeared that Magnus' holdings were second only to those of Beowulf, who owned a princely fifteen hydes.

When Magnus seemed satisfied with the extent of our tour, we rode back to the village. As we neared my longhouse, I invited him in for a cup of ale. To my surprise, he accepted.

Brita stood at the hearth, stirring a bubbling cauldron. She looked up as we entered.

"Brita, bring my guest a cup of ale, and one for me as well."

As she scurried to do my bidding, Magnus looked around with open curiosity. "Where is the byre? Hrethel always had a byre," he frowned.

"We removed it to make more room for our looms. Please sit down."

Grunting, Magnus lowered his considerable bulk onto a bench. When Brita brought his cup he drained it in one long gulp.

"Not bad, but it tastes different. What have you put in it?" he asked suspiciously.

"A few herbs. Would you like another?"

"No," he said flatly, looking again toward the far end of the house and the non-existent byre. "You may think you can survive on your own next winter without animals to warm you, but you'll be wrong, very wrong."

He started to rise, but I put out a hand.

"Magnus, we both know that Beowulf is the lord of Hrethelskeep. He has asked me to represent him in his absence, and I intend to do so, but there is work for both of us here. In fact, your official presence will be needed soon at a wedding."

His eyes widened. "Whose?" he snorted.

"Two of my people, Thorkel and Ragnhild."

Magnus stared at me as if considering. "I will have another ale," he said, in a milder tone.

I signaled to Brita who quickly refilled Magnus' cup. He drained it again and wiped his mouth with the back of his hand.

"Magnus, you say you've lived here all your life?"

He nodded.

"Then you knew Hrethel, Beowulf's grandfather? What was he like?"

After a long belch Magnus seemed in a better mood.

"Hrethel. Good man, but he spent too much time worrying. Better to take action than sit and brood."

"I'm sure you're right — if action is possible," I murmured.

"Of course I'm right!" he boomed with a grin, exposing the gaps in his crooked teeth.

"Magnus, you are clearly a man of action. Did you ever fight against Ongentheow in the Swedish wars?"

"Why do you want to know?" he began, suspicious again, but the chance to boast overcame his suspicions.

"Yes, I did, and if Eofer hadn't gotten to him first I would have killed that tough old Swede myself!" Magnus chuckled. "Quite a fighter, Ongentheow. Refused to go down until his skull was split in two."

Magnus stared at me as if to see the effect of his description, but I did not flinch.

"I wonder, do you know what happened to Ongentheow's wife after his death? I'd heard she was once a prisoner here at Hrethelskeep."

"Wife?" He frowned. "Oh yes, Ongentheow's wife. Another tough one. She took an axe to Eofer and almost chopped off an ear!"

Magnus chuckled again as if reliving a fond memory.

"She did? When did that happen?" I was all attention now.

"I don't remember exactly — when she was locked up here. After that attack with the axe Eofer had her rations cut — starved her, he did!"

My head was reeling with this unexpected information.

"But wasn't she rescued by her husband? Gunilla said . . ."

"Gunilla is an old fool," sneered Magnus. "Her mind is gone."

I opened my mouth to contradict him, but closed it. Magnus rose and stalked toward the door, where he turned and barked out, "Better think again about that byre. Oh, and the ale was good — Lady Freawaru."

When Magnus was safely gone, Ana emerged from the weaving room.

"I do not like that man," she announced curtly.

"Neither do I," I admitted, "but he's the chief in this village, so we must treat him with respect."

I lifted my still undrunk cup of ale to my lips.

"Hmph! I notice he did not give you much respect! And you went riding off with him . . ."

"Ana, I'm a grown woman and able to take care of myself," I said firmly, draining my cup.

The look on her face startled me: a mixture of concern and . . . fear?

"My dear Freaw," she said quietly, "have you ever considered what would happen to the rest of us if we were to lose you? Your safety is our only security in this foreign land."

"Why Ana . . ." I faltered, at a loss for words.

"I love you like my own daughter, Freaw, but you have many people who depend on you. You can't just go riding off with strangers!"

"Magnus isn't a stranger, he's one of Beowulf's athelings," I protested. "But, yes, Ana, I will consider what you have said. Now . . ." I yawned, "I feel strangely tired — perhaps I'll rest a bit."

Ana eyed my belly, her hands on her hips.

"No wonder, riding horseback all morning! You need to remember the child you're carrying. You don't show yet, but it can't be long before your secret is out."

She followed me behind the partition to my high carved bed. Picking up the big bag stuffed with down and feathers — one of the few things I'd taken from Wulfhaus when we departed — she gave it a shake.

"Rest yourself now, my lady. I won't let anyone disturb you."

I was not accustomed to sleeping in the daytime, but of late my energy was departing before the daylight. The bed felt soft and welcoming — like my mother's arms when I was a little girl. Sighing, I let my body sink into its embrace, and closed my eyes.

Hrethel died in this bed. I should be afraid to sleep here, but I'm not. I feel completely safe.

When I opened my eyes again, it was dark. A steady rain beat overhead on the thatched roof, some of it dripping through onto my face.

"Ana? Brita? Runa?"

I roused and drew myself up to a sitting position. Where was everyone? Surely Ana had not let me sleep through the evening meal?

"Ana?" I called again.

A face appeared at the foot of the bed, barely visible in the dim light. Eyes opened, eyes burning with hate.

"Gudfrid? Gudfrid! No! Do not curse me! I want to help you!"

Something seized my wrist and I struggled to break free.

"Freaw! Wake up! You are dreaming!"

It was Ana's voice, but the grip on my skin was cold as death.

"Ana? Is it really you?" I gasped and blinked my eyes.

Yes, there she stood, bent over the bed holding a torch in both hands. Both hands? Then who . . . or what . . . had gripped my wrist? I shook my head and my whole body shook too.

"Have you taken a chill, Freawaru? I could bring you a heavier robe, but you may want to get up now. We're gathering for the evening meal."

Ana came closer to my bed and patted my shaking shoulders

"Oh, Ana, I saw . . . such a vision. I hope never to see it again."

"It was just a dream, my lady, just a dream," she murmured as I climbed out of bed and felt for my shoes. "I've made a strong tea from those nettles you brought in. A hot cup will do you good."

My face must have shown traces of the dream-fright, for Runa looked at me closely as I took my place at the head of the table. She whispered in my ear as she filled my mug with the steaming nettle tea.

"Another omen, my lady?"

"Yes, I fear so," I answered softly.

Turning to my companions, I cleared my throat and raised my mug.

"How do you like your spring tonic?"

Saxe made a show of draining his mug, but Gorm made a face.

"Once a year is enough!" he grinned.

Ragnhild turned to me.

"My lady, would not the turning of winter to spring be a good time to hold the wedding — for Thorkel and me?"

"Exactly, Ragnhild, my very thought. But I also feel it would be best to perform our duties to the goddess in advance of your celebration. We will want her blessing on your union. We also want to win the good will of the villagers. To that end, your wedding should be an event to which everyone is welcome."

Ana frowned. "Providing suitable food and drink for such a number will tax our stores, my lady."

"Even so, it must be done," I replied. "Giving these folk something to celebrate will be a start. After that we must work together to make Hrethelskeep a stronger and safer place for us all."

At the word 'safer' Ana glanced up sharply. She did not speak, but looked at me with questions in her eyes.

Yes, Ana. I realize that the curse laid upon Hrethelskeep by the Swedish captive may affect us Danes as well as the Geats ... unless its power can be broken.

That night I let Brita remove my head covering and comb out my hair. It soothed me to have her do so, putting me in mind of the days when my mother combed and braided my hair.

"Your hair is redder — and longer — than when you were a girl," Brita observed, gently teasing out a tangle.

"Your own braids reach down to your waist!" I laughed. "We are growing older, Brita, that's all."

After Brita left, I lay awake, pondering what might lie ahead.

What should I do to placate the ghost of Gudfrid? Clearly she did not lie quietly in her grave, wherever that might be. Perhaps the proper rites had not been observed at her cremation? Perhaps there had been no rites at all? She must have died during the war with the Geats ...

Her angry spirit — where does it live? In the bright halls of Freyja, or in the dismal domain of Hel? Where should I seek her? Do I dare seek her?

Fanning the Flames

Nothing in my earlier training had prepared me for the challenge I now faced — or had it? Unferth had taught me the meaning and uses of runes. Mother had taught me the rituals needed to worship the goddess, and many rituals of healing, purification and protection. I had many means to choose from.

My thoughts drifted to... Runa. Hmmm. Could she aid me? My own women would support me in whatever I chose to do, but Runa could see what others could not. Perhaps...

Later, after everyone else had fallen asleep, I slipped out of bed. With the glow of hearth light, silently, on bare feet, I padded to Runa's sleeping bench and touched her gently on the shoulder.

"Runa?"

Her eyes flickered open, then filled with alarm. Holding a finger to my lips, I beckoned for her to rise. Groggily she did so, her dark tresses tumbling about her shoulders. Pulling her thin shift around her, she followed me into my part of the house.

"What is it, my lady? Is something amiss?" she murmured.

"No. Sit down. We need to talk."

I climbed up on my bed and patted the space beside me. Although I relied on distance, the crackle of the hearth, and Ana's snores to cover our voices, we spoke in low tones.

"Runa, first tell me how and where you were captured by the Geats. Were they Beowulf's men?"

"Yes, my lady — I mean, it was a party led by Beowulf. They came across the great gulf to our shores in Finnmark one spring. It started out with trading, but as they departed a few of the men carried off young women. I might have escaped notice had I not been playing my flute. Hondshu heard it and wanted both flute and player."

Hondshu? Where had I heard that name before? Wasn't he... yes, one of the men Beowulf brought with him to Heorot. Hondshu — he was the first man killed by the Grendel monster.

"Hondshu is dead."

"Yes, my lady, I know that all too well. He was going to make me his wife, but he sailed off with Beowulf to help the Danes and never came back!"

Her tone sounded regretful. So... Hondshu had sacrificed his life to help my people. Was a debt owed to his... widow?

"Did you want to marry him, Runa?"

"Yes," she sighed. "He was good to me, and a better match than the old chieftain back home that I was promised to!"

She sounded quite positive! I thought of my own arranged marriage to Ingeld.

"Were you to become a peace-weaver in that match, Runa?"

She giggled. "More like a bed-warmer! He was older than my grandfather!"

We both fell silent, reflecting on what might have been.

"So, Runa, what is your present position at Eaglesgard? Are you a thrall or a freewoman?"

She paused before answering.

"Somewhere in-between. I've made myself useful to Queen Hygd — who allows me a measure of freedom — but I have no status at Eaglesgard. Had Hondshu had time to marry me, I would have received his share of your father's rewards after Hondshu's death and become a woman of property. But... that was not to be. The gods are fickle..."

Her voice trailed off and she shivered. Involuntarily I put an arm around her. She stiffened, then relaxed against me.

"Runa, tell me about the woman who taught you runes."

"My grandmother? She was a shaman, a healer known throughout Finnmark. She believed I might come to share her powers in time, so she began by teaching me rune-lore."

"What else did she teach you?"

"Not much. She died shortly before the raid that brought me to Geatland."

"I am sorry for your loss," I said, caressing her hand gently. "I understand loss."

Runa returned the caress.

"I know, my lady. I read it in your face. But you will soon rejoice in a new life — in the life of your child."

Her free hand reached over to touch the slight mound of my belly.

"Ah, yes," I sighed. "That will soon be evident to all. Runa, you have keener sight than most."

I paused. Was this the right moment to delve deeper?

"Tell me, Runa, do you ever see events before they happen?"

Now it was Runa's turn to sigh.

"Oh, Lady Freawaru, I do not know. Sometimes it seems so. Then I ask myself: was it a thought of my own, or a vision sent by the gods?"

"I understand your confusion, Runa, for I share it in assessing my own gifts. But this I have learned: calling upon the goddess brings clarity and direction. Runa, I want your help in performing a ritual for the women of the settlement."

"A ritual? For the goddess? Of course, my lady!"

"Hush. Lower your voice. Now, I am going to show you something."

I reached for the oil lamp atop one of my chests and handed it to her.

"Take this lamp and light it at the hearth fire, then return to me here. Go — quietly!"

While Runa hurried to perform this task, I loosened my nightclothes and pulled down the fabric over my right shoulder. Runa soon returned with the light, her eyes sparkling with curiosity.

"Bring it closer and look behind my bare shoulder," I instructed. "What do you see?"

Runa bent over, than gasped.

"I see the shape of a feather, a perfect feather! What does it mean?"

"First set the lamp back on the chest, and I will tell you."

When she was once again seated beside me, I took Runa's hand.

"My mother believed the feather to be a mark of the goddess Freyja, signifying special powers. My mother trained me as your grandmother meant to train you — to be a seeress, a sorceress, a shaman."

I pressed her hand.

"You and I have much in common, Runa, and we can help each other. Here in Hrethelskeep I will need your eyes and ears. You have already discovered curse runes in the mead hall and that braid of hair here in the very midst of our house. Both reveal an evil power at work which must be destroyed."

I stopped, suddenly daunted by the possible enormity of the task we faced.

"I too have felt it, my lady — the sense of a heavy force that would crush out life if given a chance. I will help you in any way I can."

Runa's soft voice was a welcome counter to my own dark thoughts. I laughed quietly.

"Of course I must first convince Hygd to let you stay here," I said, mostly to myself. "Now, Runa, return to your sleeping bench and speak of these things to no one."

"Yes, my lady — and fear not: all will be well."

She slid off the bed and slipped away so quietly I could not hear her passage. Sighing, I snuffed the lamp and settled into my own bed. My heart felt somewhat lighter.

Next day after the morning meal, I gathered my women to organize a special task: preparing the stone circle for a ritual.

"It is overgrown with weeds and nettles," I explained, "which must be cleared before we can use the space. Ordinarily I would take a few thralls to do the heavier work, but we can't allow men to enter a place sacred to the goddess. Who is available today to help me?"

"How many hands do you need?" asked Ana. "And how far away is this place? I'm not eager to get on a horse again!"

I laughed. "That won't be necessary, though we will need to take some tools for grubbing out roots."

"I'll help," chirped Runa. "My back is strong!"

"So will I," said Brita, "that is . . . if Ana can spare us?"

"Yes," said Ana, "I can spare you, all of you." She nodded at Estrid, Ingeborg, and Ranhild. "It takes only one to stir a cooking pot. We can set aside the weaving for another day, my lady."

She glanced over her shoulder at our three looms, now assembled and warp-weighted.

"But is it safe for you to go there without at least one of our men?" she asked.

"Yes, I think so," I replied. "Thora and I had no problem when we went earlier. A group of six women should be safe!"

My hand went to the hilt of the dagger hanging in its sheath beneath my tunic. Ana saw the movement and nodded. So it was settled. Ana insisted that we take a jug of ale and a large wedge of cheese which she wrapped in a birch bark packet.

"Where did you get that?" I asked. "We did not bring such things with us from Heorot."

"From Rolf, Thora's husband. He has a workshop in one of those sunken huts and makes amazing things out of bark! He also told me he knows where the best mushrooms can be found."

I shuddered. "I don't think I could eat a single mushroom after . . . what happened to my brothers."

Runa looked at me curiously, but I quickly changed the topic.

"We'll need to borrow a few extra tools — perhaps Rolf could lend us another antler rake and a digging stick? Runa, run down and ask him."

"Yes, my lady." She was out the door in an instant.

Ingeborg and Estrid busied themselves gathering cloaks for each of us, while Ragnhild hurried down to the house of Sigrid to tell Thorkel where we were going. Finally we were all assembled again and ready to leave.

"Goodby, Ana. We'll be back by mid-afternoon. Don't worry about us!"

She knit her brows, but a smile lurked at the corners of her mouth.

"Goodby, my lady. It's a fine day. Enjoy your outing."

Indeed it was a fine day. A clear sky, warm sunshine, small birds twittering in the treetops — I felt like a young girl again. Beneath our feet the soft new grass was sprinkled with tiny flowers: white, yellow, pink, and purple — scattered like a carpet of stars.

I took a deep breath, delighting in the pure, fresh mountain air, so different from the salt air of the seacoast. My companions seemed to share my delight. Brita and Runa were almost skipping!

"I must admit, my lady," confessed Ingeborg, "it is good to get out of the longhouse. Ana has been working us hard these past few days."

The rake she carried over one shoulder swung dangerously close as she spoke.

"Have a care, Ingeborg! I need both of my eyes!"

"Oh, beg pardon. I'm not used to handling such implements."

As we passed other longhouses, a few faces appeared in doorways to view our progress. Thora waved to us and, further down the path, little Toke peered out from behind his mother's legs. We soon left the settlement behind, but I knew that if we kept the river to our right, we could not miss our destination.

By the time we reached the stone circle and put down our burdens, each of us was glad for Ana's thoughtfulness in sending the jug. We passed it from mouth to mouth, each woman taking a long draught.

"And now to work!" I cried. "Let's start by the stones and work toward the center, pulling or digging out whatever needs to be removed."

As we bent to the task, Runa started to sing, a wordless melody that dipped and soared like a bird in flight. My own heart dipped and soared too; it was good to feel the sun on my back, good to be working happily among my women.

By the time the sun had reached its zenith we had cleared more than half of the circle, and removed most of the stubborn vines clinging to the ancient stones. Wiping away the sweat that trickled into my eyes, I called for a halt.

"Anyone ready for a dip in the river? I'm going to bathe my face there."

Each woman stopped and turned in my direction.

"Lady Freawaru, speaking of faces, yours is quite red," said Brita with concern. "Perhaps you should sit down under those birches while the rest of us continue."

"Speak for yourself, Brita," said Estrid drily. "I need a rest too."

Ragnhild and Ingeborg instantly dropped their rakes.

"Come," I said. "Let's all go over to the river. Runa — bring the cheese!"

The water was very cold; it made my fingers tingle and stung my cheeks, but it cooled my sweating face. The moss-covered bank was soft and yielding. Spreading my cloak under the dappled shade of a birch clump, I lay down and stretched my arms and legs to relax their aching muscles. Above me the rustling leaves made their own kind of music. I closed my eyes to hear it better.

When I opened my eyes again the sun had sunk low and I lay in total shade, covered with Brita's cloak. Brita herself was looking down at me.

"Where is everyone else?" I yawned.

Handing Brita her cloak, I got to my feet, aware of the stiffness in my back and knees.

"Brita, where are the rest?"

"Over there, my lady." She pointed to a space beyond the stone circle, where I saw a wisp of smoke rising. "They are burning the weeds we cleared."

I picked up my own cloak and shook it out. "Let's join them."

As we neared the group, Brita turned and peered at my face.

"Still red. Burnt by the sun. You'll need vinegar on that tonight," she said. "But look, Lady Freawaru. We finished clearing while you slept."

She waved a hand toward the stone circle, now smoothed and shorn — fit for a ritual, and big enough to hold all the women of the village.

"Thank you, everyone!" I yawned again. "I don't know what makes me so sleepy of late."

My women looked at each other and grinned.

"Lady Freawaru," said Ragnhild, "we all know you are with child. We've know it for some time, but you seemed to want it kept secret, so we've not spoken of it. We were glad to finish this task while you — and the baby — slept."

I put my hands on my belly, which seemed to have grown much larger in the last few days.

Fanning the Flames

"I see. Well, thank you again — for your work and for keeping my secret. Now, it must be time to return to Hrethelskeep."

I could not have predicted what awaited us there.

Chapter Seven
Face to Face

Decoration on a rune stone from Lund, in Skåne, Sweden, c. 1000A.D.

"Look! Something is happening in the village — men, and horses!"

Runa's exclamation brought my head up instantly. A flicker of fear tightened in my chest. A raiding party? No, surely not, so far inland.

"Stop, everyone. Let's proceed slowly until we can see what is happening," I said. "Runa, do you recognize any of the horses?"

She shaded her eyes against the glow of the western sky.

"I think... yes, that dapple gray could be Ragnar's steed — or 'Redbeard' as you call him."

"Redbeard?" I squinted into the distance. "Then he may be bringing the thralls we asked for. Even so, let's stay close to the river, under the trees, where our approach will be less obvious."

I had been deep in thought, weighing various possibilities for the ritual ahead. So much needed to be accomplished: give honor to the goddess, ask her blessing on our crops, animals, and people in the season ahead, and unite the women of the village — Dane and Geat. I also needed to ask Freyja for her aid in dealing with the curse of Gudfrid, but that should be done privately, at a separate time, so as not to alarm others.

My body ached and my face burned. The sun seemed stronger here than back in my homeland. I must remember that in future. Ruefully, I noted that my women also had sunburned cheeks and arms.

As we drew nearer, more signs of activity gradually emerged: shapes outside longhouses, carts being unloaded — by roughly-dressed men I did not recognize. To my relief, I made out the imposing figure of Redbeard, directing it all. I was about to lead my women in his direction, when I heard a familiar voice.

"Lady Freawaru, at last you're back! You have a visitor!"

Ana stood squarely in the center of the path, hands on hips, catching her breath. She peered at me.

"What's wrong with your face?"

I put my hands to my cheeks, then my hair — full of tangles. I must look a mess — and I had a visitor? Could it be ... ?

"Hurry now! He's been waiting all afternoon! What took you so long?"

Ana was almost babbling as she hustled me along, leaving the rest to follow as they might.

"Who is it, Ana, this visitor?"

"Why, Beowulf, of course! He came back to see you!"

Beowulf? To see me? Suddenly I felt giddy, giddy with possibilities. Something seemed to open in my chest, flooding me with warmth. I blinked back tears, wiping my face with a grimy hand.

Ana glanced at my belly, protruding beneath the weed-stained tunic.

"Oh, my lady, what will you do?"

I stopped and stared at her as we reached the doorway.

"You don't think ... ?"

"Yes, I do!" She too blinked back sudden tears. "Let's get you cleaned up a bit before he sees you!"

Inside the longhouse Ana began bathing my sunburned face with vinegar. I tried to organize my thoughts.

When Beowulf named me as hostess in his mead hall, Gunilla asked if he were finally going to marry ... I wonder ...

A loud knock sounded at the door.

"Enter," called Ana.

"Beowulf!" I sprang to my feet.

"I could not wait to see you! I saw your women and knew you must be back," he declared, a wide grin on his face. He held out both hands. "Come outside, Lady Freawaru. I have a gift for you!"

Chagrined that Beowulf should see me in such a state, I nevertheless hurried to follow his command. Ana hastily tied a kerchief over my head as Beowulf and I headed for the door.

"Where? What is it, my lord?"

"Behind the longhouse. Your women are already admiring it. Come! See!"

He sounded more like Herdred than Beowulf, but hadn't I already learned that grown men could act like little boys? Giving a hasty pat to my hair, I let him lead me out of the longhouse, my hand in his firm grasp.

Women's voices, chattering and laughing, fell silent as we rounded the back corner.

There, tethered to a stake, munching on scattered tufts of grass, stood a large yellow ... cow! She raised her head, looked me in the eye, and gave a loud bellow.

"She's the best of the herd, I'm told — gives rich milk — and cream." Beowulf laughed. "Thinking of our last parting after that morning gruel, I remembered how much you liked cream! I brought her from Eaglesgard!"

"All the way from Eaglesgard?" I marveled. "How did you get her here?"

Beowulf grinned at my astonishment.

"It wasn't easy, or quick. It took three thralls to tie her onto the cart and they rode beside her on the journey to keep her calm. Now she's more than ready to be milked. Do any of your women ... ?"

"Here, my lord." Runa stepped forward with a wooden stool and a pail. "I can do it!"

I nodded approvingly. "Thank you, Runa. Brita, take note of what she does so that you can learn."

Now I turned to Beowulf, who still held my hand, and beamed at him, despite the tightness of my sunburned face.

"Lord Beowulf, what a surprise you've given us — not least the surprise and pleasure of seeing you again! Thank you for this unexpected but most welcome gift!"

He grinned again.

"I have more to offer you, my lady, much more. But forgive me. I know you meant to refresh yourself after your day's work, and I have kept you.

I'll return you to Ana, but only for a short time. We have much to discuss. I will wait for you in the mead hall, where we will not be disturbed."

We returned to the longhouse with Beowulf still holding my hand. Behind us I could hear my ladies buzzing with curiosity.

Inside, still unsettled about the meaning of Beowulf's appearance, I let Ana gently wash my face, comb my hair and change my tunic — though no piece of clothing could any longer disguise my condition. Beowulf had said nothing. Had he noticed?

"He waited inside here earlier, but when midday passed and you still weren't back, I suggested he go to the mead hall," said Ana. "I could tell he was disappointed by your absence. Clearly he has something important on his mind!"

Something important on his mind? Has he been thinking about me? He came back alone... that is, without Hygd... Oh, Beowulf, what have you come to say? But wait — perhaps it's the curse he's thinking of — the curse I've not yet taken steps to counteract...

Conflicting thoughts swirled in my brain as I headed toward the mead hall. A fresh kerchief covered my hair, as befitted my status as a married woman. Looking down, I noticed that Ana had dressed me in my finest blue tunic, the one I'd worn on my wedding day. With trembling fingers I smoothed the silken fabric. My heart thudded in my chest.

Calm yourself, Freawaru. Compose your face. Let Beowulf see you as you truly are — the daughter of a king — and queen. Oh, Mother, lend me your strength. I think I may love this man, but... does he love me?

I lifted my head, took a deep breath, and entered.

Beowulf sat in his high seat at the far end of the hall. By the torchlight that brightened the chamber I could see his face. He looked... happy ... expectant, his blue eyes shining like stars in a dark night. He rose as I approached, walking like one in a dream, and extended both arms.

"Freaw, Lady Freawaru, at last we are alone together!"

He took my freshly scrubbed hands and kissed them gently, his mustache tickling my skin.

I laughed, and with the laugh came back to my senses.

"Beowulf, my lord, I am here!"

"So I see!"

His smile, bright as the sun, dazzled my eyes.

"Freaw, I could not stay away. After I left a few days ago I could not stop thinking... of many things: of the cold and darkness of grandfather's house, of all you still needed to make the place a real home..."

My heart sank. Had he come back only to see to my comfort? To bring me a... a cow?

"... but I've already seen for myself how warm and comfortable you've made it. Why, I hardly recognized it as the same place! You bring light wherever you go, Lady Freaw."

During this speech Beowulf still held my hands in his strong grasp, squeezing them tighter and tighter. Despite my sunburn I made no move to free myself.

"Lord Beowulf, you do me honor to visit us here, when your duties at Eaglesgard no doubt require your time and attention."

His smile suddenly faded. I could have bitten my tongue.

"Yes, they do," he admitted, "but I have an important matter to discuss with you, Lady Freaw. Come, let us dine together here. You must be in need of refreshment after your long day's work."

His smile reappeared as he led me to a side table already provided with a pitcher and goblets—fine goblets of glass, not the everyday wooden mugs.

"Boy!" he called, "Bring the food."

A boy standing in the shadows scurried out the door.

Beowulf seated me, then sat down across the table so that we faced each other. Carefully he filled my goblet, then poured his own drink.

"A toast!" he announced. "Let us drink to a new and brighter future for Hrethelskeep!"

"For Hrethelskeep!" I echoed, lifting my glass, my eyes locked on his.

We drank, lowered our glasses, and looked at each other wordlessly. Finally Beowulf broke the silence.

"Freaw, I must beg a boon of you." He paused.

"What is it, my lord? I will gladly grant it, if I can."

He smiled a slow smile.

"Release your hair. Let me see your hair."

In answer I reached back to untie my kerchief. Trembling, I let it fall, then slowly undid the topknot, letting my hair tumble in waves about my shoulders. Shyly, I tilted my head to look at him.

"Ah... yes," he breathed. "It is as I remembered it." He paused again.

"Freaw, do you remember the first time we saw each other?" he began.

"Indeed I do, my lord ... in Heorot ... in my father's mead hall. I was bearing the mead cup to our warriors. You and your men had just arrived, eager to challenge the Grendel monster. I feared for your life then — we all did — but you proved yourself, killed the Grendel, saved Heorot, and sailed home with well-earned treasure."

I paused, remembering with a shiver those desperate days.

"Freaw," said Beowulf softly, reaching across the table to take my hand again. "Of all your father's treasures, you are the most precious. It was your hand I would have asked for, had you not already been promised to the Heathobard."

So, it is out ... his feelings for me, which match my own.

I drew a deep breath, inhaling the sweetness of his words, absorbing the warmth of his touch. If only ...

Ah, Beowulf, are we fated ever to meet at the wrong moment?

"Freaw," he continued, "since your unexpected appearance at Eaglesgard, I have thought of you constantly. Your presence helped me bear the loss of Hygelac. Your presence helped me see a way forward for Hrethelskeep — long neglected, I admit. You have brought the sun back into my life."

"Beowulf," I breathed softly, "what are you telling me?"

"You must know, Freaw, for I have seen an answer to my question in your eyes. I want you for my wife. Will you have me?"

I let go his hand and rose from my place, sudden hot tears streaming down my face.

"Oh, Beowulf, dear Beowulf, I would gladly be your wife, but I am not free, not free to join you. Ingeld is dead, yes, but I ... I carry his child."

Beowulf too had risen, confusion on his face. Walking to his side, I took his huge hands and placed them on my belly. His eyes widened in understanding.

"Why did you not tell me?" he murmured, his voice breaking. "What is to be done?"

Beowulf reached around to encircle me. He pulled me close, my head against his massive chest. I felt the strength of his powerful arms, heard the steady beat of his great heart. My own heart was bursting with joy and grief. Yes, I had loved Ingeld, as a young wife loves her young husband, but the deep desire I felt for Beowulf surpassed anything I had yet experienced.

He pressed against me and I closed my eyes, swaying, sinking into his body, locked in his embrace.

A cough from the doorway. "Your food, my lord."

"Set it down and don't return until I call," said Beowulf dismissively, still holding me tight.

He leaned forward, rubbing his chin on the top of my head.

"Freaw, Freaw, I've wanted to hold you for so long, so long," he murmured into my hair. "I can't let you go now."

Reluctantly I pulled back enough to look up at him.

"Beowulf, we both have responsibilities to meet. Should this child be a boy, he will be the heir to Ingeld's land and property, an inheritance I must help him secure. You, for your part, are bound to Herdred until he comes of age. Your place is at Eaglesgard, beside your king."

Even as I spoke these words, my heart rebelled against them. Beowulf gazed at me, slowly dropping his arms. His head sank.

"Duty. Again. I have always done my duty," he said bitterly. His voice was so soft I could barely hear his words. He lifted his head.

"And if the child is not a boy? What then? Or if . . ."

The unspoken 'if' hung in the air.

"I have lost a child before, my lord, and that could happen again," I said as calmly as I could manage. "If the child is a girl, I will raise her here at Hrethelskeep, as a gift from the goddess."

Beowulf studied my face.

"How long?" he asked.

"By the time of fall harvest."

"Then I shall wait — for you and your time."

Beowulf took my hands again, brought them to his lips and kissed them. I looked up at him, my heart in my eyes. His face was utterly serious, his blue eyes burning a brand on my heart.

Whatever happens, dear Beowulf, I am yours.

"My lord, are you certain of your decision? You will wait?" I looked at him closely for any sign of hesitation.

"I will wait," he repeated solemnly. Bending forward, he brushed the top of my head with his lips.

"Such a wealth of red-gold hair. You are a treasure worth waiting for, my Freaw."

During the meal that followed, a simple repast of bread, fish, and cheese, I told Beowulf of the proposed ritual to honor the goddess, of the wedding plans for Thorkel and Ragnhild, and finally of the long blonde braid found in the byre.

"How do you know it belonged to Gudfrid?" he asked quietly, stroking the fingers of my left hand as it lay on the table. I placed my right hand over his.

"Because I have seen her — twice — and her hair was cut short. No married woman wears her hair cut short."

Beowulf suddenly pulled his hand away.

"You have seen her? How? Where? She must have died years ago!"

"Yes, she is dead, but her spirit has not found rest. She came to me once ... in the latrine outside this very mead hall, and a second time ... when I lay in Hrethel's bed."

"Hrethel's bed?" Beowulf stared at me. "I was often visited by dark dreams in that bed ... could they have been caused by this curse you've spoken of?" He scowled.

"Yes." I nodded gravely. "I've been pondering ways to counter it. Some methods are more ... perilous ... than others."

"Perilous? What do you mean? Would you put yourself in danger? Freaw, I do not want to lose you!"

I have heard those words before: Ingeld ... the wolfskin ... Ingeld and Gyda in my bed ...

"Freaw, what is it? Are you seeing ghosts right now?"

Beowulf set down his glass carefully and rose to his feet.

"Oh, my lord, there are more ghosts than Gudfrid. Some of them live inside my head!"

I put my hands over my face, suddenly overcome with memories.

"Freaw, Freaw, let me help you. I am here beside you."

He was, suddenly beside me, gripping my shoulders gently but firmly as if I too were a glass that might break. I rose and turned, sheltering in his arms, savoring his touch, his smell ...

"Freaw, I would not dishonor you," he whispered huskily into my ear, "but you have awakened in me a hunger that only you can satisfy."

I heard a note of desperation in his voice. To ease the tension and his pain, I replied lightly.

"Any woman in Geatland would be your willing bed-partner, my lord."

He groaned. "Any woman? Nay, it is you I want and need. Besides..." he paused. "I have never been with any woman."

What?! Had I heard him correctly? I swung around to face him.

"Beowulf? Do you speak truly? You have never slept with a woman?"

"Do you think me less of a man for it?" His expression was anxious.

"No, just the opposite," I assured him, "but I am astonished. A man of your reputation — admired by all — a hero. I..."

"Stop!" Beowulf seized my hands and held them fast, bringing his face close to mine.

"It was not always so. As a boy I was scorned, looked down upon by my elders, for weakness and lack of ambition. Then, after Herbald died, I prayed to the gods: 'Give me strength greater than that of any Geat. Give me fame. In return I will give up the love of women. I will touch no woman with desire'."

Beowulf groaned aloud. "I have kept my vow — until now."

Stunned, I looked deep into his eyes.

"Oh, my love, you are the bravest man alive, but no man can resist the goddess of love. When she commands, you must obey."

Now he moaned. "Freaw, you are my goddess. Command me."

My lips opened to pour out my heart, but I stopped short.

Careful, Freawaru. A mistake here will cost you both, dearly. This is not the time!

"Beowulf, you have my heart." I reached up and stroked his dear face. "Now there is something more I want to tell you. When I was just a young girl, I saw you in a vision — long before you came to Heorot. Yes," I nodded at his wondering eyes, "I saw you soaring on a swan's back, coming to our rescue. You have been a part of my life since that moment."

We both fell silent.

"Now, my lord, let us return to our dinner and speak quietly of other things. We have many seasons ahead of us — I see it clearly. We will have time to chart a safe course together."

He gazed at me, the flush in his face gradually fading.

"You speak wisely, Freaw. I will accept your counsel."

Silently, we sat back down to our largely untouched meal.

Beowulf refilled my goblet, then his, and lifted his glass again.

"I drink to Freawaru the fair, wise and womanly!"

When he had drained his glass, I lifted my own.

"I drink to Beowulf the brave, kind and kingly!"

His eyes widened, then darkened.

"Only Herdred's death could put me in that position," he observed solemnly, "and I will do everything in my power to prevent that!"

He poured another goblet of ale.

"My lord . . ." I began, but he raised a hand.

"Nay, Freaw, let us use no titles when we are alone."

"As you wish . . . Beowulf." I smiled. "Now, we have . . . issues to be resolved . . . concerning leadership within the village, and individual duties. For example, who is in charge of defense, who is to supervise the thralls you brought with you, and how far does my authority extend?"

We talked late into the night, sorting out details of management and supervision. Beowulf readily agreed to put Wulfgar in charge of battle training and defense. Magnus was to oversee the male slaves and the day-to-day work of farming. My duties were to preside at village gatherings of whatever nature, and oversee the work of the female slaves. No request had been sent for Runa's return, so she would remain at Hrethelskeep during the summer.

"I will return as often as I can," Beowulf promised.

He rose to stir the embers in the hearth fire. I rose too, suppressing a yawn — which did not escape his notice.

"Freaw, I have kept you from your bed. Forgive my selfishness in wanting to keep you with me longer."

We walked hand-in-hand to the mead hall door, then stepped out into the cool night air. As I looked up at the stars, woven like a glittering net above us, I was jolted by a memory.

"Lord — that is — Beowulf, have you ever seen something in the night sky at Eaglesgard that resembled a . . . a dragon?"

"A dragon?" he echoed. "My grandfather once spoke of such a thing, but I thought it only a story to frighten children. Why do you ask?" He turned me to face him.

"I . . . I thought I saw such a creature once, but I could not be sure," I finished, lamely.

Beowulf did not seem to be upset; he resumed walking.

"Perhaps, like the aurochs and wisent that once roamed these lands, dragons have all died or gone away," he said.

"Aurochs? Wisent? What are they?" I asked in surprise.

"Aurochs were huge oxen with great curving horns. Hrethel once drank from such a horn in the mead hall, but it disappeared long ago." He smiled at the memory. "Wisent were a kind of cattle, but with shaggy heads and shoulder humps. Hrethel's father, Swerting, was said to have killed one for meat when he was a young man."

By now we had reached the door of my longhouse.

"Beowulf," I said, lifting my face to his, "I would hear more of your family's history and of your younger days here in Hrethelskeep. I hope we will talk again."

He took my hands.

"Of course. Tomorrow. May the gods keep you safe, my Freaw."

He kissed my fingertips and let me go.

That night I lay awake, reliving every detail of our reunion: Beowulf's words, his touch, the way his face changed as he spoke — but one detail did not seem to fit. What was it? Strength . . . his lack of strength as a boy. Gunilla had told me a different story. She'd said that his strength was unmatched even as a child. What could account for this difference?

And Beowulf's vow to the gods . . . What would happen to his strength if he *did* lie with a woman? What if he lay with *me*?

A stirring in my womb awakened a different line of thought. What if I had married Beowulf, not Ingeld? Then this child would be his.

Freaw, be sensible. This is foolish thinking. You must deal with what is, with things as they are.

Sighing, I drifted into sleep, feeling Beowulf's lips on my hair, hearing his voice in my ears.

Redbeard knocked on our door early the next morning. Ana admitted him, then called for me. Fortunately I was already up and dressed. He carried a bulky bag of tools.

"Lady Freawaru, will you show me what you want carved on the door posts? I'm ready to work, as we're only staying a day or two."

"Certainly," I answered, pleased with his eagerness. "I have already drawn some marks with charcoal on birch bark as a pattern. Wait here and I'll get them."

I hurried back to the chest beside my bed, where I withdrew a pouch of charcoal and several pieces of flattened bark. As I carried them back to the hearth where Redbeard stood waiting, an idea came to me.

"Redbeard, if you have time, I'd like runes carved on my own door, as well as on the mead hall door posts."

He gave a slight bow. "I'll see what I can do. Now, let's have a look at those drawings."

We sat down side by side at the table, where I traced the outlines of the runes I'd chosen for the mead hall.

"This is Algiz, a rune of defense and protection, this Eihwaz, a guardian rune, and this..."

Redbeard chuckled. "I know that one well enough! It's Teiwaz, for victory in battle! It's engraved on my own sword, it is. You know what you're talking about, Lady Freawaru!"

"Yes, thank you, I do," I acknowledged with a smile. "Now, here are the runes I'd like carved on the longhouse door: Sowulo for wholeness and Berkana for growth and fertility."

With a few strokes I added the necessary marks. Redbeard nodded, glancing at me with a grin, as if he knew a secret.

"Is that all, my lady?"

"Yes, that will be a good start. Repeat the runes in the same order each time you carve."

"Right. I'll be off then, to begin my work."

Later that morning I went to the mead hall to view Redbeard's progress. The sound of his mallet striking the chisel rang through the village. He had already finished inscribing the runes and was now working on an elaborate design of twisting serpents.

"What do you think?" he asked, stepping back from the door and wiping sweat from his brow.

"Redbeard, it's... it's beautiful!" I knelt down to look more closely, the scent of fresh wood chips tickling my nostrils. "Are those dragons? Or gripping beasts?"

"Both!" he declared with satisfaction. "Since Lord Beowulf has a dragon head on the prow of his ship, I thought he might like a few on his mead hall entrance as well."

"I do!" boomed a voice behind us.

Redbeard and I both turned. Beowulf stood, hands on hips, surveying the scene.

"Good work, Ragnar!" Beowulf clapped Redbeard on the shoulder. "But don't work too fast, old friend. I want to stay a while longer in Hrethelskeep!"

"As you wish, my lord. I believe Lady Freawaru has more work for me." Beowulf nodded.

"I think Lady Freawaru is also going to need a shed built, as she has no place for a cow in her longhouse — but that is a job for thralls, not a skilled carver like you!"

Redbeard laughed.

"Cowshed? No, that is not my line of work!"

"Indeed, my friend. Please continue what you have started."

As Beowulf and I walked away, Redbeard resumed work on his dragons.

"Beowulf, Magnus told me that we needed animals inside the longhouse in order to survive your winters. Is the cold really that bitter here?"

Beowulf did not miss a stride.

"Sometimes, yes, but I think Magnus meant only to be ... helpful. I'll have a cowshed built onto the longhouse and open a door. Magnus does not like change — but Sigfast's death has already brought change to our usual chain of command. Don't worry," he added, seeing the doubt on my face, "Magnus is a good fellow at heart. He'll get used to the new arrangements. Now, what else bothers you?"

I flushed. Were my thoughts so transparent?

"I've been thinking," I began, looking at the ground in some embarrassment, "remembering what you said yesterday — about asking Hrothgar for my hand as a reward for killing the Grendel. If that had happened, the child I now carry would have been yours."

I looked up to see his reaction to my foolish daydream, and was met with a stricken look.

"What is it, my lord?"

"Hygelac gave his only daughter to Eofer as a reward for killing Ongentheow, and it cost her her life!"

"What? Hygelac and Hygd's daughter? Why has no one spoken of this? What happened to her?"

"Come. Let's walk outside the village and I will tell you the story."

Putting an arm around my shoulders, he led me away.

Chapter Eight
Missing

Bronze age lur horn found at Tellerup on Funen, Denmark.

Beowulf held me close by his side as we walked slowly toward the river. Beneath our feet the grass was still damp with dew. Beowulf did not speak aloud, but the pressure of his arm conveyed both restraint and passion. I trembled in his firm but gentle grip. Glancing up at his face, I saw a frown constrict his brow. Was he thinking of Hygelac's daughter... or of me? I stopped and reached up to touch his cheek.

"What is it my lord — Beowulf?"

"Helga. She was about your height.... She would have been nearly your age, had she lived." He shook his head slowly and sorrowfully.

"Helga? Was that the name of Hygelac's daughter?"

Beowulf dropped his arm and turned to face me.

"Helga, yes. She was a laughing maiden with sparkling eyes; she loved to tease me. I called her my little sister, and tried to protect her as a big brother should — but I could not prevent her death!"

The last words poured from Beowulf's lips in a wave of anguish. I took his huge hands in mine, his battle-scarred hands, and pressed them to my heart.

"Beowulf, be comforted. If it will ease your pain, speak to me of Helga."

Now I led the way to the river bank and spread my cloak on a grassy overhang. Wordlessly, he dropped down beside me and laced his fingers under his chin, gazing into the stream below.

"The water took her," he began.

"What? She drowned? Here in the Göta?" I exclaimed. "But surely she knew how to swim?"

"No, not here in the Göta; it happened at Eaglesgard . . . and yes, she knew how to swim." Beowulf spoke dully, his eyes fixed on the water below us.

"Then, I don't understand . . ."

"There is much more to the story. Be patient, Freaw. I have not spoken of Helga for many winters. I cannot bring it back all at once."

I fell silent and waited for Beowulf to continue. As we sat quietly, our legs reaching almost down to the water, I recalled a long-ago incident when Unferth had saved my brothers and me from drowning—long ago, back in Heorot. Had there been no Unferth to save Helga? Beowulf's voice broke my reverie.

"Helga was still just a child when we went to war against the Swedes. She was Hygelac and Hygd's only child then. She should have been promised to a chieftain, at least, but when Eofer killed the Swedish king at Ravenswood, Hygelac rashly offered Helga as a reward."

Here Beowulf paused and groaned aloud.

"A child—a child—too young for a marriage bed!"

I opened my lips with a question, but closed them. Beowulf must be allowed to work through his grief, now that this old wound had been opened. Finally he spoke again.

"She was frightened, I know she was, but dutiful to her father. Eofer was twice her age, a rough warrior, a bear of a man—no match for a delicate girl like Helga. She submitted to the ceremony, she submitted to Eofer, but on the morning after their union she jumped into the sea and drowned herself!"

Shocked, I gave a little gasp. Tears stood in Beowulf's eyes.

"He must have hurt her. I *know* he hurt her. Men destroy women! You are not safe with us!"

Fanning the Flames

Beowulf's voice had risen and he stared at me with wild eyes.

"Beowulf! Come back to yourself! You have destroyed no one..."

Even as I spoke, echoes of Beowulf's long-ago speech in Heorot came back to me.

"I killed the sea-hag, killed Grendel's mother. I lopped off her head with the giant's sword and left her lying lifeless in her cave!"

"My lord," I said gently, touching his arm, "you are not responsible for every death. Wyrd has a hand in human affairs. If Helga chose her own death, perhaps she was fated to do so."

Beowulf continued to stare at me, but less wildly. We sank again into silence.

At length I asked another question. "What happened to Eofer?"

"Eofer? He died later in battle. No one blamed him — not even Hygelac and Hygd. No one spoke of Helga again." Beowulf gave a wan smile. "It is good to remember her now. It is good to speak her name... Helga... little sister."

His hand closed over mine.

"Freaw, all my life I have been a warrior. I have done my duty to king and comrades. I have sought fame and glory. But sometimes..." his voice trailed off. "Sometimes I want something more, something I've not yet found. What could it be?"

His face calm now, he gazed into my eyes.

"I don't know, Beowulf, but I hope you find it."

Hand in hand we walked silently back into the village.

Redbeard was still carving on the mead hall doorway when we arrived. Beowulf went off to get the cowshed project underway, but I paused to marvel at Redbeard's workmanship.

"That dragon looks ready to breathe fire!" I exclaimed.

Redbeard grinned and wiped sweat from his eyes.

"It should put the fear of Thor into any attackers," he bragged.

"Thor? I thought Thor wrestled with sea serpents, not dragons."

"Serpents, dragons, all the same to me."

I paused to consider the question that came to me. Redbeard was clearly older than Beowulf. Perhaps he had spent more time at Eaglesgard...

"Redbeard, have you ever seen a dragon at Eaglesgard?"

My question seemed to take him by surprise, for he laid down his chisel and stood up, brushing wood chips from his hairy forearms.

"Why do you ask, my lady?"

"Oh, I once thought I saw something in the night sky above Eaglesgard, something... dragon-like."

Redbeard narrowed his eyes.

"Strange," he muttered, as if to himself. "That's what Hygelac told me — not long before he went to Frisia."

We stared at each other.

"Could it have been an omen, a warning?" I whispered, my throat suddenly dry.

"You'd know better than I, Lady Freawaru. You have the gift of sight!"

I sighed. "Yea and nay, Redbeard. It does not always come when I need it," I added ruefully.

He looked at me keenly.

"Do you regularly practice your craft, my lady? Do you work at developing your skills?"

Now it was my turn to be surprised.

"What do you mean? 'Seeing' is not something I can control."

"A warrior does not become a warrior without practice," replied Redbeard. "He learns how to use the weapons he has."

These words made me recall what Unferth, my rune-master, had told me long ago: 'Each of us is a warrior, though we carry no sword or shield.'

"What are *your* weapons, Lady Freawaru?" Redbeard had not taken his eyes from my face.

"My weapons?" I echoed. "I have not drunk from the Well of Mimir, but I have imbibed knowledge from my mother and my rune-master — who both possessed more than ordinary powers."

I did not mention the feather mark on my shoulder, for I still felt uncertain about what — if any — powers it conferred. Redbeard regarded me sagely.

"Perhaps you will find Hrethelskeep a fitting place in which to develop your powers, my lady. I, for one, believe you have a destiny to fulfill here."

My mouth almost fell open at these words.

"Thank you, Redbeard, for your confidence in me. I wish everyone here shared your good opinion," I added, thinking of Magnus.

"Give them a reason to trust you! Give them a demonstration of your powers!" challenged Redbeard.

I lifted my head.

"As it happens, I am planning just such a demonstration, Redbeard: a ritual to honor the Earth Mother. All the women of the village will be asked to attend."

He smiled with satisfaction.

"That is good. Do it soon!"

"What are you two talking about so earnestly?"

Beowulf was striding toward us. Before I could answer, Redbeard stepped forward.

"We were discussing Lady Freawaru's future here. The gods must have sent this woman to you, my lord, and you have done wisely to acknowledge her powers. Hrethelskeep will be the better for it!"

Beowulf blinked in surprise.

"The lady seems to have enchanted you, old friend!"

Beowulf winked at me and clapped a hand on Redbeard's broad shoulders.

"Now, Ragnar, I need the lady's advice — about her new cowshed. Can you spare her?"

Redbeard grunted and turned back to his work, but not before delivering a parting shot: "Soon, my lady."

Beowulf tucked my arm under his and led me away, this time to my own longhouse, where several thralls were busy outside framing an enclosure of wattle and daub.

"What do you think?" asked Beowulf. "Should we make it big enough to house several cows? Perhaps a few pigs? Some sheep? I want you to be well provided for," he added tenderly.

"You know best, Beowulf. I agree that we should plan... for the future."

"Good! We'll extend the shed all the way to that manure pile." He gestured toward a large mound fringed with new grass.

"That gives *me* an idea," I said. "This would be a good place for the garden. We'll need a big one to feed all my people!"

"As you think best, Freaw. I'll have one of these fellows start turning over the dirt. You can show him how big to make your garden."

The rest of the day was spent outdoors, with my women helping me plant the seeds I'd brought with us. Beowulf disappeared from time to time, returning at intervals to examine progress on the cowshed. By the time darkness began to settle over the valley, the shed was roofed and ready. My back was aching from hours of bending over the dirt, but I delighted at the prospect of an herb and sally garden to rival the one my mother tended back in Heorot.

If she is still alive. Mother, will I ever see you again?

That night Beowulf invited me and my people to take our meal with him and Redbeard in the mead hall. To my surprise Magnus was also present. The reason was soon revealed. After all were served, Beowulf rose.

"Friends, I offer a toast: to the new hostess of this mead hall, the bearer of the cup of hospitality, the gracious Lady Freawaru. All hail!"

"All hail!" echoed the voices around me.

Beowulf now turned his attention to Magnus.

"I offer a second toast to the head man in Hrethelskeep — when I am absent. He has been given the honor of providing full protection for Lady Freawaru and her people. They are to have whatever they need to be comfortable here. To Magnus — all hail!"

"All hail!" the voices resounded.

I glanced at Magnus to see how he was taking this announcement. He looked pleased, but did not smile when I caught his eye. Magnus might yet be a tough nut to crack.

That night after Brita had left my bedchamber, Runa approached.

"My lady, how is it with you?"

"I am well, but why do you ask, Runa?"

She smiled. "There is a sparkle in your eyes today that was not there yesterday. Clearly, something has happened."

"Ah," I laughed, "you see me too well, Runa."

Then I remembered that Runa had not been present when I told Ana and my other women about the reunion with Beowulf. I cleared my throat.

"Lord Beowulf and I have reached an ... agreement. He knows that I am with child and is content to wait for the outcome. Is that what you wanted to know?"

Why am I telling this to Runa? Is she somehow bound up with my future in this place?

Runa's face brightened, then darkened.

"There is also a look on Lord Beowulf's face that bespeaks an ancient sorrow, now somewhat softened."

I marveled at the girl's perceptioin.

"You are right again, Runa."

Suddenly I found myself telling her the story of Helga and her tragic fate. Runa listened intently, taking it all in.

"Ah, my lady, in the stories of my homeland we too have a Helga, though we call her 'Aino.' She drowned herself to escape life with an unsuitable mate. It is said her voice can be heard at sea by those who sail upon it. She cries out on wind and waves, a maiden of endless sorrow."

We sat together silently for a time, thinking of Helga—and Aino. Finally I roused and shook myself.

"Runa, the ritual for the goddess—it must happen soon."

She nodded.

"I've been thinking of that flute you spoke of. Could you play it at the ritual?"

She nodded again.

"My flute is made from the leg bone of a swan, a creature of wind and waves. Its voice could be the voice of Helga, or Aino."

"A swan-bone?" My skin prickled at this, and I shivered. "I once flew with the swans at Heorot—my girlhood home. They carried me out of myself—to faraway places.

"Runa!" I exclaimed, a new idea seizing me. "We will raise up the names of women like Helga and Aino in our ritual. We will honor those women, living and dead, who have been a part of our lives."

Could that include Gudfrid? Ongentheow's wife?

Runa nodded a third time.

"Yes, my lady. The ghost-women. Yes."

Like a ghost herself, Runa slipped away into the darkness.

The next day Beowulf and I were sitting quietly in the mead hall when the door burst open. In rushed a tall young man drenched with sweat.

"Lord Beowulf," he gasped. "King Herdred is missing! You must return to Eaglesgard!"

Beowulf and I both jumped to our feet.

"Missing? For how long?" cried Beowulf.

"Since yesterday morning," panted the man, sagging as he spoke.

"Here, Aksel, sit down and take a cup of ale. You have ridden hard — and in the dark — to get here so quickly. Rest a moment, then tell us what you know."

In response Aksel sank down on one of the benches, but took only one gulp of the drink I gave him before pouring out his story

"Hygd missed him first, at the morning meal. Then she discovered his horse was gone."

He took another gulp and wiped his mouth.

"Most of us were out searching when his riderless horse returned, limping."

Beowulf's face drained of color.

"Have you searched . . . the coastline? At the base of the cliff?" He could barely choke out the words.

"Yes, Lord Beowulf. There was no sign of him there."

"It's all my fault," groaned Beowulf. "I should not have left him alone — he's still just a boy . . ."

"Maybe Lady Freawaru can help!" boomed a different voice. We turned to see Redbeard advancing toward the table.

"Lady Freaw has the Sight," said Redbeard in response to Aksel's look. "Maybe she can see something that will help us find Herdred."

Now all eyes turned toward me, frozen in consternation.

Here is another test, Freaw. This is your moment. Can you use your powers? Herdred's life may depend on it!

Slowly I walked toward the hearth, stretching my fingertips toward the flames. I focused on the fire, willing my mind to empty of all images except Herdred's face.

Come to me, my swans! Lift me up! Herdred, show me where you are . . .

For a time nothing came. I swayed in the heat and intense concentration, feeling my body slowly melt away. Suddenly a blast of cold air jolted my frame. A rocky landscape spread out below me. Then an image began to form. I saw a small face, half-hidden in darkness. Its mouth was open, crying out for help . . .

As I sank to the floor, Beowulf caught me. Gently he carried me to his high seat, settled me there and signaled for ale

"Beowulf! Herdred is alive! I know it!" Eagerly I took a sip of the proffered cup. "He is . . . trapped . . . in some sort of dark place. Are there . . . caves . . . near Eaglesgard?"

Beowulf and Redbeard looked at each other in sudden comprehension.

"The north barrens!" exclaimed Redbeard. "That rocky terrain is pocked with cavities big enough to swallow a horse and rider — one reason why no one with any sense goes up there!"

"Aksel, have the north barrens been searched?" asked Beowulf fiercely.

"No, my lord."

Redbeard erupted. "What could have possessed young Herdred to do such a foolish thing?"

"Time enough for questions later, Ragnar. We must leave at once!" Beowulf was already heading for the door.

"Wait!" I cried, rising from the throne chair.

Beowulf rushed back to clasp me in his arms, almost crushing me. When I gasped he jerked away and held me out at arm's length.

"I must leave you, my Freaw, and I don't know when I'll be able to return. Whatever has happened, Hygd and Herdred will need me. You will be safe here. Besides Magnus I've asked Rolf to look out for you as well. Now — I must go!"

In a daze I watched him rush out with Aksel and Redbeard. Redbeard looked back from the doorway to call out.

"Well done, my lady. I'll send one of your women to attend you."

Then he too was gone.

Ana found me slumped on the high seat, fighting back tears.

"Oh, my lady, Redbeard told us what happened at Eaglesgard . . . are you all right?"

"Yes. No. Beowulf is gone!" I wailed.

Ana put her hands on her hips and surveyed me critically.

"He'll be back. Even I know that! But King Herdred?"

I rose from the high seat, wiping tears from my cheeks.

"They will find him. He's not dead, he's just . . . lost."

"The gods be praised — I hope you're right," she said, lifting an eyebrow.

Suddenly I felt lighter and filled with a new confidence.

"Yes, Ana, I believe I am right. The vision was clear."

Ana's face blossomed in a broad smile.

"Thanks be to Freyja! Now you're believing in yourself — and that gives you power! Speaking of which, you'd best come see to this Aksel fellow. They left him behind to recover. He seems to be suffering from more than exhaustion."

"Aksel? Where is he now?"

"In Magnus' longhouse," she answered.

"Magnus? Why there?" Hastily I stepped down to join her.

"Apparently Magnus saw the man's lather-covered horse outside the mead hall and went to investigate. He was there when Aksel emerged and collapsed. A crowd had gathered, curious to know what was happening — myself among them. Beowulf and Redbeard left in a rush, but clearly Aksel was in no condition to accompany them."

We had reached the doorway and Ana paused to catch her breath.

"Magnus may be in charge here, but he's no healer. You'll know what to do, my lady."

As we hurried toward Magnus' dwelling, I breathed an inward prayer that I would indeed know what to do.

We found Aksel propped up against the wall on a bench, his cloak wrapped around him. His face was drained of color. Magnus looked up in annoyance when Ana and I appeared in the open doorway.

"We don't need you women," he began, but Aksel's weak voice broke in.

"Let her come in. She . . . knows things."

"Hmph! As you wish." Grudgingly Magnus stepped aside to let us approach.

I knelt beside Aksel and took his wrist to feel the heartbeat: faint, very faint, but steady. "Where do you feel pain, Aksel?"

As I spoke I began to remove his cloak — and drew back. The man's tunic was soaked with blood, not sweat as I'd earlier supposed.

"What's this? You're bleeding! What happened?"

Aksel smiled weakly.

"Just a scratch, an old wound, a remnant of our fray with the Frisians. The bleeding started after I left Eaglesgard."

"Magnus," I turned. "We'll need hot water and clean rags. Ana, run back to my chamber and bring my herb bag."

Reaching under my apron I brought up my dagger and carefully began to cut away the man's tunic. An ugly slash revealed itself on Aksel's chest. Clearly his journey on horseback had separated the flesh of the not-yet-healed wound.

"Aksel, it does not take special gifts to see that after this wound has been properly treated and dressed, you'll need a long time to rest. You could have bled to death!"

He gave a slight shrug.

"But now I have the Lady Freawaru to attend me."

I stared at him in surprise, but his eyes had closed. Just then Magnus and Ana appeared with the needed supplies. Aksel did not flinch as I bathed the wound with vinegar and mint water, then applied a compress. He moaned slightly when I wound strips of cloth around his chest and tied them tightly. Later, when I gave him a mug of burdock root boiled in milk, he sipped it slowly, and some color returned to his face.

"Thank you, Lady Freawaru," he murmured.

"Magnus, please help me lay him down on this bench. The henbane I added to the broth should make him sleep for some time."

Indeed, Aksel was already snoring hoarsely as Ana and I gathered our things to leave. I happened to glance at the binding strips Magnus had provided: finely-woven linen.

"Who made this cloth?" I marveled. "It's very fine!"

"My wife," replied Magnus gruffly. "She is — that is, she *was* an expert at the loom."

"Was?" I echoed. "Oh, Magnus, I'm sorry. I do not know your history..."

I glanced around the interior. Clearly it had not seen a woman's hand for some time: a jumble of dirty pots and bowls were stacked on the table, robes and implements lay scattered on the benches.

"Magnus, my women and I will be glad to help you tend Aksel," I began. "If you — "

"Emund's daughter cooks for me," he declared. "I don't need any other help!"

The look on his face belied his words, but I knew I must proceed with caution.

"Of course. It's just that Aksel is one of Beowulf's boon companions and I know he'd want us to give him the best of care. I could stop by this evening to change the dressing...?"

Magnus nodded involuntarily. Before he could change his mind, Ana and I left the longhouse. Outside and out of hearing, Ana burst into a tirade.

"That man . . . that man would be hard for any woman to live with! He probably worked his last wife to death!"

"Now, Ana, we don't know that. I wonder . . ."

"What?"

"I wonder if he hides his loss under that gruff exterior."

"Hmph," snorted Ana, sounding much like Magnus herself, "Everyone has losses." She shrugged "I hope this Aksel won't be another!"

Her statement startled me.

"Surely you don't think he'll . . . die? He's lost a lot of blood, but the wound was not that deep."

She shook her head. "Hard to tell. Infection could set in. He'll need good nourishment and I don't know anything about the skills of that cook Magnus mentioned."

I nodded. "For that matter, we don't know much about any of our neighbors here. We need to gather the women together soon — in a ritual that will unite us."

Ana's face brightened. "Aye. The sooner the better."

In the days that followed Aksel slowly grew stronger as his wound healed. Magnus showed himself a surprising ally, refusing to let Aksel move about or leave the longhouse without my permission — as Aksel himself later told us.

"'You won't die on my watch!' That's what Magnus tells me every morning!"

Aksel chuckled, seated at my table in my own longhouse, surrounded by my women, all of whom — even Ragnhild — had daily vied for the opportunity to tend Aksel during his recovery. Ingeborg was especially attentive, though Aksel's eyes most often fell upon Estrid. I could understand their interest, for Aksel was a handsome young man with a ready smile that showed a full set of teeth.

"Any news from Eaglesgard?" he asked.

"No, Aksel, not yet," I responded. "But fear not; all will be well."

Inwardly I smiled to hear myself echo the words of my old rune master. I noted that Aksel's eyes were clear and bright, and his face showed a healthy glow. He looked ready for . . . anything.

"Lady Freawaru, how soon will you allow me to leave?" he asked earnestly.

"Have you tired so soon of our hospitality?" I teased.

"Nay, my lady, but I want to do my part in Beowulf's court — that is, King Herdred's court."

"Tell us about the court," came Estrid's voice. "What do you do there?" she asked shyly.

Aksel seemed taken aback at the question.

"Do? Well, sometimes we go hunting — for elk and red deer, sometimes bear. We hone our battle skills . . ." here he paused and grinned. "Guess I need more practice at that!"

Ingeborg held out a circle of bread. "Fresh-baked this morning, Aksel — crisp and hot. Please have some."

As he reached to break off a piece, Estrid took his cup and filled it.

"What's this? Milk?" He almost spat. "Do you think me a child?"

Estrid's face fell, but I hurried to explain.

"She acted on my orders, Aksel. You still need to put on weight, and milk will help."

He eyed the cup dubiously. "If you say so, my lady."

Just then Brita and Runa charged in, banging the door behind them.

"Lady Freawaru, did you tell Runa she could churn the butter today? I thought that was *my* job!" Brita glared at Runa, who seemed equally wrought up.

"I tried to tell her why, my lady, but she wouldn't listen!" declared Runa, her eyes glistening with unshed tears.

"What's all this? Excuse me, Aksel, but it seems I must deal with a domestic problem. You'd better go."

Aksel rose. "I don't want to get in the middle of a female fight," he declared. "Even strong milk wouldn't help me against an angry woman!"

Flashing a grin, Aksel made a hasty exit, followed by Estrid and Ingeborg. Ana and Ragnhild quietly withdrew to the weaving room. I turned to face the two girls panting before me.

"What's this all about? You two have no business feuding like this!" I exclaimed.

"It's her fault!" cried Brita. "She thinks she can do whatever she wants. She has your favor, so she has no — no shame!"

Brita burst into angry tears, pushing away the hand Runa extended. Runa's face paled and her eyes grew large.

"Oh, my lady, I meant no harm. I just said that I should do the churning today because Brita was in her moon phase and the butter might not come." She gazed at me beseechingly.

"Where did you get such an idea?" I marveled, putting an arm around Brita's shaking shoulders.

"From my grandmother, a wise woman. She taught me many things, like feeding milk to a pet snake to bring good luck to the cattle, and ... and ... saving the afterbirth of a baby to make a good luck amulet, and ..." Runa was almost babbling. "Oh, Lady Freawaru, please don't send me away!"

Now she too was wailing. I felt like laughing at such foolishness, but kept my lips set in a firm line.

"Quiet, both of you, and listen."

With a gulp Runa swallowed her sobs. Brita dried her eyes with a clenched fist.

"I'm not sending anyone away. I need you both here in Hrethelskeep — but you must not bicker and argue like this! Runa," I addressed the dark-eyed girl standing dejectedly before me. "some of your Finnish ways seem ... strange to us, but I know you were only trying to be helpful."

She sniffed and nodded.

"Brita, Runa has been your friend since the day you rode to Hrethelskeep together. Do you remember that day?"

Sullenly, Brita nodded her head.

"I value the different skills you each possess. We must work together to make a life for ourselves here. Now, it's time for you both to get back to work. Brita, churn the butter as you always do."

Here Brita flashed a triumphant smile at Runa.

"Runa, bring me a cup of buttermilk when it's ready. I feel a bit faint. Perhaps my babe is hungry too — it's certainly been trying to get my attention this morning."

Indeed as I spoke I felt another definite kick in my midsection and placed both hands on my belly. At mention of the baby, both girls seemed to forget their quarrel.

"Oh, my lady, do you think it's a boy?" asked Brita eagerly.

"Brita, I'm sorry your boy did not get to live."

Runa's unexpected comment hung in the air. Brita stared at her in amazement.

"How ... how did you know that?" She backed away from Runa. "Did Lady Freawaru tell you I'd lost a child?"

"No. I just . . . knew." Runa hung her head. "Please, Brita, don't be angry with me again."

"I'm not. I'm just . . . surprised." Then a new thought struck her. "Runa, can you tell if Lady Freawaru's baby will be a boy?"

I held up my hand to intervene, but Runa already had an answer.

"She wants it to be a girl."

"That's enough, you two. Get back to your chores."

As they faded silently out the door, I sank down at the table to consider. Did I want a girl? A daughter to whom I could teach the skills my mother had taught me? The idea was pleasing, but I knew I had no choice in the matter. Wyrd would decide.

Chapter Nine
Invitations

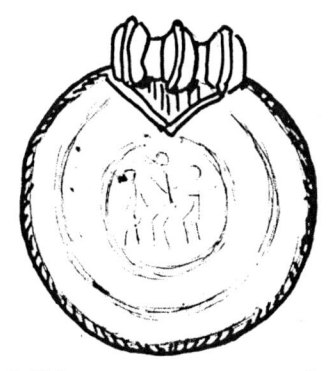

Gold bracteates, ornamentation based on Roman-inspired medallions or decorated with a representation of Odin. 5th-6thcentury. A.D.

Aksel improved so rapidly that I had to let him go, despite the long faces of Ingeborg and Estrid.

"We'll send Saxe and Gorm with him to ensure his safety on the trip. They can return with news of King Herdred."

And Beowulf, I added to myself.

In spite of this plan, the two women moped as if they were losing their best friend. Clearly they needed some new interest to take Aksel's place. Hmmm.

"Estrid, how soon is the next full moon?" I asked one morning as we set bowls out on the table.

"My lady? Why . . . in about a week, I'd say."

"Do you think that will give us enough time to prepare for a women's ritual?"

She lifted her head and her eyes brightened. "A ritual? What must we do?"

"Since you and Ingeborg are so good at making friendly talk, I thought I'd send you around to each longhouse in the village inviting all the women to attend."

Estrid's mouth opened and closed as Ingeborg entered with butter and crisp bread for the morning meal.

"Ingeborg, did you hear Lady Freawaru? We're going to help with a ritual!"

"Yes," I confirmed, "you will be my messengers to the village women. It is important that everyone attend this first gathering, so I'll rely on you two to make that clear."

"But . . . what should we say?" worried Estrid.

"Lady Freawaru," interjected Ingeborg, "Can you tell us what you're planning to do at this ritual?"

"A wise question, Ingeborg. Yes. First we'll remember publicly the women we have lost from our lives." Here I momentarily choked up, thinking of my old nurse Willa. "Then we will offer sacrifices to the earth mother and ask her blessing on our crops and animals. Finally, we'll celebrate our coming together with dancing and feasting."

That should make old Gunilla happy!

During my recital broad smiles began to appear on the faces before me. Ana, who had been stirring porridge at the hearth, cleared her throat.

"That sounds very ambitious, my lady. Are you sure you are ready to do all that?"

"Yes, Ana, I am ready!"

Despite Estrid's misgivings, the assignment I gave her and Ingeborg turned out to be surprisingly easy — due to Magnus! They reported that at every door they were welcomed, invited in, then told of Magnus' praise for the Lady Freawaru and her healing arts. If she was planning a ritual, of course they would come!

"The only one who seemed . . . reluctant . . . was Ortrud, the blacksmith's wife," said Ingeborg, otherwise flushed with the apparent success of their mission.

"Ortrud? Remind me what she looks like," I said.

"She's squat, with drooping eyes, but muscles like a man — I wouldn't want to cross that woman!" declared Ingeborg, shaking her head.

"Oh? What did she say to you?"

Ingeborg and Estrid exchanged hesitant looks.

"She, she didn't say anything at first . . . just glared at us," said Estrid. "Finally she said she had work to do and turned her back on us!"

Ingeborg made a wry face. "We noticed that she flared up when we said your name."

"Hmm," I pondered. "The blacksmith's wife is usually a respected figure in any community. Perhaps I'll talk to Thora to find out the situation with Ortrud."

I smiled. "Thank you both for your efforts. You've been a great help to me — as always."

When I knocked on Thora's door later that day, old Gunilla opened. This time she recognized me.

"Lady Freawaru! Is it time for the ritual already?"

Her voice sounded much stronger that it had on my previous visit.

"No, Gunilla, not for a few days. I need to ask you and Thora about one of your neighbors — Ortrud, the blacksmith's wife."

"What's she done now?"

Thora emerged from the dairy, wiping her hands on her apron.

"Ortrud is a prickly sort," she offered. "Magnus thinks she's deep-minded, but she's also stiff and prideful. More than one of us has felt the lash of her tongue! What has she said to offend you?"

I laughed. "It's what she has *not* said. Apparently she wants no part of the women's ritual I'm planning."

Thora laughed too. "I'm not surprised. She likes to take charge herself, not follow another's lead."

"Really? That's good to know. Perhaps I could involve her in the ritual in some way . . . I'll have to think about that. Thora, I also have another problem and I'd like your advice . . ."

"Here, sit down first." She moved a pile of robes from a bench to make room for me at the table. "Mother Gunilla, bring Lady Freawaru a drink." She turned to me. "All I have at the moment is sour milk and water," she added apologetically.

"Thank you. That will be fine," I said. The mixture might give me trouble later, but I did not want to refuse Thora's hospitality.

Gunilla disappeared into the dairy, returning with a wooden mug which she set before me, her fingers trembling. I took a sip, smiled and put down the mug.

"Now," said Thora, seating herself across from me, "What is this problem of yours?"

"It's about the sacrifice to be made at the ritual. What would be appropriate? Perhaps milk? Seeds? Something personal? What's been done in the past?"

Thora wrinkled her brow. "If you want a *true* sacrifice, it should be blood!"

"Oh, of course, a sacrificial animal — but for that we'd need an altar, and there is no altar in the stone circle."

Thora reflected. "Orm could make one for us," she said, her eyes suddenly twinkling.

"Orm? He's the blacksmith."

"Yes." Thora grinned broadly. "And he's also the husband of the proud Ortrud!"

We gazed at each other for a moment, then burst out laughing.

"What? What are you laughing about?" Gunilla appeared at the table as I rose to depart.

"Gunilla, start practicing your steps. Soon we'll be dancing in the circle! And Thora, thank you for your help."

The blacksmith's forge lay at the far edge of the settlement, far enough away to prevent sparks from setting anyone's longhouse on fire, including Orm's.

The day promised to be warm. Already my cheeks were hot from the sun. I stopped in front of the heavy door: sturdy oak bound with metal bands. There I hesitated, closing my eyes to summon an image of Hrun, my former mother-in-law.

Freaw, if you could deal with Hrun, you can deal with anyone — including this Ortrud!

Firmly I rapped on the door. When it opened I had to look down to see the scowling face of the woman before me.

"Good morning, Ortrud. Is Orm at home? I have need of his services."

The scowl deepened. "He's not here. Tell me what you want."

"Of course. May I come in?"

She peered at me suspiciously, then stood aside to let me enter. Inside it was so dark it took me a moment to make out the interior. A strong smell of smoke assailed my nostrils and I barely suppressed a sneeze. Ortrud did not offer me a seat, but I advanced to the nearest bench and sat down.

"As you know, Ortrud, I am inviting all the women of the village to take part in a ritual on the eve of the next full moon. In preparation for that we will need an altar. At present there is none in the old stone circle, so I want Orm to build one. Do you think he could do that? I'll pay him well for his work."

She snorted. "Of course he can do that! Orm can make anything! Orm!" she shouted, turning her head. "A lady to see you!"

A bear of a man shambled out of the shadowy depths of the house. He peered at me uncertainly, then straightened in recognition.

"You're the lady Beowulf brought," he declared.

"Yes, Orm, and I have a job for you."

He listened as I outlined what I had in mind. Suddenly an obstacle occurred to me which I voiced aloud.

"There is one problem, Orm. No man is allowed within the sacred stone circle, so the altar would have to be light enough for a woman to carry."

Ortrud stepped forward and pulled back her sleeves, revealing knotty, well-muscled, arms.

"I'm as strong as any man! I could carry it!"

I nodded in appreciation. "Yes, I believe you could! Just what we need!" I said, beaming approval. "Thank you, Ortrud."

"I could have a portable altar ready in three days," said Orm, getting back to business.

"That is good. Oh, and Orm, soon I will have further need of your talents. Two of my people wish to marry, so we will need a special hammer of Thor for that ceremony. I can pay you in gold or silver," I finished.

He gaped at me, then shut his jaw with a snap.

"Whatever you want — my lady. I can provide it."

On the way back to my own house I stopped to vomit into a weed patch near the path. Even so, I reached home in a good mood, both relieved and elated at my visit. I entered the longhouse to be met with an earthy aroma rising from the cook pot. Barley soup. For a moment my stomach turned again, but I went to the water bucket, took a dipper and rinsed my mouth.

"How did it go?" asked Ana, rising from the hearth.

"Much better than I could have predicted," I declared. "Thora gave me an idea which I've already put into action. Orm the blacksmith is making a portable altar for our ritual, and his wife Ortrud will bring it."

Ana beamed at me, then sobered.

"We still have to find enough food and drink for this feast you've promised. Our supplies are limited at this time of year."

Ragnhild had entered as we were talking, her face flushed with heat.

"Lady Freawaru, Thorkel tells me that Sigrid, his hostess, is quite excited about this ritual you're planning. Since her husband died last winter she has extra food stores on hand. She might be able to help. And there are others..."

"Thank you for the report, Ragnhild. Involving other women in the preparations is a good idea. But this is to be a serious ritual, not merely the prelude to a feast. We'll have real feasting later — at your wedding — which could follow soon after the ritual, if you wish."

Now it was her turn to beam.

"I do wish it, my lady. Oh, thank you!"

Impulsively she clasped me by the shoulders and gave me a little squeeze.

"I must tell Thorkel!"

Still beaming, she hurried out.

Later that day more offers of assistance came my way. Sigrid volunteered to provide mead, with Ragnhild's help in brewing it. Little Toke's mother, a shy young woman named Solveig, promised flatbread, and Emund's wife Tove salted herring. The most surprising offer came from Magnus: a young pig to use as the sacrifice. As the time of the full moon drew near, an air of excitement bubbled through the village.

To reassure the men of the village, I asked Thorkel to spread the word that their turn to celebrate would come soon, during the nine days of feasting at his wedding to Ragnhild. This prospect put a smile on every face — almost. Ana still worried about our food supply.

"We'll manage," I told her. "I had already asked Saxe and Gorm to bring back dried fish from Eaglesgard. If necessary we can send Wulfgar and Olaf hunting. Don't worry, Ana. All will be well."

My own preparations for the ritual were private. I searched through my chests for the small deerskin drum Unferth had made for me. My eyes misted as I touched the two runes painted in red on either end: Thurisaz, rune of openings, and Dagaz, rune of breakthrough and transformation.

I also consulted the rune sticks I had made myself, long ago in Heorot. Alone in my chamber I spread a white cloth on the bed, closed my eyes and reached into the fur bag, waiting for a single rune to attract my fingers. Drawing it out, I laid it on the cloth and opened my eyes. Ehwaz: rune of forward movement, the same rune I'd drawn when seeking direction for our new home. Again, my path lay clear before me.

The gods are with me — and the goddesses. Thank you, Freyja.

The next day I heard the first rumblings of opposition . . . indirectly. Thora confided to me that her neighbor Agata might not be able to attend, as her husband 'needed her at home.' Then Solveig stopped by to tell me that she might not be able to participate, but she'd send the flatbread anyway — with Thora. When I questioned Solveig briefly, it came out that her husband also 'needed her at home' that night.

"What is going on here?" I wondered aloud to Ana after Solveig left.

"Sounds to me like some of the men don't want their wives getting involved with us. After all, my lady, we are outsiders here."

"But Beowulf made clear to the village his approval and support for us. Isn't that enough?" I almost wailed.

Ana shrugged, "Being accepted takes time."

"Still," I persisted, "the whole purpose of this ritual is to bring us together. I want *all* the women to be involved!"

Ana shrugged again. "You can't force them — especially if their husbands don't approve."

She turned back to the cauldron she'd been stirring. Rabbit stew with onion to judge by the smell, which made my mouth water. For the rest of the morning I fretted, wondering what else I could do to win over the men. As it turned out, I had no need to worry.

Shortly after midday, three horses were spotted approaching the village. Emund's son Mattias, planting in one of Magnus' fields, saw them first and called to his father, who alerted Magnus, who notified me on his way to investigate.

Three horses? Could it be Saxe and Gorm returning from Eaglesgard? But who rode the third horse? I did not let the name 'Beowulf' escape my lips, but my heart beat faster at the prospect.

By the time the riders emerged into plain view, a small crowd had gathered outside the mead hall. Magnus had ridden out to meet the riders, and his big black, Nightsea, led the way. He was followed by the horses of . . . Saxe and . . . Gorm . . . and, towering above a dapple gray, Redbeard. For a moment my heart sank. Then I lifted my head to greet the newcomers.

Redbeard's face wore a broad smile as he urged his horse forward, then pulled up at the mead hall door.

"Good news, Lady Freawaru! The king is safe!"

He jumped down from his horse and embraced me eagerly.

"Herdred was found — just as you foresaw it — trapped in a sinkhole in the northern downs."

"The gods be praised!" I breathed, withdrawing from his bear hug. "And Beowulf . . . is well?"

Redbeard exploded with laughter. "Of course Beowulf is well! He and Herdred — and Hygd — have sent you gifts, princely gifts, for your help in saving the king. No, Herdred was not seriously hurt," said Redbeard in response to my questioning look, "but he would have been in a bad way had wild animals discovered him. We found him just in time!"

Gorm and Saxe now dismounted and began pulling heavy deerskin packs off their horses.

"Lady Freawaru, see what the king has sent you!" cried Saxe, pointing to the bulky object he set at his feet.

"Hold on, young fellow. Bring that bundle into the mead hall," ordered Redbeard. "We need to do things properly."

Gorm appeared at my side. "You won't want *this* package inside the mead hall," he chuckled. "Dried fish — lots of it!"

"Take that over to the longhouse," directed Ana, who had also popped up beside me. Suddenly it seemed as if the whole village had turned out, everyone eager to hear the news.

At a loss for words, I turned to join the throng trooping inside the mead hall. Redbeard took my hand and led me to the high seat.

When I last sat here, I was filled with grief. Gone now are the dread and uncertainty surrounding Herdred's disappearance, but I still yearn for Beowulf.

Fanning the Fire

Redbeard and Magnus took their places standing on either side of me. Saxe laid the bundle he carried at my feet. When everyone had assembled, I signaled for silence.

"Now, Red... I mean Ragnar, tell us what happened at Eaglesgard."

Redbeard cleared his throat and stepped to one side so that he could address both me and the expectant company. All eyes were fixed on him.

"Lady Freawaru," he began with a slight bow, "after hearing your vision of King Herdred trapped in a rocky cave, Beowulf and I took a small party of men and rode straight to the north downs. There we hobbled our horses and began the search on foot, for that is a treacherous area, with ravines and sinkholes that appear unexpectedly. We took turns calling Herdred's name and listening for a response."

Here Redbeard reached out to a nearby table, took a cup of ale, and gulped it down. He wiped his mouth with a hairy forearm.

"Beowulf was the lucky one. He heard a sound that led him to a cavity deep in the rock. By lying on his belly he could look down far enough to see something at the bottom — turned out to be Herdred!" concluded Redbeard triumphantly.

"How did you get him out?" Magnus asked the question in my own mind.

"Oh, we'd brought several lengths of sealskin rope with us, and we lowered a knotted one to Herdred. He was able to wrap it around himself and hold on while we pulled him up."

"Was he hurt when he fell into the cave?" I heard myself ask.

"Bruised and bloodied, but no bones broken. A lucky lad."

Redbeard shook his head.

"Here's the strange part, my lady." He lowered his voice and leaned toward me. "Herdred told us he was chasing a fox. Said he wanted to make a cloak out of it... for you. Said he'd just gotten off a shot with his bow and arrow when he stumbled into the cavity."

Fox? Cloak? For me? I couldn't take it all in. Redbeard nodded soberly, then turned to the faces gazing up at him.

"Herdred was thinking about Lady Freawaru when he got into trouble. Thank the gods she was also thinking about him. Without her gift of Sight, we would never have known where to look for the lad. She is the one who saved our king! I say we give a cheer for Lady Freawaru! All hail!"

"All hail!" came back the enthusiastic chorus.

Redbeard was not through, however. He strode to my chair and reached down to untie the bag at my feet. From it he lifted out a carved wooden chest and slowly opened the lid. I heard an intake of breath from the spectators and almost rose from my own chair to see what lay inside.

"People of Hrethelskeep," boomed Redbeard. "Behold in what esteem your lady is held. From King Herdred and Lord Beowulf I present to her . . . this elegant silver bowl!"

The large fluted bowl he held aloft glinted in the hearth light. As he placed it in my hands I felt its weight and noted the delicate band of entwined animals incised below the gilded rim.

A most costly and valuable treasure! I wonder if Beowulf's hands last touched it?

Smiling, I rose to acknowledge the gift.

"The king's safety is reward enough for me, but I thank King Herdred and Lord Beowulf for their generosity. I accept with pleasure this precious gift."

Redbeard was not yet finished.

"There is more, my lady. One fox does not make a cloak, but Queen Hygd also wanted to express her gratitude for your part in saving her son."

Once again Redbeard put his hands inside the bag at my feet. This time he drew out . . . a long cloak, a gorgeous fur cloak, streaked with rusty reds and tawny golds — clearly the rich furs of many a fox.

"It's beautiful!" I gasped. "But how . . . ?"

Redbeard grinned. "The queen knew you'd need a heavy cloak for our Geatish winters, so she was already having this made for you. Herdred's fox provided the final piece needed to complete the project. May I place it about your shoulders, my lady?"

I stepped down from the high seat to let Redbeard settle the cloak about my shoulders, its fringe of tails falling below my knees. As I turned to face them, another cheer rose from the people of Hrethelskeep . . . perhaps now *my* people?

This is a moment to remember, Freaw, a moment to cherish. You may now put your trust in her gift. Freyja is with you.

Later, back in the longhouse, I let each of my women stroke the soft fur, the long bushy tails, and even try on the cloak — including Brita and Runa.

"Oh, my lady," breathed Brita, "it's so beautiful. It almost matches your amber hair." Reverently she folded the cloak inside a linen sheet to place it in my clothes chest. "You looked like a queen today."

"I felt like one," I admitted. Laughing, I put my hand up to my hair to smooth back a stray wisp, and suddenly realized that I'd worn it uncovered, like an unmarried woman, since Beowulf's last visit. What did that mean?

As Brita passed her, Ana lifted a corner of the cloak. "This will need to be lined before winter comes . . . perhaps that length of yellow silk you've been saving in your wedding chest?"

"Perhaps," I nodded. "Winter is still far away. We'll have time to decide about that."

For her part Ana was most excited about the sack of dried cod Gorm carried in.

"Enough to feed the whole village!" she declared with satisfaction.

"Not my favorite," Gorm made a face, "but it will do until we can go hunting. Redbeard says there's good game in this area."

"Where *is* Redbeard?" I asked. "He seemed to disappear after we left the mead hall."

"Probably talking with Magnus," said Gorm. "Beowulf sent instructions about stocking your byre with more animals. Redbeard, uh, Ragnar was to arrange it. He's riding back to Eaglesgard tomorrow."

"Aksel . . . how is he?" inquired Estrid in a soft voice.

"Aksel is fine, though he said to tell you that he misses your pretty face." Gorm winked at me as he spoke.

Estrid crimsoned with pleasure at these words, then silently returned to her place at the loom.

A knock sounded at the door and Ana went to open it. Thora stood on the threshold, her eyes sparkling.

"I won't come in, Lady Freawaru. I just stopped by to tell you that Agata and Solveig will be able to take part in the ritual after all."

We gazed at each other in mutual understanding. I smiled and nodded as she took her leave.

Good. Now every woman in the village is committed. Freyja, thank you. With the gift of your power, I shall not fail them.

Chapter Ten
Circle of Stone

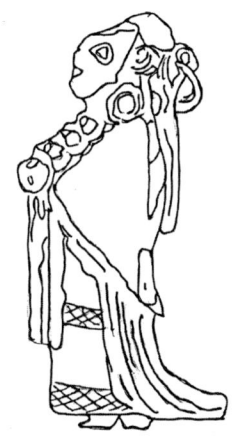

Icelandic pendant of a Norse woman, 14th century.

Dark clouds gathered overhead and a north wind swept down the valley on the morning of the ritual.

Last night the moon was obscured, and now this! Is it a sign that I should cancel the ritual?

Long faces at the morning meal told me that others shared my misgivings, though no one spoke a word. We ate glumly for a time until Ana broke the silence.

"We have hours before dusk, my lady. It could clear by evening."

"Of course, Ana." I brightened a bit. "We should all continue our preparations as planned. There is much to do!"

My words seemed to break the spell, for everyone rose from their places, and Brita and Runa began clearing the bowls. Ragnhild paused beside me.

"Thorkel says that the newly-planted fields need water, my lady. He has been hoping for rain."

I nodded wryly. "He may get his wish. Speaking of water, the bucket is empty. Runa, would you walk to the spring this morning?"

She hurried back to the table. "Yes, my lady, right away."

"I'll come with you," I said, "and assess the weather on the way."

I lifted a woolen cloak from the wall peg and followed Runa out the door, leaving my women to their morning chores.

Tiny drops splashed on my face, but the rain appeared to be scattered. I breathed in the scent of spring and pulled the hood over my head. Runa wore no cloak, but she never seemed to be cold, going barefoot in all weathers as she did now. We walked silently toward the north edge of the village where a small spring bubbled from the hillside. As we neared, we heard voices and high-pitched giggles.

"Sounds like Tove's girls," said Runa. "Ginnlaug and Gyrid. Two sillier girls would be hard to find in any village!"

"Why, Runa!" I was surprised to hear such a strong statement from her. "They're just young. They'll improve with time."

Now we could see the girls' backs. Someone was laughing.

"I hope it does spoil her plans! She acts so high and mighty, as if she runs the whole village! Mother says . . ."

Runa coughed loudly and the two girls whirled, almost letting go of the bucket they held. Ginnlaug — or was it Gyrid? — dropped her jaw as if caught stealing honey from a comb. The other finished filling their pail and set it on the ground.

"Good day, girls," I said pleasantly. "How is your mother today? I hope to see you all at the celebration tonight."

Gyrid — or was it Ginnlaug — raised her eyebrows.

"Can you control the weather too?" she asked rudely, then blushed. "Beg pardon, lady. Mother is fine, and we're . . . looking forward to your . . . ritual."

I eyed the girls calmly. One avoided my gaze; the other returned it.

"It's not *my* ritual," I said, "it's a celebration for all the women of the village."

A thought struck me. "Have you girls never taken part in such a celebration?"

"Not me," said one, poking her sister's ribs with a bony elbow, "but Ginnlaug may remember such a time."

So, Gyrid was the bold one, shorter and presumably younger than her sister.

"Gyrid," I said earnestly, looking straight into her eyes, "part of becoming a woman is learning how to treat others with respect... especially the goddesses who influence our destinies. Showing gratitude to the Earth Mother is one way to ensure that life continues to flourish in Hrethelskeep. I know you'll want to be a part of that."

Gyrid blushed and dropped her gaze, but she nodded. Without another word the two girls picked up a stout stick lying near their feet, slid it through the bail of their bucket and hoisted the brace onto their shoulders.

"Good day," mumbled Ginnlaug as they started down the path.

"See you tonight — if it doesn't rain!" giggled Gyrid.

"The gods willing," I called after them.

Runa and I looked at each other and chuckled.

"I wonder what they'll tell their mother," said Runa.

"Perhaps we'll find out tonight. Now, let's get our bucket filled and get back to the house before it *does* rain."

Rain it did, all that morning and most of the afternoon, but the sky finally began to clear shortly before evening

"What a relief," crowed Ana. "We won't have done all this work for nothing!"

Indeed the day had been a busy one. In addition to our regular work, we had bundled up dry firewood, collected pitchers for mead and water, packed bowls and blankets for the feast, a cooking fork for meat, salt for the ceremony...

"We'll look like a pack of traders," giggled Brita as she added another bowl to her stack.

"I don't want to forget something we might need," I retorted. "I want this first ritual to go well, as it will set the pattern for future gatherings. Oh, flint — we'll need flint to start the fire."

"I've already packed the starter." Runa gave me a smile. "My lady, what knife will you use for the blood-letting?"

I stared at Runa in sudden doubt. "Just my usual dagger. Why? Do you think...?"

"When I helped my grandmother at rituals," said Runa quietly, "she always used a special knife and a special bowl, reserved only for such ceremonies."

"Hmmm." I pondered this information. "I don't have a special knife, but we could use the silver bowl sent by Beowulf — and Herdred," I added hastily.

Runa nodded. "That would be fitting; such a precious object would show your reverence and respect for the goddess."

At this moment Thora leaned her head in the doorway. "May I be of help?"

"Thank you, Thora, but we have everything we need — almost."

Thora stepped inside. "Almost? What is lacking?"

I sighed. "A knife not used for ordinary tasks, a sacred knife, you might say. There's no time left to have Orm make one, so my dagger will have to do."

Thora's face brightened. "Perhaps not. Come with me to see Mother Gunilla."

Wondering, I followed her out the door, leaving my women to stare at each other in puzzlement.

Gunilla was bent over the hearth, taking a sip from the cooking pot with a long iron ladle. She looked up in surprise when she saw me enter with Thora.

"Is it time for the dancing, my lady?"

"No, not yet, Gunilla, but soon." I took her free hand. "Thora tells me you have something we might use in tonight's ritual . . . a special knife."

"Knife?" Gunilla squinted and batted away steam rising from the kettle.

"The knife in your chest?" prompted Thora.

"That old knife? Why would the lady want that?" She peered up at me.

"For the sacrifice," I answered. "I would be honored to use your knife if you are willing."

In response Gunilla hobbled over to a plain wood storage chest, dark with age, which stood against the side wall. With effort she raised the lid and slowly knelt to rummage inside. Finally she lifted out a long object wrapped in discolored linen.

"Bring it to the table, Mother, where we can see it," suggested Thora.

Slowly Gunilla rose and shuffled to the table. With fumbling fingers she unwrapped the packet to reveal a leather sheath, incised with runes.

Extending from the sheath lay a dark wood handle inlaid with a mixture of metals: silver, copper, brass, arranged in swirling designs.

"Gunilla, what a treasure! Where did you get this?" I exclaimed, reaching out to touch the lines on the sheath.

"From Hylde, Beowulf's mother," croaked Gunilla, her voice suddenly rough.

"Beowulf's mother?" I echoed. "And you have kept it all these years? Why did you not give it to Beowulf long ago?"

Gunilla sniffed. "I hope I've done no wrong, Lady Freawaru, but Hylde asked me to keep it for the woman Beowulf would one day marry."

I opened my mouth to speak, but no words came out.

"That's you, isn't it?" she asked, looking up at me.

"Yes. No. I don't know. We haven't . . ." I stopped uncertainly.

"But you will." Gunilla nodded confidently. "If you can use the knife tonight, take it, my lady. It is yours."

Tears flooded my eyes. I could barely speak.

"Thank you," I managed to croak. "Thank you, Gunilla."

I picked up the sheath and slowly drew out the blade. It gleamed dully in the hearth light.

"Rolf could polish it for you," offered Thora, "and sharpen the blade."

"Thank you, Thora, but I'd like to do that myself. A knife must come to know its owner."

"What will you name it?" asked Gunilla

"I will let the knife tell me its name — but let us see what these runes on the sheath reveal." I felt the leather carefully, tracing the lines etched into it.

"Ah, Dagaz . . . and Thurisaz . . . Why Thora! Gunilla! This is surely more than coincidence! These are the very runes painted on my drum. The gods are with us!"

Setting the knife aside, I seized a hand of each woman and raised my arms, filled with excitement.

"Wait, wait," laughed Thora. "Save the dancing for tonight. We don't want to tire Mother Gunilla in advance!"

"Oh, of course not. Beg pardon. I am relying on her to show us the steps!"

Gunilla smiled her almost toothless smile. "I'll be ready!" she declared.

I had asked the women of the village to fast after their morning meal. This was fortunate for me as well, as I could not have eaten a morsel that evening in my own longhouse. Wulfgar and our men — except for Thorkel, who always took his meals at Sigrid's house — had joined us on this occasion. The younger men were full of curiosity about what was to happen in the ritual. I gave them only the barest outline, reminding them that the rites of the goddess were secret, reserved for women. Olaf asked the question that concerned me most.

"My lady, have you ever shed blood ... that is, taken a life?"

"No, not intentionally, although I was often tempted to kill my cousin Hrothulf!"

I joined in the nervous laughter, but suddenly remembered a time when I *had* drawn blood from Hrothulf, a dark memory I kept tucked away in a corner of my mind.

"Let me give you some pointers," volunteered Saxe. "If Runa is holding the animal, have her clamp one hand over its snout and tilt up the head. Then you can make a clean cut across the throat."

I gulped and smiled weakly, fighting down a moment of revulsion.

"Thank you, Saxe. Runa, did you hear that?"

Runa smiled and nodded, looking far more confident than I felt. It occurred to me that someone else had always killed the animals that ended up in my cooking pot A knock at the door put a stop to further conversation. Thora put her head in.

"My lady? Everyone has assembled at the mead hall. We await your direction."

"Already? Thank you, Thora. We'll join you presently."

Hastily I rose, knocking over my mug as I did so. Wulfgar calmly put out a hand to steady me and spoke in a low voice.

"My lady, even if we cannot be at your side tonight, we are all behind you. Go forward with courage. You are still a king's daughter."

"Yes, and a queen's. Thank you, Wulfgar. Your words mean much to me."

Our packs and bundles sat waiting and ready beside the door. The men helped us shoulder them as we left the longhouse. Mine was the lightest, containing only my drum, Gunilla's knife, the silver bowl and a few small packets.

Outside the mead hall door we found the women of Hrethelskeep also ready and waiting. All were dressed in cloaks, as I had asked, and each woman carried a drinking cup, as I had asked. Excited chatter ceased at our approach. I made a quick mental count: twenty-six. Everyone had come.

Ginnlaug and Gyrid, who stood beside their mother, avoided my gaze. Tove herself held a cord tied around the neck of the piglet designated for sacrifice. It rooted in the grass, oblivious of its fate.

Ortrud carried a folded iron tripod and a large concave metal pan. When she saw me, she stepped forward eagerly.

"The altar. Just as you ordered." She grinned.

"So I see. It is perfect. I'll reward Orm tomorrow."

Ortrud's smile broadened even further.

Overhead the sky was fading into the long dusk of late spring. By its light we would find our way to the stone circle. Later, when the full moon rose, its silvery sheen would provide added radiance for our solemn ritual.

Underfoot the damp grass was already wetting the tips of my leather boots, but the air smelled fresh, full of life and possibility. A sudden feeling of joy surged through me, lifting me. I felt light as the swan feather tucked under my tunic. Turning to face the group. I spread my arms wide.

"Women of Hrethelskeep! We go to meet the goddess!"

A few cheers erupted.

"Yes," I nodded, "it will be a joyous celebration, but first we must prepare ourselves. We will walk to the stone circle in silence, readying our hearts and minds to enter sacred space. When we reach the circle we will stop outside the stones, near the river, and place our bundles under the birch trees. There I will direct you in what is to be done."

I paused, looking over the faces before me. Some wore eager smiles of anticipation; others looked uncertain. Gunilla stood proudly between Thora and Ana, her guides and supporters during the walk.

"Is everyone ready? Then follow me . . . to the goddess!"

Taking a deep breath, I set forth into the night.

As we walked I began to clear my own mind, to prepare myself for the ritual ahead.

Freyja, dear goddess, be with me. Uphold me, give me the strength and wisdom I need to be a leader of these people.

As I bent forward, drawing in deep lungfuls of the cool night air, an insubstantial but familiar face rose before me, pale against the darkness of the trees. Mother! She did not speak, but gazed at me tenderly. Then her lips parted. 'Daughter, Freawaru, all will be well . . . be well . . . be well . . .' Even as I lifted my fingers to touch her image, the features dissolved, fading into nothing.

Ana reached out a hand. "My lady? Are you well?"

"Well? Yes, Ana, I am well."

It seemed to me that we had barely begun to walk when the path opened into a clearing. We had reached the stone circle. Behind me I could hear Gunilla gasping for breath, so as soon as the river came into view I stopped and gave a sign. Thora and Ana gently lowered the old woman to a sitting position under the birches. One by one the other women joined us, setting their bundles on the ground and looking around curiously. I wondered how many had ever seen this ancient place before.

In the clearing the standing stones glowed softly in the half light, still damp from the morning's rain. Most stood waist-high or higher. They seemed to reach out, ready to encircle us in a spiritual embrace. But first there was work to be done.

"Runa, take this pitcher to the river and bring it back full. Brita, untie that bundle of firewood."

Each woman in my household had been given a responsibility. Now each acted to perform her task. When all was ready I lifted both arms and raised my voice, stepping back to address the assembly.

"Women of Hrethelskeep! Welcome to this holy place. We have come to honor the goddess in all her forms: maiden, mother, crone. We have come to honor our own ancestors, and those women who have preceded us. We have come to honor ourselves and all we do to make life possible. Now . . . bring your cups and form a circle, standing outside the stones. Before we begin I will enter first to purify the space, and Ortrud will set up our altar."

As the women moved eagerly to find places behind the stones, I pulled from my bag the birch box of salt Thora had once given me. Taking the pitcher from Runa, I slowly entered the circle, holding both aloft.

Ortrud huffed into the circle behind me, lugging the heavy tripod. She set it up near the center, positioning the metal pan on top. Brita followed behind her with firewood, which she arranged under the tripod, adding charcoal and a handful of wood shavings. Both women gave a slight bow in my direction as they backed out of the circle, Brita with eyes downcast, Ortrud beaming with importance.

Once again I raised my hands and voice.

"Women of Hrethelskeep, I call upon earth, air, fire, and water to make this place a sacred space for our use tonight. From the earth . . . salt." I held up the box. "To earth I join . . . water." I shook a generous helping of salt into the pitcher — "and sprinkle it to purify our space."

Suiting action to words, I walked slowly around the circle's interior, dipping my fingers into the salt water and flicking droplets against each stone. Staring eyes, transfixed, watched my every move. Retreating to the center of the circle, I set down the pitcher and took up the flint-striker hanging at my waist.

"Now I call upon fire and air."

Kneeling, I struck a spark to the prepared firewood. Soon a thin tongue of flame emerged. I blew on it gently to fan the flame, then rose.

"Earth, air, fire, and water. Our space is ready, but are each of *you* ready?" I paused to let the question sink in. "To come before the goddess is to cast aside the smallness of our human selves. To come before the goddess is to open ourselves to a greater power, a higher mystery, a deeper understanding.

"Before we can begin, we must take a vow of secrecy. Our rites here tonight are meant for our eyes and ears alone. No man is to know the nature of our revels, no word of our rites is to pass your lips outside this circle . . . on pain of punishment by the goddess! By taking part in this ritual you are taking a solemn vow of silence. Are you willing?"

Revolving slowly, I made eye contact with each woman present. No one flinched or looked away.

"Then we can begin! Set aside your cloaks and take out your cups," I instructed.

"Tonight we drink the drink of the gods: golden mead, gold as the tears shed by Freyja, goddess of love and beauty. Let the mead be poured — but do not yet drink."

This was the signal for Brita and Runa to circulate outside the circle, filling each cup with the precious honey mead prepared by Sigrid and Ragnhild. Gasps of surprise and delight ran around the circle, for mead was a drink reserved for special occasions in the mead hall, rarely available to women. I heard Gunilla's cackle when her mug was filled, and nervous giggles — probably from Tove's girls. When all were served, I lifted my own cup, a fine glass goblet.

"Women of Hrethelskeep! I call upon Freyja, the maiden goddess. Freyja, be present here in our midst, bless us with love and fertility. Friend of lovers in life, you welcome us to your hall after death. O powerful goddess, you have the power to change your form, to travel as a falcon cloaked in feathers. Behold! On my own body, the mark of Freyja!"

Loosening the top of my gown, I bared my shoulder, revealing to all the feather mark of Freyja. Walking slowly around the circle, I let each woman take a good look before continuing. From my gown I drew out a long white swan's feather.

"Any gifts I have are gifts from Freyja, maiden goddess. Now I will place upon you your own mark of Freyja. When I have touched your lips with mead from this feather, you may step inside the circle, to be joined by your sisters."

I began with Gunilla, dipping the feather into my goblet and lightly brushing her lips with the sticky sweetness. She licked her lips, then slowly, solemnly, made her way to the front of her stone and stood erect, as if years had fallen from her shoulders. Thora came next, then Sigrid, then Estrid, then Solveig, then Ana... on it went, each woman wordlessly receiving my touch as if it were a benediction and entering the circle.

Back in the center, I lifted my goblet.

"Sisters, let us drink to the goddess Freyja. Repeat after me: 'Freyja, goddess, bringer of love and beauty, we praise you!'"

"Freyja, goddess, bringer of love and beauty, we praise you!" came the refrain.

"Let us drink to the goddess — but only a sip."

Raising my goblet to my lips I took a swallow, letting the liquid trickle down my throat. As each woman followed suit, I heard "Ahs" and the smacking of lips. I set down my goblet near the altar and raised my voice again.

"Sisters. Women of Hrethelskeep. I call upon the goddess Frigga, goddess of wives and mothers. She is the guardian of our homes and hearths. We call upon her to bless our marriages. We call upon her to send us children. We call upon her at the time of childbirth. Behold, this evidence of Frigga's blessing!"

I pulled up my tunic to reveal my swollen belly, big with child. A few shocked gasps met this display, but several women patted their own protruding stomachs in mute but mutual recognition.

"My husband Ingeld is dead, but I have been blessed with this life — a gift from the mother goddess, Frigga. As many of you know well, giving birth is a mixture of pleasure and pain. We must now taste the bitter as well as the sweet."

Taking up the half-empty pitcher of salt water, I added a skinful of vinegar, swirling the two together. With this I approached the circle. Dipping the feather into the sour-salt mix, I brushed the lips of each woman in turn. Ginnlaug and Gyrid screwed up their noses, but licked their lips after the feather had touched them.

Picking up my own goblet again, I raised it high.

"We drink to Frigga, friend of mothers, guardian of the family. Goddess, we praise you!"

"Goddess, we praise you!" came the willing response, as each woman raised her cup to her lips, the taste of mead, salt, and vinegar strange on her tongue.

Now I set down my goblet, raised both arms and lowered my voice to its deepest level.

"Women of Hrethelskeep. I call upon Nerthus, Earth Mother, Great Goddess. From her womb we are born, by her we are nourished, to her we return at death. Great goddess of us all, keeper of deep mysteries, ancient crone, be present here in our blood and bones."

I paused, then called out in a high, shrill voice, "Bring in the sacrifice!"

Brita and Runa awkwardly entered the circle carrying between them the suckling pig, its mouth tied shut with cord. Runa carried the bound front legs, Brita the back. Lifting the struggling animal, they positioned it on its back on the altar pan. Runa pulled down its head, exposing the throat. Brita knelt below her, holding up the silver bowl I handed her.

I took a deep breath, my heart pounding so loudly I could hear nothing else. From my gown I withdrew Gunilla's knife. Willing myself to strike, I raised the blade.

"For the goddess!"

"Ahh . . ." a choked exhalation rose from the watching circle, mixed with shrill cries of anticipation.

Now! Hot blood spurted over my fingers as I drew the blade swiftly across the pig's throat. In fascination I watched as the creature's life drained into the bowl. The flow took a long time to cease, time enough for me to regain my composure. Taking the bowl from Brita, I held it out before me.

"Nerthus, goddess, receive our offering. Bless us, bless our crops, bless our village. Make us fruitful."

Slowly I poured a portion of blood on the ground, circling the altar, then carried the bowl to the waiting women. Dipping the swan feather into the still-warm blood, I touched it first to my own forehead, then to the forehead of Ortrud, intoning, "Blood of the body, blood of renewal, blood of life."

"Blood of the body, blood of renewal, blood of life," she whispered back, gazing at me with large round eyes.

Then, on a sudden inspiration, I added a drop of blood to the mead cup in her hands.

Tove was next, then Ingeborg. With each woman the chant grew louder: "Blood of the body, blood of renewal, blood of life!"

While I circulated, Runa swiftly and discretely prepared the pig for cooking, and Brita built up the fire. Soon the aroma of roasting flesh scented the air. When I completed the circle I raised my own goblet and added blood from the sacrifice.

"Women of Hrethelskeep, we drink to Nerthus, dark crone, mother of us all. Goddess, we praise you!"

"Goddess we praise you!" echoed lusty voices.

"Now we drink!"

As I raised the goblet to my own lips, a wave of nausea seized me, but I fought it down. Important work was yet to be done.

By now the moon had risen higher, adding its silvery sheen to the dancing light that played over us. Heat from the fire radiated out toward the circle. A few women were swaying on their feet, whether from the effects of mead or emotion I could not tell. It was time to move on to the next stage of the ritual.

"Sisters, women of Hrethelskeep," I cried, setting aside my goblet. "In this ancient place, in this sacred space, let us now give honor to those women who came before us, or who left us too soon. If you wish to honor such a woman, step forward and say her name aloud, that we may join you in celebrating her life. I will begin."

Taking a step forward, I called out: "Wealtheow, mother, queen of the Danes, I honor you."

"I honor you," came the echo.

After a brief interval Gunilla put out a tentative foot, then stepped forward confidently. "Hylde, sweet mistress, mother of Beowulf, I honor you."

"I honor you," chorused the women.

Now the names came faster: "Ermengard, sister, I honor you." "Karin, friend of my childhood, I honor you." Sobs and cries of pain rose from the circle as we lifted up each name. "Willa, nurse and second mother, I honor you." Runa found the courage to call out, "Toini, grandmother, I honor you."

When the circle began to grow quiet, I added one more name: "Helga, sad maiden, Hygd's daughter, I honor you."

By now the moon had risen fully, high over our heads. I felt the time was right for dancing.

"Sisters," I cried, "We have honored our ancestors, family, and friends. Now it is time to honor each other by joining our hands in a sacred dance. Gunilla will show us the steps."

Cackling with glee, Gunilla let Thora lead her into the center, not too close to the fire.

"Only four simple steps," she quavered. "Step forward, step back, step sunwise, step sunwise. Then step forward, step back, step widdershins, step widdershins."

With Thora's help she demonstrated the movements, slowly circling the altar. Runa had brought me my drum, and I now began to beat a slow rhythm: *pump ah, pump ah, pump ah,* deep as an ancient heartbeat. Slowly at first, with much laughter as feet tangled and shoulders bumped, the women tried the steps.

As the dancers gained confidence I increased the speed of the drumbeat and signaled to Runa. She joined me in the circle's center, raised the bone flute to her lips and began to play.

A single note rose and hung in the moonlight, piercing my heart with its aching sweetness. Unprepared for this unearthly sound, I faltered at my drumming. A momentary shock rippled through the moving circle. Then more notes, high and thin, soared and floated on the air, adding their melody to the magic of the night, a melody both sweet and bitter — like the mixture of mead and vinegar.

On played the flute, on beat the drum, on danced the women. Although I was not one of the dancers I felt lifted out of myself, a young girl again, floating high above the earth on strong white wings, light-hearted and free.

Pump ah, pump ah, pump ah, faster and faster whirled the dancing circle. Cries, sobs, laughter rose from the blurred bodies encircling me. Connected as one, we inhaled the silver night and exhaled it in song: "Goddess hear us, Goddess bless us..."

I don't know how long we danced in the moonlight, suspended in time. Gunilla brought us back to earth with a sudden collapse. Instantly I silenced the drum and Runa's music faltered to a halt. In its place a chorus of frogs could be heard, croaking lustily from the river bank.

"Mother, are you all right?" Thora bent to her side. "Are you hurt?"

Gunilla panted, trying to catch her breath. "No," she quavered," just tired — and hungry!"

Relief swept over me and I laughed. "Clearly it is time to end our ritual."

Turning to the anxious circle, I raised my arms.

"Women of Hrethelskeep, embrace your neighbor and join me in giving thanks for this night. 'Goddesses, may our offerings be received, may our lives be blessed'."

"Goddesses, may our offerings be received, may our lives be blessed," came the fervent echo.

"Our ritual now has ended," I declared. "Let us step outside the circle to take bread and meat together — and fish," I added, remembering Tove's herring.

As the circle broke up, women in twos and threes, chattering and laughing, made their way to the birch grove, where they spread cloaks beside the river. Runa and Brita brought over the suckling pig on a wooden board and Ana set to work cutting the carcass into generous portions for each woman. Solveig set out the flatbread and Tove her salted herring. Runa carried around a bucket of river water for cleansing sweaty hands and faces, while Brita distributed bowls. Soon everyone was seated on cloaks on the grass, munching and licking their fingers.

To cap the evening I brought out another pitcher of mead and circulated among the company, soothing dry throats thirsty from dancing. When I approached Ginnlaug and Gyrid, Gyrid jumped up hastily.

"May I do that for you... lady? You have already done so much for us. This has been the best night of my life!" Her eyes shone in the moonlight as she reached for the pitcher.

"Why, yes, you may," I said, adding in a lower voice, "but don't give much more to Gunilla or we won't be able to get her home!"

Gyrid giggled conspiratorially. "Thank you, lady. I won't."

Now Ginnlaug reached up to touch my elbow.

"Lady Freawaru, I've never eaten such good food. We don't often get meat at home..." She paused, glancing toward her mother who was deep in conversation with Agata. "Thank you," she concluded simply.

Two women, Laila and Marta, came up to me shyly to ask when my baby was due. They were delighted to find that all three of us would deliver at harvest time. I learned that this was Laila's first pregnancy, but Marta was an old hand with two little ones already at home. I did not mention the twins I'd lost at Wulfhaus.

When all the food and mead had been consumed, I asked Brita and Runa to carry around a pitcher of cold river water for a last sobering drink before our walk back to Hrethelskeep. As we gathered up our goods, I hesitated over what to do with the altar.

"Ortrud, do you think it will be safe to leave it here, or should we take it back to the village?"

We both eyed the heavy iron stand and pan, now scrubbed clean with sand by Brita and Runa.

"I say leave it here. After tonight, no one would dare to enter the stone circle with mischief on their minds. This is our holy place!" Ortrud spoke emphatically as she poured more water on the last of the embers.

"Yes, our holy place," I echoed. "The altar stays here."

As they rose to depart, I went up to each woman, gave her a gentle embrace, and slipped a clove of garlic into her hand.

"Plant this near the door to your house and use it to keep your family well."

"Yes, lady." "Thank you, lady."

It took much longer to return to the village than I had anticipated. Many seemed reluctant to leave the scene of our celebration, lingering in small groups, talking and chuckling. But I knew Gunilla's strength was almost gone and I wanted to get everyone home safely.

"Sigrid, Tove, Solveig . . . please help me get everyone started down the path. Those back home will be wondering at our long absence."

The reminder of husbands and children left behind had a sobering effect, and soon the group was headed toward Hrethelskeep. I asked Ortrud to lead the way this time, while I and my household slowly brought up the rear.

As we walked together, enjoying the quiet beauty of the night, Runa came padding to my side, barefoot as usual.

"Lady Freawaru, I will never forget this night. Thank you for letting me be a part of it," she breathed.

"I was glad for your help," I said, "especially your music. Your flute was magical. I've never heard anything like it before."

"Would you like to try it yourself? I could . . ."

"No, no, I'll keep to my drum, thank you, but in the future we may want to pair them again."

"Speaking of your drum, my lady, there is something that troubles me," murmured Runa.

"My drum? What about it?"

"It's that rune painted on one side, Thurisaz. I was taught to regard it with caution as a troll rune."

"Troll rune?" I searched my memory for Unferth's words when he had taught me that rune, but could only remember "a gateway between worlds."

"My grandmother said it could be used to call up demons from the underworld," declared Runa earnestly.

I looked at her in astonishment. "I don't think my rune-master would have given me that rune if it had evil powers."

Runa lifted her shoulders. "Perhaps not. But its power must be used carefully, lest you call up what you cannot control."

"Ah, yes, I will consider what you have said — but listen! Is that the sound of evil energy? The women of Hrethelskeep are singing!"

I halted on the path and bade everyone be still. Drifting back to us came lines of song:

We roam over hills drenched with dew, drenched with dew,
No care in us is found, our hearts with song are filled,
Oh goddess, guide our way, in moonlight softly glowing,
We dance over hills drenched with dew, drenched with dew.

High above the others rose the voice of old Gunilla.

Chapter Eleven
Catching the Pizzle

Fighting stallions. Detail from a picture stone, Hablingko, Götland, Sweden c. 500 A.D.

A feather dipped in blood ... a face — mother's ... women dancing in a circle ... a knife descending ... blood spurting ... Confused images swirled in my head as I struggled to rise from the depths of sleep. High above me sounded the clear, thin note of a swan flute. Bolting upright, I opened my eyes, blinking in the dim light.

No sounds of stirring came from the benches where my women lay drenched in sleep. I lay back to consider.

It must be early morning. I'm lying in my own bed, in my own longhouse. Those images — more than a dream — last night was real! Last night we celebrated the goddess with all the women of Hrethelskeep! I wonder what they are thinking this morning?

The faint taste of mead still lingered on my lips. Smiling, I turned over and closed my eyes, exhaling a sigh of satisfaction.

We were all slow to rise that morning. I heard Ana get up first, yawning and mumbling as she stirred the fire and set water to boil. When I emerged from my sleeping quarters everyone greeted me cheerfully, although Ingeborg said she had a slight headache, and none of us had much appetite for the morning gruel.

"What think you?" I asked the group. "Was our ritual a success?"

"Even if they drank too much," said Ragnhild, glancing at Ingeborg, "no one's going to complain about last night! I think you succeeded, my lady. You gave the women of Hrethelskeep an experience they'll never forget!"

"I can attest to that!" came a masculine voice from the doorway.

"Thorkel!" Ragnhild rose abruptly from her place. "What are you doing here?"

"Th-th-thanks for the warm welcome, Ragnhild. I did knock but you were talking too loud. I came to bring S-S-Sigrid's greetings to Lady Freawaru. And that's not all." He turned to me. "She wants to give you a litter of p-p-pigs from her favorite sow, as soon as they're weaned. S-S-Sigrid talks about you as if you were a g-g-goddess yourself, my lady."

I flushed with pleasure at these words. Sigrid had considerable influence in the village, so her good opinion was important.

"Thank you, Thorkel, for your message. Will you take a bowl of porridge? We don't seem to be hungry this morning."

"I've already eaten, th-th-thank you, and I must get back to construct hives for more bees. Our s-s-supply of honey was greatly depleted in making the mead for your w-w-women's ritual!"

Thorkel raised his eyes at me almost accusingly, but I chose to ignore his look.

"Very good, Thorkel, as we'll need a fresh supply for your wedding."

He brightened immediately. "How soon will that b-b-be, my lady?"

"How soon can the bees produce more honey?"

Thorkel grimaced. "It will probably take another m-m-moon or two," he said, shaking his head regretfully. "Perhaps Ragnhild could help me twist s-s-straw to make new skeps?" He glanced at his bride-to-be beseechingly.

I nodded at Ragnhild. "Go ahead with Thorkel — and thank Sigrid from me for the piglets, a most generous gift!"

The two of them had hardly left the longhouse when a timid knock was heard at the door. I sent Estrid to investigate, and heard muted voices from the entryway, but she returned alone — bearing another gift.

"It was Laila, my lady. She didn't want to come in, but she brought this bit of braid for you, said it might do to decorate something for your baby."

Estrid held out a strip of woven cloth embroidered with tiny flowers. Wiping my hands on my apron, I took the strip to examine it.

"What lovely work!" I marveled. "Laila is good with her needle. Oh, I wish she had come inside."

Estrid chuckled. "I suspect she was too shy, my lady. She seems quite young. I also suspect you'll be getting more such visitors — to thank you for the ritual last night."

Estrid was right. Later that same day Solveig stopped by with her little boy Toke, supposedly to ask how deep to plant the garlic clove I'd given her, but she also just happened to have some extra apples left over from winter storage which she thought I might enjoy — "good for your baby," she said, tousling Toke's curly hair as she spoke.

When I went to the blacksmith's to pay Orm for making the altar, Ortrud accepted my silver, but said there would be no charge to make the hammer for Ragnhild's wedding. "Our gift," she said, smiling magnanimously.

So it went for several days as almost every woman in the village made some excuse to stop by. Did I know a good cure for itch? Oh, and could I use these early greens from their garden? What would I advise for a persistent cough? One woman hinted at the need for a love potion to give to her husband. I answered their questions as best I could and accepted graciously the offerings they brought — which included a small round of cheese from Ginnlaug and Gyrid, who proudly announced they had made it themselves.

One morning both Thora and Rolf appeared at my door carrying three empty baskets.

"This one's for you," said Thora, extending the beautifully woven birch bark.

"For mushrooms," added Rolf, a tall, gaunt man with deep-set eyes and a sad mouth.

"Thank you," I said, "but mushrooms . . . ? I'm not sure . . ."

My two brothers were poisoned with mushrooms!

"If you have time, my lady, we'd like to take you mushroom hunting," said Thora brightly. "Rolf hasn't shown his secret spots to anyone in the village, but he's willing to take you with us this morning. Don't worry," she hastened to add, "Rolf's been hunting mushrooms for years and no one has ever been sickened by them."

Clearly Rolf and Thora were offering me a treat and I did not want to spoil it, but... mushrooms? Still doubtful, I hesitated. Unexpectedly Ana came to my rescue, bustling in from the weaving room.

"Mushrooms, is it? I love those crinkly ones that look like little twigs. Do those grow around here?"

"Yes," cried Thora, visibly relieved. "That's exactly what we're going to gather... if Lady Freawaru wants to come...?"

"I'll get my cloak."

It had rained the day before, so the forest floor was damp underfoot. Thora and I walked quietly behind Rolf, relishing the freshness of the morning. We seemed to be heading for the spring, but as we drew near Rolf turned toward the sun, following the base of the hill.

A sharp, pungent scent suddenly assailed my nose and I stopped to examine the undergrowth, causing Thora to stop also.

"You've probably stepped on forest onions," said Thora. "Rolf!" she called. "Wait a bit while we put a few in our basket." She turned back to me. "These are delicious sliced with greens or added to soup — a bit like garlic, but more spicy."

We paused to pull a few plants, then hurried to rejoin Rolf, who seemed eager for food of a different kind.

Food? Mushrooms? Dare I eat these 'crinkly twigs' we're going to gather?

We'd been walking long enough to start sweating when the evergreens opened up into an area of leafy shade, penetrated by shafts of sunlight.

"There!" called Rolf, pointing just ahead.

"I see it," shouted Thora, scrambling forward like an excited child. She reached down, plucked something, and returned to show me her prize: a delicately, pleated fan shape that reminded me of a piglet's ear rather than a twig.

"This is what we're looking for, my lady. If you find one, there are usually more nearby. Let's start hunting!"

Amused at her eagerness, I nonetheless scanned the ground around me closely. Yes! There's one — and another — and another. The tiny mushrooms shone like spots of sunlight against the dark forest floor. Matching Thora's actions, I dug my fingers into the dirt around each stem and plucked the moist, spongy morsels as if picking flowers. Gifts from Mother Earth!

We could have stayed longer enjoying this delightful pastime, but soon our baskets were full, and surprisingly heavy for such fragile cargo.

"This looks like a basketful of gold," I declared, gazing at the lovely yellows and tans of our treasure, "and it smells like... like what?" I asked, turning to Rolf.

"It smells like dinner!" he said somberly.

Well satisfied, we headed back to the spring, where Rolf pulled a deerskin pouch from his tunic and filled it with the icy water.

"Drink?" He proffered the bag to me first. Clearly a man of few words, this husband of Thora's!

"Yes, thank you — and thank you for showing me where to find these treasures. Your secret is safe with me."

He nodded, handing the bag to Thora when I had finished.

Back in the village we went our separate ways. Ana was delighted with my basket of gold.

"We'll cook several handfuls with a bit of meat for the evening meal," she said, "and dry the rest. These will be a welcome addition to the wedding feast in a few weeks."

"Good thinking, Ana," I responded. "You are always looking ahead."

"Speaking of looking ahead, my lady, we'll soon need to begin preparations for the baby. We didn't bring any of the baby clothes we made at Wulfhaus, so we'll have to start over."

Start over? We are starting over in so many ways, Ana.

"Yes, Ana, soon. Right now I want to enjoy a bit of rest without too many demands."

I haven't yet tackled the Gudfrid curse, but I haven't the strength just now. I need to recover from the effort required by the ritual. Above all...I need to see Beowulf again.

Ana looked at me quizzically. "I understand, my lady, but we all have our tasks. Yours is to lead us."

That night at the evening meal all my women smacked their lips over the meat and mushrooms, wiping up the last bits with flatbread soaked in the juices. I could not bring myself to touch a bite. Everything I ate lately caused a pain over my heart, and my belly was bloated with gas.

Runa often prepared teas to calm my stomach, steeping mint leaves from our herb garden with thyme and chamomile.

"I wish I had black mushrooms from the taiga," she said one day. "My grandmother swore it made the best tea, but it grows high on certain trees in the northland, and is hard to find."

"More mushrooms?" I almost snorted. "Your famous grandmother knew everything, didn't she?"

Runa frowned, but made no answer.

Why am I being cross with Runa? It's not her fault that my back is beginning to ache and I feel as heavy and clumsy as an ox.

"It's the baby," soothed Ana. "Some difficulties are to be expected."

Neither of us spoke of my miscarriage at Wulfhaus.

The matter of Ragnhild and Thorkel's wedding presented several problems. I had already promised a dowry to Ragnhild in return for Thorkel's help in getting us to Geatland, so that was not in question. Thorkel had no actual house to bring his bride to, but Sigrid was willing to share her longhouse with both of them, for a suitable price. Neither Thorkel nor Ragnhild had living relatives to sponsor them or to negotiate the bride price. After some discussion with Magnus, he agreed to stand in for Thorkel's family as I would stand in for Ragnhild's.

The biggest problem, given the time of year, would be producing enough mead for the expected days and nights of feasting and merry-making. I wondered if barley ale could be substituted for mead, but when I broached the subject to Ragnhild, her face fell. She had been standing at the loom, weaving a blanket for her bridal chest, but put down the shuttle to face me.

"I would not delay our union longer than necessary, my lady, but I know Thorkel would be disappointed not to serve the customary mead. Then, we'll need it for the honey-moon..."

I shook my head. "You'd better have him talk to the bees, for they alone can help us!"

Ragnhild looked at me thoughtfully. "There could be another way... if you'd be willing..."

"Me? How? What do you have in mind?" I asked, lifting my eyebrows.

"Thorkel has found two wild swarms in the woods," she said earnestly. "If we — that is if you — could get them to swarm to our skeps, we could harvest more honey — perhaps enough for the wedding?"

Her question hung in the air.

"Hmm... I've not tried to do that before. Let me think about it — perhaps I'll talk to the goddess."

Ragnhild's eyes widened. "Whatever you say, my lady." She turned back to her loom with a smile on her lips.

I retired to my bedchamber to consider Ragnhild's request. Had Mother ever taught me a chant to charm bees? Hmm... I closed my eyes and sat quietly. Slowly words came to me: 'valkyries... tiny valkyries... sink to earth...' And wasn't there something about throwing dirt? Yes!

"Ragnhild!"

Opening my eyes I headed for the weaving room. "Call Thorkel. Tell him I remember the words, but he must say them."

Later that day Thorkel and I practiced what he must do and say to lure the bees to his new skeps.

"You must have your skep ready, Thorkel, and a basket of earth taken from the same place where the skep will be located. Keep watch on the wild bees. As soon as they begin to swarm, throw the dirt over them and speak these words:

Sit still, you wood-wives, you valkyries,
Sink to the earth.
Never again to the wild wood fly.
I, your kinsman, call upon you.
Fulfill your duties now.
In your new home settle.
Sink. Sit. Settle.

We had to wait for two moons rather than one, but at last it was time for the wedding. I sent Wulfgar and Olaf to Eaglesgard, inviting the royal court to join our festivities. I had high hopes that Beowulf would respond, but our men returned with only three guests: Redbeard, Aksel, and — to my surprise — Jesper, Eaglesgard's scop.

"My lady," he said in his sing-song old man's voice, "I am honored to share your celebration." He made a deep bow. "Beowulf asked me to come and recount the old stories, many of which his village folk will not have heard."

Perhaps the full history of the house of Hrethelskeep? I'd like to hear that myself.

"Thank you, Jesper. You are most welcome."

I turned to Redbeard with a question in my eyes which he understood at once.

"Well met, Lady Freawaru." He lifted my hand to his lips. "Lord Beowulf could not come because he is not in residence at Eaglesgard. He..."

"Not at Eaglesgard?" I blurted. "Then where is he?"

Redbeard looked around, drew me aside and lowered his voice.

"He has gone on a mission to the Brondings, where his old friend Brecca lives and rules. He thought it wise to seek allies should the Frisians retaliate for Hygelac's raid."

"The Brondings? I do not know that tribe. Where do they reside?"

"Two days by sea along the coastline — north and west."

A sudden recollection stirred in my memory.

"This Brecca... was he not Beowulf's friend — and foe — in a famous swimming match?"

Redbeard nodded emphatically. "The same, my lady, and by reputation a doughty warrior as well."

Inwardly I shuddered. "Do you think a Frisian attack likely?"

Redbeard was silent for a moment. "No one can say, my lady, but Beowulf is strengthening our defenses. Now, I must leave you, as I see my host beckoning."

He bowed and turned to follow Magnus to his longhouse.

Hmmm... strengthening his defenses. I must ask Wulfgar what he has seen.

Later Wulfgar told me that Beowulf had ordered more long ships built to replace those lost in Frisia, and that Oskar was busy at the forge, night and day hammering out more weapons. Wulfgar added that the Frisians were not the only tribe to be feared. Rumors from the north spoke of incursions by the Swedes, an ancient enemy.

The morning after our guests' arrival, Thorkel made his formal proposal of marriage to Ragnhild in the mead hall. Magnus, Wulfgar, Gorm, Ana, Estrid, and I acted as witnesses. Thorkel pledged ten ounces of silver for the support of any children from the union and I pledged an equal amount from Ragnhild's side. The negotiations were sealed with handclasps all round.

Next came the ritual cleansing, and my first experience of this local custom, for my women and I accompanied Ragnhild to one of the saunas near the river — the same one Beowulf had shown me long ago.

Beowulf, will we someday marry? My heart misgives me that it may never happen.

Brita had built a fire below the rocks the day before, so we were met with intense heat as we entered and stripped off our clothes. From wooden pails we scooped handfuls of water to splash on the rocks, creating a steam that penetrated our pores like tiny needles. Sweat rolled down my face and dripped off my chin.

Are my women actually enjoying this? It feels strange to be exposing our bodies to each other — especially mine, so big with child.

Ragnhild moved up to the highest and hottest bench, soon followed by Ingeborg, while Ana, Estrid and I stayed on the lower level. Very soon I had had enough. Feeling somewhat overcome by the heat, I was the first to leave the sauna. Runa, waiting outside, handed me a birch bundle.

"What am I to do with this?" I asked innocently.

"Hit yourself, my lady — all over. Then I'll wipe you down with this rough towel. You'll feel wonderful, I promise!"

Shaking, I did as I was bid, but could not easily reach my legs or back.

"Here, Runa — you do it." I thrust the birch bundle at her. She took it hesitantly.

Just then Ragnhild burst from the sauna, followed by Ingeborg and Estrid, racing her to the river. Ana came last, breathing heavily. Ragnhild plunged into the icy snow-melt whooping with glee. She emerged spitting and sputtering, shaking her wet locks like a dog. Ingeborg and Estrid paused momentarily on the bank, then leapt in to join their friend. Ana stopped beside me and took the birch bundle from Runa.

"I'll get your back, my lady, if you'll get mine."

"Agreed."

After finally drying off and donning our clothes, we led Ragnhild, pink-skinned and glowing, back to our longhouse, where she was dressed in a clean tunic and apron. Brita worked scented oil into Ragnhild's long blonde hair and spread it out in waves over her shoulders. This would be Ragnhild's last opportunity to wear it unbound. I had brought a golden circlet for her to wear as a token of virginity. As I settled it on her head,

I thought of her question to me earlier that day: would she and Thorkel have children?

I was able to tell her that I saw the two of them surrounded with children. What I did not tell her was this: the children would not live long. I had striven to see more, but the explanation was not granted to me.

We had chosen Frigga's Day for the ceremony, and had erected a temporary altar of stones in a clearing near the river. This time Thorkel provided a young goat for the sacrifice, to honor Thor, and I provided one of Sigrid's fattest piglets to honor Freyja.

The ceremony began with an invocation to the gods, followed by the sacrifice. The animals' throats were cut, their blood collected, then dabbed on the faces of Thorkel, Ragnhld and everyone assembled — which included most of the village — as a purification and blessing.

Thorkel knelt on one knee and drew his sword, 'Bonebiter.' As a family heirloom it would one day be passed down to the first son. He placed a silver finger ring on the sword hilt and extended it to Ragnhild. She took both and placed the ring on her finger. Then she offered a ring to Thorkel, on the hilt of a new sword obtained from the chest of arms given to me by Ingeld long ago. He took both and placed his ring on his finger. Now it was time for the exchange of vows.

Thorkel cleared his throat nervously and began:

"Before the gods, I swear to honor you, Ragnhild, as my wife, to provide for your comfort and to make you keeper of my household. That is my pledge."

He didn't stammer! Well done, Thorkel!

Ragnhild smiled shyly.

"Before the gods I swear to honor you, Thorkel, as my husband, to provide for your comfort and keep your household. That is my pledge."

Amid cheers and halloos the two of them headed for the mead hall, the rest of us trooping after. Thorkel proudly led his bride inside. To the relief of everyone present, they did not stumble at the doorsill, for this would have been an omen of grave misfortune for the marriage. Following behind the bridal couple, Magnus and I took our places on the two high thrones at the end of the hall, he as village chief, I as Beowulf's designated hostess.

Before he and Ragnhild sat down at the table nearest the thrones, Thorkel plunged his sword into the pillar beside the high seats. It sank in at least a thumb's length, a good omen for the strength of their union.

Next came the presentation of the bridal ale, carried in by Runa in a two-handled cup provided by Sigrid. Thorkel consecrated the mead to Thor by making a sign of the hammer over it, then offered a toast to Odin, All-Father. He took a sip and passed the cup to Ragnhild, who made toasts to Freyja and Frigga before drinking. Blood from the sacrifice had been mixed into their drink.

Now it was time to hallow the bride with Thor's hammer. Orm carried in the heavy hammer he had forged, its surface chased with indentations and incised with runes. He handed it to Magnus, who presented it to Thorkel. Carefully, solemnly, Thorkel placed it on Ragnhild's lap, speaking these words:

"On this maiden's lap, Mjolnir I lay
To bless her womb that children may
In Frigga's name our wedlock hallow."

With a huge grin, Thorkel now grasped the hammer with both hands, and lifted it high over his head.

"Let the feast b-b-begin!" he crowed.

Begin it did! Trenchers of meat from the sacrifice, wild game brought down by Wulfgar and his hunters, mushrooms from the forest, dried fish from Eaglesgard, bread from days of baking, fresh vegetables from our gardens — an abundance of food now streamed into the mead hall, carried by thralls and servants. All of it would be washed down with mead, golden mead — for Thorkel's bees had done their work.

The feasting and merry-making lasted for nine days. At my own wedding I had been too preoccupied with my young husband to pay much attention to the actions of others, but here at Hrethelskeep I took delight in the antics around me: dancing, wrestling, horse-fighting, insult contests, singing, storytelling . . . I was amazed at the vigor with which the villagers took part — and at the amount of mead they could drink!

Emund's two sons, Mattias and Marten, started off the wrestling outdoors in the center of a ring of villagers. Short of stature but brawny, they stripped to the waist, grappling and grunting. Finally Marten, giving a mighty heave, threw his brother, to the cheers of the onlookers. He then challenged any young man in the circle to defeat him.

To my surprise, Olaf stepped into the ring and confidently removed his shirt. Marten sprang at him from behind and knocked him down, but Olaf rolled and twisted, quickly pinning Marten to the ground. Olaf got up grinning, and hauled Marten to his feet. I did not stay to see who would take the next challenge.

Saxe and Gorm preferred to pit their horses against each other. I was aghast that they would risk injury to their steeds, but every man in the village turned out for this contest. I heard their shouts and cheers from a distance, as I could not bear to watch such 'sport.'

Contests of words usually started in the mead hall during heavy drinking. At first I was horrified to hear participants insult each other's ancestors, but soon realized it was understood to be all in fun — much like the boasting exchanges once heard in my father's mead hall.

Each night old Jesper picked up his harp, drew his fingers across the strings, and chanted a lay — chiefly tales of battles and past heroes. One night he sang a different song, giving examples of what a wife and woman should be.

> *Women should walk in the ways of peace,*
> *Not give birth to fear and destruction.*
> *Be not like Modthryth, princess proud*
> *With vicious tongue so fierce and wild.*
> *If men did watch her daily walk*
> *She'd shape a noose to fit their necks,*
> *An ancient sword to end their lives.*
> *But she forsook her cruel ways,*
> *Sent across seas to Offa, brave.*
> *Tamed by love, they praise her now,*
> *Her generous heart, her goodness shown*
> *Like Hygelac's wife, the beauteous Hygd,*
> *Young in years but wise and knowing,*
> *Hareth's daughter, noble queen.*

One night old Gunilla grabbed everyone's attention. She rose from her table to brandish a long, dark object. Those near her choked on sudden guffaws and someone shouted, "Sleipnir!"

Odin's horse? What has Sleipnir to do with a wedding feast?

"Time to pass the pizzle," she quavered. "To win good luck, you must give us a verse, a song, a riddle — or be stuck with the pizzle!"

A roar of laughter greeted these words.

"Here, old mother, let me toss it," cried a young man at her side.

Jumping up, he took the thing and aimed it squarely at Ragnhild. She caught it awkwardly in her lap, her face turning red. Holding it out at arm's length between thumb and forefinger, she wrinkled her nose. Now I could see what it surely must be: a dried horse's penis.

"A song, Ragnhild," I called to her, "perhaps 'Spring Breezes'?"

She shot me a grateful look, then opened her lips to sing.

Spring breezes weave and whisper
All through the trees now green . . .

Her pure voice, low and throaty, momentarily quieted the boisterous drinkers.

As young lovers be
Streams flow in a hurry
No rest or worry
Until their foam meets the sea.

Triumphantly she rose and tossed the pizzle back at the young man. "Your turn," she cried.

Thorkel nodded at his bride, beaming approval, and squeezed her hand. The young man (was it another of Emund's sons?) gave us a riddle:

Honored among men both near and far
I'm brought from groves, from vales and downs.
Borne by day on wings through the air
Then bathed in barrels under roof's shelter.
I bind, I scourge, I overthrow.
Who takes me on will fall on his back
Robbed of strength, though strong in speech
Deprived of power, control of the mind.
Ask what my name is, binder of men,
Foe of the foolish, in daylight defeated.

Aksel, who was sitting in a dim corner of the hall with Estrid and Ingeborg, stood up and called out: "I know that well enough! The answer is *mead*!"

"Right you are," declared the riddler, tossing the pizzle in Aksel's direction. It seemed to be aimed at one of the two women, but Aksel gallantly intercepted it. He made a show of clearing his throat, then began to declaim loudly.

"Words to the wise: Praise not the day until evening has come; a woman until she is dead; a sword until it is tried; a maiden until she is married; ice until it has been crossed; beer until it has been drunk."

Scattered shouts of protest rose from several women in the hall and a few well-gnawed bones were flung in Aksel's direction. He grinned broadly, turned and tossed the pizzle high over his shoulder, letting Fate decide who would next receive it.

At this point my back was aching, my ankles were swollen, and the baby was kicking so fiercely I thought it would bruise my belly. As hostess it was my duty to stay in the hall all evening, but I longed to escape. Leaning toward Magnus, I whispered, "Can we end this game soon? I need to retire."

Magnus turned in gruff surprise, but softened when he saw my face. "As you wish. I'll call on the harper for one last song."

Rising, he held up his hand for silence. "Friends, let us close our carouse for tonight with a lay from Jesper, harper at Eaglesgard. What can you give us, Jesper? How about the tale of Thor in the giant's hall, dressed as a bride."

Jesper nodded and drew his fingers across the harp.

The Hurler woke, went wild with rage,
For suddenly he missed his sacred Hammer.
Then Thor to Loki: listen well:
Unmarked by men, unmarked by gods,
Someone has stolen my sacred Hammer.

I knew this tale by heart, having told it often to my brothers at bedtime, so I listened with only half an ear, letting my eyes rove over the crowd in the hall. Gunilla appeared to have the pizzle back in her possession; her wide smile expressed satisfaction with her contribution to the evening.

Chapter Twelve
Child of Ingeld

Tiny bronze fertility figure. Late Bronze age, possibly representing Freyja. Raised hand suggests goddess driving a chariot.

My first summer in Hrethelskeep passed in a haze of heat and happiness. Slowed by the weight I carried, I took time to notice the small details of my life. Long hours of daylight seemed to endow each object with a glow of color, a burst of life. I noted the sheen of Runa's crow-black hair as she stooped in the garden, picking herbs. I gloried in the hanks of yarn in red, blue, and brown piled high in a birch bark basket in the weaving room, and the white froth of milk in a wooden pail, all things which moved me strangely. Ana called it "moodiness" and said it was just part of my "condition," but I felt it was a gift from the goddess and savored each moment, even the painful ones.

One day while I was standing at my loom working on a gift for Beowulf and complaining about my back, Runa made me forget my aches with an outlandish tale.

"My lady," she said solemnly, "be glad you are not the mother of Väinämöinen, who spent thirty summers and thirty winters in her womb before being born into the sea!"

"What? Thirty years?" I gave a weary chuckle. "Who is this Väinämöinen you speak of?"

"A great shaman, a great singer, my lady. The first man born on earth," declared Runa.

"Really? I've never heard his name before." I paused to yawn and stretch my back. "Is this one of your grandmother's stories?"

"Yes," said Runa, "but everyone in my country knows such stories."

"Really?" I said again. "Someday you must tell me these stories, but today it's time for me to finish this weaving and you to fetch more firewood — Ana says our supply is low."

"Yes, my lady, right away." Runa headed for the door, then paused. "There is much I could tell you — when you are ready to listen."

She slipped out the doorway, leaving me to ponder her words.

When the first summer rain arrived, the woods and fields blossomed with fragrant anemones, and flocks of swallows began to arrive. Sheep were already out pasturing, but it was now deemed time to turn out the cows. When released from their byres the creatures took a few tentative steps, then went wild, leaping, jumping, kicking, and butting, bellowing with their tails up in the air. The sight filled me with delight and I clapped my hands like a child. Runa said the cows' behavior was due to the birch sap they'd been fed, but I knew nothing of that.

Runa and Brita were now often absent, taking our cows up to the high meadow during the day to feed on rich grass. I began to listen for their return at evening, heralded by laughter mixed with the clatter of cow bells on Krona and Krusa — for we now had two cows, thanks to Beowulf.

"What do you girls do up there all day?" I asked Brita one evening.

"Oh, I usually take a ribbon loom with me to pass the time. Runa takes her flute and sometimes plays it, but that can make the cows nervous — then we have to chase them, or coax them back. I always carry a bit of salt in my bag to entice them."

"That sounds lovely," I said dreamily. "If I were up on the meadow I'd find a warm rock and sit all day in the sun!"

Brita laughed. "Sometimes we do that too. Sometimes Runa sits and sings a sad song, but I can't understand the words — they must be Finnish."

"A sad song? I wonder what it's about. I must ask Runa."

One evening as she was helping me into bed, I put the question to Runa. She willingly repeated the words, this time in Norse. She called it "Aino's Lament," a death-song by the maiden who drowned herself to prevent an unsuitable marriage.

I went to bathe in the sea
Arrived to swim in the main
And there I, a hen, was lost.
I, a bird, untimely died:
Let not my father
Ever in this world
Draw any fishes
From this mighty main!
I went to wash at the shore
I went to bathe in the sea
And there I, a hen, was lost
I, a bird, untimely died:
Let not my mother
Ever in this world
Put water in dough
From the broad home-bay!
I went to wash at the shore
I went to bathe in the sea
And there I, a hen, was lost
I, a bird, untimely died:
Let not my brother
Ever in this world
Water his war-horse
Upon the seashore!
I went to wash at the shore
I went to bathe in the sea

And there, I, a hen, was lost
I, a bird, untimely died:
Let not my sister
Ever in this world
Wash her eyes here, at
The home-bay landing!

I had closed my eyes as Runa recited, letting the feelings evoked sweep over me.

Aino was lost to her father, mother, brother, and sister. I had no sister, but I feel a kinship with this maiden.

"My lady? Are you in pain?" Runa had stopped reciting. My eyes flew open.

"In pain? Only for the loss of Heorot and my family," I began, then stopped. Runa too had lost home and family but she did not complain. Instead she sat on a stone in the sunshine and sang sad songs.

"Runa, does singing help . . . I mean, when you're feeling sad?"

'Yes, my lady. At home . . . at home there was always singing." She smiled. "My father sang as he sharpened his axe. My mother sang as she spun wool for weaving. Young men sang as they rowed on the rivers. All the women sang at weddings . . ."

She fell silent, a faraway look in her eyes.

"I can no longer remember those faces, but I can still hear their songs," she concluded. She touched my belly gently. "You have no need for sadness, my lady. You bear new life — the start of a new family."

"Will that new family include Beowulf?" I was startled to realize that I had spoken this thought out loud.

Runa smiled again. "In time, my lady, in time."

Outside the longhouse I was amazed to see all the work being done in the fields to feed the village of Hrethelskeep. Both men and women, thralls and freemen, worked outdoors all day in the long hours of daylight. First came plowing, behind horses or oxen. Then harrowing to break up the dirt clods. Sowing of seed was usually done by the men, with the corn and barley held in baskets of woven birch bark. A kind of chant or sowing song accompanied this activity.

Rise, earth, from sleep,
Rise from your bed.
Set seeds to teeming
Set grains to growing
Thousands of shoots raise
Earth giving birth.

Cow and sheep dung mixed with chopped fir branches and moss was used to manure the fields. Horse dung was reserved for vegetables.

Midsummer came and went with the usual balefires and celebrations. Just as in my childhood at Heorot, the farmers here drove their cattle between bonfires to protect them from disease, and a few hardy souls dared to jump through the flames — mostly young men. We gave thanks to the sun for giving us light and life. Our crops and livestock were flourishing — whether due to Freyr, Thor, or Odin, I could not say, but we drank toasts to all three. For healthy children we thanked Freyja and Frigga. Above all, we thanked Earth Mother.

Midsummer was also haymaking time for both men and women. Meadow hay was mixed with leaves, moss, and lichens to provide fodder for sheep and cattle during the winter. Soon it was time to begin cutting the rye, sowing winter rye, and harvesting corn.

I noticed different methods used for the corn harvest. Most of the women carried sickles to cut the stalks, then bind them into sheaves to dry. They were careful to leave one last sheaf in the field — for Odin's horse — before threshing the stalks with clubs and flails indoors, then winnowing the grain by tossing it in a windy place. Most of the men harvested with scythes, spreading the stalks on pole frames to dry.

Regardless of the method used, each family made an offering to the dead — the 'dead share' — at the end of the crop year.

The coming of shorter, cooler days meant sheep-shearing and the start of the hunting season. Omens were consulted before any major hunt. Hunters left gifts for the forest spirits, as fishermen did for the water spirits. Animals were now allowed to graze in the harvested fields, but were brought back into their byres at night. With fewer hours of daylight, we had to light seal oil lamps indoors of an evening to do our chores.

Although my former mother-in-law had predicted that I'd never be able to carry a child to term, both Ana and I judged that my pregnancy was progressing normally — at least so far. Despite the pains in my back and wrists, despite the fatigue and lack of sleep caused by the baby's increasing activity, I settled into a blissful state, complete in myself, fulfilled in the knowledge that I carried life within me.

One day I had my first taste of salmon from the river, and thereafter developed a craving for its rich, oily flesh. When Olaf heard about this, he made sure to keep me well supplied.

In late summer I was introduced to another local treat: crayfish. The emergence of these tiny creatures along the river banks brought out young and old alike. Woven traps with small funnel-shaped openings were set out each night, baited with pieces of fish. Once caught, the crayfish were dropped live into pots of boiling water seasoned with salt and bunches of dill.

Thora showed me what to do next. The now bright red creatures were cracked open and the meat sucked out from tail and pincers. Thora dipped her morsels in melted butter and licked her fingers noisily. Soon I was cracking and licking with everyone else and enjoying it hugely.

Now that Ragnhild lived with Thorkel in Sigrid's house, I saw her much less, but she made a point of stopping by often to check on my progress. I was grateful for these brief visits, as I went out less frequently myself.

Sometimes I saw Laila or Marta outside their houses, working in the garden or tending to their animals. On such occasions we compared our symptoms and shared quiet encouragement. Our long wait would soon be over. In fact, Marta predicted that I would be the first to deliver.

"Your baby has dropped," she said one day, fixing me with a practiced eye. "You can't be more than a moon away, my lady."

Ana confirmed this when I returned to my own longhouse.

"I think Marta is right. Now you should feel less heartburn and find it easier to breathe," she added.

"Should we send word to Beowulf? I mean . . ."

"Best wait for the outcome, my lady. That will be soon enough."

Again, neither of us mentioned Wulfhaus.

I'd been told by Thora that women in Hrethelskeep gave birth in the sauna, although Gunilla had mentioned a "birthing tree" that once stood in the village center, used in olden times. I could not picture myself clinging to a tree, but I did agree to the sauna. I could remember my own mother giving birth inside the women's house at Heorot, surrounded by her women — as I would be here.

Runa fussed over me the most, shielding me from sights that might upset me and mark the baby, anything having to do with sickness, slaughter, or death.

One night after the evening meal my stomach began to cramp — not an unusual occurrence — but this time the cramps continued and became increasingly severe. Brita helped me to my chamber and stripped off my outer clothes. She helped me stretch out on the bed, where I lay like a beached whale. I sent her to make a cup of mint tea and closed my eyes.

"My lady? Are you in distress?" Runa's face hovered above me. "Is it time?"

"Surely not," I gasped. "It's too soon . . . isn't it?"

"Perhaps, but I'll get Ana anyway. Stay right there!"

Lying back, I gasped again as a wave of pain seized me. For a moment I could not breathe. Then I shouted. "Runa! Ana! Brita! Hurry! The baby — it's coming!"

The rest of that night was filled with motion. Ana and Runa helped me struggle up from my bed. Brita settled a cloak around my shoulders. The three of them helped me hobble the short distance to the sauna. Estrid and Ingeborg were already laying out blankets and Brita started a fire. Although the night air felt chill on my skin, I was already sweating.

"Relax, my lady," crooned Ana. "Breathe deeply between the pains."

They settled me on the lowest bench, leaning me against the next level. Ana pulled up my nightshift to peer between my legs.

"Barely begun. We have a long night ahead of us."

Ana was right. At first the pains came in irregular intervals, catching me by surprise each time. During one period of respite between contractions, I felt a draft and looked up to see Runa at the sauna door.

"I can do something else to help Lady Freawaru, but I must go to the longhouse. I'll be back soon." She slipped out the door, closing it carefully behind her.

Ingeborg, who had been wiping sweat from my face with a damp cloth, paused to wonder out loud, "What's that girl doing now?"

Ana shrugged. "She has strange ideas, that one . . . but she's often right."

Intent upon anticipating the next contraction, I heard their voices as if from a distance. Time seemed caught, unable to move forward, and I was caught within it. I fell into a light doze, awakened by another draft of fresh air. My eyelids flickered open. Runa.

"It will be easier for her now. I untied every knot I could find in the longhouse!" Runa cried triumphantly.

Estrid snickered, but said nothing. I started to speak but gasped as the waves came faster and faster, leaving me panting like a dog. My water broke, soaking the blanket beneath me. Soon it was time to drop onto my hands and knees on the floor, with Estrid and Ingebord supporting me on either side.

"Don't fight against your muscles," cautioned Ana. "Try to ride with the waves, pushing with the contractions."

I struggled to do as she advised and found I was better able to manage the pain. Still, the effort was exhausting. As I worked my way through the waves of pain, I reached out and clung to the nearest post. Inside me I could feel the baby moving, seeking the gateway into its new life. Fluids gushed forth, and my bowels let go. Runa cleaned everything away, pushing soft pads under my hands and knees as Ana encouraged me.

"I see the head, my lady! It will soon be over! Push hard! I'll catch the baby!"

I dropped to my elbows and pushed, straining to free the life still trapped within me. Suddenly, it shot out, and I collapsed on the floor, tears streaming down my face.

Gently Estrid and Ingeborg turned me over and Estrid began massaging my belly to produce the afterbirth.

"My baby? Where is my baby?"

"Here she is. See? We're cutting the cord now, my lady."

She? A daughter!

Ana held up a wet, tiny creature streaked with blood and crowned with a mat of dark hair. One tiny fist was clamped tight around Ana's thumb. My baby! My little girl! Her tiny lips quivered. She let out a wail, a big sound from such a tiny creature. We all laughed, and I held out my arms for my beautiful little girl. They laid her on my breast, slick with sweat.

"Inga. I will call you Inga, after your father," I murmured feeling her sweet warm breath against my skin, drinking in the miracle of her tiny body.

With trembling arms I held her up, examining her body for any signs of ... imperfection .... None. No marks of any goddess.

She will not bear that burden. Perfect. She is perfect.

With a sigh I returned Inga to my breast, where she lay blinking her tiny eyelids as if waking from sleep She opened her lips and yawned mightily, then began to nose about like a piglet. Filled with wonder at what I had produced, I hardly noticed when Runa picked up the cord and afterbirth and placed them in a bowl beside the fire, but I heard her ask:

"Should these be buried in a secret place, or dried for future use in an amulet?"

I did not hear anyone answer.

"Here, my lady, let us clean her up and wrap her in a warm blanket." Ingeborg was holding out both hands, but I was reluctant to part with this new part of me, my daughter.

Mother, wherever you are, you have a granddaughter. Her name is Inga.

Ingeborg bathed the squirming Inga in a bowl of warm water and wrapped her tightly in strips of swaddling cloth. Ana gently rubbed the baby's hair dry and fluffed it with a fine-toothed comb.

"My lady," crowed Estrid. "She has red hair, like yours!"

Inga's arrival changed everything in our household — for me. There was still weaving to be done, food to be cooked, gardens to be tended, but now Inga was my constant companion. I fashioned a sling to hold her close to my body while I worked. At night she slept in a cradle beside my bed, a beautiful cradle made by Redbeard and sent by Beowulf. The fact that he had not come in person to present it gave me pause, but I was too busy being a mother to dwell on it.

Magnus had been the first to call after Inga and I were settled. That morning I had just finished nursing and laid Inga in her cradle when there came a knock at the door. Ana admitted Magnus and directed him to my chamber. I was surprised and mystified to see that he carried the hammer of Thor used at Ragnhild's wedding.

"Show me the child," he said brusquely.

"She is sleeping just now," I said. "Will you take a cup of ale?"

"Later. I must see if the child is sound. It is my duty."

I stared at him in bewilderment. "What do you mean, Magnus?"

He drew himself up and puffed out his chest.

"If the child is ... defective ... in any way, it is my duty as head of the village to ... banish it," he declared, staring at a spot above my head.

"Banish it? You mean smash it with that hammer? You'd do that?" I bristled all over, immediately on the defensive.

Magnus shifted his weight. "It is my duty..." he began again.

"Never mind your duty!" I cried, rising in agitation. "Here — see for yourself — this child is perfect!"

Snatching Inga from her cradle, I pulled off her wrappings and held her up. Magnus took her gingerly. Inga immediately gave a howl and began kicking and struggling. Then she peed all over his hands.

"Her lungs are healthy enough," said Magnus, hastily handing the babe back to me, "and she appears to be normal."

Caught between outrage and amusement, I stifled my retort and thrust a wiping rag into his hands.

"Of course she is normal," I snorted, pulling my wailing infant close to my breast.

"In that case," said Magnus, "it is my duty — nay, my pleasure — to welcome her to the village. May the gods be with you ... what did you say her name is?"

"Inga," I spat.

"May the gods be with you, Inga. Welcome to Hrethelskeep." Magnus raised the heavy hammer slowly above our heads, moving it up, down, and sideways. "There. My duty is done. Now I'll take that cup of ale you offered."

I stared at him in amazement. "So, the hammer...?"

"Is for blessings. Defective children are exposed in the forest."

When Magnus was gone, Ana and I shared a moment of mixed hysteria and relief.

"That man..." she began.

"... was 'only doing his duty,'" I finished. "Inga has been accepted into the village. It is now her home — officially. Thanks be to the gods!"

Inga's arrival gave me a welcome new focus, for all through that autumn Beowulf did not come to Hrethelskeep. From time to time we heard news of the court, usually from Aksel, who paid frequent visits to our longhouse. Both Estrid and Ingeborg lavished attention on him, but it was not clear whom he favored most.

We women were busily preparing winter garments for the cold season ahead. We padded my fox cloak with a layer of wool, then a lining of silk, and made a warm head covering from two more pelts provided by Gorm from his hunting. We also constructed ankle-length cloaks for all of us, made of felted wool and finished to suit each woman's taste: mine dyed with woad to a deep blue, Ana's left in its natural brown, Estrid and Ingeborg's bleached to grey. These we lined and quilted with down or feathers for added warmth.

Thora told us that besides his farming Emund was a shoemaker, and that one of the sunken huts near Orm's forge was his tannery, marked by the smell of urine used in treating hides. From him we ordered winter shoes made of reindeer skin with the hair left on. Emund showed us his specialty: he used skin from the reindeer's hind leg at the knee joint, which provided a toe for the shoe. Then he sewed other skins on both sides of the instep, placing the animal's dewclaws on each side of the heel. This prevented the shoe from sliding on slippery surfaces. I was delighted with his ingenuity, and paid him well for his work.

Inga was an easy baby. She took to the breast immediately and slept long hours between feedings. She seemed to grow pinker and plumper with each passing day. Laila, who had also given birth to a daughter, was not so fortunate. Her little girl was colicky and difficult to nurse, remaining pale and sickly. Although she had passed Magnus' initial examination, it was not a surprise when Laila's baby died in its third moon. Marta, who had produced twin boys, coaxed Laila to help her by acting as wet nurse to the second infant. Overnight Laila's depression lifted, and thereafter the two women spent much of their time together.

Snow had already begun to fall when Beowulf unexpectedly appeared in Hrethelskeep, bearing more gifts. The best gift was Beowulf himself. My heart turned over when I heard his voice at my door. Hastily rising, I handed Inga to Estrid and refastened my tunic.

Estrid hurried off to the weaving room, where Ingeborg was already working. Interrupted in her feeding, Inga began to wail loudly. Before I could say "Come in," Beowulf burst through the door, stamping snow from his boots. He was dressed in a fur-trimmed cloak as red as a rowanberry. His face lit up when he saw me standing, motionless, beside the hearth.

"Freaw, forgive my sudden entrance. I could not wait to see you!"

Flinging aside the cloak, he swept me into his arms, pressing my milk-filled breasts against his huge chest. In the distance I could hear Inga still howling, but Beowulf was not taken aback.

"I congratulate you on a healthy child," he chuckled. "The babe has strong lungs!"

"Beowulf," I managed to cry when I could speak. "At last you've come!" I drew in a deep breath, taking in his scent and the cold of outdoors.

"Dear Freaw, how I have missed you," he murmured huskily. He held me out at arm's length. "You are more beautiful than ever, my Freaw. Bearing a child has given you a bloom, a glow — you are a very goddess!"

He lifted my fingers to his lips and kissed them one by one. Tears filled my eyes and flowed down my cheeks as I hungrily devoured his dear face, so full of tenderness.

"I came as soon as I could," he declared, pulling me once again into his arms.

I could have stood there forever, locked in his embrace, lost in his love, but Inga was wailing ever more loudly. My babe was calling me.

"Excuse me, Lord Beowulf, I must see to the child."

Instantly Beowulf dropped his arms, disappointment on his face.

"As you wish, Lady Freawaru," he said in a formal tone. "I would not come between you."

Behind him I could see Ana standing near my chamber shaking her head violently, but I did not then understand her meaning. I called to Estrid to bring me the baby, now red-faced and screaming. To my surprise, Beowulf intervened, taking the child and cradling her in his great hands as he spoke in a low voice.

"So this is Inga. Well met, Inga. You must learn to know your friends from your enemies, little one. I am a friend. I am Beowulf."

Inga stopped in mid-scream. She took a long, shuddering breath, then relaxed in his hands, her normal color returning.

"What's this, my lord? Know you how to charm? Inga is usually afraid of strangers," I declared.

"But I am not a stranger," he replied, "at least . . . not any longer. I hope to see more of you both, you and Inga. I see she has your hair color." He smiled, a clear smile, and handed Inga back to me.

"When you are free, Freaw, please join me in the mead hall. Until then I must speak to Magnus and to Wulfgar — who I hear has been doing an excellent job of improving the young men's battle skills."

He bowed and turned to go, picking up his cloak.

"Beowulf?"

"Yes?"

"Thank you — from both of us."

He nodded, then left the longhouse.

Beowulf was barely out the door before Ana came flying up to me like an angry hen.

"Freaw! How could you treat him so?" she flashed, hands on hips.

"What do you mean? What did I do?" I asked in genuine bewilderment.

"You put your child before your man, that's what you did!" she stormed.

"And if I did, what's wrong with that?" Now I was the one to bristle.

"No man will stand for it! He will leave you flat — alone with your child — that's what's wrong!"

I stared at Ana in disbelief.

"But you saw how he took her, how he held her . . ."

"Another man's child!" Ana was almost spitting. "You've been fortunate thus far in Beowulf's generosity, but you should not presume too much!"

"Ana, surely you are wrong. Surely his heart is big enough to love us both?"

Inga had begun to wail at Ana's loud voice, and I was almost wailing myself.

Just then Brita and Runa entered, but stopped in mid-stride when they saw Ana and me in heated conversation.

"Redbeard . . ." began Brita, then fell silent.

Glad for this interruption, I prompted her to continue.

"Yes? Redbeard . . ."

"Is collecting the tribute owed to Eaglesgard, from the summer harvest," she said.

Runa chimed in. "He says the customary contribution is one out of every nine portions, but we aren't sure how to figure that."

Given a practical problem to solve, Ana turned her attention to the two women.

"I'll sort it out. Where is Redbeard now?"

"Outside the mead hall, loading carts for the trip back," said Brita.

Trip back? Beowulf may not intend to stay long! I must pull out my surprise and see him immediately ... but should I go alone or take Inga with me?

A glance at Ana's face decided the question.

"Estrid? Ingeborg? Where are you? I need one of you to take the baby!"

Beowulf was still conferring with Magnus when I slipped inside the mead hall, bearing my gift. He nodded toward the front table.

"We won't be long, my lady. Please take a seat. There is wine ready for you."

Nodding in return, I settled myself to wait but did not touch the wine, preferring to drink it with Beowulf. The hall felt damp and chill; it smelled of sour ale. Under the table my feet encountered a scattering of bones.

I must send Brita and Runa to clean in here. I've been neglecting my duties since Inga was born. Hmmm. Wine. What a surprise ... I wonder why Beowulf is offering wine on this occasion?

Suddenly Magnus' gruff voice startled me.

"... can't sit here and wait! We'll join forces. Just tell us when!"

I lifted my head to hear more, but the two men were heading for the door. When Beowulf joined me, his face looked grim, but a smile soon lightened his features.

"Freaw. We are alone again."

He held out his arms. I rose and melted into them, nestling my head against his beard. As we held each other in blissful silence, I made no move to break away. Finally he lifted my chin with his fingers and gazed deep into my eyes.

"Freaw, my Freaw, we have much to consider, and my time in Hrethelskeep will be short, but let us sit and drink and open our hearts to each other."

Gently he seated me and took his place across the table.

"What is amiss, Beowulf? I heard Magnus speak of 'joining forces.' Are you — are we — in danger of attack?" I gazed at him earnestly, my heart in my eyes.

"There is always danger," he began, pouring wine into our glasses, "but I don't think it is immediate. The Frisians seem to be content with killing Hygelac." Here his voice broke and he paused. "The danger that concerns me comes from the north, from the Swedes, who still seek revenge for the death of Ongentheow."

"Ongentheow?" I burst out. "Gudfrid's husband?"

Beowulf looked puzzled for a moment. "Gudfred? Oh, yes, the wife." He nodded. "Ongentheow's two sons, Ohther and Onela, have been raiding along the coastline north of Eaglesgard. They could not easily attack us from the sea, but they might try to come inland."

"How far inland? Do you think ... Hrethelskeep?" My voice caught at the name of my adopted village.

"Unlikely — especially with winter approaching. Still, we must be armed and alert."

Seeing my stricken face, Beowulf rose and came to stand behind me. Removing my head cloth, he buried his face in my hair. As he breathed in its fragrance, recently scented with herbal oils, a thought struck me and I turned my head.

"Beowulf, you mentioned the name 'Onela.' My father's only sister was married to a Swede named Onela. Could it be the same man?"

Beowulf straightened. "Your father's sister? What is her name?"

"Yrs," I answered, "or Ursula. Father never spoke of her, but Mother once told me her name and said she'd been married into a royal house long before I was born."

Beowulf resumed his seat and lifted his glass.

"This is good news, my Freaw, although I do not know what use we can make of it at present. Let us drink to future possibilities! Wes heil!"

"Wes heil!" I echoed, glad to have contributed useful information.

We drank and set down our glasses. Beowulf's hands reached across the table to take my hands. I had not drunk wine for many moons, and the taste lay strange but sweet upon my tongue. I licked my lips to savor it. Beowulf smiled.

"You like it? I brought it as a gift especially for you, traded a fur for it on my last trip to the south."

"It's delicious, a very special treat," I acknowledged. "I also have a gift for you, Beowulf. It has kept me company during your absence; now it is ready to join you at Eaglesgard."

Beowulf looked mystified as I reached under the table and brought up one of Rolf's beautifully woven birch bark containers.

"A travel pack? I have ..."

"Nay, my lord. Look inside."

Beowulf undid the lacings on the top and lifted out a length of woven linen. Shaking it out, he held it up and peered at it closely. "It's a tapestry," he said at last.

"Do you recognize the story?" I asked, suddenly doubtful of my skill.

"I see . . . a dragon . . . and a warrior . . . it must be Sigurd!" cried Beowulf, his face lighting up. "Sigurd was my childhood hero! This is a fitting image to decorate my hall at Eaglesgard! Thank you, dear Freaw. A man would have to travel far to find another woman as skillful and as beautiful as you!"

Dropping the cloth on the table, he leaned forward and enfolded me in another embrace. When we finally resumed our seats, I had a different topic to explore with him.

"Beowulf, speaking of travel, what of your friend Brecca? We heard that you'd paid a visit to the land of the Brondings."

Beowulf grinned from ear to ear. "Brecca, yes. Still up for a challenge, just as when we were boys."

I grinned back at him. "I still remember the talk at Heorot about your famous swimming contest, and Unferth's attempt to deny your victory."

Beowulf took another draught of wine and laughed.

"Apparently there are several versions of that story being told. I will tell you what truly happened." He leaned back and closed his eyes for a moment.

"It did not start out as a swimming match, but a challenge to see which of us was the better man at fighting sea-monsters."

He paused, a grin spreading over his face.

"It was agreed that whoever reached shore first after his battle would receive the prize of victory—the gold chain King Hygelac wore around his own neck! That morning the sun rose red over a stormy sea, but we flung ourselves into it, clad in chainmail with swords in hand. Soon we were separated by the waves and I saw Brecca borne off in a different direction."

"I was carried to a great cliff towering above a place that swarmed with sea-dragons, many-armed polypi and horrible nixies. I fought them off, stabbing through their scales. One dragged me down to its cave, but I stabbed it in the heart and swam with it to the surface. Long was the journey back, for I was far from home."

Here Beowulf stopped to take a deep breath.

"Brecca reached shore first and claimed the gold chain; that is true. But when King Hygelac and all his court saw the monstrous corpse I dragged ashore, they proclaimed me a champion braver and bolder than Brecca. Hygelac gave me his own sword, Nägling, with its gold hilt and runes engraved in gold—sure to bring good fortune to its owner."

Beowulf took a long drink and wiped his lips with a sleeve. We sat in silence for a time, each of us reliving his past adventure. Then my mind turned to matters of the present.

"How is Herdred? And my sister Hygd?"

"They are well, both are well," he said, but shook his head. "Herdred is determined to become a man overnight, and he sometimes acts as rashly as his father. Herdred needs the guidance of a firm hand... which brings me to our present situation."

He took another drink and cleared his throat.

"As Hygd has pointed out to me, if war should come you are safer here in Hrethelskeep than anywhere else. And you have the child to raise, as I have Herdred to oversee at Eaglesgard. We both have our duties..." he trailed off, his eyes misting.

I swallowed hard. "Yes, we have our duties. I understand, Beowulf. We must remain apart — for now."

He nodded. "I'm glad you understand. These are uncertain times. We must be strong to meet whatever comes."

He got up and went to a wall bench stacked with travel packs. From one he withdrew a roll of leather and brought it to our table.

"Hygd sends this for baby Inga." Unfolding the end, he revealed a long string of large, brightly colored glass beads. "She said it could be a plaything now, and a necklace later."

"How thoughtful," I murmured, fingering the cold, shiny baubles. "Please give her my thanks."

"And this is from Herdred." Beowulf unwrapped another fold and removed a tawny pelt, a fox fur. "The boy is obsessed with hunting, though no longer on the north downs!"

Beowulf's face grew thoughtful.

"Freaw, your gift of sight should be nourished; its use may be crucial if war comes to us. I've been thinking... I think you should attend the Great Blōt at Uppsala, the sacrifice held every nine years. All the shamans of the north gather there."

"A blōt? At Uppsala? When does it happen and where is this place?" I asked in confusion, trying not to focus on the word 'war.'

"By my reckoning it will be held after two more winters. Uppsala contains a great temple dedicated to the gods, and it is the seat of power of the Swedish kings. It's located far to the north, on the east coast of this country."

"The Swedish kings?" I repeated. "I thought they were your enemies!"

"Now, yes, but that could change . . . perhaps with your help." He paused. "I too have a distant family connection with the Swedish line through my father's tribe, the Waegmundings. Perhaps . . ." he let his words hang in the air between us.

Now I recalled something else from long ago.

"Beowulf, I believe there was such a blōt at Heorot during my childhood. Willa, my nurse, kept me inside the whole time, saying the sacrifices were not fit for a child's eyes."

"You are a child no longer, Freawaru. You are woman grown."

Beowulf smiled and squeezed my hand gently. "For now, let us enjoy our brief time together, and you can tell me all about your baby." He poured the remaining wine into my glass.

Beowulf and Redbeard left the next morning, with thralls driving a string of ox carts laden with tribute. My heart sank to see them go, and I moped about all day "like a lovesick mooncalf" as Ana put it. My other women kept a respectful silence, but toward evening Runa sought me out with a suggestion.

"My lady," she began, holding out a branch of some sort. "In my country we have a test to see into the future: this rowan twig."

"A twig? How is it used?" I asked, only mildly interested.

"You put it into the fire and watch to see what oozes out. If it's honey — that is, sap — you can expect a wedding. If blood, there will be war. If water, peace will continue. My grandmother said it never fails. Do you want to try it?" She held out the twig.

Did I? I was not sure I wanted to, but . . .

"Yes! Set it into the flames!"

She did so, placing the twig at the edge of the hearth fire. We both watched in fascination as the twig trembled in the heat, then smoked. A drop of something emerged on the tip and I put out a finger to catch it. Although painfully hot on my skin, I focused on the droplet. It was turning color, turning . . . blood-red. War!

With a shriek that startled Inga from her slumber, I flung the drop away and stuck my finger in my mouth to soothe the burn. War? Could it be? Savagely, I turned on Runa, ordering her out of my sight, but the horror had been planted.

Chapter Thirteen
Rings and Riddles

Mask on a gravestone dedicated to a man who fell "when kings fought".

The next morning I rose feeling unrested, weary after a fitful night. Bloody images had populated my dreams, and I could not shake a feeling of foreboding. When Inga woke with a hungry cry, I rose and slowly put her to suck, welcoming her insistent mouth, her tiny body so full of life.

I will protect you, Inga. I will preserve you, no matter what the cost!

The violence of my thoughts surprised me, bringing to mind Ana's words of yesterday. What would I do if I had to choose between Beowulf and Inga? I shuddered, causing Inga to lose her grasp momentarily. She gave a wail of dismay, then latched on again with determination.

That's right, my daughter. Hold on to life!

At the morning meal my women were subdued, speaking little. The rumor of war had run through the village like wildfire, though no one could say who had first spoken of it. When Runa came in with fresh milk for our porridge, she avoided my gaze, her eyes downcast. Ana looked at Runa, then at me.

"What was that commotion you two had last night? Were you disturbing our lady, Runa?" she asked sharply.

Before Runa could open her mouth, I replied. "We were casting omens — and the result did not please me."

"Omens, is it?" cried Ana. "Surely you don't need Runa to cast omens, my lady. Your own methods have worked fine in the past!"

I stared at Ana. Of course . . . my runesticks!

"You're right, Ana. I will consult the runes — immediately."

Rising hastily I hurried to my chamber. Taking one of the keys that hung at my waist, I unlocked the small chest containing my rune bag. As I sat down on the bed to open the bag, I chided myself for my foolishness of the previous night.

Runa's head is full of strange beliefs and practices. You know nothing of her background except what she has told you. That grandmother she talks about could have been a witch rather than a shaman — if she even exists!

Settling myself, I closed my eyes, trying to frame the question to be asked. Will there be war? Will there be war soon? How soon? Will war come to Hrethelskeep . . . to Eaglesgard? In frustration I opened my eyes and shook my head to clear it. Then I heard a voice . . . my mother's clear voice. 'Freawaru, do not ask the runes. Ask the goddess. Call upon her to guide you.'

"Thank you, Mother," I breathed. "I will."

Rising, I tucked the rune bag inside my tunic and went to rejoin my women, still sitting at their meal.

"I must go to the stone circle, today. Who will come with me?"

Ana's face filled with alarm, but Estrid and Ingeborg rose eagerly.

"I will!" cried each.

"What about Inga?" asked Ana, getting up slowly. "She'll need to be fed long before you can walk there and back again. Now that you're a mother you can't just go running off when it takes your fancy!"

I paused. Ana was right. Having a baby did add constraints to my life, but . . .

"'I'll take her with me!" I cried. "She'll sleep most of the time anyway, and I can introduce her to the goddess!"

Ana started to frown, hands going to her hips.

Fanning the Flames

"I don't like it. Here we've just been hearing of possible attackers, and you want to go off alone with the baby!"

"Not alone. As you can see, Estrid and Ingeborg are willing to come with me. If you like I'll also ask Wulfgar or one of the other men to accompany us."

"Humph! Well, if this is turning into an expedition, we'd better get busy."

At that moment Brita and Runa entered from the dairy with long faces.

"Can we come too?" asked Brita timidly.

"Wait, wait," I cried. "This is to be a private visit. I need to consult the goddess about these rumors of war . . . and get some answers."

"My lady," said Runa quietly, "will you need a sacrifice for the goddess?"

"A sacrifice? Hmm . . ." I faltered, unsure, then had an inspiration. "Yes, but it will be a personal sacrifice: a lock of my hair."

Estrid and Ingeborg looked horrified, but Runa nodded in approval.

"Well chosen, my lady, a sacrifice indeed."

Ana opened her mouth to object, then closed it, then opened it again.

"You'd best wrap up . . . there may be snow again from the looks of the sky, and you'll need a bit of food and drink — especially for the men. I'll get something ready."

I sent Brita to speak to Wulfgar. She soon returned with Wulfgar, Gorm and Saxe. Having three large men standing beside the hearth suddenly made our longhouse seem much smaller. Wulfgar wore a long dark cloak, and his legs were wrapped in leather. He held a spear in one hand and had slid a knife into the top of one legging.

"What's this all about, my lady?" He stood at attention, his face serious.

"Ana thinks we need protection to walk to the stone circle, and I've been wanting to confer with you about our defenses here at Hrethelskeep."

"I see." He bowed. "I am always at your service, my lady. Are you ready to leave now?"

"Yes, just as soon as I gather up Inga. She's going with us."

Wulfgar's eyes widened in surprise, but he said nothing. Ana bustled up with packets of food and a jug, which she thrust at Saxe and Gorm.

"Don't be drinking it all on the way going or you'll be thirsty on the way back," she admonished.

Saxe winked at Gorm. "Don't worry, Ana. I'll keep an eye on it!"

Underneath their short cloaks I noted the glint of sword hilts. I had not seen Saxe and Gorm for some time and was amused to note that Saxe had grown a luxurious mustache, which he clearly groomed with great care. Gorm was now wearing his hair in two plaits on either side of his face. Wulfgar had retained his usual full beard and bushy eyebrows. To my mind he looked like the fierce masthead carved on a fighting ship. Surely we would be safe in the company of these men!

Outside the longhouse the air felt crisp and clean, with just a hint of moisture from the low clouds above us. I took a deep breath, glad to be free of the wood smoke spiraling from our hearth. It was good to be out of doors again. It was good to have my body back as well! Inga lay nestled in her sling above my heart, a warm talisman.

Wulfgar and I set off walking together, followed by Saxe with Estrid and Gorm with Ingeborg. Wulfgar carried his spear at the ready and glanced from side to side as we left the village and entered the forest, but we neither saw nor heard anything alarming. Gradually I began to relax and enjoy the day, but there were serious questions I needed to ask.

"Wulfgar," I began, slowing my steps, "what is the danger to Hrethelskeep? And what defenses do we have in place should there be an attack?"

He slowed his pace to match mine.

"With the men no longer working in the fields, we have available a substantial fighting force. They're already been drilled in the use of sword, spear, and battle-axe, and I've seen to it that every man has a sturdy shield."

I gulped. "Are there watch guards posted? On every side of the village?"

Wulfgar shook his head. "Given our location in this broad valley, we could see anyone approaching from the mountain sides to the north and south. Because of the heavy forest in this country an enemy force would have to come by river — from the east or west."

I nodded, absorbing this information.

The river, yes. It flows west — to Eaglesgard, to the sea. "Wulfgar," I stopped and turned to face him as another thought struck me. "Beowulf said that Eaglesgard could not be easily attacked from the sea, but do you think...?"

"...that the Swedes might attack Hrethelskeep first, then continue on to Eaglesgard? Yes, that is what I would do if I were in command."

Fanning the Flames

"But why would these Swedes want to harm us? " I cried, hugging Inga closer to my breast.

"Old feuds live on, my lady. You should know that well from your experience of the fatal feud between Hrothgar and Ingeld."

My mouth fell open and hot tears sprang to my eyes.

"Do you wish to shame me, Wulfgar? Me, Freawaru, the failed peace-weaver?"

Behind us the sound of chattering voices stopped abruptly.

"Nay, my lady, you misunderstand me." Wulfgar shifted his weight uneasily. "I meant that once a feud is set in motion it grinds on relentlessly. No one man, no one woman, can stop it."

I stared at him, blinking back tears. "So... you think we are doomed?"

"Nay, I did not say that. Much depends on the timing of the attack. Right now I have hunting parties out to the east and west, on the alert for signs of any intruders." He paused, looking at me closely. "If you can use your special powers of sight to learn any details of what to expect, we can better prepare our defenses."

"That's exactly why we're going to the stone circle," I said, lifting my head higher. "I will consult the goddess. She will help us."

Let me be right. Our lives may depend upon it!

By the time we reached the sacred stones Inga was awake and hungry. The rest of my companions looked hungry as well, so we spread our cloaks under the now-leafless birch trees beside the river and settled under the pale midday sun. Gorm and Saxe took turns patrolling the area while Wulfgar and the rest of us ate our cheese and bread, washed down with good barley ale.

Thank you, Ana.

Estrid and Ingeborg shielded me when I put Inga to nurse. Finally I was ready to begin our work, and I called everyone together.

"We women will enter the circle, while you men stand guard — at a distance," I directed. "It is forbidden for you to see any part of our ritual."

"Agreed," said Wulfgar, "but your safety is my chief concern, my lady. Call out at any time if you need help."

"Agreed," I echoed.

Wulfgar, Gorm, and Saxe melted into the surrounding trees as I and my women prepared to enter the stone circle. Ingeborg carried my ritual things and Estrid carried a small bundle of sticks for the fire. The iron altar made by Orm sat exactly in the center of the clearing where it was left last spring. Our request for new life had been amply fulfilled since that time. Now it was a question of preserving life.

We had set aside our cloaks as the day warmed. I adjusted the sling to place Inga over my heart in order to have both hands free. Thus far she had been perfectly content to feed and sleep.

Taking the salt box from Ingeborg, I stepped inside the circle and cast a few grains toward each of the four directions: north, east, south, and west. As I did so, I invoked the goddess.

"Goddess, be with us in this sacred space. Hear us. Grant us the wisdom we seek. Open our eyes to see what must be seen."

I beckoned to Estrid, who slowly, reverently, entered the circle.

"Place the firewood directly atop the altar."

When she had done so, I took the flint at my waist and struck a spark to the dry tinder. A curl of smoke rose up, then a small tongue of flame.

"Ingeborg, you may enter."

After she had joined Estrid and me in the circle, I lifted my arms to the sky.

"Goddess, you are a bringer of life. Behold this child, your gift to me. Behold Inga, daughter of Freawaru."

Slipping my child from her sling, I held Inga aloft. She stirred, but did not waken as I returned her to my breast. From the bag Ingeborg carried I withdrew the special knife used at our spring ritual and handed it to her. Removing my head linen, I shook out my hair, which tumbled about my shoulders in waves of red and gold.

Bending my head, I nodded to Ingeborg. With one hand she lifted a heavy curl from the front of my face and held it out. With the other hand she drew the knife across the curl, severing the golden strands. For a moment she stood transfixed, holding the hank of hair aloft like a trophy. Wordlessly, I took it from her.

"Goddess, I offer you a prized part of myself, this lock of hair."

Gently I laid the lock on the altar fire. It sizzled and curled and caught fire. The three of us watched in silence until the lock was entirely consumed. Then I addressed my women in solemn tones.

"Estrid and Ingeborg, it is time for me to leave my body. I must fly to the goddess to discover what I can of the enemy and their movements. You will surround me and uphold me as I enter the trance. Remember any words that escape my lips. Catch me when I return to earth."

Fanning the Flames

Estrid cast a frightened glance at Ingeborg, but both nodded.

"We will not fail you, my lady, but what of the baby?" questioned Ingeborg.

"She will be safe with me. Let us begin. Goddess, be with me!"

I closed my eyes and began to hum a wordless melody, revolving slowly inside the circle of my women's arms.

Come to me, my swans! Lift me above this world! Show me what I need to see!

I turned slowly, sometimes brushing against one of the women, but never stopping... turning... always turning.

A blast of cold air hit my face and sent a tremor through my body. I was rising... higher, ever higher, into a region as cold and dark as death. Clutching Inga ever more tightly, I rose, fighting for breath. My cheeks felt numb, and frost seemed to block my throat and nostrils. I struggled.

Freyja, spare us! We are flesh and blood!

Slowly the darkness lessened, the air grew warmer, and I could breathe easily again. Below me a great light appeared which grew and spread, filling my vision.

"Bright! So bright! I cannot see!"

Blinded by the brilliance below me, I sought to escape, but my wings beat against solid flesh, and I plummeted to earth.

In a daze I reached out blindly. I felt myself lying on my back on something soft, but I could see nothing. My body shivered uncontrollably, still held in the grip of an icy hand. Muted sounds broke through to me: Estrid's voice crying "My lady, my lady, come back! Speak to us!" I heard Inga's wail at my breast. Someone wrapped a cloak around me and my tremors gradually lessened. Finally I opened my eyes. I lay cradled in Estrid's lap with Ingeborg bending over me.

"You're back, my lady," she said. "You're safe. Take your time now."

Inga had no such patience. In response to her continued cries I sat up and fumbled at my tunic, baring a breast to meet her demands. As Inga settled in to nurse, I returned to myself, pulled back into the world again.

"Did I speak during the trance?" I asked, trying to clear my head. Estrid and Ingeborg repeated the few words they had heard, and I pondered them carefully.

"'Bright'? Yes, I remember a blinding glare. It felt like staring into the sun."

"Did you... see the Swedes?" asked Estrid hopefully.

"No . . . no. Let me think: darkness, then light in the midst of darkness, brilliant light. What could it mean?"

"It sounds like a riddle," offered Ingeborg.

"A riddle, yes, and runes can reveal the answer to riddles," I cried. "I will add *galdr* to *seiðr* to unravel this riddle."

Shifting Inga back into her sling, I opened my tunic and reached for the rune bag tucked inside.

"Where is my head cloth?" I asked, looking about.

"Here, my lady." Ingeborg pulled it out of her pack.

"Spread it on the ground before me, please."

Closing my eyes again, I slipped my fingers inside the bag, waiting for a single rune stick to find me.

Ah, here it is — perhaps the answer to this riddle.

Drawing it out, I laid it on the head cloth. We all stared at the object.

"What is it, my lady?" Estrid eyed the stick as if it were a snake.

"*Isa.* Ice." I answered. "A force of nature, beyond control."

"Ice?" murmured Ingeborg. "Ice is bright, blindingly bright."

I stared at her. "So it is. And ice is only formed in the dark of winter! Estrid! Ingeborg! I think we may have found part of the answer. Ingeborg, call back the men!" Exultant, I rose.

"Wulfgar, Gorm, Saxe, the ritual is over. Come join us," called Ingeborg.

She and Estrid stretched and shook themselves, then began to gather our things. As we left the stone circle, I spoke a few words of closing.

"Goddess, we thank you for the light you have given. Let the circle be closed. Blessed be."

On the way back to Hrethelskeep I told Wulfgar what I had learned. He grasped its significance immediately.

"They will attack in winter, after the ice has frozen solid. I don't know when that happens in this country — probably after Yule. I'll ask Magnus. Thanks to you — and the goddess — we'll have time to be well prepared. Well done, my lady!"

We arrived at the longhouse with smiles on our faces. Ana took the baby and fussed over her, but clearly Inga had not suffered from her outing. Her cheeks glowed with color and her eyes were as bright as stars. Not ice.

A few mornings later we woke to a changed and muted world. When I opened the door for a breath of fresh air, I discovered a world of snowy white. Stepping outside, my boots sank in snow up to my ankles. More flakes were falling on my hair and eyelashes; I stuck out my tongue to catch one and laughed out loud in childish delight. I'd never seen this much snow at Heorot! A thin layer already covered the roofs of the longhouses and snow lay thick on the boughs of evergreens. Familiar paths had almost disappeared under a layer of white.

From somewhere nearby I heard the sound of stomping feet. Looking through the falling flakes, I saw Rolf outside his door, tramping down the snow. Cupping my hands I called out to him.

"Good morrow! How long do you think this will last? It's so . . . beautiful," I said, lacking the words to say how I felt.

"All day — or longer," he called back, then stamped his way toward me. "Do you have a good supply of firewood? I could send one of the thralls to cut more if you need it."

His beard and mustache were flecked with frost, as if he'd been outside for some time.

"Thank you, Rolf. We have enough on hand to last for several days."

A gust of wind swirled around the corner, blowing snow in our faces. I sputtered and spat, my cheeks stinging.

"It feels colder than usual," I muttered to myself, then smiled at Rolf. "Tell Thora that I'm working on a new weaving pattern if she'd like to see it . . . but this might be a good day to stay indoors," I finished, looking about.

He nodded soberly. "We may have no choice — this could be the first storm of the winter."

"Winter? So soon? I always feel closed in when winter comes," I admitted.

Rolf chuckled. "Soon it will be time to bring out the skis. Then you won't feel closed in!"

"Skis? I haven't thought of those in years. I'm not sure I'd remember how to use them." I blew on my hands and rubbed them together.

"You don't ski?" Rolf shook his head in amazement. "You'll have to learn all over again. Anyone here can teach you — but we should talk of that later. You are getting cold." He turned to go, then paused. "Do you skate?"

"No, I don't skate," I said, laughing ruefully. In truth I felt mildly inadequate. "Thanks for your offer of help — with the firewood."

He nodded mutely, heading back to his own doorway through the swirling snow.

Inside my own longhouse I was still grumbling at myself when Runa and Brita came in to serve the morning gruel.

"Skis... skates... will I have to learn all over again?" I muttered.

Runa's eyes lighted up at my words. "Skiing, my lady? I haven't skied in years, but I'd love to do so again. I could show you..." she began, but I cut her off.

"I do know about skates — those horse bones you tie to your feet to slide over the ice. But why anyone would want to do that, I don't know."

I looked around the table at my women. "Have any of you used skates before?"

Estrid nodded. "I tried when I was a girl, but I always fell down. There was never much ice to practice on around Heorot."

Ana sniffed. "Good for breaking bones, if you ask me. I've seen it happen."

"My lady," said Runa shyly, "the men in my village back home often competed with each other to see who could skate the best. It was a manly skill they took pride in."

"If it's a manly skill, we women don't need it," declared Ana emphatically. "Now, to more important matters: we need to refill all the lamps today." She glanced up at the roof vent, where snow filtered in, falling into the fire with a hiss. "Our outside light will be dimmed by this snow, so we'll need a lot of oil to do our work."

Later that day Runa came to my side as I was nursing Inga.

"My lady," she began, eyeing me tentatively.

"What is it, Runa? Do you have something to teach me?"

"I just wanted to say that skis give you the freedom to move about in the winter-time. I love gliding over the snow — it feels like flying!" Her face beamed as she spoke.

"Flying? Really..." I considered her words. Perhaps Rolf was right. Perhaps I should learn how to ski again.

Fanning the Flames

It turned out to be Thora who taught me, although it was Rolf who fashioned a pair of skis for me from lengths of spruce and leather straps. When the snow storm cleared, a thick layer of white covered the hillsides above the valley. Thora pronounced it a perfect day for my first lesson.

Sunlight sparking on the crystalline crust almost blinded me, but Thora led me to a level space at the foot of the hillside overhung with evergreens so laden with snow that their lower branches reached to the ground. The cold air stung my nostrils, and I pulled a woolen scarf over my nose.

"We'll start out on the flat," said Thora in reassuring tones, "and wait until you're comfortable here before heading up on the slopes."

Up? On the slopes? Is she teasing me?

Just learning how to walk on these sticks was difficult enough. Bundled up in woolen cloak, mittens, and reindeer boots, it was hard to move at all. I felt as awkward as I'd been in the final days of my pregnancy.

"Don't worry," laughed Thora, as I floundered beside her. "Soon you'll be skimming over the slopes like Skadi with her bow and arrow."

"Skadi?" I echoed. "Wasn't she the giantess who married a sea god?"

"Yes," nodded Thora, "a mountain woman wed to a man of the sea — an unlikely pair, like some I could name!" She chuckled. "Rolf and me, we're as different as day and night, but we get along. Now, watch what I do."

She demonstrated as she talked. "Use your poles to steady yourself. Start by shifting your weight to the right foot. Then slide your left foot forward. That's it. Now shift your weight to the left and bring your right ski forward. That's it ... you're getting it!"

By the time we got back to Thora's house I was winded but exhilarated. *I am learning how to ski!* Gunilla had a kettle of steaming barley soup waiting for us, even though the evening meal was hours away.

"It's best to keep something hot going in the winter — for emergencies, you know," said Thora as we sat at the table.

"Take another cup, Lady," urged Gunilla. "Good for your milk."

"My milk? Oh, yes, for the baby. Thank you, I will."

As we drank, I brought up Thora's reference to Skadi.

"Gunilla, you know the old stories better than we. Why did Skadi marry Njord?"

She set down her cup and wiped her lower lip.

"By mistake. When she was given her choice of any god, she was only allowed to see their feet. She chose the most beautiful pair, thinking they must belong to Balder. She was wrong. They were Njord's feet!"

Gunilla cackled with glee and broke into a fit of coughing. As I waited for her to recover, a knock at the door drew our attention. It was Brita, looking worried.

"My lady, you'd better come. It's Inga. She's wailing pitifully and won't be comforted."

I rose at once, bidding Thora and Gunilla a hasty farewell. It would be many days before our skiing lessons could be resumed.

Inga's howls reached my ears outside the longhouse, and I hurried to enter. Inside Ana was jiggling the baby, pacing back and forth as she tried to calm her.

"I think it's just gas, my lady, but she is very warm and I knew you'd want to see to her yourself — once you'd finished playing in the snow."

Ignoring Ana's last comment, I took Inga and carried her to my bed chamber. She continued to howl as I unwrapped her bindings. Her little body did feel a bit hot, but when I wrapped her loosely and put her to my breast, she began to nurse, her howls subsiding into little gasps and gurgles. As she fed, I closed my eyes and leaned back, letting my mind wander... An image of feet came to me, a pair of beautiful feet. I sighed. Did they belong to Beowulf?

That winter more snow fell on Hrethelskeep than I could have imagined possible. Deeper and deeper grew the drifts, as wind from the north howled over the mountains and down into our valley. And the cold! I had never felt such cold! I soon learned that Magnus had been right about the byre: having animals next to our living space added much-needed warmth. How glad I was that we had accepted Beowulf's offer of the additional structure!

Krona and Krusa had to share the byre with our sheep and pigs, but the cows had their own stalls and an abundance of meadow hay. It became my habit to visit them each morning, stopping by the half-door to lean in and call their names. It gave me a good feeling to know that no matter the weather, we would always have milk and butter available to us.

Fanning the Flames

Inga continued her fretfulness, refusing any of the herbal solutions I dripped on her lips. As the winter wore on, she was sick repeatedly: colds, coughs, fever, colic . . . Earaches were the worst, and they always struck at night. Inga would progress from whimpering and pulling at her ears to outright screams that tore at my heart. At such times I would lift her from her cradle, position her upright against my body, and hold warm compresses to the side of her head.

Other babies in the village were sick as well, some sick unto death. Marta lost her younger twin despite all our efforts to save him. He gasped out his life in his mother's arms. My grief for her was mixed with the memory of losing my own twin boys long ago at Wulfhaus. Now I grew terrified at the possibility of losing Inga.

One night Inga's ragged breathing kept me from sleeping. I listened, pondering what else I could do for her. As I lay beside her, worn with worry, I closed my eyes, just for a moment . . .

A rush of wings fanned my cheeks. Slowly I opened my eyes. A tall woman, a beautiful woman dressed in white feathers stood on a sledge pulled by enormous cats, cats as big as reindeer! Stunned, I sat up. Could it be Freyja, wrapped in her falcon cloak? Yes!

"Goddess, help me! Help my child!"

She drew closer, her icy breath enveloping me. One white arm reached out. Long slender fingers, fingers that grew and grew, encircled my Inga, my baby.

"No! No! Spare her! Spare her and I'll do anything! I'll make more sacrifices to you . . . I'll give up . . ."

What more can I offer? In horror I watched as the icy fingers lifted my baby from her cradle . . .

"No! Stop!" I blurted, convulsing in panic. "I will . . . I will . . . I will give up Beowulf! I swear it!"

I must have been shouting, for I woke to find Brita and Runa on either side of me, shaking me gently.

I bolted upright, gasping, "Is she dead? Is she dead?"

"Who, my lady? No one is dead. You've been having a nightmare, that's all," soothed Runa.

"Inga? My baby!" I cried, springing out of bed.

"See, my lady, she's here in her cradle," said Brita, "sleeping soundly. Your cries did not wake her. See for yourself."

I reached down to touch Inga's soft, downy cheeks and feel the steadiness of her breathing. Her skin felt warm, but no longer hot.

"The fever is gone — thank the goddess," I cried, tears streaming down my face.

"Thanks to you, my lady," said Runa quietly. "That poultice you put on her chest at bedtime has drawn out the congestion."

I stared from face to face, wondering. Was Runa right or had the goddess spared my child?

The goddess — I made a vow — about Beowulf — I made a vow.

Shivering, I sank back on the bed, letting Runa and Brita cover me with furs, but sleep did not return to me that night.

Chapter Fourteen
A Winter's Journey

Design from a picture stone found in Uppsala, Sweden, c. 700 A.D.

After my vow to give up Beowulf, Inga's problems gradually lessened. She began to thrive, putting on weight and sleeping through the night. What had caused this? Had I truly seen Freyja in my dream vision? Had she heard my vow? I could not be sure, but I could not ignore my words. Having bargained for my child's life, I must now keep my part of the bargain.

No attack came from the north that winter or the next. Rumors told of King Othere ill or on his deathbed with two sons, Eanmund and Eadgils, waiting their turns at the throne. Perhaps internal conflicts kept the Swedes away from us. Whatever the reason, I was grateful for a time of peace.

During this time I saw little of Beowulf. He appeared infrequently at Hrethelskeep, conferring with Magnus and Wulfgar, then stopping by to see me and the baby for a few precious hours. The first time we met again face-to-face, I was stricken with doubt and remorse.

What have I done? How can I give up Beowulf? I love this man!

Wrapped in his arms, I let silent tears fall against his chest, but managed a wan smile when he released me.

"I miss you, my Freaw, every day," he breathed into my hair. "I would see you more often if I could." He did not speak of the duties that kept him away.

Our previous agreement to live apart helped me hide my inner turmoil, but Beowulf seemed to sense that something had changed. He gazed at me with questioning eyes, but I had no answers to give him.

Beowulf happened to be present when Inga's first tooth appeared. Runa urged me to mark this event with a special ceremony, explaining her belief that Inga would now acquire a guardian spirit, which must be welcomed appropriately. Since Beowulf was visiting, we prepared a feast and offered toasts to all the gods, giving thanks for Inga's first full year of life.

Runa presented her with an amulet, a small woven bag containing Inga's dried birth cord. This made me recall Runa's question at the time of Inga's birth: "What should be done with *these*?" and I asked her the whereabouts of the birth sac itself.

"I buried it," she whispered to me, "high in the meadow under a rock. Now, no one can use it against her," she added triumphantly.

I smiled approvingly and thanked Runa for her vigilance.

She could be right to hide it. Anything which protects Inga is welcome.

Beowulf had started calling Inga "little fox," given her dark, alert eyes and the reddish hair that wreathed her face. Fortunately he had never seen her red-faced and crying! He found Inga a happy child who recognized him at each visit. When she ran to him, he would scoop her up, hold her before his face, and pretend to bite her fingers. She would laugh, reaching out to tug at his beard and explore his face with her tiny hands.

Inga daily dragged around the fox pelt given her by Herdred. She even slept with it every night. On his visits Beowulf used it to tease her, tickling her face with the white tip of the tail as she laughed and tried to pull it away.

The joy Beowulf brought to our lives made the longhouse seem to glow with special warmth. Such moments filled me with a bittersweet pang, knowing we could never be a family . . . if I kept my vow.

Fanning the Flames

Inga had passed her second winter when Beowulf made a proposal: join him on a journey to the Great Midwinter Blōt in Uppsala. We were sitting at a table in the mead hall, alone except for a servant at the door, our faces lit by the flickering hearth fire.

"Is Hygd going?" I asked immediately. "Or Herdred?"

Beowulf shook his head. "Hygd thinks Herdred is still too young to witness such events; she wants to keep him close at home." Slowly he shook his head again. "The boy is growing up fast. We can't protect him forever. She will have to face that soon."

Inwardly I sympathized with Hygd. Protecting my child was my highest priority.

"How would we travel? How long would it take? May I bring Inga? May I..."

Beowulf held up his hand to interrupt the torrent of questions.

"You'd best leave the child here with your women. The journey will be long, and may be difficult, but..." he held up his hand again as I opened my lips to protest "it is important that you be presented to the Swedish court as a seeress of the Geats, one who can see into the hearts and minds of others, one who can predict the future... a woman of power!"

My mouth stayed open as I listened to his words, but I shut it with a snap as a momentary panic seized me.

"Beowulf, would I be required to give a public display of my... my gifts?"

"Yes, that might happen." He reached over and took my hands. "I have faith in you, my Freaw. You have powers that I and others do not. Together we could show our enemies that we are strong, not an easy target!"

I nodded, now understanding the real reason for this journey. It pleased me, that word: 'together.'

"Very well. If it will prevent a war, I'll do it!" I declared, surprising myself with the firmness of my voice. At my next question, Beowulf laughed.

"What should I wear?"

"Ah." His face glowed. "Your best gowns and furs! You could wear that fox cloak that Hygd gave you. Yes, bring that. You will look as splendid as a goddess."

I smiled in response, glad for his words, but still unclear about the whole plan. "Who will ride with us?" I asked.

"I will choose a company of men from Eaglesgard and Hrethelskeep. You will need one or two of your women and a servant."

Mentally I surveyed my women.

Estrid and Ingeborg will want to come. Brita can wait on us — no, she hates riding horses. Better take Runa instead. Ana can look after Inga. Ragnhild is expecting her first child, but not for many moons. She can help Ana...

"Freawaru?"

Coming out of my reverie, I looked into Beowulf's eyes, deep pools of blue. For a moment I felt a tingle of pleasure that reminded me I had not truly given him up. I swallowed and tried to smile.

"Yes?" I managed to say.

"Freaw, no harm will come to you on this journey, I swear it. I would give my life for you!"

'And I for you!' my heart cried out, but I knew my heart to be a traitor. Had it not already traded Beowulf for Inga?

"What? Tears? Don't you believe me?" Beowulf's voice reached me from a distance. "Come here. Let me hold you."

He rose from the table, opening his arms to me. Blindly I rose and walked into them. We stood, breathing as one, locked in our love. I did not, could not, speak of my vow to give him up.

The days that followed were busy with preparations. We would need food and supplies for the journey itself and animals to sacrifice when we reached the temple. I was curious about this temple, for in my experience sacrifices always took place in the open. As we were leaving the mead hall one frosty morning, I asked Beowulf about this. His reply was grim.

"You'll see many sacrifices out-of-doors at Uppsala, hanging from every tree! Nine of every available creature."

"Every creature?" I repeated. "Does that include...?"

"Yes," said Beowulf matter-of-factly, "that includes humans. Captives of war, mostly."

I shuddered, remembering the horse sacrifice at Heorot where a young thrall had been slain and hung in the bog as an additional offering to the gods.

"Why nine?" I asked, to take my mind off this memory.

Beowulf looked at me in surprise. "For Odin, of course, Odin who hung for nine nights on the world tree as a sacrifice to himself."

"Oh, yes, I remember my rune-master chanting the words to me: 'I hung on the tree for nine long nights ... wounded by my own blade, bloodied for Odin.'"

I shuddered again. "So . . . bloody Odin will be worshipped at the temple."

"And Thor," said Beowulf, "he is the god most favored by my own men. But Freaw, it won't be all blood and death. There are great wonders to be seen at Uppsala: the great tree that never dies, the golden images, the sacred horses . . ."

"Horses? What kind of horses?"

It had been months since I'd ridden Burningfax. I'd fallen out of the habit while I carried Inga, and later she had taken so much of my time . . . I suddenly realized that I was eager to mount a horse again.

"Frey's sacred horses are white," Beowulf was saying, "white stallions that have never been ridden."

Frey? Oh yes, Freyja's twin brother.

"And will the horses be . . ." I looked up in sudden dread.

"Sacrificed? Yes. That is their destiny."

I bowed my head. Horses. A true sacrifice. Then I spoke aloud. "What animals shall we take to sacrifice?"

Beowulf reflected. "A market is usually set up where animals can be bought, but we won't depend on that. We'll bring our own animals: a few goats, some sheep and of course boars for the three main gods."

"We'll have quite a caravan!" I laughed. Then a different thought came to me. "Beowulf, will there be other women at this blōt? Are women allowed to take part in the ceremonies?"

He did not answer immediately. We had been walking toward my longhouse. Now we paused at the doorway. A shadow passed over Beowulf's face.

"I have only experienced one Great Blōt, back when I was a young warrior accompanying King Hygelac. Hygelac . . ." The memory brought pain to his eyes, but he smiled as he turned to face me directly. "The ceremonies at the temple were open to everyone, man and woman alike, but I don't remember seeing many women," he admitted. "They may have conducted their own rituals in secret, separate from the temple."

"Only a few women?" I asked. "What were they like, these women?"

Beowulf reflected, seeming to search his word hoard.

"Strange," he said at last, "and powerful . . . not like other women. One was said to be a witch."

His voice dropped on the last word. I frowned in mock indignation.

"Beowulf! Do you think *me* a witch?"

"You?" He laughed and shook his head. "Of course not! But you do have... powers."

He opened the heavy door and held it for me to enter. As I stepped past him his lips brushed my head and he murmured, "My Freaw, your power over me is undeniable."

I trembled at his words, for I still lacked the strength — or the will — to tell him of my vow.

Of the men at Hrethelskeep Beowulf chose Saxe, Gorm, and Olaf to join our party. Magnus had declined earlier, saying he was too old for such foolishness. Wulfgar agreed to direct the defense of the village in our absence, should it be necessary — with Magnus' help, of course.

One evening at bedtime as Runa was combing out my hair, I told her that she would be accompanying me to Uppsala. She was both surprised and excited.

"Shall I bring my flute?" she asked, carefully working out a tangle.

"Yes, and I will pack my drum and rune bag. We must be ready to meet any challenge."

Runa returned the comb to my chest and came around to face me.

"My lady," she said, wrinkling her brow, "if we are going to the seat of the Swedish kings, might we seek news of how Gudfrid met her end? That might help us resolve the curse she laid on Hrethelskeep."

"I've been thinking the same thing, Runa. That braid of hair you found — I will include it in my pack."

I did not then foresee how important that braid would become in helping us meet the challenges of our expedition.

At first Estrid and Ingeborg were not keen on making the trip, but when Beowulf mentioned Aksel as one of the men he'd selected from Eaglesgard, they showed more enthusiasm. I had thought Ana would disapprove of the trip, but she seemed eager to have little Inga to herself. She did admit that Ragnhild's help might be needed on occasion, but she cheerfully assured me that Inga would be well cared for in my absence. I had no reason to doubt her.

Aksel, Leif, and Lars soon joined us from Eaglesgard. I had hoped to see Redbeard among the company, but Beowulf said he had specifically asked him to take charge of Herdred while he was away. One evening during our preparations for the journey, I found the three men inside the mead hall and asked them for news from the court.

Lars, a short, stocky, powerfully-built fellow, looked strangely at Aksel, whom I already knew well, and at Leif, an older man with deep-set eyes and bristling brows. No one seemed willing to speak. Finally Aksel took the lead.

"My lady, Queen Hygd regrets not joining you. She wanted to come, but . . . ." Suddenly he had no more words for me.

". . . but Beowulf wouldn't let her!" blurted Lars.

"What Lars means," said Aksel, frowning at his companion, "is that Hygd was needed in Eaglesgard—to support King Herdred."

"That's not what I heard," countered Lars. "She accused Lord Beowulf of wanting more time alone with this lady . . . not that I'd blame him!"

He gave me a look that was almost a leer. Aksel raised his hand abruptly as if to strike Lars, but I struck first—a different blow.

"Lars Larsson, your tongue may one day bring your death upon you! You will not return unscathed from Uppsala! Let my words be a warning to you!"

The smug look on his face faded, quickly replaced by confusion and finally, fear.

"So, you *are* a witch!" he muttered. "Hygd thought as much."

"No," I answered calmly, "I am not a witch, but you are a fool if you know not when to hold your tongue. I expected better manners from one of Lord Beowulf's men."

Lars dropped his eyes and sullenly turned away, but now Leif spoke up, seizing Lars by the arm and pulling him forward.

"This lady is owed an apology," he said firmly.

Like a sulky child Lars mumbled a few words, ending with ". . . meant no disrespect."

"I accept your apology, Lars. Let us be friends. We have a long journey before us."

Outwardly I smiled. Inwardly I wondered.

What is amiss here? Why has Beowulf chosen this man as part of his honored guard? Could Lars have some secret connection to the queen? He talks as if he is her champion!

Aksel and Leif hustled Lars away, and I exhaled in relief.

Do I have an enemy in Beowulf's camp? This exchange may not bode well.

On the morning of our departure we bade farewell to those staying at home. Ana put on a brave front, but I saw tears glistening in the corners of her eyes.

"Take good care of Lady Freawaru," she called out the door. "Bring her back safe."

Under a heavy sky, a few flakes of snow were falling, partially masking the shapes of our group in the dim light. Beowulf, who stood just outside next to Frostmane, handed the reins to Gorm and came to the door.

"Don't worry, Ana. It is customary for all hostilities to cease during the Great Midwinter Blōt. We should all be safe, wherever we are."

Ana grunted, but did not respond.

Little Inga seemed to sense the coming separation and had clung to me desperately for days. I had told Inga that I would be gone for a time, but I knew not what 'gone' meant to a child who had always had her mother at her side. Brita and Ragnhild stepped forward to distract her with her beloved foxtail when I made my exit from the longhouse. I felt both anticipation and foreboding, delight and dread, at the trip that lay before us.

When will I see my child again? When will I see Hrethelskeep again? May the gods protect us all during this journey!

The runes I had consulted earlier seemed favorable — except for Gebo, which could be interpreted in more than one way. Gebo indicated a gift, but did it mean a gift which would come to me or a gift which must be given to the gods? I could not tell.

We were setting out in the depth of winter. Dark, cold days had followed even darker, colder nights. I felt as if we lay trapped in the frozen grip of Ymir, the frost giant. What better time to seek the aid of the gods, to show our reverence for their life-giving powers? To Uppsala we must go!

Beowulf had explained that the midwinter sacrifices always began on the second full moon after the winter solstice. Light from the moon could help supplement what little sunlight we would get during the short days of midwinter. He also told me that our route would take us across the breadth of the country, from its west coast to its eastern shore, for Uppsala lay close to the sea.

We would start out following the River Göta, heading north and east. He said we would encounter great lakes, other rivers, and vast forests along a trail that had been used for countless generations.

"Will we meet other travelers on this route?" I asked, somewhat reassured that the way was well known.

"Possibly," he said, "and we may find shelters along the way — if they have not all collapsed over the years. I remember staying in such places when I rode with Hygelac."

I wore long leather breeches under my gown, borrowed from Thora's Rolf. Estrid and Ingeborg had chosen to wrap their legs in strips of wool. My women and I wore our reindeer boots, but Runa had borrowed another idea from Thora. During our first winter at Hrethelskeep, Thora had taught us how to use moss to keep out the cold that seeped through cracks in the walls. Now Runa put the moss to another use: stuffing it inside her thin leather shoes for added warmth.

Originally Beowulf had planned for his three men to lead the way, followed by us riding side by side. Estrid, Ingeborg, and Runa would come next, then the four sledges loaded with tents, provisions, and animals for sacrifice. These were pulled by sturdy fjord horses, a long-ago gift to Beowulf from his friend Brecca. Four thralls rode these horses and four more thralls huddled in the sledges with the sheep, goats and pigs. Our rear was to be guarded by Saxe, Gorm, and Olaf.

The darkness and the depth of snow required a change of plan. To break through the drifts piled waist-high along the river, the fjord horses and all the thralls, carrying torches, were sent ahead to open a trail. Behind them Aksel, Lars, and Lief also carried torches to light the way for the rest of us.

What a noisy caravan we made: the bleats and squeals of the animals, the muffled tramp of horses' hooves, the shouts of the thralls as they whipped their mounts — all could surely be heard from a great distance. Any enemy lurking nearby would have advance warning of our coming.

Beowulf has assured us that attacks and reprisals will be set aside during this time. May he be right!

From somewhere in the distant past a voice echoed in my consciousness: "All may yet be well."

I fixed my eyes on the torchlights ahead, wavering in the chill air, and urged Burningfax forward. Having spent much of the winter inside our dark, smoky longhouse, I was happy at first to be outdoors in the crisp, clear air. Wrapped in furs and layers of clothing, I felt reasonably warm. Sitting straight and tall in my saddle, I turned to smile at

Beowulf. He seemed deep in thought, so I turned my attention to our surroundings.

I could see the outline of bare birch trees quivering in the rising wind. Snow-clad firs lining the river towered over us like sentinels guarding our way. Occasionally a blanketed bough would release its load, showering us with cold, wet crystals. Beside us the Göta kept up a low gurgle, rippling over rocks between the icy shelves on either bank. From somewhere overhead a raucous crow noted our passage.

This land is beautiful, but it is a harsh beauty.

I shivered, then shifted in the saddle, settling myself for a long ride. The wind stung my face, and I reached up to pull my fur hood over my forehead. Burningfax gave a snort and lowered his head into the wind.

Cold. Cold. Cold. I'd never experienced such cold! Despite my furs and cloaks and leather breeches, the cold seeped into my very bones. Wind-whipped tears froze on my cheeks and my breath turned the rim of my hood into a ring of crystals. The only warmth came from Burningfax, who gamely forged ahead, sometimes turning his head to whinny at Frostmane.

From time to time I looked back at my women to see how they were faring. Estrid and Ingeborg looked miserable, but Runa appeared oblivious to the frigid conditions. In mute misery I rode on, my head bowed. When the pale sun stood high overhead, Beowulf called out, turning in his saddle. "Take heart! We will stop soon to build a fire and warm ourselves."

I nodded, unable to speak. By the time we finally halted, I felt stiff with cold, numb from head to toenail. Beowulf put out a hand to help me as I awkwardly dismounted. I walked about stamping my feet to regain feeling in my toes. Estrid and Ingeborg were doing the same. None of the men appeared to notice our discomfort.

Under Beowulf's direction a fire was started with wood and tinder hauled on one of the sledges. Some of our men broke branches from nearby trees to add fuel. My women and I huddled around the blaze, our teeth chattering. Runa helped set up a tripod and a cauldron of venison stew over the fire.

Ah, hot meat for the belly! That will restore our flagging spirits!

Silently I thanked Ana for preparing this travel food in advance of our journey. It was far too cold for much outdoor cooking! We ate noisily, stabbing chunks of frozen crisp bread into our bowls of stew as we stood in a circle around the fire. Suddenly Runa laughed and spoke.

"Look at us! We're eating as ravenously as a pack of wolves!"

"Wolves?" Shuddering, I stopped chewing and turned to Beowulf. "My lord, are we in danger from wolves on this journey?"

He too paused. "Wolves are always on the hunt in winter, but they would not attack a party as large as ours — besides, we are well armed," he concluded confidently.

One of the thralls tending to the horses let out a kind of squeak and blurted, "Wolves?"

I glanced in his direction. *Neither the thralls nor the animals have weapons!* The man was shivering, but whether from cold or fear I could not tell.

"Beowulf, tell me again: how many days will it take us to reach Uppsala?"

He frowned. "If we don't make too many stops, I'd say six or seven days."

Six or seven? Can we survive such a journey in this brutal cold?

My teeth were beginning to chatter again, but I clenched my jaws firmly together and tried to smile. Once back in the saddle I was surprised and pleased to find that I felt somewhat less uncomfortable. The trail ahead had become less difficult too, as if others had recently passed this way before us. Now Aksel, Lars, and Leif took the lead; the thralls and sledges fell back behind me and my women.

Perhaps, with Beowulf beside me, I can go anywhere and do anything!

Despite my determination to treat this as a grand adventure, my endurance was being severely tested. I tried to set a good example for my women, but Runa was the only one who seemed truly comfortable in her surroundings. The four of us shared a tent each night, glad for the warmth of our bodies and our sealskin bags. Sometimes we heard the howl of wolves, but their calls sounded far away, and our men took turns standing guard at night, pacing beside a small fire to keep warm.

As I lay awake I thought of Inga, wondering how she was faring without her mother, wondering if she missed me as much as I missed her... I prayed she was safe and warm in Hrethelskeep. Sometimes I had other thoughts, allowing myself to wonder how it would feel to reach out a hand and find Beowulf lying beside me, to listen to his breathing, a steady reassurance in the night. I banished such thoughts as quickly as they came, but still they came...

Runa and Estrid slept nearest the outside and Estrid complained bitterly, but Runa said not a word, rising each day as if she had slept on eiderdown beside a cozy hearth fire.

"How do you manage?" I asked her one morning.

"Manage what, my lady?" She looked up from lacing my reindeer boots. My own fingers had felt too stiff to do it, and my back too sore to bend.

"This, this trip with all its hardships," I said. "You remain cheerful while the rest of us are full of complaints!"

Runa laughed, tugging at the frozen laces.

"When I was a girl my grandfather took me with him while herding reindeer. I got used to the cold. Now it reminds me of happier days... There! You're ready!" She got to her feet, rubbing her hands together briskly.

In the days that followed we saw signs that other travelers had preceded us: the mark of sledge runners, a ring of ashes inside a wind shelter. Once we came upon the bones of a horse, one of its forelegs clearly broken. Wolves and carrion feeders had stripped away the flesh, leaving only skeletal remains.

One of our horses kicked a thrall and the man limped heavily thereafter, but he was still able to work and rode with the animals when we travelled. Another thrall complained of possibly frostbitten toes, but overall our group was faring well.

An unexpected delight came in the nightly displays of dancing lights in the northern sky. More than once we looked up from our campfire to see wavering bands of green and purple shimmering overhead.

"That's Thor waving his hammer," suggested Saxe at our first sighting.

"Or Valkyries," declared Aksel, "flying over our world looking for worthy heroes to take to Valhalla."

"But there is no battlefield here," I objected, "and I hope it stays that way!"

My women nodded in agreement, but the men's eyes brightened as if they were always ready for a fight.

Not until we came to the great Lake Vänern did we see another party. It was midday when we approached this vast sheet of ice, brilliant even in the weak sun. Beowulf called a halt and instructed the men to attach ice shoes to the horses' hooves.

Grateful for this respite, I dismounted, stretched my back and shoulders, and looked about. I could not be sure, but there appeared to be a large group of riders far ahead of us, almost lost in the glare of ice.

Glare. Ice. Suddenly I knew that I had seen this place before. Then it came to me: my vision — danger on the ice. Could we be in danger here? Now?

"Beowulf!" I called, interrupting him as he supervised the attachment of short iron spikes to the horses' hooves. "I sense danger!"

He strode forward, searching my face, then took my hands in his.

"Freaw, the ice is still very thick this late in the winter. You can see where others have already crossed." He gestured toward several wide paths clearly visible on the surface of the ice. "We are safe."

"No, I don't mean the ice. I mean . . . attackers," I finished, feeling a bit foolish but nevertheless determined.

"Where?" Beowulf looked over my head, then turned toward the frozen lake. "I see no one, except other travelers. Calm yourself, Freaw. We are safe, and we are nearly halfway to Uppsala."

He released my hands and returned to the other men.

Am I being foolish? But the vision was clear.

I raised my hand to my eyes and peered into the distance. Only a band of travelers. Beowulf must be right.

"Yes, my lady, I see them too." said Runa, coming to my side. "Headed for Uppsala."

"Beowulf says we'll reach Uppsala soon, that we've come almost half way," I told her, rearranging my furs. "Whatever we find there will be welcome after this long, hard journey!" I cried.

Runa lifted a hand as if to caution me. "The real challenges may lie ahead of us," she said quietly.

I stared at her and nodded. "From what Beowulf has told me, we are riding into the enemy's stronghold — into the heart of the Swedish kingdom," I said quietly. "We must be ever watchful for hints of hostility behind masks of hospitality. We must give the Swedes no excuse to attack us."

Runa nodded in return. "I will be watchful, my lady, I promise."

When I first introduced Burningfax to the ice of Lake Vänern, he balked, eyeing the slippery surface with distrust. Gradually the example of the more experienced horses gave him the confidence to set a cautious foot on it. Soon he was stepping out with the rest.

That day as we rode on, clattering over rough ice ridges and finally past the lake into thick forest, the weather began to soften — or had I just grown more used to it? No, others were noticing it too. Ingeborg threw back her hood and Estrid actually smiled. Beowulf said nothing, but urged his horse into a quicker pace.

We rode through another forest, we crossed another frozen lake, we found another forest, a river, and finally emerged onto a plain dotted with low hills. On the sixth day of our journey we began to breathe in moist air and sniffed a salt tang in the wind from the east. Our horses increased their speed, as if sensing a destination near at hand. Beowulf, however, grew more cautious, calling out to the three men in front and halting our party — to listen.

"For what?" I asked, patting Burningfax as he stamped impatiently.

"Other horses," he said. "Other travelers. We don't want to surprise anyone unnecessarily. By now most parties should have reached Uppsala. By my reckoning we should be arriving midway through the sacrifices."

Just then Aksel rode up to confirm Beowulf's supposition. "A party of horsemen just ahead, over that next rise, my lord. I'd say ten or more."

Beowulf nodded. "Keep a short distance behind. Give them space. We don't want to suggest anything hostile."

Aksel nodded in return and rode back to rejoin Lars and Leif. As we resumed our progress at a slower pace, I questioned Beowulf further.

"Why are we arriving at the midpoint of the blōt rather than at the beginning?"

He grimaced. "To save you and your ladies from some of the horror of the daily sacrifices: nine of each living creature. By the time we arrive the trees will already be full of carcasses — frozen, of course. They won't smell ... much."

My mouth fell open. *So he is serious about this: Trees. Full of ... carcasses ... corpses.* I asked no further questions.

"Remember, everyone," Beowulf called out, "Stay together and be alert, but wear a cheerful face. Take no unnecessary offense at whatever you encounter. We come in peace to worship the gods ... and we hope to depart in peace as well."

In an undertone to me he added, "May the gods be with us, and may Freawaru show her powers."

I gulped.

Long before we saw the houses themselves, we saw spirals of smoke rising from a sea of longhouses. I tried to count the long, thin plumes, but lost track as they faded in and out. Uppsala must be a great settlement indeed to have so many houses! As we drew nearer, my stomach tightened in a knot of fear.

What will we find here? How will we be received?

Chapter Fifteen
Uppsala

Swedish tapestry depicting the gods Odin, Thor and Freyr, 12th century.

Although I judged it to be only midday, light was already fading when we approached Uppsala. For as far as I could see a stout palisade fence rimmed the settlement. At intervals stood heavy wooden gates. From one of these gates a man on horseback emerged and rode toward us, a tiny figure in the waning light. As he drew closer I saw that he wore full armor and carried a sword.

At Beowulf's signal we reined in our horses. His three men in front fell back to join us, forming a shield around me. We sat in silence, waiting. As Burningfax stamped and snorted, my heart leapt wildly. *Stay calm, Freawaru. Be strong.*

The guard halted abruptly. "Hail, strangers. State your names and your purpose here," he barked.

Beowulf moved forward a step on his mount. He spoke calmly but clearly.

"I am Beowulf, son of Ecgtheow. I serve King Herdred of the Geats. We come from his court to represent him at this Great Blōt. These," he indicated with a sweep of his hand, "are my men."

The guard looked us over, taking his time.

"Your name is known to me, Lord Beowulf, but who are these women?"

Now I nudged Burningfax forward one pace and drew myself up in the saddle.

"I am Freawaru, daughter of King Hrothgar of the Danes, wife of Ingeld the Heathobard. I come as a seeress of the Geats. These are my women."

The man's eyes widened, then narrowed.

"Hrothgar, eh? And Ingeld? We'd heard they were both dead!" he said bluntly. "Nevertheless the king will want to see you. He is not in residence at the moment, but his sons will greet you in the mead hall. Come. I'll show you where to leave your carts and provisions and the stables for your horses. Follow me."

He turned and rode off without a backward glance. We followed, passing through a wide gate which slowly closed behind us, pushed by panting thralls. I noticed other guards staring at us as we passed by. Thus we entered the strangeness of Uppsala.

Uppsala! I had never seen so many houses, so many people packed into one place! The lanes were filled with men of all description, on foot and on horseback. Some wore costumes strange to me. I saw baggy pants and tight-fitting vests beneath their open cloaks, and they wore boots up to the knee.

"Those are likely Rus," murmured Runa coming up beside me. "They live beyond the Baltic Sea."

No one seemed to take notice of us new arrivals — except for one individual who caught my eye: a tall, gaunt man in a dark cloak. Something about him seemed familiar, but he was soon lost to sight as our party pressed forward through the throng.

After seeing our horses stabled, carts stowed, and space made for our thralls in the crowded lofts above the animal pens, we were escorted to the mead hall by our guard, who called himself 'Stig.' Othere's hall was clearly the largest building in the settlement, rising above the surrounding houses like a great bird sheltering its young. Like my father's hall its outer walls gleamed with gold in the torchlight, for by now darkness had fallen.

At the entrance Stig delivered us to the hall guard, who beckoned us forward, pushing open heavy double doors. As we stepped inside, we were met with a blaze of torchlight, our faces bathed in heat from a roaring hearth fire. The blast of sound was almost as great, for the hall was filled with men drinking, laughing, talking, and quarreling.

As we traversed the length of the hall, Beowulf and I in the lead walking hand-in-hand, the noise gradually fell away. We stopped at the far end before two elaborately carved thrones. Lounging on them, drinking horns in hand, sat two young men. One, a beardless fellow with pale hair, sat up and gave a loud belch.

"Nels, what have you brought us?"

The guard made a low bow, then waved his hand at us.

"Lord Beowulf of the Geats. Lady Freawaru of the Danes — and also of the Geats."

Now the other young man sat up. His hair was darker and he stroked a thin mustache. I judged him to be the older of the two.

"Beowulf, eh? I've heard of you. You're a monster-killer they say. Too bad you're a Geat, but welcome to Uppsala — especially welcome when you bring us such beautiful women!"

This was not at all what I had expected! Where were the manners of a royal court? My eyes narrowed in indignation, and Beowulf's hand settled atop his sword hilt, but he spoke in a conversational tone.

"Thank you, my lords. I should warn you that Lady Freawaru can divine men's secret thoughts, and is formidable when angered."

Now both young men sat up even straighter and exchanged looks. The darker one rose and made a slight bow.

"Eanmund and Eadgils at your service, my lady. On behalf of our father, King Othere, we welcome you to Uppsala."

I bowed in return. "Thank you, my lords."

You will have reason to thank the Geats one day when your father is gone!

Where did these words in my head come from? Yet, I sensed disaster ahead for these two young fools!

Now a deeper voice spoke from behind me as another man stepped forward.

"Freawaru of the Danes? Would you be Hrothgar's daughter?"

This man looked to be older than Hrothgar himself. He spoke with authority and carried himself like a king.

"Yes, my lord, I am Freawaru, Hrothgar's only daughter. How do you know my father?"

He chuckled, a dry laugh without mirth. "I am Onela, married to your father's only sister." He chuckled again, turning toward Eanmund and Eadgils. "Nephews, this lady comes from a royal house. You will do well to treat her with great courtesy." His tone was sharp.

During this exchange Beowulf and the rest of our group had stood quietly, awaiting the outcome. Now Onela spoke again.

"Your aunt and I would be honored to entertain you — and your women — in our longhouse during your stay in Uppsala, if that would please you?"

His words were gracious, but his eyes shone with a sinister intensity. For a moment I could not speak, seeking the intent behind his invitation. Finally, curiosity about the aunt I had never met overcame my caution.

"Thank you, my lord. I accept with pleasure — that is," I turned back to Beowulf — "if my companions are also given suitable lodgings."

Onela bowed. "Of course. I am sure my nephews can arrange that. Uppsala is full of celebrants, but we always have special places for warriors such as Beowulf."

Again he smiled the smile that was not a smile. Eanmund and Eadgils now roused themselves.

"You men there, make room at your table for Beowulf and his men. We will all drink together and hear their tales!"

Drink? What we really need is hot food at the end of our long, cold journey!

Beowulf apparently shared my thought, for he spoke a few low words to Nels about arrangements before signaling our men to join him at a table. To me he whispered, "Go with Onela, but be on your guard. Tomorrow we will know better where we stand with the Swedish court."

We bowed to each other and I bowed to the two brothers before allowing Onela to lead me from the hall. Estrid and Ingeborg were chattering excitedly behind us, but Runa kept silent. I hoped she was taking note of each person we encountered, so we could later compare our observations.

"My longhouse is quite near," Onela was saying at my side, "and I'm sure you'll welcome the walk after a day of riding." He took my elbow, steering me along. "Your aunt will be pleased to see you — even though your arrival in Uppsala was not expected. We had heard ... but there will be time later for talk, after meat."

Meat? Suddenly I felt ravenous. Meat would be most welcome! As we walked out into the frosty night, the cold air only whetted my appetite.

Onela's longhouse was almost as large and splendid as the mead hall. When we entered, I looked around discreetly. Fine tapestries lined the walls and the benches were topped with thick furs. Wonderful aromas rose from steaming cook pots. I sniffed: some kind of fish soup, and boiled pork.

Servants scurried about carrying food to the long table set beside the hearth and setting out bowls and glasses — real glasses, not wooden mugs. I counted a dozen places. A large household to feed! Onela beckoned a serving girl to bring us towels and wash water.

"Refresh yourselves, ladies, while I fetch my wife." He disappeared behind a partition at one end of the house.

Now I was in a quandary. Runa's dress did not reveal her status as a servant, but it would not be proper for her to dine with us and our hosts. Apparently she sensed my dilemma, for she said softly, "I'll see if any help is needed with the serving," and slipped away.

The woman who entered on the arm of her husband looked older than my mother, but her years sat lightly upon her. She was dressed in a dark blue wool tunic edged with gold thread over a finely-pleated white kirtle. Between silver brooches hung a string of beads: crystal, amber, carnelian, and more silver. Clearly Onela could afford to adorn his wife with fine jewelry! A few wisps of white hair strayed from a fine linen head cloth embroidered with runes.

Runes! I must find out how else she uses them!

Her clear, gray eyes observed me shrewdly, but when she spoke her voice was low and soft.

"So . . . Freawaru. My brother's daughter. Welcome."

She glided forward to embrace me. I felt the thinness of her body under its rich trappings, but her grasp was strong. Her scent suddenly filled me with nostalgia for my old home in Denmark. She smelled of dried herbs — just like Mother after she'd prepared an herbal remedy for one of our family members.

"Aunt Yrs," I said, gently disengaging myself and making a low bow.

"In this country they call me 'Ursula,'" she replied, extending her hand. "Come. You shall sit beside me at meat and tell me of Heorot." She led me to the head of the table.

That night I took an instant liking to this unknown aunt of mine, but was mindful of the need for caution. Although tempted to pour out my heart to her, I gave Ursula only the barest outline of the events at Heorot — and at Wulfhaus, for she had heard of my marriage to Ingeld.

"So, they are gone. Hrothgar, the brother who carried me on his shoulders when I was a girl. Ingeld, the man who should have been your mate for life. Destroyed by each other in a futile feud..." Her voice trailed off. "We shall speak more of this later. Now you must be longing for your bed."

At these words the weight of the day seemed to settle on my shoulders.

"Yes, Aunt Ursula. I will welcome bed — especially a warm bed. Thank you for your most gracious hospitality."

I looked around, realizing that we two were the only ones left at the table, which had already been cleared. Onela had disappeared. I heard Ingeborg and Estrid talking softly somewhere in the background.

"Benches are ready for you and your women." Ursula pointed toward the long side wall. "Your servant has gone with my house thralls to the loft over the byre. Tonight everyone in my house will sleep in safety." She smiled at me warmly. "Your arrival is a gift from the goddess, Freawaru, a gift from the goddess."

I awoke with a gasp from a dream in which Aunt Ursula's sweet face had changed into Gudfrid's face: wild-eyed and muttering curses.

Gudfrid! I must learn more about that woman — how she lived, how she died.

Rubbing sleep from my eyes, I sat up and looked about. Two women stood by the hearth, stirring something in the large iron cauldron hung over the fire. One of them was Runa. I beckoned to her and she came quickly to my sleeping bench.

"Did you rest well, my lady?" she asked in a low voice.

"Yes, Runa, better than I have for many nights. But tell me..." I looked around at the other benches where blanketed forms lay snoring and lowered my own voice. "What did you learn from the servants last night? Anything that will help us?"

She made a wry face and knelt beside the bench to speak into my ear.

Fanning the Flames

"Your aunt is held in high regard, but your uncle is feared by many. There are whispers that he has been slowly poisoning the king. No one has seen Othere in the mead hall for months."

Hmmm. Mere servants' gossip? I wonder... Yet it was Othere's sons who greeted us in the mead hall, not Othere himself.

Aloud I said, "Thank you, Runa. I will take porridge as soon as it is ready."

Runa returned to the hearth. I rose and began pulling clothes on over my nightdress. A rustle from the end of the room caught my ear and I turned to see Aunt Ursula emerging from her chamber, dressed much more simply that she had been the day before. She saw me looking at her plain attire and came forward.

"Onela wants us all to attend the sacrifices today, and I do hate getting bloodstains on my best gowns!"

My stomach tightened. I blurted out, "We brought animals for sacrifice. Will they be used today?"

"You'll have to ask your uncle. He is in charge of such things. It will be our duty — nay, our pleasure — to show you the temple and its surroundings." She turned to the servants at the hearth. "Is the gruel ready? We'll need to feed our guests and get an early start on the day."

As we ate, I asked Aunt Ursula about the runes embroidered on her head cloth.

"I noticed that you chose runes of good fortune and protection: Gebo, Eihwaz, Algiz. Are you the rune-mistress here?"

Ursula laughed, a true laugh. "No, not at all. Those were the favorite runes of my former mother-in-law, who put them everywhere. Even the benches, including the one where you slept, bear such inscriptions."

I froze. *Her mother-in-law? That would be Gudfrid!*

Casually I said, "My former mother-in-law had no such love for me. She was a difficult woman."

Ursula sighed. "Mine had a very hard life, even as queen. She lost her husband in a war with the Geats when I was just a young bride. That was years ago, yet I feel her restless presence every day."

"Do you?" I exclaimed. "Perhaps her spirit has not found peace, perhaps..."

I was interrupted by the entrance from outside of Onela, followed by Beowulf! He gave me a reassuring grin as he paused beside Onela, shaking snowflakes from his hair.

"Good morrow, ladies. Today we honor Thor with our sacrifices," announced Onela. "You are all invited to witness the proceedings and take part as you wish."

I shivered. *So, at last I am to see the temple and its gods. But what of the goddess? That is another topic I must explore with Aunt Ursula.*

We women rose from the table and began to pull out cloaks and furs from our traveling chests. I held up the fox-fur cloak for Beowulf's approval, but he shook his head and mouthed 'save it.' Apparently the trial of my powers would not come today.

Outside the longhouse our horses were waiting. I greeted Burningfax with affection and swung myself into the saddle like a practiced horsewoman.

"The temple is located on the other side of the River Fyris," explained Ursula as we rode, "closer to the sea and the site of the great burial mounds."

"Mounds?" I echoed. "I see only one in the distance, but it's the biggest one I've ever seen!"

"That would be Ottar's mound. Others will follow. The temple area is sacred, reserved for the bodies of kings."

"Does Ongentheow lie there?" I asked, then immediately regretted my rashness.

"No, his body was never recovered from the war — one of Gudfrid's many sorrows," said Ursula soberly.

We crossed the shallow river at an icy ford. Above us a leaden sky promised more snow. As we gained higher ground, I squinted my eyes looking east. A tall shape like a ship's mast emerged out of the morning mist.

"What is that?" I asked Ursula, pointing.

"The Great Tree," she said reverently, "the tree that lives evergreen. Have you not heard of it?"

"I know of Yggdrasil, the World Tree," I answered. "Surely this is not the same tree?"

"Who is to say?" murmured Ursula. "At the base of The Great Tree lies a well fed by a sacred spring. Rites to the goddess take place there. Healings have happened there. It is my favorite place," she concluded, then fixed me with a questioning look. "Do you worship the goddess?"

"Yes, oh yes! She has put her mark upon me..."

I was about to say more, but Onela and Beowulf now urged their horses forward and we were obliged to follow.

Soon we came upon a clearing dominated by a tall, looming timber structure, roofed but open on one side. Wind-whipped snow obscured the view, but as we drew near the clouds parted momentarily and a burst of sunlight illuminated the interior.

"Behold, the temple!" cried Onela.

I gasped in amazement. Tilting back my head I gazed in awe at three gigantic statues, three tall wooden pillars carved and heavily gilded, reflecting the sunlight with blinding brilliance, three gods seated on a triple throne.

The central figure brandished a huge hammer. Thor. To his right sat one-eyed Odin in full armor with a handful of weapons. To Thor's left sat Freyr, clasping his own enormous penis.

Only gradually did I become aware of human figures kneeling at the base of each statue. I looked at Ursula inquiringly.

"Priests," she whispered. "They attend the gods during the festivals, offering up each day's sacrifice."

Sacrifice? Ah, yes, the purpose — one purpose — of our journey.

Our group dismounted, handing the reins to attendants who appeared as if by magic. Onela led us forward, a hushed group, treading the now-falling snow. I regretted that Runa could not be with us, so I tried to fix every detail in my mind to tell her later.

The temple was situated at the edge of a large open area. Clustered to one side stood a few low buildings, balanced by a grove of trees on the other. Towering above everything, The Great Tree spread its massive branches. It was hard to believe that such a place existed, yet here I stood, in its very heart. Behind me I heard excited whispers from my women, and Saxe giving a long whistle of astonishment.

"What are your thoughts, Freawaru?" Onela's voice brought me back to the present. He was gazing at me with a curious expression — respectful, yet arrogant.

"I am filled with wonder, Lord Onela, and fear, almost. This place is overwhelming, yet splendid."

He smiled in apparent satisfaction. "A fitting response from the daughter of King Hrothgar." He paused. "You may call me 'Uncle'."

I gave a slight bow. "Thank you, Uncle."

Beowulf now joined us. "What is the order of the ceremony, Lord Onela? We have brought a fine boar to be sacrificed whenever you deem it appropriate to offer it."

Onela acknowledged Beowulf with a slight tilt of the head.

"The creatures already chosen will be sacrificed first, starting with a cock and ending with a slave. It will take most of the day to slay them and hang them in the sacred grove. After that, your offering will be welcome."

Slaying. Hanging. Steady, Freawaru. You can no longer hide from slaughtering as you did when a child. You are a woman grown, a king's daughter.

Beowulf shot me an understanding look and turned to address Onela.

"Perhaps the ladies could be excused until this evening, then?"

Onela's retort was immediate and emphatic.

"No! I wish to give Lady Freawaru the honor of taking part in the ritual. She may slay one creature of her choice."

Me? Is this some sort of test?

"I would not choose to slay a horse, nor to take a human life," I heard myself say.

"As you wish," said Onela, bowing. He turned away to give orders to a group of men approaching from the side buildings and motioned for Beowulf to come with him.

I felt a slight pressure on my arm. Aunt Ursula.

"Pick the smallest; it will bleed the least," she murmured.

"Have you done this before?" I asked in surprise.

"No, women are not usually participants, but I've witnessed many sacrifices. Your uncle seeks to honor you . . ." She paused, looking in his direction. "I wonder why?"

A crowd had begun to assemble in front of the temple, but except for those in our own group, there was not a woman in sight. Behind us flames crackled as bonfires were lit all around the clearing — a welcome antidote to the damp chill of the morning.

Within the open-sided temple, priests were setting up tall iron lamps and filling them with oil. Soon their flames added wavering light and somber shadows to the giant statues looming over us. As I looked about, searching for Beowulf in the crowd, a different man caught my attention: the same man I'd seen among the throng upon our arrival in Uppsala.

"Pardon me," I said to Aunt Ursula. "I think I see someone familiar..." Abruptly I separated from our cluster of women, drawn toward the stranger only a few paces away.

His back was turned to me as he stood between two men of enormous height and girth. These giants were dressed in skins and furs, reminding me of animals. As if feeling my eyes on him, the cloaked man slowly turned. I took a step back and inhaled sharply. Could it be...?

"Freawaru? Lady Freawaru!" The man stepped forward and made a deep bow.

"Unferth? Unferth, it *is* you! What are you doing here, old friend?"

Unferth's dark, deep-set eyes with their crazed, faraway look gazed back at me out of a face thinner than the one I remembered.

"I could ask the same of you, my lady, but I presume you are here to honor the gods — as are we."

He beckoned to the two hulking figures who came up to stare at me with open curiosity. One wrinkled his nose as if sniffing the air; the other drew a hand across his mouth as if tasting something bitter.

"Let me present my companions, Bodvar Bjarki and Hjalti," said Unferth. "This is the Lady Freawaru, daughter of our late king, Hrothgar."

Both men bowed. A multitude of questions swirled in my brain, but one rose uppermost. I could not restrain myself.

"Unferth. Does my mother live?"

He paused before answering. "Truthfully, I do not know. She left Heorot shortly after your departure. She did not reveal her destination."

Mother... alive... gone... where could she be?

By now Estrid, Ingeborg, and Ursula had joined us. My women were clearly astonished to see Unferth again, but nodded without speaking. When I introduced the men to my aunt, she looked at Unferth sharply.

"So, you are the representative from King Hrothulf's court? I heard Onela speak of you."

King Hrothulf. Hearing that title and that name together smote my heart.

Unferth bowed. "Yes, my lady, we have come from Denmark at the invitation of the Swedish court."

A note of warning sounded far back in my brain. On the one hand, what could be more natural than two royal families renewing old ties? Yet, why now?

Ursula took my arm and nodded to Unferth. "You must excuse us. Lady Freawaru is to take part in the ceremony this morning and she needs to make her choice of sacrifice."

Unferth's eyes widened, but he gave another deep bow and let us pass. Ursula steered me toward the row of low buildings beside the temple. As we neared them I heard grunts and bellows, barks and bleats.

"Here are the separate enclosures for each creature to be sacrificed," Ursula was saying. "You may wish to examine them before making your selection."

She nodded curtly at the first attendant we encountered. He quickly swung open the shed door and I peered into the dim interior. It looked to be a byre like any other, with stalls, mangers and feeding troughs enclosed with wattle fencing.

In sequence I inspected all the possible offerings: roosters, cats, dogs, sheep, goats, pigs, oxen, and horses. I shook my head when the last attendant eagerly offered to display the human offerings shackled inside a shed no larger or taller than the rest. Like the other attendants the man's dirty face, layers of rags, and cropped hair marked him as a thrall, but he flashed a toothy grin. Perhaps he felt grateful to have escaped the fate of the captives he guarded.

What should I choose? If I'm to show strength — of will and character — it should be a large animal. Perhaps a pig? A goat? In the stories Thor travels with goats...

Closing my eyes, I mentally felt inside my rune bag. My fingers closed on... Uruz! The wild ox! Transformation! Death releasing new life!

"The aurochs," I said aloud. "I mean, the ox. I choose the ox."

"Well done," beamed Ursula. "Let's find Onela and tell him."

The rest of the morning passed in a blur. We watched as, one by one, each creature was brought from its shed, briefly sprinkled with water from the sacred well, then presented to the priest who stood before Thor's statue, knife in hand. A low stone altar at the foot of the god stood ready to receive the victim.

The knife rose. The knife fell. Blood spurted forth, to be caught in a sacred cup. After streaking his cheeks with blood, the priest poured the rest of it at the base of the statue, uttering prayers to Thor, giving thanks for his protection in the past, entreating his favor in the days ahead. Each creature's remains were then carted off to be hung in the grove nearby.

By midday the cock, the cat, the dog, and the ram had been offered up to Thor. Between sacrifices our group visited one of the bonfires to warm our hands and faces and pass around provisions from our travel packs. Cold food on a cold day. I shivered, longing for the hot porridge we'd sampled that morning. Beowulf noticed me trembling and came to stand beside me.

"Are you worried, my Freaw, about your role in this blood-letting?" Frowning he put his arm around me.

"No, I'm just cold," I replied. "I am ready. I have been shown the jugular vein that I must sever. I know what to do and I will do it."

Beowulf looked at me with admiration in his eyes.

"Freaw, you are unlike any woman I have ever known!"

I wrinkled my nose and smiled.

"I will accept that as praise, not criticism, my lord."

Beowulf had opened his mouth to reply when Onela approached, looking somewhat distracted.

"Lady Freawaru, it is time to prepare for the sacrifice of the ox, and my wife insists that you be provided with a protective apron. Please come with me."

Obediently I followed my uncle, with one backward glance of reassurance at Beowulf.

By the time the ox was brought out, I had taken my position beside the priest. We stood to one side of the altar, facing the approaching animal. The priest held a heavy hammer, its handle inlaid with gold in a lightning-bolt pattern. I held the sacred knife, its long, curved damascened blade wiped clean of blood from the previous sacrifice. Two thralls led the ox up to the altar with a rope tied to each horn. The priest raised the hammer high over his head.

"Thor, mighty thunderer, we dedicate this bull to you!"

The hammer came down squarely on the beast's forehead with a chilling thud. The ox, still partially held by the ropes, sank to its knees. I stepped forward and took a deep breath. After the attendants raised the lolling head, I drew the knife blade forcefully across the bulging vein in its neck. Blood poured out in a steaming torrent onto the altar stone. I exhaled in relief.

There! It is over! I have done my part!

The priest caught some of the blood in his cup, then dipped a finger. He daubed his own face, then carefully marked my cold cheeks with the hot blood.

As I approached our group, waiting nearby in the clearing, my women stared in awe at my blood-streaked face.

"How soon may I wipe this off?" I murmured to Aunt Ursula.

"Not until tonight. Wear it with honor. You've created quite a stir, my dear. Look around you."

I turned my head to find many eyes upon me. A few men were muttering and shaking their heads, but several gazed at me with open admiration. Unferth was one of them. He left his companions abruptly to come up and bow before me.

"Lady Freawaru, you continue to astonish me," he declared, with something that looked almost like a smile.

"Unferth? Well met in this place. Freaw told me you were here in Uppsala." Beowulf strode up to clasp Unferth by the shoulders. "How long are you staying?"

"We leave in three days to return to Denmark — after the final sacrifice to Odin."

"You and your companions must join me and my men in the mead hall tonight."

"With pleasure, my lord."

Beowulf inclined his head toward me. "Unferth, what did you think of Lady Freawaru's performance today? Was she not impressive?"

Unferth nodded. "She has learned her lessons well. She no longer needs a teacher."

I flushed with pleasure at all this attention, but the next sacrifice was about to begin — the horse sacrifice, which I wished to avoid.

"Aunt Ursula, would it be discourteous to leave now?" I whispered hoarsely.

"Yes," she said simply, "but we do not have to witness the remaining sacrifices at close range. Come. Let's move back toward the fire."

Although I tried not to look, I caught a glimpse of the horse being offered to Thor: a dun-colored horse that looked much like my own Burningfax. I also heard its whinny before the hammer descended. As for the human offering, I saw only a thin, dark-haired fellow who looked as if he'd been drugged — possibly a kindness offered to captives slated for sacrifice.

Why do the gods demand sacrifice? Or ... do they? Perhaps it is only we humans who desire the spilling of blood.

Darkness had long since fallen over the clearing when it came time for Beowulf to offer the boar we had brought from Hrethelskeep. It was a fine fat pig with formidable bristles and long, sharp tushes.

"We will eat well in the mead hall tomorrow," observed Onela, eyeing the boar.

"So, it will not be hung in the grove?" I asked innocently.

"No, only the official sacrifices performed by the priests go there. All others are used to provide meat for the celebrants — like your group," he explained. He appeared to be in an expansive mood.

"Uncle," I began, then paused. What I really wanted to ask could wait for another occasion. "Uncle, thank you for the honor you paid me — allowing me to be a celebrant."

With the help of our men, Beowulf managed the boar sacrifice gracefully and cleanly, slitting the animal's throat before it had time to struggle or register alarm. At last, this long ordeal was over.

On the ride back into Uppsala I spoke not at all. Although emotionally exhausted, I maintained a queenly bearing as Burningfax carried me safely home. Home? Yes, home for the moment. That night we all sought our benches immediately after meat. I slipped into a dreamless sleep.

Our second day in Uppsala was not a repeat of the first. After the morning meal I stopped Uncle Onela as he was about to leave the mead hall and asked if I could see Freyr's sacred white horses — before they were all sacrificed. He seemed gratified by my interest.

"I cannot take you myself, as I must preside over today's ceremonies in honor of Freyr. If Beowulf and his men care to join you, I'll provide an escort to take you to the place where the horses are now being kept."

"I would like that very much. Thank you, Uncle." Then, almost as an afterthought, I asked the question that had been lurking in my mind. "Uncle, why does King Othere not appear at the sacrifices? Is he ill?"

Onela's face betrayed no emotion, but his voice took on an edge.

"That is not your business, my lady. I have taken his place — temporarily — during the festival." He raised an eyebrow. "Have you not been treated well here?" His eyes bored into mine.

"Yes, very well. I just thought if he is ill, I have herbs in my bag..."

"Think you we have no healers in Uppsala?" He almost spat. "My own wife is a mistress of herbs. Now, about those horses..."

He turned and barked an order to one of the house thralls, who hastily scurried out the door, followed by Onela himself.

When I queried Estrid and Ingeborg, they displayed no interest in horses of any kind. They wanted to stay inside with Ursula and try their hands at a new weaving technique she had mentioned. Runa looked at me beseechingly, but I could think of no excuse for her to join me.

Beowulf and all six of our men arrived shortly thereafter, eager to see the famous horses dedicated to Freyr. With them came Stig, the guard who had met us outside Uppsala upon our arrival.

"Not on duty today?" I asked pleasantly.

"No, my lady. With the festival more than half over, there are fewer newcomers to inspect."

Stig looked much less intimidating by daylight than he had in the dark. A sallow, pimply fellow, he wore no armor today and carried no sword, but he was full of enthusiasm for Freyr's horses.

"They are one of the glories of Uppsala!" He declared with pride. "You've never seen anything like them!"

"Too bad they are slated to die," I murmured. Stig looked shocked.

"Oh, no! We must give all possible homage to Freyr. He is the father of our land, the founder of our royal line! No sacrifice is too great to honor Freyr! He brings us life, good health, and good fortune!"

"I see, I see," I smiled. "Well, lead us to them!"

Mounting Burningfax, I settled myself gingerly in the saddle. Once again riding beside Beowulf, I set off happily, looking forward to what the day might offer. It was another frosty morning, but one with streaks of sunlight sparkling on the snow. Once again we crossed the river, but this time we skirted the temple area, passing near the sacred grove with its latest offerings. We paused briefly to honor the sacrifices.

Crows and kites fluttered above the branches laden with half-frozen forms. On the ground vultures clustered around fallen remains, pecking at pieces on the blood-stained snow. One human figure caught my eye. From its clothes I recognized the ragged slave sacrificed yesterday.

His eyes were already gone and his face hung in scraps. I shuddered and turned away from the gruesome sight.

Stig noticed my aversion and laughed out loud. "You'd like it even less at night, my lady. Rats! Hundreds of 'em crawling over the carcasses. Why, they..."

"Stig, tell us about the horses," interjected Beowulf. "Do you breed them here, or trade for them abroad?"

"Both," replied Stig. "They come from distant lands. I'm told the Arabs race 'em in the desert."

By now we were nearing a fenced enclosure containing a barn as long as a house. The stable doors stood open.

"You are in luck," called Stig. "They've been let out for exercise."

I narrowed my eyes against the sunlight, but gradually detected several white forms that blended into the snow-covered pasture. One high-spirited stallion neighed and reared, pawing the air with its hooves. We reined in our own horses beside the palisade fence.

"How beautiful!" I breathed in awe. Some of the elegant creatures trotted toward the fence at our approach, snorting through unusually wide nostrils. Their smooth coats appeared both white and black to me, for I saw dark skin beneath their light hair. We sat for a time, gazing at these handsome beasts.

"So, one of these will die today?" I asked Stig.

"Yes, one each day in which Freyr is honored." He nodded emphatically. "But as you see we have both mares and stallions for breeding stock."

Mentally I stroked the long, silky neck of the stallion, wondering how it would feel to ride such a glorious creature.

"Stig, have *you* ever tried to ride one?" I asked.

Stig gave a harsh laugh. "Me? Only if I wanted to die! No man — or woman — is allowed to mount a horse sacred to Freyr!"

"Thank you, Stig," said Beowulf. "We need to get back. I'll be offering a boar to Freyr later, and some of my men wish to witness the earlier ceremonies."

I saw Saxe, Gorm, and Aksel nod their heads, so I turned my horse away from the fence. Soon we were riding back toward Uppsala.

Our men headed straight for the temple, but Stig and Beowulf accompanied me back to Onela's longhouse. Then they too departed. It was not until the next day that I heard a full report — from Olaf — of what took place that day at the sacrifices to Freyr.

We were standing beside the door inside Onela's longhouse. Olaf had brought me some items I'd requested from our sledges.

"The sacrifices followed the same order as yesterday," he began, "but at the end it erupted into lewd songs and wild dances." He shook his head. "One priest dressed like a woman made advances to the male priest, pulling up his tunic and thrusting out her — his — hips. The male priest must have hidden a long stick under his cloak, which he waggled in front of him like Freyr himself! Some of the drinkers watching laughed and cheered. Not me. I was glad you were not present, my lady. It was no place for a woman of dignity."

Olaf's face had turned scarlet during the telling of this story. I nodded sympathetically.

"I had heard that Freyr's rituals could be somewhat... crude. But tell me about Beowulf. Was the boar sacrifice well executed?"

Olaf brightened. "Yes, my lady. Beowulf chose a splendid boar — the golden one, you remember it — everyone who saw the animal remarked on its size and virility — like Freyr's own Gullinborsti, they said."

It pleased me to hear that Beowulf's second sacrifice had gone well. Dismissing Olaf with my thanks, I returned to the hearthside.

During that second day in Uppsala I too was busy, inside Onela's longhouse talking with Aunt Ursula about her mother-in-law, Gudfrid. As Ursula stood at her loom I pulled up a stool to sit beside her. Cautiously I revealed a few details about what I suspected to be Gudfrid's curse, touching lightly on her captivity in Hrethelskeep. Ursula listened attentively before responding.

"Her spirit was strong — and bitter after Ongentheow's death. She wanted to die with her husband, and raged against the Geats for sparing her."

"How *did* she die?"

Ursula looked around to see if anyone were near and lowered her voice.

"She drowned herself. In the sacred well. Beneath the Great Tree."

"Drowned? How horrible! But, was there a funeral pyre? A proper burial?"

Ursula bit her lip. "Some would say so. I would not. You must understand..." She turned to face me. "It was a time of confusion and uncertainty. The kingdom was in upheaval. Warring factions sought the throne. The proper burial of one old woman was not a high priority — for some." She gazed at me sadly. "The fate of Gudfrid has lain on my heart for many a winter. Perhaps, Freawaru, you have been sent by the goddess to help Gudfrid find rest — at last."

"Perhaps. Aunt, I will do what I can. Will you help me?"

"I will, but we must wait until the cycle of sacrifices has ended. Then the temple ground can be ours."

We embraced, sister and daughter of Hrothgar.

Our third day in Uppsala was a day dedicated to Odin. I knew that Unferth would surely attend the ceremonies for the god he worshipped above all others, so I sent word to Beowulf that I wished to go to the temple that day. Once again my women were content to stay with Ursula.

"One bloodbath was enough," declared Estrid. "How can you stand it, my lady?"

"It is my duty to 'stand it'," I said firmly. "Besides, I have much to ask Unferth about conditions back in Heorot."

"Heorot," sighed Ingeborg. "Don't you miss it sometimes, my lady?"

"Of course, but my life — our life — is with the Geats now. Have you been unhappy in Hrethelskeep?"

Ingeborg and Estrid looked at each other. Ingeborg spoke.

"No, my lady, but it would be nice to experience court life again."

"Do you mean you'd like to see more of Aksel?" I teased. Both flushed. "After this trip perhaps we'll all see more of court life," I said. "Now, I must get ready for today's ceremony."

Chapter Sixteen
Putting to Rest

Bronze amulet representing a priest of the cult of Odin, c. 800 A.D.

"You've not yet worn your red fox cloak, my lady. Would you wish to display that treasure today? You may need it." As Runa held up the tawny coat of pelts for my consideration, her face held an unspoken message.

"Hmm. Yes, thank you, Runa, I will. I too have a feeling this cloak may be useful today."

Runa looked at me closely. "Have you received a vision, my lady?"

"No, not exactly, but I sense something unusual in this place. More and more I feel that Uppsala is inhabited by spirits. I wonder. Could they be the spirits of those sacrificed in the temple? For two nights I've heard voices, cries and whispers, in my sleep. One voice is growing stronger. It may be . . . Gudfrid's," I concluded hoarsely, my throat suddenly constricting.

"Oh, my lady, should you go out today? Are you in any danger?" Runa touched my elbow lightly as if to hold me back.

"To live is to be in danger, Runa. Yes, I will go out, prepared as much as I can be for whatever lies ahead. Hand me the cloak."

When we arrived, the now familiar temple ritual had already begun. On this occasion the priest of Odin presented a dark and ominous appearance, for he wore a black hood that covered most of his face. His voice, cold as ice, cut through the morning fog as he offered the first sacrifice.

"Odin, we invoke your presence," he intoned. "Grant your followers courage, wisdom, and victory in battle. We sacrifice this life in tribute to your powers, great god."

I did not flinch as the knife descended and blood spurted from the cock's throat onto the altar stone. Beside me Runa drew a quick breath, but her eyes shone with curiosity as she looked about, taking in every detail of her surroundings. To our mutual satisfaction, Runa had been allowed to join me today. Aunt Ursula had urged me to take along a female attendant, saying that it was not fitting for a woman of my status to be alone in a crowd of men.

The usual throng of worshippers had gathered before the temple; others stood in small groups around the bonfires, for the fog was chill. Beowulf and I led our group to one side where Unferth and his companions stood waiting, as if expecting our arrival.

"We meet again, my lady." Unferth made a deep bow. "Do you wish to wield the knife again today?" he asked upon rising.

"No, no more of that, thank you," I responded lightly.

"Then perhaps you would be willing to undertake a different challenge — as a favor to your admirers?"

Perplexed, I took a step back. "What do you mean? What kind of challenge?"

"I've been talking to Lord Onela. He wishes to witness the gifts he's heard about — your gifts from the goddess."

"Uncle Onela? He's said nothing to me..."

Beowulf now joined the conversation.

"Lady Freawaru, I too spoke to Onela of your gifts, at the mead hall last night. I told him of your visions, of your role in finding the young king when he was lost. I told him that you are a seeress, a woman of power. Why, even now you are wearing the proof — see, Unferth?" He gestured to my fox, fur cloak. "This was her reward from Queen Hygd for finding the lost Herdred."

"If Onela wishes to test my powers, why is he not here himself?" I asked in some exasperation.

"He is, my dear."

I turned to see Onela advancing, wearing that thin-lipped smile of his. Two heavyset, serious-faced men accompanied him.

"May I introduce two of King Othere's councilors? Lord Kjell and Lord Jörgen. They too are curious about your powers."

Something like panic rose in my throat. I swallowed hard to force it down.

What will these men require of me? Why did Beowulf not warn me that this was coming?

As if reading my mind, Onela answered my questions.

"To make this a true test, we did not give you time for advance preparation," he said, smiling. "Here is what we propose. Unferth has told us that you met his companions only yesterday and have no knowledge of their background or lineage."

Onela beckoned for the two men to step forward.

"Tell us, Lady, if you are willing, what is revealed to you when you study their faces? What can you tell us of their past, or their future?"

Onela stepped back, leaving a wide space between me and the proposed subjects.

Ignoring them, I stepped forward and faced Onela squarely.

"My lord, the goddess is not a servant who will answer to your bidding or mine. Only in moments of extreme need or when faced with matters of dire consequence do I call upon her. Such a calling is not undertaken lightly, and requires certain rituals to be successful."

Straightening my shoulders, I lifted my head.

"You are my host and my kinsman, Lord Onela, but I am not yours to command. Furthermore, this public confrontation is unseemly." I gestured to the growing circle of curious onlookers. "If there is information you seek, let us find a more private setting — for your good as well as mine. You might not, for example, wish the whole of Uppsala to know that you have failed to honor a sacred ancestor whose spirit even now roams abroad — your own mother!"

Onela's eyes widened. He had opened his mouth to speak, but at my last words he closed it suddenly and held up a hand as if to forestall further disclosures.

"I have a small room near the temple, a private chamber. Let us retire there. Come."

Onela's small chamber was sumptuously fitted with furs and hangings. Its hearth radiated warmth, and jugs of ale sat ready on a low table. It made a stark contrast to the holding pens nearby. As we entered, Onela noted my surprise.

"So, there are some things you do *not* foresee," he commented dryly.

"Indeed, Uncle — yet I am honored to receive what the goddess reveals to me."

Our men were bidden to wait outside as Onela, the two councilors, Unferth and his two companions, Beowulf, Runa, and I crowded into the narrow space. Instinctively I positioned myself at the head of the table, flanked by Beowulf and Runa. Onela stood opposite me, the councilors to his left, Unferth and his companions to his right. This arrangement put me in mind of pieces on a game board. I made the opening move.

"Lord Onela, you wish for a demonstration of my gifts, but the challenge you have set can be met without resort to the goddess. To begin with this man . . ." I pointed to Bodvar Bjarki. "As his name, 'Little Bear', his dress and his manner all indicate, he is a shape-shifter, a warrior who can fight in animal form. Am I right, Bodvar Bjarki?"

The giant man shifted his weight and growled, "Yes, you speak true."

I smiled. "Bodvar, you are fortunate in your powers. No doubt you will one day become a great king's champion. As for you . . ." I pointed to his companion, "your name and appearance have changed, but I recognize in your face a stripling once called 'Hott,' the butt of bones and abuse at Hrothulf's table. What have you tasted, Hjalti, that has altered you so?" — for the man continually wiped his lips.

Hjalti's mouth fell open. "Dragon's blood," he croaked. "Bodvar made me do it!"

His hand went to his mouth but he jerked it down, frowning fiercely as laughter escaped from the spectators.

"Fear not, Hjalti, you too will one day earn your fame as a warrior — if you stay beside your friend here. Now . . ." I looked squarely at Onela, "are you satisfied, my lord?"

Onela made a slight bow from his end of the table. His eyes locked on mine.

"An impressive performance, my lady. I congratulate you."

"Thank you, Uncle. I have questions for *you* concerning Gudfrid — but we can address those later. Now I wish to speak with Unferth, for news of Heorot."

Onela glanced at the two councilors, who turned away from me sharply as if to avoid my gaze. Did they fear me? Beside me Beowulf murmured, "Well done, my Freaw."

"Have you heard enough, my lords?" Onela was heading for the door. "You may use this chamber as long as you wish, my lady." He bowed and led out the rest of the group, leaving Unferth and me together with my companions.

I asked Runa to pour ale for the three of us, but Beowulf declined it, withdrawing to a bench beside the door. Unferth and I raised our cups in a toast of friendship.

"I cannot stay long, Lady Freawaru. I brought a special horse to offer to Odin, and Onela is graciously allowing me to assist the priest in its sacrifice."

"Unferth, just what is your relationship with Onela?" I blurted.

He fixed me with his hooded eyes. "We may become allies, my lady. But, you have questions about Heorot?"

"Yes, I do." I said, noting Unferth's polite but rapid change of subject. "Tell me about Hrothulf. What is he like, as a king?"

Unferth took a swallow of ale and wiped his lips.

"Hrothulf is not now the man you once knew," he began.

"Really? Is he worse?" I snapped.

"No. Better." Unferth smiled broadly. "After he took the blow to the head that I delivered, he changed."

I stared at Unferth, remembering the butt of the axe head descending, buying time for me and my people to escape from Heorot.

"... more warriors every day, many of them berserkers, and the mead hall has been rebuilt. Heorot once again shines with its former glory!"

I could scarce believe my ears, but I had other questions. "Unferth, what of my brothers? Were they given proper burial?"

Unferth nodded. "Yes, before she disappeared, overseeing the funeral pyre was your mother's last act."

I was about to ask for details of mother's disappearance, when a knock sounded. Beowulf opened the door to reveal Stig.

"Lord Onela sends word that your sacrifice is next, Lord Unferth. He bids you hurry."

Unferth rose, bowing apologetically. "I have answered your questions, Lady Freawaru. Now I must go—but you may wish to see the horse I've brought. It may look familiar. Please come...?"

With a glance at Runa and Beowulf, I followed Unferth out the door.

From one of the holding sheds an attendant led out a beautiful dappled gray horse. The handsome, well-muscled beast reminded me of father's old warhorse, but Gullifax had been sacrificed at father's funeral pyre, on the burning ship. I looked at Unferth in perplexity.

"The son of Gullifax," he explained. "This stallion has been my special care, raised to become an offering to Odin." He nodded in satisfaction as he stroked the animal's powerful withers.

"Then how can you bear to give him up?" I exclaimed.

"For Odin, no sacrifice is too great!" he cried. "The pain of loss adds to its value as an offering."

Mutely I absorbed these words, recalling the dear old days when I rode behind my father, clinging to his back. In silence I watched Unferth conduct the horse to Odin's altar, but I looked away as he joined the priest in its ritual slaughter. Hearing a sob behind me, I looked over my shoulder to see Runa standing with bowed head.

Looking up, she murmured, "So this is what I've been missing? I do not need to see more, my lady. May we go now?"

"No, we must wait until the official sacrifices have been concluded. Then Beowulf will be offering the boar we brought. After that we will go."

Runa bowed her head again.

This time Beowulf sacrificed a black boar, leaner and smaller than the previous two offerings.

"Not enough meat to feed all the warriors in Valhalla," commented Unferth, who had stayed to witness our sacrifice.

"Our boar cannot regenerate each day like Odin's Sæhrimnir, but it was fattened on acorns, so its meat should be flavorful," I retorted. "Perhaps you'll be sampling it in the mead hall tomorrow."

"Nay, I must leave in the morning to return to King Hrothulf's court," said Unferth.

"So soon? I had hoped for more talk."

A sudden thought struck me.

Hrothulf. Is he still my enemy? Should I fear him?

"Tell me, Unferth, when you get back to Heorot, if you speak of me at all, what will you say of me to King... to Hrothulf?"

Unferth gave a slight bow. "I will tell him that Hrothgar's daughter has become a vǫlva, a seeress, respected and feared by all who meet her. Now I must go. Farewell, Freawaru."

For a moment we looked at each other, our shared history holding us a moment longer. What was it he had said about the pain of loss?

Once again we part. Unferth, I will miss you. You have brought back precious memories.

"Farewell, old friend."

Unferth turned and disappeared among the worshippers leaving the temple grounds.

"Come, Runa. It is time for us to leave as well. Let us find Beowulf."

That night Onela joined us women in the longhouse after the evening meal.

"Lady Freawaru, my wife tells me that you have a matter of importance to discuss with us?"

Ursula nodded and rose from her place at the table.

"We can talk in my chamber," she said, leading the way.

Onela pushed aside the heavy wine-colored tapestry draped over the doorway and we entered a spacious bedchamber, lit with oil lamps on shelves around the walls. He let fall the drape, closing out the clatter of crockery being cleared and distant voices. Pointing me to an elaborately carved chair in the corner, he and Ursula seated themselves on the ornately carved bed—a fine one, I noted, but no finer than my bed in Hrethelskeep.

"Now," he said coldly, "what is this talk of Gudfrid?" He leaned back, crossing his arms.

"Lord Onela, Uncle, I have seen your mother in Hrethelskeep. I have heard her voice here in Uppsala. Her spirit has never found rest."

Onela stared at me in obvious disbelief.

"What right have you to speak of my mother? She died before you were born. You know nothing of her!"

"She came to me, Uncle, I did not seek her. From the land of the dead she calls out to the living. We must heed her cries. Look!"

From inside my tunic I pulled out a small package of dark blue cloth. Placing it on my lap, I unfolded it to reveal the contents: a long, faded braid of once-golden hair.

Ursula clutched Onela's arm and gasped. "Husband! Your mother was missing one braid! That's how we identified the body in the well."

Onela glared at me. "How did this come into your possession?" he demanded.

I rose, carried the cloth to Onela, and placed it in his lap. Then I told him of its discovery in the byre, of the nightly visitations by his mother's spirit, of her rune-curses dug into the benches at Hrethelskeep. He listened with bowed head as I gave my account. Slowly he lifted the braid, feeling its weight, then gently stroked its silky softness.

"My mother. I have not thought of her in years."

When he raised his eyes, moisture glistened in the corners.

"I have doubted you, Freawaru, but I see that you have gifts — significant powers — that I and others do not." He took a deep breath. "What should be done? What do you recommend?"

"Aunt Ursula and I wish to perform a ceremony after the festival is over, a ritual to appease Gudfrid's angry spirit. But something lasting should also be done."

I paused. "Uncle, to be forgotten is to cease to exist. Your mother longs to be remembered. You could give her what she wants," I said quietly. When he nodded, I continued.

"Perhaps a stone erected in her memory, a memorial stone raised by her two sons?"

A slow smile began to lift the corners of Onela's thin lips.

"I see. A public monument, a pious tribute from dutiful sons — who happen to be the kings of Sweden!" His smile bloomed. "You are a gifted woman, Freawaru, and a clever one. But why should you bother yourself with this matter? How does it benefit you?"

"As I said, Uncle, I did not choose this task, it was thrust upon me."

Onela was silent for a time, looking from me to Ursula, who placed an arm around his shoulder. Finally he spoke.

"I give my permission for you and Ursula to use the temple grounds for your ritual. I will even consult my calendar to see if the chosen day is propitious for a sacrifice. And I will erect a memorial stone on behalf of Othere and myself," he concluded with a wry twist of the lips.

"You have shown courage, Freawaru, in bringing this matter before us. Should I thank you — or the goddess?" His eyes narrowed.

"Uncle, as your nine-day festival has shown, we all seek the good will of the gods. The goddesses are no less powerful."

Onela rose and made a low bow.

"I go to rejoin our guests in the mead hall — and to savor more of that excellent pork you Geats brought us." A true smile spread across his face. "Goodnight, ladies."

He gave Ursula a gentle embrace, then lifted the tapestry and left the chamber. Ursula came over to put her hands on my shoulders.

"Thank you, Freawaru. Your uncle is a hard man to sway, but you have impressed him." She frowned. "Onela is much like his mother. I pray that our efforts to appease her will be equally successful."

The next morning Ursula invited me and my women to join her and her women in the sauna.

"A ritual cleansing is necessary after all that bloodshed," she declared, shaking her head vigorously.

I gladly accepted the invitation and soon found myself in a steaming bath-house surrounded by sweating bodies. Carefully, slowly, I drew in deep breaths of the thick, moist air, letting it fill me and cleanse me, inside and out.

Runa assisted Ursula's servants, pouring water on the hot rocks and softening birch bundles in the steam for later use. When I looked around I saw other women stretching their backs and rolling their shoulders. Ah, yes — after the tension generated by the past few days, the sauna provided a welcome release. Blissfully I shut my eyes.

Suddenly a hand touched my shoulder. I looked up to see Ursula gazing down at me in amazement.

"What's this I see? What's this mark below your shoulder?"

"You see what I cannot, Aunt, but I am told it is the mark of Freyja, a sign of her presence in my life."

Ursula climbed down to sit beside me, her plump thighs pressing against mine as she whispered in my ear.

"Thanks be to the goddess. You have been blessed, my dear. Now I know why you were chosen to be her messenger. Tomorrow we will gather in her name to give Gudfrid a proper farewell."

She squeezed my thigh with surprising strength, then called to her servants. "More steam!"

The next morning a small group of women gathered beside the sacred well, under the Great Tree: Ursula and three of her women, and Estrid, Ingeborg, Runa, and I. Without the usual crowd of worshippers, the temple grounds were notably bare and empty. Black against the trampled snow, low mounds of ashes marked the location of past bonfires. We had brought our own fire with us in the torch I carried.

The heavy, dark temple, scene of so many grisly sacrifices, was almost transformed now by slanting rays of winter sunlight, but we turned our backs to the temple, focusing instead on the Tree of Life and a special altar which had been erected for our use. Without speaking, we formed a circle around the stone altar.

Ursula stepped forward with a silver flask, from which she poured oil into the altar's shallow bowl. I ignited it with my torch. The flame spread, filling the bowl with fire. I handed the torch to Ingeborg, paused, then called aloud.

"Freyja, great goddess, be with us in this place. We assemble here to honor you, and, with your blessing, to honor our sister, Gudfrid."

Now Ursula handed me the wrapping containing Gudfrid's hair. Gently I removed the braid and laid it on the bed of flames. Stepping back, I loosened my headcloth to reach the lock I had tied off previously. Estrid handed me the sacrificial knife. Severing the red-gold curl, I placed it in the bowl of fire. Ursula too separated out a lock of hair, white this time, and leaned forward toward my knife. Soon three lengths of hair lay curling in the flames. We drew back from the acrid smoke that spiraled upward.

"Goddess!" I cried, lifting my arms, "We give you a part of Gudfrid and a part of ourselves. We beseech you: receive Gudfrid into your keeping. Give her rest in the house of the dead. Welcome her into Fōlkvang."

Ursula too raised her voice in supplication. "Gudfrid of the golden braids, fly to the arms of Freyja and shelter there. Be now at rest, leaving us in peace."

At a nod from me, Runa drew out her flute and played one, long, lingering note. I lifted my voice to join it and soon a song of sorrow rose in the air, a keening wail. We mourned the death of a woman unknown to some of us, yet a woman like ourselves with a woman's joys and sorrows.

When the lamentations ceased and the smoke subsided, Ursula reached inside her cloak and drew out a small leather bag. Opening the drawstring, she put a thumb and forefinger inside, withdrawing a dark substance which she sprinkled liberally on the remaining fire. Immediately a sweet smell arose, replacing the previous acrid aroma.

"Cinnamon," she said, "obtained from the Rus in trade. It is rare and costly — Gudfrid's favorite spice."

Everyone drew a breath, inhaling the sweetness. Soon nothing remained of the three lengths of hair. Quietly we drew back from the altar and turned our faces toward Uppsala.

On the night before our departure from Uppsala, I was once again invited to Aunt Ursula's bedchamber — for one last talk, "woman-to-woman" she said. I started to take a seat across from her, but she put an arm around my waist and drew me to sit beside her on the bed.

"Freawaru. Hrothgar's daughter. You have become very dear to me in these past few days." She gazed at me with affection. "I was not blessed with a daughter — and all my sons have died," she confided, lowering her eyes. Then she looked up and smiled. "I would like to give you something of mine to take back with you — in memory of our time together, and... to keep you from danger."

Reaching behind her neck she untied her head covering, a pure white cloth edged with embroidered runes. She laid it in my lap.

As I touched the finely-woven cloth, tears sprang into my eyes.

"Thank you, Aunt Ursula. I will treasure this always."

Turning toward her, I reached out both arms and we met in a warm embrace. When we disengaged, Ursula gave a low chuckle.

"Gudfrid's runes of protection. May they cancel all her curses and keep you safe on your journey home. Now," she said rising, "you will need more provisions for your travels. I've already had my servants pack a barrel of our best Baltic herring, and Onela is providing two casks of ale."

"Thank you again, dear aunt." I rose to join her. "I must confess that I had doubts about coming to Uppsala, but your hospitality has made me feel most welcome."

Ursula took my arm as we turned toward the doorway.

"I hope you won't wait nine years before returning to us."

"Nine years? Oh, yes, the next Great Blōt. Who can say? If the goddess wills it," I responded.

"Just a moment." Ursula paused beside a long, low chest against one wall. "I should show you Onela's rune staff, the calendar he spoke of earlier."

She bent over, using one of the keys that hung at her waist to open the chest. Lifting the lid, she reached down, took out a long object wrapped in linen, and laid it on the bed.

"Go ahead. Unwrap it."

Curious, I folded back the cloth. Inside lay a long wooden staff carved with three long rows of repeating runes and other symbols. I stared in awe at this repository of time.

"Onela could give you more details, but I know that it holds a record of solstices, equinoxes, and moon cycles. Onela gets it out every year to mark the first full moon after the winter solstice — the first day of the Great Blōt."

"Did he carve these runes himself?" I asked in wonder.

"No, not Onela." Ursula chuckled again. "Gudfrid. She was the rune master at court."

"Gudfrid?" I looked at Ursula. "What an amazing woman, what a powerful woman!"

Ursula nodded. "As are you, Freawaru, but do not be tempted to use your powers wrongfully. I am no seeress, but I fear that dark days may lie before you. Onela..." She stopped and lowered her voice. "Onela does not love the Geats!"

I gave her a wry smile.

"I think Beowulf is well aware of that, Aunt. And I have had visions of war hanging over us. We must face what comes to us as best we can," I concluded. "Now, goodnight, Aunt. We will say our final farewells in the morning."

Once again we embraced and I left her chamber, holding the head cloth against my heart.

Despite our affectionate parting, I spent a restless night under Aunt Ursula's roof. For a long time I lay awake, reviewing all I had experienced during our stay in Uppsala. Finally I drifted into fitful sleep.

When I opened my eyes again, I stood alone at an open door, looking into a vast, snow-covered landscape. Not a sound came to me. Stepping out, I did not flinch as my bare feet met the cold snow, but walked steadily toward the open river.

How can I cross? Even as I asked the question I found myself on the other side, rapidly approaching the temple. In the distance a dark, wide stain was spreading toward me over the snow.

Black-robed priests flew over my head, fluttering toward the sacred grove. There they circled, dark crows above a carrion feast. Human bodies hung from every tree — hundreds of bodies — trickling blood that swelled into a river, crimsoning the snow, covering my feet, lapping at my ankles.... I screamed, but made no sound.

Suddenly I stood amidst the grove, bodies suspended all around me. Directly before my eyes hung Ana, her throat slit. No! Not Ana! In horror I recoiled, bumping against another body. Thora? No! I whirled to face... Wulfgar... then Brita... then Magnus.

Is there no escape? Above me the crows cackled wildly. I reached out blindly; my fingers touched a small body, a child's body, its face grimaced in a rictus of death. It was... Inga. No! Not my child!

With a shriek I bolted upright, panting and sweating, to find myself still on a sleeping bench in Onela's longhouse. Nearby my women had roused and were stumbling sleepily to attend me. I sat frozen for a moment, then trembled, shaking off the horror.

"Just a dream... a terrible dream... but it is over," I said at last. "It is time to go home."

The next morning when Beowulf and our men came to collect me and my women at Onela's longhouse, I noticed that Lars' lips were bruised and swollen. Taking Olaf aside, I made a discreet inquiry.

"What happened to *him*?" I asked, inclining my head in Lars' direction.

"Oh, he ran into Stig's fist last night in the mead hall." Olaf bobbed his head in evident satisfaction.

"Why? What caused the fight?"

"You, my lady," said Olaf cheerfully. "Lars made a disrespectful remark about you being a witch. Stig set down his ale cup, stood up, knocked Lars off the bench and sat down to resume drinking." Olaf was grinning from ear to ear. "Don't worry, my lady. Lars can't say anything else against you — he lost a front tooth."

Aghast at this turn of events, I nonetheless smiled inwardly.

So, Stig stood up for me! Apparently I have at least one friend among the Swedes. But I do not need Lars as an enemy among the Geats!

"Thank you for the information, Olaf. I'll make a poultice for Lars' mouth at our first stop on the journey homeward."

We made our farewells briefly, for the weather had turned again, promising snow, and Beowulf wanted to get an early start. Aunt Ursula embraced me tenderly, and reached up to touch a bit of the head cloth tucked beneath my fur cap.

"May the goddess go with you, my dear," she murmured.

Onela gave a formal bow, then bent to brush my cheek with his lips.

"May the goddess help you discern your true friends from your enemies," he said gravely. As he looked up, his eyes strayed to our group, mounted and ready to depart.

Can he mean Lars? Has he heard of the mead hall incident? Or... is he looking at Beowulf?

"Goodbye, Uncle. I will remember you always with the greatest affection."

How wrong I was in that pronouncement.

Chapter Seventeen
Battle on the Ice

Great iron battle axe inlaid with silver wire from Mammen, Jutland, Denmark.

After our return from Uppsala, I expected my life to continue as it had before the journey: raising my daughter, overseeing my household, exercising leadership in the village, and welcoming occasional visits from Beowulf. For a time this pattern continued.

Beowulf was taking every possible precaution to ensure the safety of the Geats' kingdom. He formulated specific plans to counterattack any Swedish assault, whether it arrived by sea or over land. Provisions were set aside to feed an army on the move. The smiths at Eaglesgard and Hrethelskeep worked daily producing more weapons, and more armor. At both settlements, any male big enough to hold a sword engaged in training for combat.

During this time I sought desperately to penetrate the mists that hid the future from my eyes. Over and over I came up against a wall of white and a sheet of ice. Only once did a new image enter my vision: I saw the wooden sword Herdred had used as a child being cast into the flames.

What could this mean? I asked myself. Am I seeing the past, instead of the future? When no clear answers came to me I often despaired, but over time the threat of war gradually receded from my consciousness.

Inga was a girl of six winters when it started, the same age I had been when the Grendel monster invaded Heorot. The summer before we had heard the news of King Othere's death, of the Swedish throne being usurped by his brother Onela, and of Othere's two sons' flight to Geatland in search of protection. Despite Beowulf's warning of the danger involved in sheltering royal refugees, Herdred had taken them in.

We heard all this from Aksel, a frequent visitor at Hrethelskeep since he had begun courting Estrid. We were standing outside, for I and my women were weeding in the garden when he rode in on his big roan horse. Aksel had little good to say about the Swedish princes.

"That Eanmund expects to be waited on constantly and given the best of everything. He demands rather than accepts the hospitality of the court. And Eadgils is worse, if possible, but in a sly, underhanded way. He tries to make you feel as if you're not doing enough for him, that he deserves more than he's getting."

Aksel spat in disgust.

"Why does King Herdred let them stay at Eaglesgard?" inquired Estrid, flushing with pleasure at Aksel's arrival.

"King Herdred has a generous heart and only sees good in others," said Aksel. "He could not turn away these suppliants, especially since they were wrongfully deprived of their kingdom." He shook his head. "There will be trouble. From what I've heard of Onela, he won't tolerate any challenge to his position — and as long as they are alive, Eanmund and Eadgils will be threats!"

Onela. Uncle. Do you remember Freawaru?

I still thought of Herdred as a child, but Aksel informed me that the king was now a young man grown taller than his mother and eager to make his own decisions. Too eager, perhaps. Aksel shook his head again.

"Beowulf sends word that Hrethelskeep should put its men on fighting alert. I've already spoken to Wulfgar — and I'll be able to stay for dinner," he concluded, with a look at Estrid's face. Immediately her fading smile reappeared.

We spent an anxious summer waiting for hostile signs from the Swedes. Autumn came and went; slowly we began to relax our vigilance. Soon it was Yule and time for the annual slaughter of domestic animals for winter use. All around me the clearing bristled with activity: cauldrons being hung on tripods over open fires, racks of fish being set to smoke over other fires, dogs barking, children squealing with excitement as they ran among their mothers. I was in the midst of cleaning entrails for sausage-making, a new method of food preservation introduced by Runa, when we heard the distant rumble of hooves.

Hastily wiping my hands on my apron, I called, "Inga? Where are you? Come here!"

A giggling someone grabbed my knees from behind. I whirled to catch her up and shake her gently before setting her down.

"What are you playing, child?"

Inga's blue eyes shone bright with merriment.

"War, mother! I'm a Geat and Toke is a Swede. I can't let him catch me!"

"No, you can't let him catch you," I repeated, my heart in my throat as the sound of horses drew nearer. "Run inside now. Ana has a treat for you!"

Without hesitation Inga turned and ran for the door of our longhouse. Instinctively I felt for the knife hanging inside my dress. From the sound, I judged there to be many horses, many more than the usual small band of visitors.

They are coming from the south. Can they be Swedish warriors? Have they already overcome Eaglesgard?

Panic rose in my throat. All around me other women had stopped their work, lifting their heads and looking about in alarm. Someone shouted.

"Where are the village guards? Where are our men?"

Suddenly Gorm burst into the clearing, panting.

"It's a war party, but it's our own — Beowulf and the men from Eaglesgard. Quick! We'll need to gather provisions and join them! We're heading north!"

Beowulf? North? I don't understand.

Other men were flooding into the clearing on foot, Magnus and Wulfgar in the lead. All wore battle gear. I ran forward to meet them.

"Wulfgar, what's happening? What have you been told?"

Wulfgar's face looked grim but resolute.

"It's what we've been waiting for, my lady: war with the Swedes. Training is over! A large army is coming from Uppsala, led by Onela. We must intercept them before they can reach Hrethelskeep!"

He sounded almost glad, eager for a fight. My mouth fell open and my hand flew to my chest. For a moment I could not breathe.

War! Has it come to this?

"Women, the time we dreaded is here—but we are ready," I cried, recovering. A number of women had clustered around us, seeking direction. "Pull out the provisions we prepared, pack the wagons with food and other supplies—but do it quickly so our men can join Beowulf's warriors."

Ragnhild, who had given birth to her first child a month earlier, ran up to Wulfgar. "Not all our men are leaving, are they? You won't need—Thorkel?"

"No, no," said Wulfgar in reassurance. "We'll leave behind a home guard with Magnus in charge of defense, but we'll need every other able-bodied man in the village to join Beowulf."

Behind Wulfgar I saw Saxe and Gorm leading up horses, and thralls pulling out the sledges we'd used for the trip to the Great Blōt. How long ago that seemed now! In another moment Beowulf himself appeared, riding beside Herdred and the two Swedish princes. Bringing Frostmane to a halt, he swung down from the saddle to envelop me in his strong arms.

"Freaw," he cried, releasing me, "Time is short. You must be strong. We go to war against Onela's forces."

"How do you know they are coming?" I cried breathlessly.

Beowulf almost smiled.

"Stig sent me a message—by a trusted thrall. Stig was loyal to King Othere and secretly supports Othere's sons."

My eyes widened. "Stig? Not the guard who..."

"...defended you at Uppsala? Yes, the same man," replied Beowulf. "According to Stig, Onela planned to set out after Yule on the new moon. That means he will be leaving Uppsala soon. We will intercept him at Lake Vänern. Surprise is our best chance for victory."

Lake Vänern. A battle on the ice. Just as I saw it.

"How many Swedes will you face?" I asked anxiously.

"Enough," he said gruffly. "With the men from Hrethelskeep added to our ranks we will be a formidable force. Nevertheless, while we are gone, arm all the women."

My head reeled as I took in the implication behind his words, and my fingernails dug into his forearms. With a conscious effort I strove to control the trembling that seized my body.

"I'll do all I can," I croaked.

"I know you will. Now, I need a word with Magnus before we go."

Go? So soon? Will you be gone ... forever?

"Wait!" On impulse I pulled off my head covering, the cloth embroidered with Gudfrid's runes. "Take this with you and wear it on your person. It's for protection."

Beowulf glanced at the cloth in surprise, but took it from my trembling hands and tucked it inside his tunic.

"You'll wear a byrnie into battle, won't you?" I implored desperately, not caring that I sounded like a mother admonishing her child.

"Yes, of course. Our mail shirts are loaded in a sledge with our helmets and weapons. Fear not, Freawaru. I will return to you."

He pulled me close in another embrace and kissed me hard on the top of my head.

"Now I must go."

Next I sought out Herdred, sitting tall and proud on his horse. Despite the beginnings of a mustache on his upper lip, his cheeks wore the bloom of youth.

"Freaw!" he called out. "We meet again! Look! I can carry my father's sword now!" He pulled back his fur cloak to reveal a long scabbard strapped to his waist.

"Greetings, my king. I pray it will serve you well."

Reaching up, I touched his knee, but further words deserted me.

"Don't worry, Freaw. We'll show those Swedes how the Geats can fight! I promised Eanmund and Eadgils that I would protect them, and I will keep my word!"

I stared mutely at Herdred, dark thoughts flooding my mind.

Young man, this is no time for mead-hall boasting! You may be leading your people into disaster — like your father before you!

As I tried to manage a smile, a vision, an image of his boyhood sword perishing in flames, suddenly passed before my eyes. I blinked.

"King Herdred ..."

"Yes, Freaw? What do you see?"

"I see ... that you've grown," I finished lamely.

Herdred laughed, a clear, ringing, boyish laugh.

"Yes, I am a man now! Farewell, Freawaru! I go to war!"

He wheeled his horse and rode off to join the other men pouring into the clearing. Soon he was lost to my sight. As I watched him go, I felt a choking sensation and suddenly realized: Herdred is the one in most danger, not Beowulf!

Eanmund and Eadgils glanced at me in recognition and gave token bows from their horses, but I spoke not a word to either. Had these two not brought war upon us? Even if they were the rightful heirs to the Swedish throne, did they have the right to involve us in their conflict?

The reproachful faces of my two dead brothers unexpectedly rose before me. They too had been denied the throne by a usurper. Did I not wish to destroy their destroyer? Shaken with these thoughts, I moaned in confusion.

Unferth once told me that Hrothulf was more fit to rule than either of my two brothers....Would not Onela be a better king than either of the two princes? Yet Uncle Onela might kill my beloved Beowulf—just as my father killed my husband!

Runa's strong hand on my shoulder brought me back to the moment.

"My lady, our men are leaving. You should bid them farewell."

Runa's face looked anxiously into mine.

Beowulf had been shouting orders, lining up men and horses. All the wagon beds had been lifted off their wheels and placed on sledges to travel better over snow. Now Beowulf took his place beside Herdred at the head of the line, Eanmund and Eadgils just behind them.

"We ride to war!" cried Beowulf. "May the gods be with us!"

"May the gods be with you!" I shouted, running forward and lifting my arms to the sky. "May you ride to victory!"

"Victory!" echoed the warriors.

"Victory!" shouted the remaining villagers, although tears streamed down many a face.

As the procession began to move, a small figure burst from the doorway of my longhouse: Inga, followed by Ana, at a run.

"Beowulf," cried Inga, darting forward, but her voice was lost in the din of horses and groaning sledges. "Beowulf," she sobbed, now running to my side. "Will he come back, Mother? Will he return to us?"

"If the gods are willing." I gathered my child in my arms and held her close.

In our "home guard" Magnus and Orm would command a handful of old men and young boys. All were trained in the use of sword and battle-axe, and two of the boys were good shots with bow and arrow. All had sturdy round shields of wood, but only Magnus and Orm owned metal helmets. A few owned spears. I had noticed several bundles of spears in Beowulf's cart and bundles of arrows.

Of course! Beowulf wants to use the open ice on Lake Vänern for a long-range attack!

When the last sledge had disappeared, I shook off my reverie and called out to Magnus.

"Yes, my lady?" Magnus approached briskly, his age falling away with each step. The threat of war seemed to have given him new life.

"Are there swords enough to arm the women, as Beowulf requested?"

Before he could reply, Ana spoke, suddenly appearing at my side.

"Swords? Shouldn't we be thinking about the children? Maybe collecting them in one place where we can defend them as a group?"

"Lady Freaw, Lady Freaw, you must call upon the goddess to protect us!" shouted a voice from the edge of a growing crowd of agitated women, pressing around me.

I looked beyond them to the clearing spattered with blood and offal.

"Quiet, everyone. We'd best finish our butchering first and clean up this mess. Tonight we can meet in the mead hall to make further plans. What say you, Magnus?"

"I agree," he said gruffly. "Listen to Lady Freawaru, all of you. She speaks wisely."

Despite the gravity of the situation, I felt a flush of pleasure at Magnus' words. We exchanged bows and he left abruptly. Each woman returned to her interrupted task of the morning. I reached down to touch Inga.

"Come, little one. You can help me. It takes more than two hands to fill sausage casings."

My hands trembled as I picked up a length of intestine. Suddenly I seemed to see a man sprawled on the ground, his belly split open, entrails exposed.

No! Beowulf! I cannot lose you!

Had I cried aloud? I glanced at Inga, but her face showed no alarm.

Goddess, what have I done? By giving up Beowulf to save my child, have I doomed him? Spare him ... save him! Beowulf, you must come back to me!

Hot tears splashed on my fingers. As I reached up to wipe them away, Inga laid her soft hand on mine.

"Don't worry, Mother. He'll come back."

I managed a weak smile. "Of course he will."

Oh Beowulf, come back and make me your wife! I'm ready now — to go with you and spend the rest of my life with you. Come back, my love!

By nightfall our work was finished. As the early dark of winter descended on Hrethelskeep, in every longhouse oil lamps were lighted and hearth fires stirred, to cook our food and raise our spirits.

That evening every free woman in the village entered the mead hall and took her place among friends and neighbors. The older women, including Sigrid and Ortrud, took places near the front. Thora, her neighbor Solveig, and her friends Agata and Tove sat down next, followed by the younger women; among them were Ragnhild with her new son Torvald, Marta with her twins, and Laila — who I noticed was pregnant again. Gunnlaug and Gyrid helped herd in the children, including Inga, for Ana had chosen to assist old Gunilla, now totally blind and barely able to walk.

An air of dread and anticipation hung over the hall, for almost every woman had seen a son or husband follow Beowulf off to war. Our remaining men and boys clustered to one side as Magnus, Orm, and I took our places in the facing chairs at front. At a nod from Magnus, I opened the assembly.

"People of Hrethelskeep, hear me! We place our trust in Beowulf and our men, but we must be ready to defend ourselves if it should come to that."

Murmurs of agreement rippled across the hall.

"The men are well armed," I continued, "but we women have only knives of various sorts. Orm here is offering swords to all who wish to wield one. The choice must be yours."

I heard a few gasps and a shout or two from the women seated before me. A tall figure rose and signaled for my attention.

"Yes, Sigrid?"

"Lady, begging your pardon, but we must also consider a danger here at home: our thralls! Some of them might be glad to see us destroyed by the Swedes — and would even help them! I personally locked my slaves in the cow byre tonight. Others might want to follow my example!"

Now Ortrud stood up.

"Any thrall who lifts a hand against me will get his head split open! I can wield an axe as well as any man!"

Nervous laughter greeted this announcement. Both Sigrid and Ortrud sat back down, apparently satisfied with their contributions. Magnus rose next.

"First, I would advise each family to hide its treasures — if you haven't already done so — until the danger is past. Next, you women can help keep watch, taking turns with the men. We'll need guards posted day and night. Come talk to me if you are willing and able." He looked at me. "Anything else, my lady?"

"Yes. We must prepare a sacrifice to the gods. I ask each household to contribute an offering. We can use our slaughtering space to hold the ceremony. I will also consult my runes for further direction."

Nods of approval met this announcement.

"You'll need a new altar for the sacrifice," said Orm, rising from his chair. "I will make it — and I have the swords ready at my forge."

So it was settled.

Magnus and I were the last to leave the mead hall that night. The energy he'd displayed earlier seemed to have left him, and I noticed a definite limp as we walked together toward my long house.

"Now comes the hard part," he said.

"What do you mean?" I hazarded a hand on his arm. He did not shake it off.

"Waiting — that's the worst. I'd rather be in the thick of the fray than waiting for it to begin," he growled.

"You would be a formidable fighter in any fray, Magnus. I'm glad you're on my side."

He stopped and turned to look at me in the half-moon's light.

"I am. It's our side now. Good night, my lady. Here is your door."

Before I could respond, he had walked away, still limping.

Runa met me at the entrance. "Oh, my lady, I've heard an owl cry three times. Do you think it's an omen?"

I sighed wearily. "Probably just another hunter seeking its prey. Come outside with me for a moment. I'm not ready to go in yet."

Obediently Runa fetched a cloak and slipped outside to join me in the semi-darkness. Breathing in the frosty air, I closed my eyes, trying to clear my mind of all but this moment, a moment of peace.

"Look, my lady! What's that crossing the moon?"

My eyelids flew open. "What? What did you see? Tell me!"

"Something...a huge thing with wings...not a bird...flying across the moon's half face. It seemed to be trailing...smoke?"

"What do *you* think it was?" I asked, my heart racing with recognition.

"I've never seen anything like it before, but...could it be a dragon? It put me in mind of a dragon...." She shivered.

I put my hands on her shoulders. "Yes, it could be. I saw one in the night sky above Eaglesgard, trailing smoke and fire."

"Fire?" She shivered again. "Let this not be an omen that we will perish by fire!"

"Runa! The Swedes may try to set our homes on fire—just as the Heathobards destroyed the mead hall at Heorot! We must defend against fire! We'll instruct every family to bring up buckets of water from the river to store in their houses and we'll get Orm to open the hole in the ice with his hammer. This was a lucky omen, Runa!"

"Are you sure you have read it aright, my lady?" she asked meekly.

"Whether I have or not, there is a clear warning here. Tomorrow we will alert everyone to the danger of fire."

On the morrow we did just that, adding one more layer of protection to the defense of our homes. We had previously piled snow against the outside walls of our longhouses to keep out the cold. The snow could also protect against fire, and the buckets of water be used for saving our roofs.

As for saving our treasures, my women and I had already done our best to secure them, burying strongboxes under my bed, my jewels in a trench beneath the looms, and bags of silver beneath the dung heap in the yard.

"Those Swedes will have to 'eat dirt' to find this treasure," Brita had chuckled.

Women in pairs took turns standing guard during the day, with boys and old men taking their positions at night. We held a public sacrifice to appease the gods of war, both Tyr and Odin. When I consulted the runes, they told me only of 'standstill' and 'disruption.' We were as prepared as we could be. Now, we must wait. I selected a sword from Orm's forge, a stout double-edged blade. I named it 'Blood-drinker.'

Many tense days later I was standing with my women at our looms trying to concentrate on the pattern before me, when I heard an urgent knock on the door, followed by a blast of cold air and Thora's gasping voice.

"Freaw! My lady! They're coming!"

Whirling about, I dropped the shuttle, cold fear clutching my heart.

"Who? Who's coming? Beowulf — or the Swedes?"

Thora met me with open arms and a broad smile.

"Beowulf! Our men!" She clasped me in a sudden embrace, her cloak rough and cold against my skin. "Solveig and I were standing watch near the north edge of the village when we saw a red fox streak out from the dark pines framing the river road. We wondered what had frightened the animal. Then we caught a flash of sunlight on metal — and held our breaths — until I recognized Beowulf's horse: Frostmane, right enough, with his gilded collar!"

She paused to catch her breath, her face suddenly darkening. "The line of riders is moving slowly. Perhaps there are wounded . . . perhaps . . . my Rolf?" She gulped.

"Let's find out! Runa! Run tell Magnus! Brita! You and Ana stay with Inga! I'm going!"

Hastily grabbing a shawl, I ran outside, Thora right behind me. Bright sun on the snow momentarily blinded me and frigid air made my eyes water. I blinked, and blinked again. There — emerging from the forest — Beowulf?

Running, I almost collided with Orm and Ortrud, each carrying a battle-axe.

"It's Beowulf!" I shouted, blinking back tears.

"So Solveig said, but it's best to be sure," replied Ortrud grimly. "It could be a trap!"

Goddess, may it not be so! Let it be Beowulf, sound and whole!

"Nay, it's Beowulf," shouted Thora. "See? Here he comes!"

Following the line of her finger, I saw three horses at the head of a line of men. Even at this distance I could make out Beowulf's figure, but who were the other two? Half-blinded by tears of joy, I ran forward, all thoughts of dignity and position forgotten.

Beowulf, you're alive! You've come back!

Behind me I heard shouts and cries as villagers streamed out to welcome home our warriors. I now recognized the two riders flanking Beowulf: Wulfgar and Redbeard. Their faces were grave, etched with exhaustion. These were not the faces of conquering heroes.

Breathless, I faltered, slowing to a stop. What could be wrong? A horse and rider came from behind me and galloped by: Magnus on Nightsea, riding out to meet the men. I watched, unsettled, as he joined Beowulf, exchanged a few words, then turned his stead to accompany the group into Hrethelskeep.

Behind their leaders a line of horse-drawn sledges and silent men on foot tramped over the snow—fewer men, it seemed to me, than those who had set out over two weeks ago. Who was missing? Suddenly I remembered the handsome young man flashing his sword and boasting of victory: Herdred. Herdred was missing. With a cry, I ran forward.

"Beowulf! What of Herdred?"

Beowulf approached slowly. Bringing Frostmane to a momentary halt, he leaned down.

"The king is dead. We have his body. Come to the mead hall. We'll talk there."

Flicking the reins, he rode on, leaving me speechless in the center of the road. I was still standing there when Olaf rode up.

"Allow me, my lady." He scooped me up onto his horse, settling me in front of him. "Beowulf is oppressed with grief just now. I'm sure he did not mean to be discourteous."

Glad that Olaf could not see my tears of shock and dismay, I whispered my gratitude.

"Thanks be to the gods for your safe return. And the rest of our men . . . ?"

"All accounted for, my lady. We had little chance to test our battle skills—but you'll hear everything in the mead hall."

We rode in silence the rest of the way into Hrethelskeep, passing villagers with joyous faces. I saw Rolf hugging Thora and Thorkel cradling his infant son. I saw Ana holding up Inga, who was waving to Beowulf, but I saw him ignore them both. I saw all this as if in a dream, my throat dry, my heart constricted.

The king is dead. Beowulf is sunk in grief. What can I do to help him?

"Let me down at my longhouse, Olaf. I'll need to oversee preparations for a suitable welcome."

"I hope that means hot food. I haven't thawed out in days!" Olaf declared with a grin in his voice.

"Yes, it means hot food — and plenty of ale. We also have a good supply of bread. You won't go hungry."

When I entered the longhouse, Brita and Runa were already busy at the hearth, setting cauldrons to boil. Ana hurried to my side, her face full of questions.

"What's the matter? Beowulf did not even look at us!"

"I know. He could barely speak to me. The king is dead, Ana. Herdred is dead."

Ana's eyes widened and her hand flew to her mouth.

"No! Can it be? But . . . they came back . . . ?"

"I don't know any more than that, Ana. Beowulf is to explain it all later at the mead hall. Right now we must prepare to feed a host of exhausted, disheartened men. Where are Estrid and Ingeborg?"

She sniffed. "Gone to see their sweethearts, I expect — Estrid to see Aksel and Ingeborg to Gorm."

"Gorm? I didn't know she fancied him — but more of that later. We must start our cooking."

I looked around the room. "Inga? Where are you? Come here, little one. You can help us."

She came out of the byre, wiping her hands on her dirty apron.

"I was petting Krona. Mother, what's wrong with Beowulf? I waved at him and he didn't wave back."

I pulled her onto my lap, smoothing her hair and wiping her sweaty forehead.

"Beowulf is sad, my dear. The king — his dear friend — is dead."

"Oh," she said. "Oh. I'm sorry. I'll be sad too."

After the warriors were fed, the women and other villagers crowded into the mead hall to hear Beowulf's report. He, Wulfgar, and Redbeard took places in the facing chairs. I sat with Magnus and Orm at the head table, cleared of food but supplied with jugs of ale and drinking cups. I had been too busy to eat, and had no appetite anyway.

Most of the faces around me showed relief and there was open rejoicing at the return of our men — but how could this have happened?

Our men safe, but the king dead? No opportunity to speak with Beowulf privately had presented itself, and I was heartsick... for both of us.

How could Beowulf possibly explain the king's death without bringing shame on himself and his comrades? First Hygelac — now Herdred — he'd sworn to defend them both. Now they were dead and he lived. I did not wish him dead — far from it — but to lose one's honor was worse than death! In an agony of suspense I waited to hear what he would say.

When Beowulf finally rose to speak, a hush fell over the hall. He stood quietly for a time, staring into the distance. At length he opened his word hoard.

"Geats, Danes, people of Hrethelskeep, by now you know that King Herdred is dead. I will tell you the manner of his death as best I can, and of the part played by your brave men in the fight against the Swedes."

I closed my eyes to hear him better, for the haunted look on his face twisted a knife inside me.

"Our plan was sound: to surprise Onela's forces at Lake Vänern, giving us space for a battle in the open. We reached the lake in four days' time and set up camp along the western shore. An icy fog hung in the air, but we could see the glow of fires in the distance, and knew the Swedes must be encamped on the eastern shore. We spent the night under extra furs, lighting no fires to give away our position.

"During the night a fierce gale blew in from the north, knocking over tents and carrying off our standard. Nevertheless we set out on the morning of the fifth day in full battle gear, to surprise the enemy. The wind was picking up snow from the ice and hurling it in our faces, but we pressed on, intent upon attacking before the Swedes were aware of our presence.

"The storm intensified as we advanced, swelling into a ground blizzard that wiped out any sense of depth or direction. We could barely see each other, and the wind howled louder than any human voice. I led our men, with Herdred on my right, Eanmund and Eadgils on my left."

The Swedish princes? Where are they? I'd forgotten all about them!

"Suddenly, out of the swirling snow Onela appeared right in front of us. Seeing the two princes, he roared 'Rebels!', drew back and hurled his spear, but it was deflected by Eadgil's shield. Now the four of us closed on Onela and his two champions.

"My sword met Onela's; for a moment the storm subsided and we could see each other face to face. Onela's champion attacked me, a momentary distraction. Then I saw Onela's sword draw blood from Eanmund's arm. Suddenly Herdred, with sword raised, jumped in front of me, shouting 'Glory to the Geats!' Onela cut him down with one stroke to the neck."

I gasped, as did those around me. Beowulf had dropped his head, but now lifted it, his face grim.

"I caught the king as he fell toward me and shouted to the princes to hold off Onela, but Eadgils had disappeared, and Eanmund was suddenly run through by Weohstan, one of Onela's champions."

Beowulf's face darkened.

"At that moment horns blew from every direction and we knew we were surrounded. Onela's voice cut through the storm. He cried, 'Beowulf! You are outnumbered! Give up this battle. I have no quarrel with you. By Odin I swear it! We have what we came for: the rebel princes. Take your boy-king and return to your own country in peace!'

"I was ready to raise the battle cry 'Fight to the death!' when the storm whipped up again, battering us with howling wind, blinding us with blowing snow, so ferocious that I could not tell one man from another or see my hand before my face!"

Beowulf shook his head in amazement at the memory.

"I carried the king away from the front line, but he was already gasping out his life in a fountain of blood. I held him in my arms as he died. Alas, alas for young Herdred!"

Beowulf stopped speaking and turned away, holding his face in his hands. When he had recovered somewhat, he drew himself up and faced the crowd.

"When this howling, blinding storm monster finally abated, the Swedes were gone. We searched for bodies on the ice, but found none. The only warriors who died on the field of battle that day were Herdred and Eanmund. Eanmund's body was gone — no doubt taken by the Swedes — Eadgils may have been taken captive — I cannot say. No one else in our band was even injured."

Redbeard rose and came forward to stand beside Beowulf.

"The gods had a hand in that battle, I swear it. Odin — or Thor — was against us. There is no other explanation. I've never seen a storm like that in my whole life!"

Now Wulfgar rose, clearing his voice.

"When the Swedes departed, we were left with no enemy to fight, but Beowulf had already saved King Herdred's body so that we could take him back to Eaglesgard for a hero's funeral. He died in battle, a brave warrior, worthy of a place in Valhalla."

Beowulf's face lightened momentarily and he opened his lips again.

"The Swedes could have attacked us after the storm cleared, but they did not. With the two princes in his hands, I believe Onela will keep his oath — to leave us in peace."

Beowulf lifted his head high.

"Now, let us honor all our warriors, assembled here. Each man and each woman in this hall tonight was ready to shed blood defending home and family. Let us drink a toast to our brave band!"

He held out his goblet, which was quickly filled by a waiting servant.

"Wes hail, brave warriors!" He lifted his cup high.

"Wes hail, brave warriors!" came the ringing reply.

"We drink to your courage." Beowulf drained the goblet.

"And now," said Beowulf, his voice choking, "I offer words of praise for King Herdred. He was a brave young king. He gave his life to keep his word. He died defending his guests, the Swedish princes."

Beowulf's face contorted in a deep scowl.

"One day the Swedes will taste my sword again! Revenge will come!"

He shook his head as if to clear it of heavy thoughts.

"In the morning we folk from Eaglesgard will depart, taking the king's body with us. All who wish to do him honor may assemble outside the mead hall to view his body and bid him farewell. Now I bid you all good night."

His head sank forward on his chest, and I half-rose from my seat, but Magnus gently pulled me down.

"Later, my lady. He'll be all right."

I sat quietly as the hall slowly cleared. Many villagers came up to express their grief at the loss of the king and to thank Beowulf for the safe return of their husbands and sons. Beowulf received their words with a still face, almost as if his spirit had left his body. I feared for him.

Finally, when only a few remained, lingering to talk among themselves, I rose. Beowulf's eyes met mine and he crossed toward me.

"Don't go yet. I need to talk to you."

The voice was almost the voice of the Beowulf I knew, but his face held little tenderness.

"I will stay." I looked at him hopefully.

Shall I tell him now of my readiness to marry? Would it lighten his grief? Or should I wait for a better time?

When the hall was empty save for the two of us, Beowulf took my hand and drew me down to sit on a bench beside him.

"Freaw, I have a favor to ask."

"Yes, my lord? I mean, Beowulf?"

"I want you ... I need you ... to come back to Eaglesgard with me. I do not wish to face Queen Hygd alone, bearing the dead body of her only son. Having your company may ease her pain. It would help me as well. Please say you'll come."

These were not the words I'd hoped to hear.

Does he only want me to soften the blow for Hygd? Does he care more for her feelings than my own?

"I don't know... you said you're leaving in the morning? And I have Inga to consider — could I bring Inga with me?"

Beowulf barely hesitated.

"No, I think not. The sight of your living child might deepen Hygd's grief for her dead child."

"I see."

Yes, I do see. You place Hygd before me! Still...

"Beowulf, I will come, but if I should be asked to make an extended stay I must be allowed to send for Inga and the rest of my household. Agreed?"

"Agreed." The shadow of a smile softened his face.

Now it was my turn to make a request.

"Beowulf, may I see Herdred's body? He was... dear to me." I gulped as a lump rose in my throat, cutting off further words. Beowulf nodded

"He's not a pretty sight. I did what I could to make him look less... distressing... for Hygd."

Hygd again? Don't be petty, Freaw. How would you feel if you were to lose Inga?

Stifling my own distress, I left the mead hall hand-in-hand with Beowulf. He led me outside to one of the cart-sledges that had formerly held weapons and armor. It was draped with a single cloak. Aksel, standing vigil beside it, nodded to us and slipped away.

I was not prepared for the stab of anguish that assailed me when Beowulf uncovered the sledge. Herdred was laid out in full armor, one hand across his mail shirt, sword at his side, his helmet resting beside his head. He could have been sleeping in his own bed, except for the extreme pallor of his face. I gasped, tears springing into my eyes.

"Herdred, young friend, you grew up too soon and were cut down too soon! Your Freaw mourns for you!"

Reaching down I touched his cold, still face, and noticed a kerchief wound around his neck, a stiff, bloody kerchief edged with runes.

"Why, that's the cloth I gave you, Beowulf, for protection!"

Looking up, my eyes met his.

"Would you had given it to Herdred — but it's too late for that now." Beowulf sounded close to tears. "We've kept the body cold to preserve it for the funeral pyre."

Suddenly Beowulf drew me close. Pushing back my head covering, he buried his face in my hair.

"Freaw," he choked, "I failed Hygelac and now Herdred. When the light flickered out of the king's dying eyes, a great darkness came over me. I fear it will never leave me."

His body heaved with silent sobs as he clung to me, giving vent to an agony of grief and guilt.

Chapter Eighteen
Return to Eaglesgard

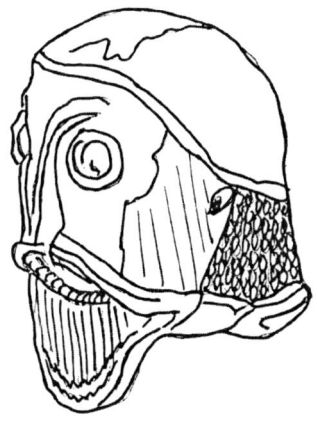

Detail of a carving on a wagon in the Oseberg ship burial.

There was little time for sleep that night. After a tender parting from Beowulf, I returned to the longhouse to rouse my women. They had retired for the night, but all except Inga were still awake.

"Ana! Brita! Everyone! I need your help! On the morrow I leave with Beowulf—for what could be a lengthy stay at Eaglesgard."

They rose hastily to help me pack and prepare provisions. While they worked at the hearth, I called Runa into my bedchamber to unearth one of the strongboxes under my bed.

"Will you need your jewels too, my lady?" Runa was kneeling on the floor scraping at the soil with an antler tip. I considered the question.

"No, I think not—not yet—but I may need them later—for a wedding."

"A wedding?" Runa rose, shaking dirt from her apron. "Do you mean . . . you and Beowulf?"

"Hush, Runa. Keep your voice down. Say nothing to anyone. It's only a possibility."

Why not? If I declare my unconditional love for him, will not Beowulf reply in kind? Being together at Eaglesgard could be a boon for us, the opportunity we need.

"Has Lord Beowulf spoken . . ." began Runa, but I held up my hand.

"Hush. He has spoken, but not of marriage. I know he loves me, but on this trip it will be my duty to help him comfort Queen Hygd."

Runa looked me full in the face. "Will Beowulf become the next king? Will you become his queen?"

"Queen?" My voice faltered. "I do not know. There is Hygd to consider . . ."

"Yes, there is Hygd. My lady, who are you taking with you to Eaglesgard? You'll need an attendant."

"Why, you, Runa. Since Hygd is your rightful mistress, she has every right to expect your return, and I . . ."

Runa's eyes suddenly filled with tears.

"Oh, my lady, I'll follow you anywhere, but please let me serve you, not Hygd. She has other women to do her bidding!" Runa sank to her knees.

Taken aback at the intensity of Runa's plea, I put out a hand to raise her up.

"Calm yourself. Nothing has been decided. We will confront the circumstance when we get to Eaglesgard." *I must face many challenges when I get to Eaglesgard.* "Now, finish your digging so we can both get some sleep tonight."

Early the next morning I woke Inga to explain the situation. She was curled in a warm ball on her sleeping bench. At my touch she opened her dark eyes and smiled up at me sweetly.

"What is it, Mother? Why do you look at me that way?"

With a stretch and a yawn, she tumbled out of her robes. I sat down beside her, pulling the robe around her shoulders as I murmured in her ear.

"Inga, my precious, I must leave you for a time."

Inga jerked away, her eyes clouding. "Leave me? Why, Mother?"

I cupped her chin in my hand, noting how much she'd grown to look like her father.

"I must go to help Beowulf say goodbye to the king and to comfort the king's mother." I reached out to stroke her hair, still damp from sleep, but she leaned away.

"I want to go with you! Take me with you, Mother!"

I sighed. "I can't, Inga. Ana and the other women will take good care of you while I'm gone — just as they did when I went to Uppsala."

She nodded, but a fat tear rolled down one cheek. Fiercely she wiped it away with the tail of the fox pelt she slept with every night.

"This is a sad time for everyone, my dear, but we must be brave. I will either return to you soon, or send for you to join me — I promise."

I held out my arms and she melted into my embrace. When we parted, I picked up the worn pelt.

"Inga, do you remember who gave you this?"

She shook her head.

"King Herdred. It was his birth gift to you."

Her eyes widened. "The same king who is dead."

"Yes, the same." A tear began to trickle from my own eyes.

Inga gazed at me thoughtfully. "Mother, may I see King Herdred before you leave?"

Her question took me by surprise.

"Why, yes, you may, but why?"

"To say goodbye and to give him this." She held out the pelt.

This time my eyes flooded with tears. "Of course, my dear. Now let's get some breakfast."

It was a somber line that gathered outside the mead hall that morning. Our breath hung in icy clouds before our faces, for the day was bitterly cold. I had dressed in layers, topped with my fox fur, as Beowulf thought it might give Hygd pleasure to see it again. Redbeard stood quietly by the sledge as villagers wrapped in woolen cloaks filed slowly past King Herdred's body. Several placed small tokens on his chest: an amulet, a silver coin, an apple, a packet of salt.... At the end of the line Inga asked Beowulf to lift her up. As he did so, holding her securely in his huge hands, she laid her beloved fox pelt at Herdred's side.

"Goodbye, king," she whispered, her eyes round as she stared at the still body.

Before setting her down, Beowulf gave Inga a fatherly hug.

Could you one day become her father, Beowulf? Can we ever become a family?

At Inga's urging, her friend Toke asked to be lifted up next. He carried a small wooden sword — the toy he used when playing Swedes and Geats with Inga — which he laid carefully beside Herdred's hand.

"Goodbye, king," called Toke in his little boy's voice. "I'm sorry you're dead."

Beowulf set Toke down carefully, stood up and wiped his eyes.

"Thank you, children, for your tributes."

He turned to address Redbeard. "See to it that all the tributes are properly collected, my friend, and cover the king's body. It is time to depart." Now he turned toward me. "Are you ready, my lady?"

"Yes, my lord."

I turned to face my household and the other assembled villagers. Inga stood in front of Ana, ready to wave her farewells. Her face showed neither fear nor sorrow, but my own face was not so composed as I knelt to give my daughter a final embrace.

"Farewell, my dear one, my Inga. May the goddess be with you and protect you always."

"Farewell, Mother. Come home soon!" She kissed me on the lips, her mouth soft and warm.

I rose, my eyes glistening, loath to part from my child. Redbeard courteously took my arm and led me to our waiting horses. He helped set me on Burningfax, then climbed up on his own horse. Like a man in a dream, Beowulf mounted Frostmane. Aksel and Leif mounted the two horses hitched to Herdred's sledge. After them Runa would ride next to Lars, followed by the rest of the warriors from Eaglesgard.

Slowly we began to move out, leaving Hrethelskeep — for how long? Questions flooded my mind even as I wiped away the tears that flooded my eyes.

What lies ahead? Who will be king? Queen? Most important, will Beowulf and I be together?

We spoke little on the ride to Eaglesgard. The wind and cold made conversation difficult, and Beowulf seemed in no mood to share his thoughts. Redbeard, however, was full of talk as he rode beside me.

"Tis a great favor, you coming with us, Lady Freawaru. You'll be a great comfort to the queen."

I was not so sure of this, but kept my doubts to myself.

"Thank you, Redbeard. I look forward to seeing once again the great eagle you carved above the mead hall door."

Speaking of the eagle put me in mind of another flying creature, and a statement slipped out before I realized I had spoken.

"Tell me of dragon sightings."

Redbeard turned toward me in the saddle and wiped away the ice that had collected around his mouth.

"Yes, there have been recent sightings, but how did you know? Ketil reported fire in the night sky just before we left for Hrethelskeep. We thought it a sign portending the battle to come." He gave me a piercing look. "What do *you* think, my lady?"

"If an omen of disaster, it might have foretold the death of King Herdred."

Redbeard continued to fix me with his gaze.

"We need you at Eaglesgard, my lady. In these difficult times we need your special gifts."

We subsided into silence, each thinking our own thoughts.

As we neared the settlement, a pair of armed sentinels rode out to meet us. Seeing Beowulf, they greeted us joyously. "Where's King Herdred?" shouted one. In silence Beowulf gestured toward the sledge, now draped with Herdred's cloak. Understanding, the two men bowed their heads, turned and joined our procession.

When we came in sight of Eaglesgard, Beowulf momentarily halted the line to address Redbeard and me.

"I will ride ahead and speak first to Queen Hygd. Take Herdred's body to the mead hall. I'll join you there later."

Despite the cold, it seemed to me that everyone in Eaglesgard poured out of doors upon our arrival, as eager to welcome home their men as the villagers of Hrethelskeep had been. Ketil, older and grayer than I remembered him, came up to clasp Redbeard by the shoulders after he dismounted.

"Greetings, old friend. It is good to see you safely back!"

Young Erik took the bridle of my horse and helped me down, his eyes shining.

"Our warriors are back! With the Danish princess! This is a grand day!" he exclaimed. "Our men must have made short work of those Swedes!"

Not wishing to dash his enthusiasm, I said nothing of the battle or its losses.

"You will hear all when Beowulf comes to the mead hall," I told him, managing a slight smile. "Thank you for your courtesy."

With the appearance of Aksel and Leif beside the draped sledge, the clamor of voices trailed off.

"We've lost our king," announced Aksel. "Herdred is dead."

This blunt announcement was met with sudden silence, then a keening wail poured forth from the woman I recognized as Signe, Herdred's old nurse.

Now Redbeard and Ketil took charge, directing the disposition of men and sledges, sending people back to their longhouses, ordering a feast for the evening meal, and escorting me into the mead hall where a most welcome fire blazed on the hearth. After they left with a promise of food and drink to be delivered, Runa joined me, vigorously rubbing her arms and legs.

"Are we to stay here tonight, my lady?" She looked around the dim interior as if re-orienting herself to once-familiar surroundings.

"I don't know, Runa. Everything depends upon Beowulf — and Hygd. We must wait."

Suddenly exhausted, I sank down on a nearby bench.

"Let me remove your shoes and rub your feet," murmured Runa. "Bread and ale are on the way. You'll feel better soon."

I let Runa attend me, grateful for her familiar presence in this still strange place — once Hygelac's hall, then Herdred's . . . and now? Even before the food arrived, I had drifted into sleep.

When I awoke, the hall was no longer empty. From the far end, near the throne, I heard voices; the name that echoed down to me was . . . 'Beowulf.'

Runa appeared with basin and towel.

"I'm glad you're awake. It is almost time for the welcome feast and the hall will soon be filling with people. It's also time to freshen up."

I yawned, stretched, and splashed water on my face.

"Have you seen Beowulf?"

"No, my lady, not yet, but Redbeard says he'll soon be here."

"Lady Freawaru?" A voice and a face not familiar to me now claimed my attention, as a young woman approached us.

"Yes?"

"I am Dagmar, my lady, one of Queen Hygd's women." She gave a slight bow. "She sent me to see if you need anything."

The girl's eyes were red-rimmed and her voice hoarse. I rose to face her.

"It is good of your gracious lady to think of me in the midst of her sorrow. Please tell her that I share her grief — and I'm here to be of service to her in any way I can. How... how does she fare?"

Dagmar gulped and took a deep breath.

"When she heard the bitter news the queen collapsed, screaming; then she raged and raged. She is calmer now, but moves like one in a trance."

"Is Lord Beowulf still with her?" I asked anxiously.

"Yes," said Dagmar simply.

"That is well. When grief is fresh it is best not to be alone." My mind flew back to the dagger in Hrun's hand after the death of Ingeld. "Will the queen appear at the feast tonight?"

"I know not, my lady. She puts her trust in Beowulf now. It will be as he advises. In truth..." she paused, "... it was Lord Beowulf who sent me to you. Now, if you have no need of me, I shall return to the queen."

"Certainly. Thank you, Dagmar. You may go."

Beowulf. Hygd. How painful Herdred's death must be for each of them! Yet Beowulf still thinks of my welfare.

"Runa, help me dress. Oh, I wish we'd brought my jewels — I want to look my best tonight!"

Hygd did attend the feast. As she entered the mead hall on the arm of Beowulf, a hush fell over the assembly. She was pale, but walked with quiet dignity, staring straight ahead. She was finely dressed, wearing the gold necklace that Beowulf had brought back from Frisia. Her face was set, as if willing itself to maintain control. I marveled at her composure, thinking how distraught I would be if I were to lose my Inga.

When the two of them reached my table near the thrones, she stopped and turned toward me. Respectfully I rose to embrace her, and whispered tenderly, "Sister. May the goddess be with you."

Beowulf seated Hygd at the head table, taking his place beside her. She lifted her head and drew herself erect, gripping the arms of the chair tightly. Slowly Beowulf rose to speak.

"People of Eaglesgard," he began, "we gather tonight to mourn our fallen king and to honor the warriors who followed him into battle. Let us first take meat and drink together; then you will hear all that befell on our expedition."

He sat down abruptly and Hygd signaled for the serving to begin. During the meal I ate little, my eyes seeking Hygd's. She kept her eyes lowered, making little effort to taste her food. Beowulf betrayed no emotion as he ate and drank mechanically. The sound of other voices enclosed us in a comforting web, but I sat in suspense, awaiting what the night might bring. Beside me, Redbeard patted my hand sympathetically.

"Courage, my lady," he murmured. "We must all show courage."

Why, that's exactly what I told Inga! Am I behaving like a frightened child?

Other words now came to me, Unferth's words from long ago: 'We are all warriors, though we carry no visible weapons.' Straightening my shoulders, I gave Redbeard's hand a firm squeeze.

"Yes, I am ready to do my part."

Beowulf's recounting of the battle on the ice added no new information. I listened with closed eyes, re-envisioning each detail: the storm, the slashing sword, Herdred falling . . . a scream . . . My eyes flew open as Hygd's screams pierced the hall.

"No! No! The gods have cursed me! Cursed me!"

She had risen from her chair, wildly clawing at her cheeks. Instinctively I jumped up and ran to her, grabbing her wrists. She struggled for a moment, then collapsed against me, in a shudder of sobs. Beowulf too had risen, but stood stricken, as if powerless to move.

"Beowulf, help me!" I cried, struggling to hold up the queen.

Slowly he came to my aid, gently taking Hygd by the shoulders and guiding her back down into her chair. She sank forward, her face in her hands, rocking back and forth and sobbing convulsively. I looked searchingly around the hall for Hygd's women. Concern for the queen shown on every face. Signe rose, then Dagmar and a third woman I did not recognize. I beckoned them forward, and turned to Beowulf.

"My lord, may we retire with Queen Hygd? We will take her back to the women's house and stay with her."

Beowulf nodded, his face drained of color. The pain in his eyes made me wince.

"Yes, take her, please," he said in a husky voice. "Your presence may be what she needs now. Do whatever you can to bring her comfort."

"I will," I whispered, looking into his dear face with all the love in my heart.

As Signe and I reached for her arms, Hygd shook us off, rising from her chair with head held high.

"I don't need your help!" she burst out, then swayed and staggered forward.

Gently we supported her on either side as we made our way through the assembly, followed by murmurs of sympathy and pity. Runa joined us as we left the mead hall. In the open air Hygd revived; she shouted curses, railing against the gods — and me.

"You, proud princess, are supposed to be the seeress. Did you not foresee Herdred's danger? Why didn't you protect him? You have failed me — everyone has failed me! Herdred is dead! My son, the king, is dead!"

The four of us finally managed to get Hygd into her house, where she collapsed on the bed, spent, and closed her eyes as if to shut out the reality of Herdred's death.

"Signe, do you have any chamomile in your herb stores? A tea made from that should induce sleep and perhaps lessen her pain."

"We do, my lady." She turned to the fourth woman. "Kirsten — fetch that bag from the cooking house." She turned back to me. "I'll prepare it immediately."

I sat with Hygd all through the night. Her women tried to keep watch with me, but gradually drifted into sleep. While Hygd remained awake I talked to her in low tones, trying to soothe her and implant happier images to replace the brutal picture of the sword slashing across Herdred's throat.

"He is beyond pain now . . . He did not suffer . . . He died in an instant . . . Herdred died as he wanted — in battle — a hero's death . . . Now he feasts in Valhalla with Hygelac — father and son together . . . Herdred's courage gave honor to the Geats . . . You raised him well, Hygd."

Sometimes I dozed, but woke to assess Hygd's breathing and color. *It has been a great shock, but Hygd will recover. Then what will she do?*

Early the next morning, when it was apparent that Hygd was more herself, I was shown to a bed in a nearby longhouse. Runa came with me and found a place on a sleeping bench. She had stayed beside me all night, bringing bread and ale at intervals to fortify me. I fell asleep instantly. Thus it was that neither of us was present when Hygd called Beowulf to her side.

A loud cough by Signe brought me to the surface from a deep, dreamless sleep. I opened my eyes to see her bending over me, a strange look on her face. Immediately I sprang up.

"What is it? Has Hygd...?"

"Calm yourself, my lady. It's not Hygd. It's Lord Beowulf; he wants to see you as soon as you're ready to receive him."

"Beowulf? Of course I'll see him! Runa! Wake up! I need your help!"

Signe backed away discreetly as I dressed and Runa arranged my hair in a fresh braid. Snow was sifting through the smoke-hole, but the air felt slightly warmer.

"Signe, how long have I slept? What has been happening?"

"It's almost nightfall, my lady. The council met to decide on a new king and the queen is in much better spirits."

Ah, decisions have been made. Beowulf is coming to give me the news! My heart beat faster in anticipation.

Signe disappeared. Moments later Beowulf entered, shaking snow from his hair and cloak. I met him at the door with a smile of gladness, but Beowulf's face reflected a mix of emotions I could not read.

"Freaw, we must talk — alone."

"Of course, my lord." I nodded to Runa, who left quickly. When Beowulf made no move to embrace me, I said, "Come sit by the hearth and warm yourself, my dear."

Silently Beowulf took a seat at the table and gestured for me to sit across from him. He raised his head and looked at me with pleading eyes.

"Freaw, they have asked me to be king."

I half-rose from my place. "As they should! You are clearly the right man to lead the Geats!" I cried with enthusiasm. "Do you remember what my father foretold for you? He said that the Geats would one day choose you as their king."

Beowulf nodded, a faint smile passing briefly over his features.

"Freaw, there is more. Hygd has asked me to marry her."

"Marry? Hygd?"

His words fell like blows. I gasped, flinching as if struck. For a moment I could not breathe and my stomach rose into my throat.

Fanning the Flames

Beowulf was speaking again, earnestly. He reached across the table to take my hands.

"Freaw, I have not given her an answer. I had to talk to you first. Freaw, you know my heart lies in your keeping, but I believe it is my duty to honor Hygd's wishes. I did not save Hygelac ... and now Herdred ... I have failed—failed twice. I must not fail again. It is my duty!" he concluded with a sob, his grip almost crushing my fingers.

I stared at Beowulf in anguish, unable to speak. When I could find my voice again, I began to argue.

"Beowulf, you take on too much responsibility! You are not to blame for the loss of Herdred—or of Hygelac. Each one risked his life knowing that death could be the outcome. Each welcomed a warrior's death. Besides, I..."

Suddenly stricken, I fell silent, my eyes blinded. Beowulf freed my hands and reached up, wiping away the tears that coursed down my cheeks. Then he leaned toward me.

"Freaw, you yourself once reminded me of my duty to support Herdred's kingship, even as you were mindful of your responsibility to raise young Inga. We both heeded the call of duty in the past. Is it any different now?"

My mouth twisted in pain at the bitter irony in his words. "Yes, yes, it's different! I love you! Completely! I want to be with you always! I thought the time had finally come when we could be together!"

Beowulf regarded me gravely. "And what of Hygd?"

I shook my head vigorously. "I don't know, I don't know!"

Once again tears started to flow as I blurted out, "Do you love her?"

Beowulf gave a deep sigh.

"No, but it is not a question of love, Freaw. Hygd is the queen; she has the right to command me. The welfare of the tribe must also to be considered. We Geats are a small band. Strong leadership is essential for our survival."

He sighed again, then gazed directly into my eyes.

"Freaw, I once asked you to be my wife..." He shook his head slowly. "That is no longer possible. Will you release me—to marry Hygd?"

My heart almost stopped beating. Clutching the edge of the table, I closed my eyes and took a deep breath.

Can I do this thing? Must I give him up—again?

Exhaling slowly, I opened my eyes.

"Yes, Beowulf, I release you. Do what you have to do."

Suddenly I stood up, sending the bench clattering. "Please go now," I cried, "and send Runa to me."

I turned away from him, for I could not look at Beowulf, could not bear to see if his face showed sorrow . . . or relief. As I stood with head bowed, I felt his arms wrap around me. Looking down, I saw clenched fists and felt the tension in his powerful arms.

"Freaw, goodbye to our dream. I will love you always," he whispered.

Unclenching his fists, he stepped back. I heard the fading sound of his footsteps. Then he was gone and I was alone — trembling — suddenly racked with cold — feeling more alone than I had ever felt before.

Moments later Runa entered to find me retching into a bucket.

"Oh, my lady, what's wrong?"

She hurriedly found a cloth to wipe my face, then wrapped me in a sleeping robe as I shivered uncontrollably in her arms.

"Hygd," I gasped. "Beowulf will marry Hygd!"

Runa held me tighter as I shook and sobbed, her voice low.

"As I feared," she murmured.

"Oh, Runa, what-what am I going to do?" I wailed between chattering teeth.

Her reply was blunt, but kind.

"Survive, my lady, and carry on — as we all must do."

Both Hygd and I recovered somewhat in the days that followed. I avoided all unnecessary contact with Hygd — and with Beowulf. Herdred's funeral pyre was constructed and his body burned with all due ceremony. I stood at a distance from the crackling flames as the offerings from Hrethelskeep were added, watching Toke's toy wooden sword burn, blackening next to a fox pelt that crisped and curled. I thought of Inga held high in Beowulf's arms, her nose being tickled with the tip of that tail. My Inga. My heart gave a sudden lurch at another thought.

You vowed to give up Beowulf — to save Inga. Now you are being forced to keep your vow! Freyja, goddess, is this your punishment? For my betrayal?

To any observer my grief for the loss of Beowulf could easily be construed as grief for Herdred. I once looked up to find Hygd staring at me intently, as if trying to penetrate the mask of my stony face. I did not shirk in showing her respect, but only Beowulf and Runa knew the anguish that lay on my heart.

The choice of Beowulf as the Geats' new king came as a surprise to no one, but the announcement of his proposed marriage to Hygd was another matter. Eager to find a cause for rejoicing after Herdred's death, all of Eaglesgard was caught up in preparations for the ceremony. I watched impassively, speaking little, feeling absent from my own body — until the morning that Hygd sent for me.

Kirsten escorted me into the queen's bedchamber, a spacious room at one end of her longhouse. I knew it only from my all-night vigil, and looked around curiously at the hangings on its walls — finely woven tapestries. I wondered if Hygd remembered that night of fitful sleep and raving, but did not speak of it

Hygd was dressed as if for a public appearance in a soft woolen kirtle of light blue, overlaid with a barley-colored apron. She wore her hair loose, tumbling over her shoulders in waves of gold streaked with gray. Her cheeks had healed, betraying only slight signs of their desperate rending.

"Sister Freawaru." She rose to greet me, her eyes bright, almost feverish. "My women tell me you have shown great concern for my welfare. I thank you, and I thank you for your vigil, for staying with me through that ... dreadful ... first night."

I nodded and bowed, my throat too dry to speak. Hygd patted the bed.

"Come. Sit beside me and take your ease."

I settled myself stiffly near her and tried to swallow. I could not help thinking that soon she and Beowulf would be together, perhaps on this very bed. Hygd took my hand and smiled.

"Freawaru, sister, Beowulf and I want you to be our honored guest at the wedding ceremony — and we invite anyone else from Hrethelskeep who would be free to attend."

Clever. She frames my defeat as an honor! I wonder ... is this some sort of peace-offering?

"I thank you ... Queen Hygd."

The word 'sister' would not form on my lips. I had hoped to escape the ceremony altogether, but now there seemed no way to avoid it.

"But do you accept?" Hygd's voice cut through my thoughts. "Your blessing on our union is important ... to us both. Surely it is little to ask after all that Beowulf has done for you and your people!"

Hygd's voice had taken on an edge. I looked up slowly.

"Yes, yes of course. I, we . . . will be honored. Now, I have much to attend to. With your permission I will leave for Hrethelskeep immediately to convey your invitation and make my own preparations."

Hygd patted my knee as if I were a docile child.

"That is well. I'll ask two of our men to escort you." She paused. "By the by, I've noticed that Finnish thrall often in your company. Has she been useful?"

"Finnish thrall . . . Runa? Yes, she has been a great help to me. Do you have need of her?"

Anxiously I awaited her answer.

"Not at present, but I may need more women to attend me if — no, when — I bear Beowulf a child."

My mouth almost fell open at these words. I stole a sideways glance at the lines on Hygd's face and the silver streaks in her hair.

"The Geats need Beowulf to lead them," she was saying, "but they also need an heir to continue his line. I will give him a son!'

She rose, smiling brightly, triumphantly I thought. I also rose, nodding, and let her embrace me before I left the chamber, my mind reeling. I was still incredulous at Hygd's announcement when I entered the longhouse which Runa and I now shared with Signe. Runa was standing alone at the hearth, dipping a bowl of porridge. She looked at me questioningly.

"What does the queen want now?"

I paused only a moment.

"A baby — with Beowulf!"

Runa dropped the ladle, staring at me wide-eyed.

"But, she's too old — isn't she?"

I shrugged, removing my cloak and hanging it on a peg.

"Hygd doesn't think so. She is determined to give Beowulf a son, an heir to carry on his line."

Runa scowled. "Does she think to replace Herdred?"

I sighed. "I cannot say what Hygd thinks or feels. I can barely look at her. I'm always wondering if she knows of my love for Beowulf and disregards it — or is acting in innocence."

Runa cocked her head sideways at me.

"My lady, you and the queen are two strong women used to getting your own way!"

I sighed again. "Runa, it's time to leave Eaglesgard — for the moment. We are to carry an invitation to Hrethelskeep to attend Beowulf and Hygd's wedding. We will leave tomorrow."

As promised, two men, Aksel and Leif, were released to accompany Runa and me back to Hrethelskeep. Our trip was made unexpectedly difficult by an early thaw; we encountered muddy ruts under a thin skin of ice and snow. Even so, as we rode eastward my spirits began to rise. Soon I would see my Inga again and feel her soft arms around my neck. On the other hand, I faced the unpleasant task of telling my women about the coming union of Beowulf and Hygd. Runa seemed to sense my ambivalence.

"Courage, my lady," she murmured. "All may yet be well."

I turned to look at her, then spurred Burningfax ahead without a word.

Our arrival came as a welcome surprise to my household. As I entered the longhouse Brita and Inga were emerging from the byre. When she saw me, Inga flew into my arms with a glad cry.

"Mother! Mother! Krona has a new calf! And look — I've lost a tooth!"

She grinned broadly, showing me the empty space. Kneeling, I hugged her tightly. Estrid and Ingebord left their looms to greet me, followed by Ana, walking slowly with a slight limp.

"Welcome home, my lady. We did not expect you back so soon," said Ana, looking me up and down appraisingly.

Releasing Inga, I stood. "This will be a short visit, for I must return soon."

"What is the news from Eaglesgard?" clamored Estrid. "How is . . . Aksel?" She reached to take the cloak from my shoulders.

"You can ask him yourself, Estrid. He and Leif are outside putting up the horses, but will join us shortly."

Estrid's face beamed at this news.

"And Queen Hygd?" inquired Ingeborg quietly. "How is she taking the loss of her son?"

"She is over the initial shock," I said, biting my lip before continuing. "Hygd has something else to occupy her mind now. She is to marry Beowulf."

Everyone except Inga gasped and gazed at me with wondering eyes

"But you . . . but he . . ." sputtered Estrid.

"Stop, please. Say no more. Their union may be for the best — for everyone." I choked on the last word, but managed a weak smile. "Looking on the bright side, you are all invited to the wedding."

Wordlessly Ana embraced me, her warmth a welcome balm. When she released me, her eyes were bright with unshed tears. I stepped back in consternation.

"What's wrong, Ana? Are you in pain?"

She shook her head slowly. "No more than usual. It's this weather — bad for my joints — but I'm fine, my lady. It is you I'm thinking of."

"Dear Ana, you are always thinking of others. But why haven't you told me about this problem? We must seek a remedy in our herbal stores. I'll look into it immediately!"

Ana shook her head again. "Some things can't be helped, my lady. Some things must be endured."

I stared at her in silence. *Are these words meant for me?* The arrival of Aksel and Leif at the door ended our conversation.

Later that day I conveyed the wedding invitation to Magnus, Wulfgar, Ortrud, and Thora, with a request that they repeat it to their neighbors. Once the news was disseminated, an air of expectation spread over the settlement. I could not share in it, but decided to make the best of the situation. First, I had Brita unearth the jewels buried beneath the looms, which Runa then rubbed to sparkling brilliance.

"Oh, my lady, you'll be more beautiful than the queen!" gushed Estrid as I settled the web of gems atop my hair.

"No one will be looking at me," I said dryly, "at least I hope not."

Goddess, give me the strength to survive the coming ordeal!

Next I chose a quiet, private moment to consult my runes. I had not attempted a three-rune reading since Ingeld's fateful departure from Wulfhaus to attack my father's mead hall. I spread my white cloth on the bed and closed my eyes, ready to divine my fate. Before I reached into the bag to select the first rune, I mentally reviewed my present situation.

The Geats are at peace. My household has found a home in Hrethelskeep. Inga is safe, with a secure future. My position is respected and honored, and I still have the gift of foresight — sometimes. Now enters a new element: the marriage of Beowulf to Hygd. What effect will this have on me and my family?

Invoking the wisdom of Odin, I whispered, "Great giver of runes, guide my hand as I seek my fate. Reveal to me what I need to know." Slowly my fingers closed on one particular rune-stick. Removing it and laying it on the white cloth, I opened my eyes. Raido. Rune of journeys.

Yes, we have made a journey, we Danes, to find our present home.

A second time I reached into the bag and drew forth a rune-stick. Gebo. The gift of union, of partnership.

Yes, again. This matches the action to come: Beowulf and Hygd will be joined as partners, king and queen. Now, how will their union affect my life?

With trembling fingers I reached inside the bag a third time, searching blindly as tears welled up behind my eyelids. At last I felt an answer within my grasp and slowly withdrew it. Nauthiz. Nauthiz? Troubled, I stared at the crossed lines, trying to recall Unferth's long-ago instruction: 'Constraint... necessity... limitation. Troubles and setbacks can be your teachers. Accept them and use them to restore balance to your life.'

Ruefully I wiped my eyes and gently tumbled my rune-sticks back into their bag, whispering, "Whatever Wyrd may bring, I will always love you, Beowulf."

Thinking of Beowulf, I knelt on the floor and pulled out from beneath the bed a small chest which contained the silver bowl he had once given me. Lifting it out, I marveled again at its simple beauty: so perfectly shaped, so delicately incised. On impulse, I set it down carefully on the chest and reached for the jug of water that sat beside my bed. Pouring its contents into the bowl, I breathed a silent prayer: *Freyja, Goddess. Come to me, show me what I need to see!* Expectantly I bent over the bowl.

For a time I saw only my own reflection: dark eyes and parted lips. As I concentrated, the face began to blur and change. Gradually two images formed: the backs of a man and woman, naked, walking hand in hand toward a strange slab of rock. The rock was covered with rune-like markings, symbols... I made out a ship, the sun, a warrior... On the woman's shoulder I saw the image of a small feather. The tall man turned to face her. His beard was white. Beowulf.

With a cry I jumped up, knocking over the bowl and spilling the water on my gown. What can this mean? I whispered to myself, trembling all over. Do we yet have a future together? Carefully I returned the bowl to its chest and placed the chest back under my bed. When I left the bedchamber I felt calmer and lighter, better equipped to face the days ahead.

The group which represented Hrethelskeep at the wedding consisted of Magnus, Wulfgar, Saxe, Estrid, Ingeborg, and me — and, of course, Runa. We were present for the ceremony and stayed for five of the nine days of celebration. Staging a wedding in the midst of winter put a strain on Eaglesgard's resources, but Hygd had refused to wait more than a decent interval following Herdred's funeral pyre. I might have been the only one present who knew the primary reason for her haste.

Estrid and Ingeborg stood beside me in the mead hall as we watched Beowulf lay the hammer of Thor in Hygd's lap and declare their union official. At the wedding feast, I surprised myself by rising to offer a toast.

"To Beowulf and Hygd. May their union be a blessing to the Geats. May their reign bring peace and plenty to all. Wes heil!"

"Wes heil!" shouted the assembled guests.

Hygd beamed in approval, but Beowulf's face wore only a forced smile. He seemed uneasy at the banquet, looking away whenever our eyes happened to meet. One part of me wanted him to share my suffering, but a better part wanted his happiness. Even so, it was hard to look at him and Hygd together, seated side by side on their thrones. Married. King and Queen of the Geats.

When we finally returned to Hrethelskeep, I threw myself into work: starting a new tapestry on one of the looms, taking inventory of all my dried herbs, teaching Inga how to pattern braid . . . Inwardly I longed for warmer days, for the chance to run out of doors without boots and cloaks, for a wild gallop on Burningfax. Runa had returned to my household after Hygd spoke no further of her; now she and Brita began to resume their old bickering. When the first green shoots broke through the sea of mud and slush that surrounded us, we were all more than ready for spring.

Barely two moons later, when I and my women were outside planting the sally garden, two messengers arrived in haste from Eaglesgard: Aksel, and — to my surprise — Dagmar. Straightening from my work, I greeted them in alarm.

"Welcome — but what is amiss? You have clearly ridden hard to reach us!"

"It's the queen. She needs you," declared Aksel, sliding off his horse. He reached up to help Dagmar dismount.

"Come into the house where you can refresh yourselves and we can talk. Inga—" I turned toward my daughter, standing in the middle of the garden staring at the newcomers. "Stay here with the others and help Brita finish that row."

At a wave of my hand everyone returned to their tasks. Wiping my hand on my apron, I led our guests inside. After offering them basin and towel and a cup of ale, I addressed the reason for their visit.

"What is it the queen wants from me?"

"You'll have to ask Dagmar," said Aksel. "I'll go outside and keep your ladies company!" He grinned, bowed, and started to whistle as he headed for the door—no doubt to seek out Estrid.

I drew Dagmar to a bench near the hearth and we sat down together. She looked perplexed, as if not sure what to say or how to say it. Finally she began, solemnly looking down at her hands.

"My lady, this is in the strictest confidence. The queen is . . . troubled . . . by her inability . . . that is, she has not yet . . . conceived a child with the king." She finished in a rush.

"Does she bleed? Are her cycles regular?" I asked calmly.

"Yes, no, that is, her cycles appear to be . . . waning. And there is . . . another problem . . ." her voice trailed off.

"Yes?" I encouraged her gently.

"There is . . . a lack of . . . attention from the king."

"Oh? And what is it the queen wants of *me*?" I asked, my heart turning over.

"She hopes you can provide some tonic, some potion to help them both?" Dagmar looked up at me hopefully.

So. Hygd wants a magical mixture to increase her fertility and a love potion for Beowulf!

I almost choked on a strangled laugh rising in my throat. When I regained my composure, I spoke in low tones.

"There is danger in such tonics and potions. Does the queen realize that?"

"Oh yes," said Dagmar earnestly. "She instructed me to tell you that she would risk anything to bear her husband a son!"

"I see." For a moment I felt almost sorry for Hygd, so desperate that she had sent to her rival for help. Should I help her? Or hinder? Could I help her?

I reached out to touch Dagmar's hand. "There are remedies one could try — for both problems — but I cannot guarantee results."

"Oh my lady, you must try! The queen is counting on you!" Dagmar had risen, wringing her hands.

"Is she? Her confidence may be misplaced, but — yes, I will try what I can do." Now I too rose. "Come with me to the drying shed where my herbs are stored. I will make a careful selection — to aid the queen."

Dagmar put her hand timidly on my arm.

"You remember, my lady that this ... problem ... is to be kept private? No one else here or at court is to know."

I raised my eyebrows. "Does that include Beowulf?"

"It does," said Dagmar emphatically.

Inside the shed I lit several oil lamps to give us good light and began to take down bags from the shelves, opening each and sniffing the contents. In my head I heard Mother's voice: 'Mistakes can be dangerous — even fatal. You must be attentive to details.' Slowly I began to set aside the herbs I would take: flaxseed, motherwort, valerian, crampbark, henbane, pennyroyal.... Dagmar watched me in awe, as if I were a priest performing a ritual. Suddenly I felt humbled by the project I was undertaking.

Freyja, goddess, be with me and guide me. Save me from error. Protect me... from my evil thoughts.

Chapter Nineteen
Hammer of Death

Charm from Iceland depicting Thor gripping his hammer, 11th century.

Back in Eaglesgard I steeled myself against my first sight of Beowulf, but he was absent when Runa and I arrived — out hunting with his athelings, according to Hygd. She welcomed me with open arms and hustled me into her bedchamber, dismissing the thrall who'd lighted oil lamps along one wall. Still it was cold enough to see our breath, and I did not remove my warm cloak. Hygd spoke in low, urgent tones. "Sister Freawaru, your presence here tells me that you are willing to help me produce an heir. What is your plan?"

Surprised at her abruptness, I hesitated.

"Please tell me, Queen Hygd, if I understand the situation correctly. You need an aid to increase your fertility and perhaps a . . . potion . . . to increase desire?"

"Yes!" Hygd clasped her hands together. "I've already tried the remedies concocted by my own women, and nothing has helped. Your knowledge and skill are now my only hope!"

I sat down without speaking, once again on the very bed she must share with Beowulf.

Can I do this thing? Now that I am actually here, I have my doubts!

I tried to clear my head and address the matter as a practical problem.

"Have you tried mallow?" I began.

"Mallow?" Hygd scowled. "We use the roots in a tea to relieve coughing. How could that help me conceive?"

"Boiling the leaves in ale produces a stronger infusion," I said, "but there are other aids as well. A caudle* of parsnips, whose root is shaped like a man's member, may be drunk. And there is always . . . brooklime."

"Brooklime?" Hygd looked doubtful. "Isn't that . . . dangerous?"

"Yes," I said soberly, "it can be dangerous if not carefully controlled."

Hyyd leaned toward me, her eyes imploring." I put myself in your hands, my sister. I will do whatever you say. I will do anything to get with child."

I gulped. Such trust made me uneasy. What if I failed? Or worse, what if I harmed the queen?

"With the help of the goddess, I will do what I can," I whispered, lightly pressing Hygd's hand beside me.

In the days that followed I strove to help the queen achieve her goal. We started by appealing to the goddess. One night during a full moon Hygd and I performed a private ritual in a rocky but sheltered nook beside the sea. We kindled a small fire on the bare rock and sacrificed a lock of Hygd's hair, invoking the goddess Freyja, asking for her help to make Hygd's womb fruitful again. The next day I started Hygd on a course of brooklime and begged Freyja to bring on the moon blood Hygd would need to conceive. I also prepared a poultice of henbane to bind on Hygd's left thigh; according to Runa this never failed to produce a male child.

I do not know which of these measures was responsible, but by the next full moon Hygd's cycle had resumed. Now I had to address the delicate matter of Beowulf's involvement.

Under the bed which Hygd told me she shared with Beowulf I placed runes of binding and increase. Together Hygd and I sacrificed a piglet to

---

* A thickened and sweetened hot alcoholic drink somewhat like eggnog.

Freyr and had the heart cooked and served to Beowulf. To Hygd I served the caudle of parsnip from tubers I'd brought with me.

As spring began to blossom, returning green to the land, Hygd too blossomed, for she missed her cycle and shortly thereafter began to experience queasiness of a morning. I was not present when she revealed her pregnancy to Beowulf, but I hoped it brought him joy. Personally, I was torn between relief that my efforts had been successful and jealousy that Hygd was to bear the child of the man I loved.

I kept to myself, seldom leaving Signe's longhouse, and did not enter the mead hall during my entire stay at Eaglesgard. Runa brought in our meals, and we dined together in companionable silence. As soon as Hygd felt secure enough, we would return to Hrethelskeep.

On the morning of our departure I heard an unexpected knock on the door. Opening it, I stood face to face with Beowulf. For a moment I stood stricken, speechless.

"May I enter?" he asked quietly.

"Of... of course, my lord. Come in." Turning, I nodded to Runa, who faded into the background.

Beowulf stepped inside along with a breath of warm air. Involuntarily I reached toward his hand, then quickly pulled back. Overwhelmed with emotion, I swallowed hard and tried to still the trembling in my limbs. Beowulf stood immobile, staring at me as if trying to solve a problem.

"What have you done, Freaw?"

These words, so unexpected, shocked me into speech.

"Done? It is you and Hygd who have done it, my lord — conceived a child to carry on the Geatish line! You must be..."

I faltered as his eyes bored into mine and a low growl escaped from his throat.

"Hygd and I? Freaw, I have slept with Hygd only once, on our wedding night. What dark magic have you used to produce this ... this unnatural quickening... so many moons later?"

Now it was my turn to stare.

"You slept with Hygd ... only once? I don't understand," I cried, bewildered. "I thought you wanted a child!"

Beowulf reached out to place his huge hands on my shoulders.

"Freaw, I could not do it. I could not betray my love for you — even though duty required it."

"Oh my dear!" I melted into his arms and buried my face against his great chest. "I tried to help Hygd for your sake — for love of you!"

We swayed, locked in a tender but grieving embrace. As I clung to him, words once spoken by Hygd floated into my head: 'I will do anything to get with child!' Suddenly I broke away to look up at him.

"Beowulf, do you have any reason to doubt Hygd's faithfulness?"

His face darkened. "Should I? That could be one explanation..."

I raised my fingers to his lips. "No," I said, "Let us thank the gods for this... this blessing for the Geats, and do not question it. The ways of Wyrd are beyond our understanding."

Beowulf held my gaze, searching my face.

"You may be right, Freaw. Hygd seems genuinely happy now, and I..." he paused. "I won't think ill of her."

Gradually his face brightened.

"Thank the gods? Yes, we will celebrate this... blessing... at the midsummer balefires. Hmm... a child — a son — an heir." Beowulf shook his head. "I never thought to see this day."

"You will have many moons to wait," I cautioned. "This child won't be born until Yuletide."

"Yuletide," he repeated slowly. "A double cause for celebration." He took my hands in his. "Freaw, will you return to us then? I'm told you are leaving Eaglesgard this morning?"

I nodded, suddenly eager for my own house and its familiar faces. "Yes, my lord, I will return at Yule and bring my household to join in the celebration — but if Hygd should need me before then, you have only to send word."

"Dear Freaw, your strength and your kindness do you honor. Thank you for your generous heart."

Bending, he kissed my hands, then raised his head. "Farewell, my Freaw. May the gods go with you."

"Farewell, my lord Beowulf. May the gods be with you — and with Hygd."

I had expected Aksel and Leif to accompany us back to Hrethelskeep, but to my surprise it was Lars and Leif who came to our door later that morning.

"Estrid will be disappointed," whispered Runa in my ear. "I am too, as I'll have to ride beside that rude fellow again!" She gestured toward Lars.

But Lars surprised us both by taking a place at my side as we set off on horseback. As he gave me a crooked grin, I noted that he had lost even more front teeth since his encounter with Stig's fist at Uppsala.

"Good morrow, Lars. I welcome your company," I said blandly.

"Mos' women do," he mouthed and gave me a strange smile, as if he knew a secret.

Ignoring his comment, I urged Burningfax into a trot. Soon Eaglesgard with all its challenges was left far behind me.

We arrived in Hrethelskeep to find the village in an uproar. Marta's little boy Per had just narrowly escaped a gruesome death! I had hardly entered the longhouse when Ingeborg, Estrid, and Ana, each eager to claim a part in the drama, began to regale me. According to Ana, Per had accompanied his mother to the spring, which now trickled slowly from the hillside as winter relinquished its grip. As Marta waited patiently to fill her bucket, the chlld wandered toward the edge of the forest. When a lone wolf suddenly appeared, Marta cried out a warning, but the wolf sprang forward, snatched the boy's arm in its jaws and dragged him toward the trees.

Estrid now picked up the story. "Oh, my lady, it was fortunate for both Marta and Per that Olaf was also in the forest! With one well-aimed arrow he brought down the fearsome creature and saved the child!"

"We heard the whole story when Marta arrived at our longhouse seeking aid for Per's mangled arm," continued Ingeborg. "We bathed the arm with healing herbs and wrapped it loosely with strips of linen."

"Well done! All of you!" I cried, joining the group gathered outside around Olaf and the wolf's carcass. It was a big one, with a beautiful coat and strong white teeth, now stained with blood. Inga tumbled out of the longhouse with Brita behind her. She ran up to clasp me around the legs, then squealed at the sight of the wolf. With a tentative finger she reached out to touch it. Memories flooded over me.

"Your father killed such a wolf long ago. Its skull hung over his mead hall, which he called 'Wulfhaus'."

Inga looked up, curiosity in her eyes. "My father? You never talk about him, Mother. Why is that?"

I knelt and drew her onto my lap, leaning down to stroke her sweaty face.

"The memories are ... painful, my dear. As I've told you before, he died before you were born. But now that I think of it ... Ana," I turned. "Did we bring that pelt from Wulfhaus when we came to Geatland? I can't remember..."

Ana looked over from where she stood beside Marta and the boy, crooning words of comfort.

"Yes, my lady. It's packed in the bottom of one of your chests. Do you want it?"

"Not now, but perhaps later. I have an idea. Please come inside, all of you, and take a seat."

When everyone had trooped into my house, I motioned to Per.

"Come. Sit beside Inga and I will tell you a story — about Tyr, the god who bravely put his hand into a wolf's mouth."

Per stopped whimpering and climbed up to join Inga on a bench. Gently she put her arm around him.

"Long ago, when the gods were young," I began, "the trickster god Loki slept with a giantess. Their union produced three monsters. One was a huge wolf named Fenris. For a while the animal was kept as a pet, but when it grew bigger and bigger, fiercer and fiercer, the gods decided that it must be put on a chain. By now It was too big and strong for anyone to hold it down while the fetter was attached. Finally one god volunteered: Tyr, the god of war, the god whose rune is etched on many a sword blade."

Per's eyes were as wide as Inga's; he was listening intently, as were all the adults gathered around my hearth.

"The gods asked the dwarves to fashion a magical fetter. It was made from the footfall of a cat, the spittle of a bird, the breath of a fish, the roots of a mountain, the beard of a woman, and the sinews of a bear. Tyr assured Fenris that the binding would not hurt or hinder him. As a pledge of his truthfulness, he offered to place his hand in the wolf's mouth."

"Ooooh!" squealed the children, wriggling in anticipation.

"When the shackle was made fast, Fenris could not break it. Realizing that he'd been tricked, he immediately bit off Tyr's hand, leaving him with a bloody stump. So..." I concluded, "You were lucky, Per. You still have your hand, your arm, and your life!"

Olaf slowly stood and addressed the wide-eyed little boy.

"Per, how would you like to help me skin this wolf? I could use some help," he said, winking at me over the boy's head.

"Mother, can I?" Per's eyes were shining as he appealed to Marta.

"Yes, you may. Thank you, Olaf—and all of you," she said shyly, looking around at my women.

I rose, followed by the listeners, who soon took their leave. When they were gone, Inga approached me, her own eyes shining.

"May I see the wolf skin, Mother? Father's wolf skin?"

"Yes, of course. Come. We'll look for it together."

That night Inga went to sleep with the pelt from Wulfhaus tucked beneath her, the tail clutched in her hand.

A day or so later Runa, Estrid, and Ingeborg were sitting beside the hearth winding wool onto spindles for weaving, while Ana and I were busy at the looms. Inga sat beside Runa, idly switching the tail of the wolf pelt. Runa paused and looked up.

"I've been thinking about the part played by the bear in making that shackle for Fenris. Does anyone here know how the bear lost its tail?"

Estrid snickered. "Bears don't have tails—do they?"

"Not now," responded Runa calmly, "at least not much of one, but my grandmother told me that bears had very long tails—once upon a winter."

Estrid and Ingeborg smirked, their expressions dubious, but Inga dropped the pelt and reached up to touch Runa's arm.

"Tell me, please, Runa, how *did* the bear lose his tail?"

Just then Brita stuck her head out of the byre to call out, "I want to hear the story too!"

At my nod she entered to join the group, bringing the smell of our animals.

"It happened like this," said Runa, her fingers flying as she continued her work. "In the old days the animals could talk to one another and they had friends and enemies just like us. One animal was very smart: Foxy. Another animal was not so smart: Bear. Even so, the two were often together.

"One winter's day Foxy was enjoying a feast of fish which he had stolen from an ice fisherman's sledge, when Bear happened by and called out, 'Where did you get that big fish, old friend?' 'Why, I caught it at the lake,' answered Foxy. 'Could you show me how to catch such a fish?' asked Bear, his mouth watering. 'For you, old friend, I will share my secret,' declared Foxy. 'Just go down to the lake on a clear, cold night, put your tail into the hole which the fisherman has made in the ice, and sit there without moving until morning.'

"Thanks, friend Foxy, I'll try it right away,' said Bear, and indeed he put Foxy's advice to the test the very next night — a clear, cold night with a sky full of stars. After pushing his tail into the fisherman's *avanto*, he sat very still. When the water in the hole began to freeze, Bear felt little prickles all over his tail, but he was pleased, thinking that fish were nibbling at it.

"When morning came, Bear tried to pull out his tail, anticipating a great catch. He yanked and tugged, tugged and yanked, but his tail was frozen fast in the ice. Soon Foxy came loping by. 'Help me, old friend,' cried Bear. 'I can't get loose!' Immediately Foxy ran to the fisherman's hut and yelled, 'Bear is stealing your fish! Bear is stealing your fish!' The fisherman rushed out with a stout stick and began to beat Bear, who strove mightily to free himself from the ice.

"At last, with a mighty heave, Bear wrenched himself free and ran off toward the forest, but his tail had snapped off and remained in the ice. And that is why, from that day to this, Bear has always had a short, stubby tail." Runa smiled broadly. "Stars, moon, sun — my tale is done."

Inga laughed out loud; then she sobered. "Fox was mean to Bear. I wouldn't want a friend like that!" Picking up the wolf pelt, she stroked its fur thoughtfully.

Brita stood and stretched. "I'd better get back to cleaning out the byre, but tell me this, Runa: have you ever seen a bear?"

Runa looked up. "Yes. My people revered that animal. My grandfather once killed a bear to save his own life. The men in the village made a great sacrifice afterward to appease the bear's spirit. Grandfather hung one of its claws over our door to fend off evil."

We all stared at her, imagining the sharp tips of a great claw. Ana shuddered.

"Puts me in mind of that . . . that Grendel."

A shiver ran down my own back, but I shook it off.

"No more stories today. The Grendel is long dead — and so is its dam. We are safe in Hrethelskeep now, thanks to Beowulf."

My women nodded vigorously in agreement. "Thanks to Beowulf."

Soon it was time for our midsummer bonfires, and a time for public celebration of Queen Hygd's pregnancy. Inga and Toke gathered armfuls of broken branches from the riverside to toss onto the blazing heap in the clearing outside the mead hall. They reminded me of my two young brothers in their childhood days, and tears sprang to my eyes.

Strange. I have not thought of Heorot for many seasons. Hrethelskeep is now my home.

Toasts were drunk to the queen, to the king, and to the Geats in general. We basked in the warmth of the fires and the peace that Beowulf had won for all our people.

Shortly after this celebration came the first of many requests I was to receive over the summer to visit outlying farmsteads. I was asked to make pronouncements about the future of a couple soon to wed, to predict the success of the fall harvest, to recommend healing remedies for the sick, even to settle quarrels between neighbors. Runa and one or two of our men accompanied me on these trips. Over time she and I developed a special ritual for such occasions, using her flute or my drum. We even made a special cloak of animal skins for me to wear.

Back in Hrethelskeep I occasionally consulted my runes for a long-range prediction, hoping to see what lay ahead for me, my household, and . . . for Hygd. The rune which presented itself most often was Pertho: a rune of mystery with varied interpretations. Apparently I was being told to wait with patience for whatever would unfold.

Inga grew a full head taller than Toke that summer, although he was the older of the two. She seemed to shoot up like a young willow, all arms and legs, but with none of the awkwardness sometimes seen in girls her age. Toke followed her everywhere, a willing participant in whatever she wanted to do.

One day after they had been playing Geats and Swedes, Inga asked me an unexpected question. I was seated beside the hearth sorting herbs for drying, when she came in, sweaty-faced and breathing heavily.

"Mother, was my father like Beowulf?"

Taken aback, I paused to gather my thoughts. Inga's dark eyes never left my face.

"Ingeld was tall and strong like Beowulf," I began, "and his fame as a warrior was unquestioned."

Inga frowned. "Did he like little girls? Would he have liked me? Beowulf likes me!"

I sighed. "I'm sure Ingeld would have loved his daughter, had he lived to see her. He loved me, your mother."

Did he? Yes, he did, but he loved honor more — and paid the price for his choice!

"Mother? Don't cry! I'm sorry, I did not mean to hurt you!"

Inga, big as she was, had crawled onto my lap and thrown her arms around my neck.

"Am I crying?" I shook my head in surprise and hugged my daughter gently, then released her.

"Speaking of Beowulf, let me show you the tapestry I've started — as a gift for the baby he and Hygd are expecting."

Obediently Inga slid off my lap and followed me into the weaving room, where I showed her my charcoal sketch on sheepskin of a child at the helm of a longboat.

"My own mother once wove such a design — when I was just a child," I said quietly.

"Grandmother?" Inga looked at me inquiringly. "Tell me her name again."

"Wealtheow," I said.

"Wealtheow," repeated Inga slowly, "another person who died before I was born?"

"Perhaps not. Someday I may be able to answer that question. Now, it is time for me to work on this tapestry, and I hear Toke calling for you outside. Give me a kiss, then run and play."

Inga's soft lips touched mine before she bounded out of the longhouse.

Spring, summer, autumn came and went with no major disturbances to mar our tranquility. An occasional visitor from Eaglesgard brought news of the queen's developing pregnancy, but no request for assistance. All must be well. Our fall harvest was bountiful, easily providing the annual tribute due the king. We gave thanks to Freyr and Freyja for the fertility of the land and for continued peace. Soon the cold and Yule were upon us.

After completing the usual slaughter and butchering of animals for our winter stores, I and my household prepared for the journey to Eaglesgard. Beowulf had invited Magnus and several other villagers to attend the Yule celebration as well as we Danes, so our party was a large one, requiring horse-sledges. Thorkel and Ragnhild chose to stay behind, for their infant son was sickly.

Heavy, wet snow had fallen the night before our departure. Some tree branches sagged to the ground; others dropped showers of snow on our heads as we passed beneath. My mood was joyful as I breathed in the fresh winter air, wrapped in furs against the cold, Burningfax frisking and snorting beneath me. Wulfgar and Magnus led the way as we left the village. Inga rode in a sledge, bundled between Ana and Brita, but Estrid, Ingeborg, and Runa rode horseback along with the rest of our men.

During the journey I thought back on all that had happened since our arrival in Hrethelskeep: our women's rituals, Beowulf's declaration of love, Inga's birth, the sacrifices at Uppsala, Onela's attack, Herdred's death, Beowulf's marriage, and Hygd's pregnancy.

Life is a struggle, but there is much to savor in times of sweetness. Thank you, Freyja, for all you have granted me.

Upon our arrival in Eaglesgard, we were directed to various longhouses where we would lodge during our stay. My women and I were welcomed by Signe, my former host.

"How is the queen?" I asked, after we had settled in and warmed ourselves at the hearth.

Signe frowned. "Very large, my lady. I fear she may be carrying twins. I hope you plan to stay for the birthing?"

"Yes, Signe, I do."

Twins? I lost twin boys at Wulfhaus! I hope Hygd has a better outcome!

When I saw Hygd in her bedchamber shortly before the welcoming feast, my first reaction was one of concern. Besides her huge belly, her hands looked puffy and her face bloated. After an awkward embrace, I asked, "How are you feeling, Queen Hygd?"

She laughed a tired laugh. "Big. Heavy. My head hurts and my eyes are blurry—but in one more moon this will all be over, thank the gods!"

Her answer jolted me, for her symptoms did not seem normal.

"Are you still feeling the baby?" I asked cautiously.

Hygd brought her face close to mine, as if trying to focus. "Indeed! He kicks vigorously every night, keeping me awake!"

Suddenly she groaned and pressed both hands against her back.

"Should you be attending this banquet tonight? Bed rest might be more advisable," I said anxiously.

Hygd groaned again. "You may be right, but I want to greet our guests and sit beside Beowulf in the high seat as usual." She smiled weakly. "Thank you for your concern, my sister."

That night Hygd did indeed sit beside Beowulf, but she did not stay long. When she excused herself and summoned Dagmar and Kirsten to help her out of the hall, I too rose from my place at a front table, but Hygd bid me stay and enjoy the feast. I sat back down as whole roasted pigs were carried in and served to each table.

Salty pork? Not a good dish for one in Hygd's condition! Has she been eating this all winter?

The evening was far advanced and I was considering a return to Signe's house to rejoin Inga, Brita, and Runa, when Signe herself bustled into the mead hall and hurried to my table.

"Lady Freawaru, come quickly! The queen is stricken!"

Signe's face was white, her eyes wide with fear. Startled, I rose, my eyes turning toward Beowulf. Should he be told?

Signe was pulling at my arm. "Hurry! Hurry!"

We almost ran from the hall, leaving behind us a wave of consternation.

Hygd lay on her bed, her face twitching. Suddenly her body went rigid, hands clenched and eyes bulging.

"Help her! Help her!" begged Signe. "I don't know what to do!"

"Nor do I," I admitted, staring in horror at the queen, whose jaw now began to open and shut violently. Her whole body shuddered and she made a sudden movement as if to fling herself off the bed. Signe and I were barely able to restrain her.

"Dagmar! Kirsten! Help us!" cried Signe.

Hygd's face contorted, turning purple, and blood-tinged foam drooled from her mouth. Dagmar screamed at the sight; Kirsten backed away without speaking.

"She's stopped breathing! She's not breathing!" cried Signe. "Do something!"

Frantically I placed my hands on her chest and pushed. Hygd exhaled loudly and resumed breathing, but she did not open her eyes. As suddenly as it had started, the convulsion stopped.

"Hygd? Hygd! Can you hear me? Speak to me!" I implored, of what I now feared was the dying queen.

A stir and tramp of feet behind us signaled the arrival of Beowulf. He pushed past Dagmar and Kirsten as he charged into the chamber, staring wildly at the still form on the bed.

"What's happening? What's wrong with Hygd?"

"Beowulf, I fear she is dying!" I cried, my eyes stinging with sudden tears.

"My lord," croaked Signe hoarsely, "it may still be possible to save the baby. Shall we try?"

Beowulf whirled to face me. "Must I choose? Hygd or the chlld? Can't you save them both, Freaw?"

I gulped. "I'll do what I can, Beowulf. This goes beyond all my experience, but I will try . . . Signe, fetch me brooklime and pennyroyal!"

For most of that night Hygd hovered between life and death. Our attempts to induce labor only brought on further convulsions, impossible to control. Shortly before dawn the queen died.

When Hygd's women sent up a keening wail, Beowulf immediately appeared in the doorway.

"'Is she . . . ."

"Hygd is gone, my lord. Your queen is dead."

Exhausted, I staggered back, then rallied to pull the women out of the chamber, intending to give Beowulf time alone with Hygd. Signe, however, shook me off vehemently.

"No! There is still a chance to save this baby! We must cut to the womb!"

Beowulf's face drained of color as he backed away, out of the chamber.

"Stay, my lady," barked Signe. "I'll need your help. Kirsten, fetch clean towels. Dagmar, hand me the birthing knife. We must act quickly!"

I could hardly bear to look as Signe's knife split the taut skin of Hygd's belly from navel to crotch.

"Hold back the skin flaps while I make the next cut," instructed Signe. "Kirsten, use a towel to staunch the blood."

Kirsten fainted, dropping like a stone, but Dagmar snatched a towel and pressed it against the pulpy mass exposed by Signe's knife. I steeled myself to avoid joining Kirsten on the floor as Signe used her blade a second time and put her hand into the new opening.

"I feel a leg!" she crowed, as fluid gushed from the cavity. "Dagmar, wrap a towel around my other hand so I can get a better grip!"

Scarcely breathing, we watched in fascination and dread as Signe gently pulled. Two legs. Buttocks. A body. A head. Signe held up the baby and gave it a smart smack on the bottom, but it gave no cry. Its face was blue, the eyes shut tight. I saw a tiny penis. A boy. Dead.

Signe began to shake, her mouth opening in a strangled wail. Tenderly I took the baby from her, the cord still attached, wrapped the child in a clean cloth and laid it on Hygd's breast. Reviving Kirsten, Signe sent her for water and strips of linen with which to clean and bind Hygd's body. Signe was so exhausted she could barely stand or speak. It fell to me to give Beowulf the news.

I found him pacing furiously outside the longhouse, oblivious to the wind and snow. Beckoning him inside, I took his cold hands in mine.

"Hygd gave you a son, my lord, but he did not survive. I am sorry."

Beowulf received my words in silence, his eyes already red-rimmed and swollen. Finally he spoke.

"May I see her now?"

"Yes, my lord."

Later that morning after Beowulf had left and the news of the double deaths had spread shock and grief over the settlement, her women bathed Hygd's body in herb-scented water and dressed her in a white gown that matched the pallor of her skin. They arranged her body, the baby in her arms, readying both for their rebirth in the funeral fire.

When I finally staggered back into Signe's longhouse at mid-morning, Inga approached hesitantly, then flung her arms around my waist.

"Oh Mother, Mother, don't ever die!"

I stroked her hair, loosened her grasp, and slumped to the floor. Signe and Ingeborg helped me rise and walk to a bench, where I collapsed and gave myself up to sleep. Overcome with grief and remorse, I slept through the rest of that day and through the night. I did not wish to awaken even then, but Inga insisted.

"Mother? Mother! Open your eyes!"

Slowly I raised my lids to see Inga's face hovering above me, her eyes filled with tears. Shaking my shoulders, she cried, "Don't leave me, Mother, don't leave me!"

Groggily I sat up.

"Inga? I'm here, child. I've not left you."

In a sudden spasm of pain, the reality of Hygd's death struck me full force. *Hygd is gone. She and her child. They are gone forever.* Drawing Inga to my breast, I nuzzled her head with my chin, murmuring, "Child, child, be comforted. We are here ... together. You are safe in your mother's arms."

I tried to put on a brave face for Inga and my women, but Hygd's death and my inability to save her or her child shook me to the depths. In my mind I relived the horrific scene over and over.

What did I do wrong? What else could I have done? Where was the goddess? Was Wyrd to blame?

A long-ago vision floated up from memory, a vision I'd seen shortly after our first landing at Eaglesgard: Hygd's body covered in blood, writhing on a bed of pain. Perhaps it was her fate to die?

Shock and grief swept over the settlement. All thoughts of celebration were forgotten as everyone, Geat and Dane alike, reeled from this sudden, unexpected blow. Beowulf shut himself up in his quarters for a time, finally emerging to direct the building of a funeral pyre at cliff's edge, near the spot used for Herdred and Hygelac. All three, gone. Of the House of Hrethel, only Beowulf now remained.

Hygd was laid out on the bed on which she had died, covered by my cloak of fox pelts — my offering. Four men lifted the bed onto the platform just before the pyre was lighted. Fresh snow had settled on the timbers, making them slow to ignite. Darkness was approaching by the time it fully caught fire. Hygd's women had added her fine gowns, warm cloaks, gold rings, silver bracelets, and twisted collars to the pyre, along with tools for spinning and weaving. Beowulf sacrificed her favorite horse. With a groan of exertion he placed it on the pyre himself. The men of Eaglesgard stood stony-faced around the pyre, except for Lars, who wept openly. I thought better of him for this honest expression of grief.

"Good-bye, my sister," I whispered, as Hygd's body and that of her child disappeared in smoke and fire, spiraling up into the frosty night. "Good-bye."

Two days after the funeral pyre, Redbeard sought me out. He wanted my help in reassuring and guiding the settlement. With the queen dead and Beowulf in seclusion, he feared that Eaglesgard might go adrift, like a rudderless ship.

"But I'm an outsider," I protested.

"People here respect you," he began, "and we need to restore the normal order of daily life. Circulate among the women. Speak of Hygd openly and give others a chance to air their grief. Join me in the mead hall. We'll ask Jesper to tell the Geats' favorite stories and sing their favorite songs. Above all," he continued earnestly, "we need to help Beowulf resume his duties as leader of the Geats. You can reach him, my lady. He will listen to you."

I listened. I took a deep breath. Finally I agreed to do what I could.

I sought to comfort Beowulf at every opportunity. Although I knew that only time could lessen the deep pain that laid him low, I grew alarmed when I heard that he was asking the harper to sing 'Hrethel's Lament' night after night in the mead hall. One night I slipped inside to hear it for myself. Jesper was chanting the lament, but I could not see Beowulf in the dark interior.

> *The crime is great, the guilt is plain*
> *But nothing can be done, no death,*
> *No vengeance, no requital, none.*
> *My son has slain my son.*
> *The harp is silent, hope forgotten.*
> *Each morn remember and despair,*
> *My home a wasteland, emptiness.*
> *All cheer, all pleasure lost and gone*
> *Nothing helps, not word nor hand*
> *Nor sharp-honed blade, nor war nor hate.*
> *My son has slain my son.*
> *The harp is silent, hope forgotten.*
> *Lay me down on a bed of sorrow*
> *Leaving life and grief together.*

When my eyes adjusted to the dim hearthlight, I saw Beowulf seated on his throne, alone, his head in his hands. When I approached, Jesper withdrew. Beowulf lifted his head, his eyes dull and unseeing.

"It's me, my lord, Freaw."

"Freaw? Freaw, it's my fault. I killed Hygd." He choked back a sob. "I never should have touched her! It's all my fault!"

Now he broke into great sobs, his shoulders heaving. I knelt beside him, waiting for the spasm of recrimination to pass. When it spent itself, I placed both hands on his knee.

"Beowulf, you are adding to your own burden. Hygd would not want you to blame yourself! She rests in the house of Freyja now, where she has found peace. She would want peace for you as well."

The face he turned to me was not Beowulf's face. For a moment I saw Hrothgar, my father, his face distorted in agony over the loss of his comrades to the Grendel.

"Your people still need you, my lord. They need your help to carry on, to go forward after this great loss. They . . ."

"Do *you* still need me, Freaw?" interrupted Beowulf, seizing my wrists. "I need you, but I will not destroy you as I destroyed Hygd!"

He spoke so fiercely I recoiled. Pulling free, I stood, choking back a sob.

"Beowulf, Beowulf, if there is blame to be placed, lay it on me," I cried. "I helped Hygd in her quest to conceive a child. She called me 'sister,'" I sobbed, "but I failed her, Beowulf, I failed her in her time of need."

Now my own tears began to flow in a torrent. Rising, Beowulf encircled my shoulders with his great arms and held me fast. I had been holding in my own grief for days, but now let it pour forth freely: grief, guilt, pain, and sorrow. Locked in each other's arms, we mourned our loss together.

When at last he was able to speak, Beowulf said, "Freaw, I have a great boon to ask of you. Could you, would you, stay in Eaglesgard through the rest of the winter? The people need you now, and I want you here beside me."

I did not answer immediately, conflicting thoughts racing through my head. Finally I voiced my misgivings.

"What would be my position here, Beowulf? Your people might be outraged if I seemed to be assuming Hygd's place, so soon after her death."

"My honored guest?" offered Beowulf. "You could act as hostess in my mead hall here when I am absent, just as you have done at Hrethelskeep. Come spring I will build you a new longhouse — big enough to hold all your people, if you like."

"Very generous, my lord. Let me talk to my household," I paused, then smiled. "I know it would make Inga happy. She's very fond of you."

At the mention of Inga, Beowulf's face softened.

"Dear child — she's a younger version of you, dear Freaw."

The decision to go or stay was taken out of my hands when the weather worsened. A storm blew in with blizzard force, piling snow in great drifts up to the roofs of the houses and making travel impossible.

In the long, dark days that followed, I seldom saw Beowulf, but when I did he gave me no cause for concern. I did not fear for him until Wulfgar came stamping a path to my door one gray morning. He told me that Beowulf had once again locked himself in his quarters and was now refusing food and drink.

Packing a basket and wrapping myself in my warmest cloak, I struggled through the snow behind Wulfgar to Beowulf's longhouse. Only a thin thread of smoke rose from the smoke hole. Upon entering, we saw that no lamps were lit; the only light came from the hearth.

At the door to Beowulf's chamber I took a packet from the basket before handing it to Wulfgar, then knocked softly on the door.

"Beowulf," I called. "It's Freaw. May I enter?"

"Better you don't. I'm not fit company. Better I'm left alone." His voice sounded hollow and hopeless.

"Not better for me, Beowulf. I love you. I want us both to go the same way. Please see me." I lifted the latch. "I'm coming in."

"If you must."

I pushed open the door. With the light from the outer room I could just make out Beowulf sitting in his nightclothes on the edge of the bed.

"May I join you there?"

Beowulf motioned for me to come over. Closing the door, I made my way to the bed and sat down near him.

"You show great love for me, Freaw," he said heavily.

"As you have shown me in the past, my love. I do not want to live if you are dead."

I put a piece of the seaweed I'd brought into my mouth and began to chew loudly.

"What are you doing?" asked Beowulf. "Are you chewing something?"

"Yes, I'm chewing seaweed. Signe told me it will hasten my death so that I won't have to live so long without you. I have enough for us both. Give me your hand."

He did. I gave him a strand and went on chewing. In a moment I heard him doing the same. A little later I called out to Wulfgar for water and he brought a drinking horn to the door. I met him and took the horn for a long drink.

"Beowulf, would you like a drink?"

"Yes, this seaweed has made me very thirsty."

I passed the horn to him. He took a great draught, then spat.

"We've been tricked!" he cried. "This is milk!"

Beowulf bit a piece from the rim, then flung the horn aside.

"Our plan has failed," I cried, "but I have another. Now I want us both to stay alive, long enough for you to compose a verse in Hygd's memory and to carve it onto a rune-stick. Then, if we still want to, we can die."

Silence, then a long, low chuckle from Beowulf.

"As you wish, Freaw. I will follow your plan."

After that there were no more solitary retreats on Beowulf's part, and despite the winter gloom, life at Eaglesgard took on a more cheerful cast. But the event which finally lifted Beowulf's depression arrived quite unexpectedly—from the sea.

A ship appeared below Eaglesgard one clear, crisp day, bearing Eadgils, the Swedish prince. All were amazed.

"We thought you dead, or captured by Onela's forces in the battle on the ice," declared Beowulf when Eadgils was brought before him. I happened to be inside the mead hall and stayed in the shadows to listen.

"I *was* captured that day, my lord, but Stig helped me escape during the army's return to Uppsala. I was gone before Onela could miss me." Eadgils smirked, throwing back his long, tangled locks.

"What brings you back to Eaglesgard?" demanded Beowulf suspiciously.

"I have been amassing forces for a renewed attack on Onela," declared Eadgils. "Brecca of the Brondings has pledged a hundred men, likewise Hrolf Kraki of the Danes. I invite you and your men to join us."

Beowulf squinted at Eadgils as if considering. "But the seas will be frozen around Uppsala. How do you propose to get there?" he queried.

"By land—by horse and sledge—just as we did before—but this time with a much greater force! I am determined to take back the kingdom that is rightfully mine—and avenge the death of my brother! Will you join me?"

Eadgils' pose was challenging. I shivered, wondering how Beowulf would respond.

Beowulf rose, shouting, "By the gods! I will join you! I will avenge the deaths of Herdred—and of Hygd!"

Every man in the mead hall leapt to his feet, shouting and shaking his fist. Beowulf called for food and ale; soon the hall was filled with the cheerful sounds of men eating, drinking, and laughing together. I slipped out unnoticed to carry the news to my women.

At first I was horrified by the prospect of more war, and more death—my mind in turmoil

We've been living in peace, in no immediate danger from the Swedes. Now this Eadgils arrives, stirring up battle-lust among the Geats, whetting their appetite for revenge—just as Starcartherus incited the Heathobards to attack Heorot. That resulted in the death of my husband!

It's the same old story: men charge exultantly into battle, leaving women behind to worry and wait. Just when Beowulf and I might finally forge a life together, this happens! Is our path to be blocked again? If he goes to war, like Ingeld, Beowulf may be killed!

By the time I arrived at Signe's longhouse, to be greeted first by Inga, my focus had shifted. *Beowulf is the king, responsible for all his people's safety. It's not only the Geats; he wants to protect you too, Freaw, you and Inga.* Still, it was with a heavy heart that I reported what I had heard to my household.

The prospect of battle seemed to enliven every man at Eaglesgard. Even Magnus, who'd been grumbling for days about the need to get back to Hrethelskeep, swore that if he were younger he'd show the Swedes what a real warrior could do! When I consulted Wulfgar about his wishes, he answered without hesitation, "We'll follow Beowulf, my lady."

To Beowulf himself, who invited me to sit beside him at the next night's feast, I observed that he had once given this advice to my father Hrothgar: "It is better to avenge dear ones than to indulge in mourning forever." Admittedly, this was followed by my sigh of resignation.

Beowulf nodded eagerly, giving me a smile that lit up his whole face.

"'I am glad you understand, Freaw. This time we'll put an end to the Swedish threat that's been hanging over us. No more talk! This time a decisive battle!" He grinned. "According to Eadgils, Hrolf Kraki is sending twelve of his champions, including several berserkers!"

"Hrolf Kraki was once Hrothulf, my cousin and my enemy," I said dryly. "I hope he keeps his word, Beowulf."

As it turned out, both Hrolf Kraki and Brecca kept their word and each sent their hundred men to join Eadgils and Beowulf. Profit and plunder motivated many, for Eadgils had promised rich rewards to those who helped him win back his kingdom. Others were simply eager for fame and glory.

The army that massed outside Eaglesgard surpassed any sight in my experience. An entire camp was set up at the edge of the settlement, with rows of tents pitched for the warriors. As always, bringing up horses from the harbor was difficult and slow. Among the men working at this task were Unferth's former companions, Bodvar Bjarki and Hjalti. I was outside supervising the distribution of provisions when I saw them and stopped to stare. Bodvar returned my look.

"By the gods, it's Lady Freawaru! Well met, my lady! King Hrolf Kraki sends you his greetings!"

"He does? Beg pardon, Bodvar. I bid you welcome to Eaglesgard. Is Unferth with you?"

"Not this time, my lady. King Hrolf could not spare him."

"I see. How fares King Hrolf?"

"He's well, my lady. Please excuse me. I must finish my work." He bowed and turned. "Come, Hjalti, we have three more horses to bring up."

Hjalti bobbed his head at me as he followed Bodvar back toward the cliff.

Before the army's departure, Beowulf asked me for a rune reading. We chose a quiet early morning in the empty mead hall, where a thrall had built up the hearth fire for our meeting. Beowulf, having never seen me consult the runes before, was curious about the procedure. He sat down across from me as I spread my small white cloth on the table.

"I will pull three runes from my deerskin bag and lay them out in sequence right to left," I said. "The first rune will indicate our present situation. The second indicates the action called for. Finally, the likely outcome will be revealed by the third."

"Freaw, I respect your gifts, but you say 'likely' for the outcome?"

"Yes, my lord." I nodded. "The gods never fully reveal all that is to come. Shall we begin?"

"Yes."

"First we must invoke the giver of the runes." Closing my eyes, I raised one arm and intoned: "Great Odin, guide my hand. Grant me the wisdom to read aright the message sent."

Still with closed eyes, I thought of all the men and horses gathered at Eaglesgard. Reaching into the pouch, my fingers closed on a rune. Without opening my eyes I laid it on the cloth, then reached for another and laid it beside the first. The last rune seemed to avoid my fingers, but finally one fit itself into my hand and I drew it forth. Only when I had placed the final rune beside the others did I open my eyes.

Beowulf leaned forward eagerly. "What do they mean?"

I scrutinized the three runes lying face down before me and turned over the first.

"This is Isa, the ice rune. It speaks of a period of waiting, a freeze of action, with events at a standstill."

"The death of Herdred — and now Hygd — these have brought me to a stop," murmured Beowulf. "What comes next?" he asked, his brow wrinkling.

"Patience, my lord. I'll turn over the second rune. Ah, it's Raido, the journey rune. This rune advises forward movement."

Beowulf's face brightened. "The action required is a journey? A journey to attack the Swedes!"

"So it would seem," I said, "but the third rune holds the crucial message." Slowly I turned it over.

"Tyr's victory sign!" crowed Beowulf. "Every warrior knows that sign!"

"Yes," I confirmed, "it is Teiwaz, rune of the war god, giver of battle courage. This rune calls for action, for conquest."

We gazed at each other in growing awareness.

"At last!" Beowulf rose to his feet. "At last! The gods are with us!"

I too rose as Beowulf came around the table, wrapped his arms around me, and lifted me off my feet.

"Thank you, my Freaw! The goddess be praised for your special gifts!"

"The runes are a good omen, my lord, but no guarantee."

Fanning the Flames

I and my people decided to travel behind the army on the frozen Göta as far as Hrethelskeep. Saxe and Gorm were sent ahead with Lars and Leif to alert the village. A few days of sunshine had recently softened the snow, making it easier for men, horses, and sledges to break a path to the river. Still, when the army set forth from Eaglesgard, it would be the depth of winter and their journey a test of endurance.

On the morning of departure, Ketil took me aside, his face solemn.

"My lady, while I was on duty outside the mead hall last night, I saw something I knew you'd want to hear about . . . in the night sky."

"In the night sky?" I echoed. "What did you see?"

"A long tongue of flame — perhaps a dragon, or something like it?"

"May it be an omen of success," I exclaimed, "foretelling doom for our enemies!"

Ketil nodded. "Like Thor's thunderbolt? Yes, that could be it." He continued to nod vigorously, a grin spreading across his face. "Lady Freawaru, we need you here. I hope you'll return to Eaglesgard come spring."

I grimaced. "First we'll see what the winter brings." Unspoken was the yet-to-be-determined fate of our army.

We set forth on a crisp, cold day, but not a bitter one, for the wind was down. By travelling in the van of the army, my group found the way easy. Magnus and Wulfgar led us once again, followed by Runa and me. Estrid and Ingeborg's horses pulled the sledge where Inga sat wedged between Ana and Brita. Our young men rode at the rear.

By midday we had reached Hrethelskeep. Accompanied by Magnus, we women returned to our longhouses. The rest of the men went on with Beowulf. No time was spent on leave-taking, with Eadgils urging on the men. I had bidden Beowulf goodbye before we left Eaglesgard. Now his fate, and the fate of hundreds of other men, lay with the gods.

Thora was the first to visit us upon our return, arriving at our door with a kettle of steaming soup, fragrant with herbs.

"Chicken — with dried rosemary — but no mushrooms — just the way you like it." She smiled. "Welcome home, my lady. We've missed you, all of you."

Inga rushed up to hug Thora before she could relinquish the kettle.

"Where's Toke, Thora? I have so much to tell him! There was a BIG funeral fire, and mama let me watch it, and Beowulf told me . . ."

"Wait, wait, Inga. Let Thora put down her kettle," I admonished. "We have the rest of the winter to tell our stories!"

Thora laughed, hanging the kettle on an iron hook over the hearth. "I'm glad to hear that. From what Saxe told us, I thought you might be returning soon to Eaglesgard." Her voice held a question.

"Beowulf did ask me to stay," I confided, "but until we know the outcome of this attack on the Swedes, nothing can be decided."

Thora's smile disappeared. "I could hardly believe it when Saxe and Gorm brought us word of this second campaign," she blazed. "At least Rolf stayed home this time — his mother is so sick I wanted him to be here for her passing."

"Gunilla? What's wrong? She seemed well enough before we left!" I exclaimed.

Thora shrugged. "Old age and bad lungs, I'd say. At night she can barely breathe."

"Oh, Thora, I'll go to see her right away. My women can tend to the unpacking."

"Have your soup first," instructed Thora, turning toward the door. "I'll tell Gunilla to expect you. She will be pleased."

Gunilla was pleased by my visit, but also confused about the reason for my long absence.

"Did you finally marry Beowulf?" she quavered, reaching out her bony fingers.

I took her hands. "No, Gunilla. Beowulf was married to Hygd — but she died in childbirth."

"Your child? With Beowulf?" She began to gasp for air as a fit of coughing seized her.

"Here, Mother, try a cup of this mallow tea." Thora lifted a mug to the old woman's lips and she managed a few sips.

"Rest yourself, Gunilla," I soothed. "There's no need to talk now. We'll have time later."

I glanced at Thora, who shook her head. Clearly, the old woman might soon be gone.

A few nights later Gunilla died in her sleep. I wept to hear it, remembering Gunilla in earlier, happier days. More deaths followed, including that of Thorkel and Ragnhild's infant son. Thorkel had followed Beowulf to war, and was not present to comfort his wife when their baby died.

Fanning the Flames

"Oh, my lady, will Thorkel return to me?" implored Ragnhild. She had joined me and my women in our longhouse one dark afternoon. "Can't you use your sight to find out what's happening in the war?"

I sighed. "I have tried, Ragnhild, I have tried, but all I can see is ice. Somehow the ice has a role to play in this battle."

Ice. Once again the battle between the Geats and the Swedes was decided on the ice of Lake Vänern. When the army finally returned, after almost a moon's absence, their sledges bore dead and wounded. Among our men, cheerful, faithful Saxe and Gorm had been slain, as well as Emund's son Mattias; Olaf was alive but badly wounded. Thorkel returned unscathed, as did Wulfgar. Beowulf's comrade Leif had been killed in the battle, and Aksel wounded, but Beowulf himself—Beowulf lived!

Overjoyed to see him whole and safe, I did not ask for details of the battle, nor did he offer any, only stopping in Hrethelskeep long enough to assure me of his survival and announce a complete victory over the Swedes. Onela and all his men had been destroyed. Eadgils had returned to Uppsala in triumph to claim the throne

Many Danish and Norse warriors had gone on to Uppsala with Eadgils to form his new fighting force and receive their promised rewards, so our army was smaller by half upon its return. I noticed Bodvar Bjarki and Hjalti among the men returning with Beowulf, and Brecca's two sons, Edvard and Erik. The latter stood out from the rest of the men due to their bright red hair and beards. Apparently, for some men, defeating the Swedes had been glory and satisfaction enough.

We heard a few details from Olaf as he began to recover. Runa seemed especially fond of Olaf, for she tended him night and day. When told of the deaths of his long-time comrades, he wept, but gave a glowing account of their prowess in battle.

"When I was injured by a spear thrust," he told us, "Saxe carried me to safety while Gorm fought off attackers. Then Saxe ran back to join him. They were filled with battle-lust, laughing and shouting. Now they are gone . . . to Valhalla." His eyes misted. "I wish I could join them."

"Nay, nay, Olaf. They died with honor, and you are needed here in Hrethelskeep," I said, smoothing back the hair that fell over one eye, but inwardly I too wept for our companions, now lost to us.

One funeral pyre was erected to honor those slain in battle. Together the village mourned the deaths of our three brave young men.

Wulfgar gave us a fuller account of the battle one night in the mead hall. Young and old alike crowded inside, eager to learn the full story, to hear every detail of this great victory over their enemy of many generations. Toke's mother let him join Inga at our table, and the two sat wiggling with anticipation, delighted to be up so long past their bedtimes. Light from all the torches brightened our faces and created flickering shadows on the walls above. When everyone had found places and settled in to listen, Wulfgar rose and strode forward to stand beside the high seat.

"Somehow the Swedes learned of our coming," he began, "and we lost the element of surprise, but we did reach Lake Vänern in record time. Eadgils and Beowulf sent out two men to test the ice for depth and stability. They reported it safe for men, but feared it was not safe enough for the additional weight of horses. We therefore tethered our mounts behind trees on the shore before continuing our advance. A strong wind at our backs whipped our banners and swept the ice clean of snow."

Wulfgar paused to take a long draught of the ale offered by a waiting servant.

"We soon saw Onela's forces advancing from the north. When, at last, they were within spear range, Eadgils signaled the charge, blowing a blast on his horn. Beowulf threw the first spear, dedicating our victory to Odin. Then he drew his sword and we clashed head-on with the Swedes."

Wulfgar stared ahead as if reliving that moment of impact. Beside me, Toke and Inga shivered.

"Several berserkers with battle-axes fought beside Beowulf and Eadgils, helping them cut down the first wave of Swedish soldiers, The rest of us in the front line, led by Brecca's two sons, fought with sword and spear."

"Where was Onela?" I interrupted.

"Onela? He led the second wave of Swedes — all on horseback." Wulfgar gave a wry smile. "That was his undoing, for the ice suddenly cracked and gave way; fissures spread rapidly and the ice tilted in great slabs, delivering him and his men to the icy waters that would be their grave."

I gasped, as did many in the hall.

"Our own men narrowly escaped the same fate, but we drew back in time." Wulfgar's eyes narrowed. "I saw Onela drown. I saw him clawing at the edge of the ice, being dragged under by the weight of his furs and armor. He and his army were swallowed up in the dark waters of death. The Swedes will bother us no more."

For a moment there was utter silence. Then shouts of triumph rang out. I could not join in the celebration that followed, for my thoughts flew to Aunt Ursula, whose husband would never return.

Chapter Twenty
Breath of the Dragon

Dragon head belt end mount of bronze gilt, found at Vendel, Uppland, Sweden, c. 600 A.D.

For the rest of the winter we folk in Hrethelskeep turned inward, gradually absorbing our losses and not looking too far into the future. New life arrived when Marta gave birth to a healthy baby girl, welcomed into the community by Magnus.

We had occasional contact with Eaglesgard when Aksel came to visit Estrid — always accompanied by Lars. Since surviving the recent battle, Lars had grown increasingly morose and withdrawn. It was Aksel who one day brought us news that two Swedes had shown up at Beowulf's court seeking sanctuary: Weohstan and his young son, Wiglaf.

"Weohstan?" I searched my memory. "Wasn't he the one who killed Prince Eanmund in the first battle on the ice?"

"The very one," said Aksel, wiping his lips. He was seated beside Estrid as we took our evening meal in my longhouse. "As you can imagine," he continued, "his life was in danger after Eadgils returned to power, and he also claims kinship with Beowulf through mutual ancestors in the Wægmunding tribe."

"Did Beowulf welcome him?" asked Estrid, smiling up at Aksel.

"He did, and he agreed to accept the son into fosterage."

"How old is the boy?" I inquired.

"Seven, I believe — the usual age." Aksel turned to look at Inga, slurping her soup. "Will you be sending your daughter to be fostered soon?"

"Inga?" I rose in agitation. "Never! I will not part with my child!"

"Beg pardon, my lady. I did not mean to upset you," said Aksel meekly. Into the silence that followed, Inga dropped her own question.

"Mother, when are we going to see Beowulf? I miss him!"

When I could find my voice, I answered, "I miss him too. In the spring we will consider a visit to Eaglesgard."

Smiles around the table — except from Ana — revealed this to be a welcome possibility.

"What's wrong, Ana? Don't you like the hospitality at Beowulf's court?"

Aksel was clearly teasing Ana, but she spoke matter-of-factly.

"It's cold. It's windy. To get there you have to ride a horse or be bundled in a sledge. We have all we need here at home!"

Everyone laughed at this succinct assessment — except Inga, whose face wore a pout.

"I still want to go, Mother."

So do I, child. So do I. Aloud I said, "Where is Lars? He is missing his meal."

Aksel waved a hand toward the door. "He may be with Wulfgar. Lars seems to have lost his appetite since — since Leif was slain." Aksel leaned forward and lowered his voice, as if inviting our confidence. "You know they were fighting side by side on the ice. Leif took a blow meant for Lars. Now Leif is dead and Lars can barely live with himself."

"Oh, I did not know," I exclaimed, then reflected. "We all lost dear ones in that battle." The laughing faces of Saxe and Gorm rose before me. "May we have peace now. No more killing!"

"By the gods, may it be so," murmured Ana. "No more killing."

Spring came early, as did a message from Beowulf repeating his invitation to come to Eaglesgard — permanently. I decided to hold an all-village meeting in the mead hall one chilly evening, to sort out the possible repercussions of such a move. I asked Magnus and Wulfgar to join me in front of the high seats. As I stood there surveying the faces before me, I saw men and women in work clothes and children wrapped in sleeping robes looking up at me expectantly, their eyes reflecting the light from the hearth fire. Our neighbors. My friends. It would be difficult to leave them.

In an earlier conversation with my immediate household, I'd learned that Ana, despite her loyalty to me and Inga, wanted to live out her days at Hrethelskeep.

"Forgive me, Freaw, but I'm tired," she'd said. "I don't have another move in me. After all the travelling we've done together and the changes we've endured, I just want to sit by the fire in this very place. I'm settled here now. Let me stay."

"Oh Ana, dear Ana. You have been a second mother to me!" I'd cried. "I owe you so much! If it is your wish to stay here, of course you may stay! I'll see that you are well looked after." And so it was agreed.

Ingeborg confided in me that Tove's son Marten had recently begun to court her, and she had a mind to encourage him; therefore she would stay with Ana if it came to our separation. Thorkel and Ragnhild wished to stay and continue their efforts to start a family. Estrid, of course, wanted to join Aksel at Eaglesgard. Wulfgar and Olaf declared they would abide my decision. As thralls, Brita and Runa had no decisive voice, but Brita made it clear she wanted to stay with Ana, while Runa was steadfast in wanting to follow me. Inga had already declared her preference: to live near Beowulf.

Now, larger issues must be addressed. Would Magnus continue as chief of the village? Who would preside in the mead hall? Who would lead the women in rituals to honor the goddess? In the mead hall we talked far into the night, as I made sure that each adult had a chance to be heard.

Magnus was of a mind to hand over leadership to Wulfgar, saying he had reached the end of his fighting days. With Gunilla gone, he was now the oldest member of the settlement, and looked every year of his age. Orm and Ortrud supported Wulfgar, as did all the landowners, so that matter was easily settled. I was pleased and relieved when Wulfgar accepted the role of chief, for it meant that Ana and Ingeborg would always have a person of influence to support them in the village.

To lead the women's rituals I proposed Thora, with help as needed from Ingeborg and Ortrud.

"Thora encouraged and guided me in re-establishing the practice when I first came to Hrethelskeep," I said. "It is fitting, I think, that she continue this work in my absence. She knows the rituals well, as do Ortrud and Ingeborg. They will provide strong leadership."

At these words, Thora graciously nodded her acceptance, and Ortrud rose to speak.

"Lady Freawaru, when you first arrived, I was suspicious; I had my doubts about you, but you've helped all the women here to grow stronger. You will be missed, but now we are well able to carry on without you. Thank you for what you've given us." She sat down abruptly.

After some further discussion we decided to leave open the question of mead hall hostess, allowing Wyrd to have its way. As I gathered a sleepy Inga in my arms to leave the hall, Tove's two daughters approached me respectfully. Without my noticing, Ginnlaug and Gyrid had grown from gangly girls into full-figured young women.

"Lady Freawaru," began Ginnlaug, "we've been thinking that you'll need more women to go with you to Eaglesgard. Why not take us?"

I looked doubtfully at their eager faces.

"We'll work hard, my lady, and obey your every command!" said Gyrid earnestly.

"Does your mother know of this?" I asked, searching for Tove's face in the departing throng. "Doesn't she need you at home?"

"She would be honored for us to serve you, my lady. She said so," declared Gyrid.

"Well... I will think about it." I spoke cautiously, not sure I was ready to assume responsibility for such spirited young women.

"Thank you!" they chorused, and ran off to find their mother.

Now Olaf came up to me and gently took the sleeping Inga from my arms.

"I'll carry her, Lady Freawaru. She's too heavy for you."

"Thank you, Olaf. And what will you do, now that Wulfgar has decided to stay in Hrethelskeep?"

He bit his lip as if to hold back tears. "I'll go with you, my lady. With Saxe and Gorm gone—better not to stay."

Dismayed, I put out a hand to touch his shoulder. "I miss them too, Olaf, but we must look forward, not back. Going to Eaglesgard will open a new life for all of us."

He nodded silently and we left the mead hall together.

A few days later I visited each family in the village to say goodbye, leaving a packet of herbs or a basket of apples at each house as a parting gift. At every door I was warmly welcomed and invited in for a sip of sour milk or a mug of ale. At Rolf and Thora's house I lingered longest. So much had been shared with this dear couple — and with Gunilla, whose absence I felt keenly.

"Thora, would you please look in on Ana occasionally?" I implored. "She'll be lonely with only Ingeborg and Brita for company." *As you are lonely now, dear friend, without Gunilla.*

"Of course, my lady. It would give me great pleasure." Her eyes were moist as she spoke.

"And Thora, at the rituals — remember Gunilla, remember to dance!"

She smiled. "Yes, my lady. Though the heart be heavy, our feet may dance."

We left Hrethelskeep on a fresh spring morning as birch leaf buds were just beginning to open. Beowulf had sent Lars and Aksel with thralls and carts to help us move our household goods, including my strongboxes, a loom, and one of our two cows. Runa had chosen Krona over Krusa, saying that Krona did not kick when milked.

It was a happy-sad leave-taking despite assurances that we would return frequently to visit. Solveig brought her son Toke to say goodbye to his playmate, and Thora appeared with a birch bark packet.

"For your journey," she whispered. "I will miss you."

"I'll miss you too, dear friend. This will be a time of adjustment for all of us."

We clasped hands, then embraced.

Olaf had invited Inga to ride behind him on his horse. She was delighted by this unexpected treat, as she had expected to ride in a cart with Ginnlaug and Gyrid. Estrid and Runa would ride beside Olaf and me. As we mounted, Ana's voice rang out in a blessing:

"May the gods go with you. May you journey safely."

While others turned their faces toward the sea, I took a long look back at what had been my home.

As we rode, I thought of our first landing in Geatland.

Once again we are starting over. When we arrived on Beowulf's shore, we were ten, eleven counting Brita. Now we are only three, five with Inga and Runa. A small band, but enough. Surely we will find friends in Eaglesgard.

Eaglesgard was indeed colder and windier than Hrethelskeep, but spring along the sea coast had its own special flavor: the taste of salt tang in the air. It made me think of ships and sailing. It awoke in me a longing to lift my wings and fly above the waves, soaring free of earthly cares.

"Spring frenzy," Ana called it, but she was no longer at my side to offer caution. In her place I now had Signe. Shortly after our arrival, I and my women had settled into her longhouse. She told us that no one felt comfortable staying in Hygd's former quarters, which had remained empty for the rest of the winter.

"Such a waste," signed Signe, shaking her head.

Unsure whether she referred to the loss of Hygd or to Hygd's house, I hesitated, then stated the idea forming in my head.

"The location, so close to the mead hall, would make it convenient for preparing feasts. Why not convert Hygd's house into a cook house? And perhaps use her bedchamber as a drying and storage room for herbs?"

Signe stared at me in surprise, then slowly nodded her head.

"A good idea, my lady. Perhaps enough time has passed to address the matter with Beowulf?"

"I'll find an early opportunity to speak to him about this sensitive topic," I said.

Speak to Beowulf I did, when he came to Signe's door to welcome me and my women. After a warm greeting he listened patiently to my idea.

"A separate cook house? It's time we had one! Already you bring new life and change to Eaglesgard!" He smiled. "As promised, there will be a new house built for you, Freaw, but I'll send Redbeard over so you can instruct him in any alterations you deem necessary to create a cook house." He smiled again. "Will you join me tonight in the mead hall?"

I returned his smile. "With pleasure, my lord, but right now I have work to do."

Beowulf chuckled and turned to go. "Women's work, eh? Never done!" Women's work indeed! Spring meant time for planting and cleaning and airing and an opportunity to wash our hair in the river. Spring also required a formal ritual to ensure fertility for crops, animals, and people. Much work lay before me, but I was full of anticipation and energy.

First I directed a thorough cleaning of Hygd's former house, which set off a flurry of activity throughout the settlement. Soon almost every rock and shrub in the vicinity was covered with clothes or bedding spread out to dry in the sun. Walls grimy with soot were scrubbed with lye water. Hearth pits were scrubbed with sand and new fires laid. When our houses were clean and well aired, we washed ourselves.

I led a troop of women and girls to the saunas. There we stripped and basked in the hot steam, then snatched up our clothes and rushed to the river, where we plunged into the icy water, gasping and shrieking. Swirling our tresses, we dived and floated, then rubbed soap in each other's hair, finally submerging ourselves to rinse. As my mother had once done for me, I washed Inga's hair before tending to my own. Gyrid and Ginnlaug splashed happily with the rest, having lost their shyness in the midst of so many women. Drying off and donning our clothes completed this celebration of spring.

Finding a time and place for the fertility ritual was a more difficult matter. Given the rocky terrain around Eaglesgard, garden plots and pastures were located some distance from the settlement, with forested areas even further away.

"Where do you usually hold your observances?" I inquired of Signe.

"We sometimes went to a meadow east of the settlement, but during Hygd's pregnancy we stopped."

"I see. Signe, is there an area nearby where no one goes?"

"There's the oath stone, but that's sacred to the men . . . ." Her voice trailed off as she seemed to consider. "There's also a place beyond the burial mounds, full of ancient stones. That place is seldom visited." Her eyes widened. "You don't think . . . ."

"I do think!" I exclaimed. "Could you take me there today?"

Walking with Signe among the standing stones, many of which towered over our heads, I marveled at their appearance of great age.

"These were here long before my time," observed Signe.

Weathered gray slabs, they stood like jagged teeth amidst a rocky meadow. Tiny blue and yellow wild flowers flourished at the base of several stones. A few bore faint runic inscriptions, but most were stark and bare.

Turning slowly in a circle, I breathed in the sea air and lifted my arms to the sun. "Signe," I cried. "This is a place of power! I feel it in every sinew, every bone! This would be a perfect place for our gathering! Here we will praise and give thanks to the goddess and invoke her blessing on Eaglesgard."

Later that spring, when light and darkness stood in balance, we held a sunrise ritual among the standing stones. There I learned the names of many women I had not previously met: Liv and Elsa were young mothers with babies at home; Lise and Lempi unmarried sisters living with their mother, Anki, and grandmother, Greta. There were others, but it would take time for me to learn all their names. Fortunately, now that we no longer had to fear the Swedes, a time of peace stretched before us — time for learning names, time for rituals, time for feasting and dancing, time for Beowulf and me.

Beowulf was steadfast in his determination to shield me from all harm — including harm from himself should we marry, for he was still haunted by the memory of Hygd's death in childbirth. He built a new longhouse for me and my household near the edge of the settlement; he and I lived in our separate abodes but saw each other daily. I sat beside him at the mead hall feasts, and presided there in his absence, but he made no move toward intimacy.

He is not yet ready, I told myself. I must wait for his lead.

When it became known in the surrounding countryside that I had taken up permanent residence in Eaglesgard, I once again received requests to visit and bring the gift of my special insights to outlying farmsteads and families. Following ancient custom, I sometimes rode in a wagon to make these visits, recalling the peace and plenty promised to those who worshipped Nerthus, the Earth Mother.

As news spread of the Swedes' defeat, more and more warriors flocked to Beowulf's court, eager to win fame under such a renowned leader. Beowulf was generous in rewarding his raiders with gold rings, and soon attracted many thanes to his standard. He was generous with his time as well, personally instructing young Wiglaf in the arts of battle. He also doted on Inga, refusing her nothing.

Over the years that followed, Inga grew to be a high-spirited, beautiful young woman, with hair that grew ever redder as mine faded toward gray. Young Wiglaf had caught her eye, and the two often walked together along the coastline of an evening, while light still glowed in the western sky.

Once Inga told me they'd seen a strange flash of light as darkness fell, not green or purple like north lights, but almost a flash of fire. This stirred old, unsettling memories, but I set them aside, content to enjoy the sweetness of this time of peace.

Estrid and Aksel were joined in marriage shortly after our return to Eaglesgard, and she soon gave birth to a baby boy. Back in Hrethelskeep, Ingeborg decided that Marten was not her best choice for a husband. Instead, she married Wulfgar, and now sat beside him in the high seats of the mead hall. Ana, despite her aches and complaints, had otherwise settled in to old age, allowing Thora's cheerful presence to lighten her days.

Lars continued his surly behavior, growing more bitter each year. One of his thralls, a Swedish captive taken in the second battle on the ice, became the butt of Lars' abuse. After one savage beating, this unfortunate man ran away from his brutish master. Slipping out of Eaglesgard on foot, he headed for the north downs, confident he could not be tracked over the barren rock.

There, when darkness fell, he sought refuge in an opening in the rock and stumbled upon an ancient cave filled with a foul reek, but heaped with wondrous treasures: jeweled swords, helmets, byrnies, filigreed standards, rings and collars and cups of gold that gave off their own light. Dazzled, he seized a gem-studded goblet and fled from the barrow, fearing its owner might soon return. Back he sped, back to Lars, bearing the cup to placate his master, and bearing doom for Eaglesgard.

We learned all this much later, after Beowulf and I had joined as one, after the devastation brought by the dragon.

It was a golden autumn afternoon when Beowulf came to the cook house and invited me to join him for a horseback ride. I was glad to slip away, leaving Signe in charge. We had been busy for days baking flat bread and brewing mead for use during the winter. I had not ridden Burningfax for almost a moon.

Before we set out, Signe prepared a bag of bread and cheese and a skinful of ale. "In case you get hungry," she said. "And take cloaks!"

"We'll be back before the evening meal," I assured her, "but I'll take this with thanks."

No vision warned me that these words were the last we would ever exchange.

"Where are we headed?" I asked as Beowulf helped me mount Burningfax.

"I want to show you a special place, unknown to most people here. I discovered it years ago when we were searching for Herdred."

"The north downs?" I asked. "I thought that was a dangerous place for horses — and their riders!"

"Freaw, you know I would not expose you to danger! Nay, we will skirt that area of caves and sinkholes, following the coastline to the north. Our destination is an ancient site — possibly a holy site — but you will see for yourself."

Mounting Frostmane, he touched his heels to the horse's side and we set out merrily, ready for adventure. There was no discernible trail as we rode past rocky promontories, through forest and meadow, taking our time as we enjoyed the day and each other's company. The sun was still high in the sky when Beowulf slowed Frostmane and gestured ahead.

I looked carefully, but saw only slabs of smoothly sloping rock, barely visible above the grassy meadow. I shook my head in puzzlement. "I see nothing unusual."

"Just wait. We'll stop here and tether the horses."

He helped me dismount, then tied our horses to one of several birches that shimmered in the afternoon light, their leaves like small gold coins. Taking my hand, he led me to the nearest rock and pointed down.

Gradually I made out shallow lines, figures and symbols scattered across the granite rock face: ships, men sailing ships, oxen, sun disks, more ships, men with plows, animals, men with giant penises, men and women clearly having sex.

"*Hällristningar* — rock pictures," said Beowulf, grinning. "I thought that you, of all people, could best reveal their meaning."

Wide-eyed I looked back and forth from Beowulf to the carvings.

"Beowulf, these must be very, very old — almost beyond human memory. What a treasure! It's as if our ancestors are speaking to us!"

"Look here," said Beowulf. "What do you make of these small depressions, hollowed out of the rock at regular intervals?"

I bent low to examine the rock, running my fingers lightly over the cup-shaped depressions, a thumb's width and depth. An image began to form in my mind, an image that made my cheeks flush. Slowly I rose, filled with the vision. I had seen this image before: a naked man and woman walking hand in hand toward these very rocks.

"Beowulf," I whispered, "we have been here before — but not in this lifetime. Priest and priestess, we coupled here to bring new life to our tribe." Shaken by this glimpse into the unknown, I trembled, barely able to breathe. "These cups were made to hold offerings to Freyr and Freyja; they were meant to hold ... male seed."

Silently we stared at each other. I could feel heat rising from my loins, spreading into every fiber of my being. I had waited so long ... I was suddenly aflame, burning with desire to give my body to this man. Reaching up, I slipped off my headcloth, undid the top knot and let my hair fall in waves to my waist. Beowulf stood transfixed.

"Freaw," he said thickly, his voice hoarse with emotion. "Freaw, you are the goddess. Command me. Be my guide — but do not ask me to plant my seed in those rocky cups!"

Beowulf threw back his head and laughed exultantly. When he opened his arms, I stepped into them. Pulling myself tight against him, I felt his hardness and knew his desire matched my own. I lifted my head and he pulled me up, pressing our mouths together. Our kiss was almost savage. And long.

Finally I struggled free to get a breath. As his embrace loosened, I could again touch the ground. His hands slid down my flanks and came to rest on my hips.

"I love you," he breathed, "and — may the gods forgive me — I want you! I have always wanted you, Freaw. My vow and my duty have denied us both, but now, together in this sacred place, I can no longer resist you or my passion for you. All I desire is to have you completely, now and always."

His face was suffused with tenderness, his eyes full of tears.

"Freaw, my love, be my guide."

Taking his big hands, I directed him in slowly disrobing me. After removing my cloak, I unfastened first one, then the other of my brooches and placed them in his hand. As he dropped them to one side, my apron fell to the ground. Gently Beowulf helped me pull my gown and shift over my head. Now I stood naked before him, bathed in the golden light of afternoon. I reached out to touch his belt buckle.

"Let me," he chuckled. Shrugging off his cloak, he spread it on the ground, then removed his belt and tunic; last of all, he let fall his trousers.

I gazed in awe at this god-like figure. Beowulf—my king, my love! I turned and lowered myself onto the cloak, still facing him.

"Come." I extended my hand.

Beowulf stepped forward and knelt beside me. I lay back, stretching out full length, and took his hand. "Lie with me."

He hesitated, then lowered himself beside me. Again I took his hand and placed it on my breast.

"Kiss me, my love."

Tenderly, his lips met mine. Then I guided his hand from my breast down to my loins. Despite the years of abstinence, my woman juices had begun to flow. *Freyja, thank you*! Now panting in anticipation, I cried out, "Beowulf, I am ready. Now!"

I closed my eyes in bliss as his body settled gently over me. Relaxing, I accepted him deep inside me.

When we woke, sated with love-making, the sun had slipped low over the distant sea. A light fog hung in the air, enfolding us in a magical blanket of fulfillment and serenity.

"Beowulf, it's late," I whispered with a shiver. "They'll be worried about us back at Eaglesgard."

Beowulf yawned and turned toward me. "It's not safe to travel in the dark. We'll have to spend the night here, and make our return early in the morning." He sat up. "I'm hungry. Did you bring any food?"

I laughed and pushed him away playfully. "Yes, thanks to Signe, I did."

"Freaw, you're shivering! I'll make a fire to keep you warm. We can sit side by side wrapped in our cloaks, and I will sprinkle golden leaves on your beautiful hair. We will feast and make love again—like those ancient kings and queens of the hällristningar!"

That night we ate and drank and laughed beside the fire—and made love again.

Beowulf and I woke with the sun on a clear, fresh morning. After refreshing ourselves from a nearby spring, we mounted our horses for the return to Eaglesgard. On the homeward journey we spoke little, but Beowulf frequently leaned over to stroke my hair. Both of us were filled with wonder and gratitude for what we had experienced.

As we came out of a forested area into an open meadow, I looked south to the horizon.

"Beowulf, look at that strange low cloud!"

"That's not a cloud, Freaw, that's smoke! And it's coming from Eaglesgard!" He kicked Frostmane into a gallop.

We rode as fast as we dared. My heart was pounding, filled with panic and dread.

What's happening? A raiding party? A Frisian attack? Is Inga safe? What will we find at Eaglesgard?

Even from a distance we could see that the mead hall was gone, so too the cook house. Only smoldering heaps marked the places where they had stood. Stunned, I took in the devastation. Heorot, all over again, but worse! This time my child, my Inga, might be among the victims! I leaned forward, searching anxiously for my longhouse. Had it been spared?

As we drew nearer I saw that Signe's house still stood, and those nearby looked intact, but others were reduced to blackened frames. The ground itself looked blasted by fire, and a stench of death hung over the settlement. As we rode in I saw bodies and carcasses lying on the ground, some burnt beyond recognition: dogs, horses ... people.

Smoke still rose from several houses and people with buckets could be seen trying to douse the embers. Weeping figures wandered among the buildings as if dazed by the carnage. As I jumped down from my horse, one soot-stained figure staggered toward me. It was Olaf. He blinked and rubbed his eyes.

"Freawaru? Is it you, my lady? Thank the gods! We feared you were dead — killed by the dragon on its way to Eaglesgard."

"A dragon? A dragon did this?" Beowulf was instantly at my side, seizing Olaf by the shoulders. "What happened!"

"Wait!" I cried. "First tell me: is Inga safe?"

Olaf nodded wearily. "Yes, my lady, she is safe. Houses on the edge of the village were spared when the dragon blazed its path." He turned to Beowulf. "You'll find your athelings meeting in council in Signe's house. They will be relieved to see you alive, and they can tell you what happened. Now excuse me. I've been sent to round up slaves and carts to remove the dead."

Olaf squared his shoulders and left to take up his gruesome task. Beowulf hurried toward Signe's house as I hurried toward mine. Halfway there I met Inga, Runa, Ginnlaug, and Estrid, all carrying buckets. When she saw me, Inga gave a glad cry and rushed forward to embrace me.

"Mother! Where have you been? I thought I'd never see you again!" She burst into tears and buried her face in my neck, sobbing like the little girl she had once been.

"Didn't Signe tell you?" I murmured tenderly, my arms around her. "I was with Beowulf. We spent the night together at a sacred site."

As I looked up, Runa came forward, then Ginnlaug, followed by Estrid with her little boy. Ginnlaug's face was ashen.

"Oh my lady, the dragon killed Signe — and Gyrid!" she wailed. "They were working late in the cook house when blasts of fire came down from the sky. They were burned alive!" She too burst into great sobs. "I'll never see my sister again!"

"Gyrid? Signe? Both lost to us?" I shuddered, releasing Inga to comfort Ginnlaug, even though she had long since grown to womanhood.

"Surely the gods are against us,' wailed Estrid, "sending this scourge to destroy us!"

Suddenly all the night sightings, all the intimations I'd been given in the past flooded over me.

"I should have foreseen this!" I cried. "I should have warned the settlement! I am to blame..."

"Stop, my lady!" It was Runa's voice. She had stood silently during our outbursts of emotion, but now stepped forward.

"You are not to blame for this catastrophe. Even now the athelings are questioning the culprit — one of Lars' slaves. I saw him being marched into the council chamber with a rope around his neck!"

We gawked at Runa in astonishment.

"If that is the case, we will soon hear of it from Beowulf," I said.

We did. Later that evening, after all the fires had been quenched, Beowulf called a meeting of survivors, outside Signe's longhouse. Most of the village had escaped the dragon's wrath. Only a few unlucky ones had been blasted with its fiery breath — including Ketil and several young thanes who'd been drinking late into the night inside the mead hall. Even so, each death was a death to be mourned — and avenged.

Lars forced the Swedish slave to repeat his story of running away, finding the cave and stealing the gold cup. Beowulf listened attentively, then decreed that the thief himself must lead the way to the dragon's lair.

"There I will fight the beast," declared Beowulf, who then looked around the gathering. "Oskar, are you here? I'll need a new shield — one made entirely of iron. Linden wood will not hold against a dragon's breath."

Oskar rose. "I'm here, my lord. I'll begin work immediately."

"Very good." Beowulf looked again around the assembly. "I will choose a company of champions, eleven in all, to join me in the fight. Eleven warriors most eager for glory." He paused to let his words sink in. "As soon as the shield is ready, we will set out."

When the meeting was over, I approached Beowulf.

"My lord, let me help you. Let me see the dragon."

"See the dragon? What do you mean, Freaw?"

"I believe that if I can hold the goblet stolen from the dragon's hoard, I may be able to envision the dragon itself. Then you would know what sort of monster you will face."

Beowulf's eyes widened. "That would be a great help, Freaw, but if you do this, is there a risk for you?"

"Not more than I'm willing to take — for you. Will you arrange to get the goblet?"

"Yes, I will." He smiled.

Suddenly shy, I asked another question. "Will you join me tonight, my lord?"

He smiled again, but ruefully. "I no longer have a roof to offer you, Freaw, and I would not ask you to sleep again on the bare ground!"

"To sleep in your arms is all I ask," I responded, "and I have a plan. My women will sleep in Signe's house so that you and I may be alone in mine — in a bed. Will you come?"

He hesitated only briefly. "Yes, I will come."

That night watch guards were posted around the settlement and every household prepared many buckets of water in case of another attack, but no dragon disturbed our rest. Each night that followed brought dread and foreboding, but still the beast did not return. I was reminded of the long nights at Heorot waiting for the Grendel monster to attack. Were we to face such a time again?

Oskar labored night and day to produce the shield Beowulf needed. The young thanes argued and boasted among themselves, each sure that he would be chosen as one of the lucky eleven. Beowulf sent scouts to survey the damage in the countryside. Their report was grim: fields burned and farmsteads blasted, with great loss of lives and livestock. The dragon had scorched a path of destruction all along the coastline. Fortunately, due to its inland location, Hrethelskeep had been spared.

Reeling with shock and grief myself, I strove to be strong for Beowulf, who took the attack even harder. He spent the daylight hours with his athelings and thanes, salvaging what could be used from storehouses and stockpiles, sending Aksel to supervise slaves in the clean up, comforting survivors as best he could. By nightfall he looked exhausted. Still, he joined his men in Signe's house — now the designated mead hall by day — for a flagon of ale before retiring to my side.

Our passion for each other had not abated, but our love-making was now overlain with a blanket of sorrow — and, in Beowulf's case, remorse.

"Was this a punishment for breaking my vow?" he muttered one evening. "Yet Odin has his Frigga; may I not have you?"

In our private moments he revealed other misgivings as well.

"Freaw, I feel no fear, but my heart is heavy. I am still not too old to wield a sword, and Nagling has never failed me, but I sense . . . I sense that death may be near. Like Hygelac, I wish to die in battle, as a warrior." Reaching over to stroke my cheek, he murmured, "Freaw, you mean more to me than I have words to express. I would be loath to leave you, but my duty is clear."

I tried to dispel his gloomy thoughts with the warmth of my love, but I too feared for Beowulf's life, especially when I learned that he was determined to attack the dragon alone, keeping his champions in reserve. When I protested his plan, he fixed me with a reproachful gaze.

"Freaw, it is my fault that the dragon's attack took so many lives and caused so much destruction. If we had not gone off together, I would have been here to defend my hall and my people. As king of the Geats it is my responsibility to pursue this fight alone."

To this argument I had no reply, but I could at least assist Beowulf by trying to envision the dragon. Lars grudgingly relinquished the golden cup, and I instructed Inga and Runa in how to help me enter a trance state. We chose a time at mid-morning, among the standing stones. While Inga beat a steady rhythm on my drum and Runa played a soft, dream-like melody on her bone flute, I revolved slowly in a circle, holding the cup in both hands.

"Freyja, great goddess, come to me now. Enfold me in your cloak of feathers, fly me to the dragon's lair. Protect me as I view the beast, and bring me safely back. I will honor you and praise you all my days, dear Freyja."

As the sun beat down upon my head I began to perspire, sweat beading on my forehead. The cup grew heavy and hot in my hands. Steam... steam rose around me. Then, I saw it: a great coiled snake-like dragon coated with enameled scales, lying atop its treasure hoard. Its jaws opened wide, revealing sharp fangs, but as it writhed and convulsed I thought I saw a whiteness on the under belly.

Its eyes gleamed yellow as the huge head moved back and forth, back and forth, counting and recounting, searching for the missing cup. Suddenly its eyes fixed upon me; flame gushed forth from the creature's throat. The cup in my hands grew hotter, hot as a burning brand. With a shriek I dropped the cup, then fell, landing on the dry grass at Inga's feet. The flute faltered, the drumming stopped.

"Mother! Are you all right?" cried Inga in alarm.

"Patience. Give her time; she must recover," I heard Runa say.

As the vision faded I sat up, drenched with sweat.

"Oh Mother, your hands!" cried Inga. "Are they burned?"

I held them up and examined them as if they belonged to someone else. "No, Freyja has preserved me." I paused. "I have seen the dragon! I must tell Beowulf."

That night in our bedchamber I told Beowulf all that I had seen.

Wiglaf, now a grown man, was among the warriors chosen to accompany Beowulf. He was chosen last after he begged Beowulf for a chance to use the weapons bequeathed to him by his father, Weohstan. His selection completed the eleven, all young warriors eager to prove themselves in an heroic battle.

Finally — or all too soon — the new shield was ready: tall as a man and made of solid iron. Only Beowulf himself could lift it. On the fateful morning I helped Beowulf array himself in mail shirt and helmet, but I was not prepared for what happened next. Opening a small wooden chest, Beowulf took out a great gold collar which he clasped around his neck. I gasped.

"Isn't that Hygd's collar? The one that Hygelac..."

"Yes," said Beowulf grimly. "The one Hygelac wore when he was killed in Frisia. I wear it today in his honor, for it may be that we will meet again... soon."

I blanched at the implication.

"Beowulf, although your beard is gray, you are still far stronger than any other man! Go forth with a stout heart, my love. You have been a good king to your people, and they — we — I — would be loath to lose you."

Beowulf nodded somberly.

"Freaw, it is no boast for me to say that I have never known fear. I am older now, but I will fight again to defend my people and for the glory of winning. I would use no weapon if — like the Grendel — the beast could be killed with my bare hands. I will carry sword and shield to stand against its shooting flames. My heart is firm, Freaw, my hands calm. Wyrd will decide the outcome."

Giving me a final embrace and a long, tender kiss, Beowulf released me.

"Goodbye, Freaw, my love."

"Goodbye, Beowulf, my dearest. May the gods be with you."

I tried to speak cheerfully, but fear clutched at my heart. As Beowulf walked down the path I wanted to run after him, to fling my arms around him and beg him to stay, but I stood fixed, rooted to the spot.

Courage, Freaw, you must show courage. You cannot stop him. Be worthy of his love and trust.

All of Beowulf's warriors had assembled to accompany him on the trek to the dragon's lair. Lars and the unlucky servant led the way: the thrall on foot with a rope around his neck, preceding Lars on horseback. Beowulf and the chosen eleven followed close behind. As I watched them depart, I prayed fervently: *May the gods protect you, Beowulf! May they bring back all alive!*

Returning immediately to my bedchamber, I pulled out my rune bag and tried to compose myself.

"Odin, Freyja, hear me, be with me. Guide my hand to reveal Beowulf's fate."

Drawing a deep breath and closing my eyes, I reached into the bag. My trembling fingers fastened on a rune, which I drew forth and laid on the pillow where Beowulf's scent still lingered. Slowly opening my eyes, I looked down to see... Thurisaz. I stiffened. Oh, no... Thurisaz is a troublesome rune, generally regarded as unpleasant in nature, and with many possible meanings. I considered.

It could be seen as a thorn—something sharp and evil to touch—like the dragon's tooth? Runa called it a troll rune and associated it with giants, but I remembered Unferth's teaching that Thurisaz could indicate a gateway between worlds. Could those worlds be... life... and death? My heart froze. Returning the rune to its pouch, I rose to leave my chamber.

That morning, to still my fears, I joined the other women in harvesting what was left of our ravaged herb garden. Now and again I stopped to raise my head and listen. Was that a cry? A shout? A roar? Faint sounds rose above the distant murmur of the sea. Each fired my imagination.

Have they found the cave? Has the dragon attacked? Is Beowulf battling alone? Have his chosen champions joined the fray?

It was almost midday when a lone horse and rider galloped into Eaglesgard. It was Aksel, with the news I'd been dreading.

"Lady Freawaru!" he cried out, "Lord Beowulf has been wounded! He may be dying! Come quickly if you wish to see him yet alive!"

Dropping my basket, I grabbed the hand he extended and swung up behind him. As I clasped his waist, Aksel gave spur to his horse, shouting, "Hold on!"

The ride seemed interminable, an endless nightmare of agony and suspense. I tried to question Aksel, but he had few details to give me.

"We were watching from a distance, my lady, on a ridge where Beowulf had bidden us stop and await the outcome. Led by the thrall at spear-point, he and his champions strode on to the cliff's edge. There they stopped and Beowulf seemed to disappear. We saw rising steam, then flashes of fire. We also saw Beowulf's men turn and run for their lives toward a nearby wood—all except one, who also dropped out of sight below the cliff edge."

Aksel turned briefly to glance back at me.

"My lady, it was Wiglaf who reappeared, shouting at the cowards who had fled. I caught the words 'wounded' and 'poison.' That's when I took horse to come for you."

"Thank you, Aksel. Well done. I pray we are not too late!"

As we thundered along the clifftop, I invoked every god and goddess I knew: Let him live! Let him live!

When we reached the site where the greater part of Beowulf's men were gathered, we quickly dismounted. They parted to let us through, their faces grave. Aksel and I scrambled down a rocky slope to reach the ledge below. There on the ground I saw Wiglaf bending over Beowulf. Around Wiglaf's neck gleamed a golden collar — Beowulf's collar. I gasped. This could only mean ...

"No!... No!... No!..." Bent double, I sank to my knees.

Beowulf. Beowulf is dead.

Chapter Twenty-One
Facing the Future

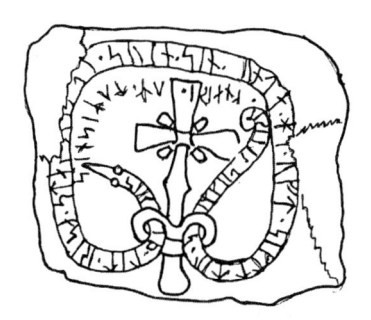

Mervalla stone in Södermanland, Sweden, commemorating a fallen warrior.

When at last I opened my eyes they would not focus, but I realized that Aksel was kneeling beside me.

"What . . . ?" I whispered. Then it all rushed back to me. Starting up wildly, I headed for Beowulf's body, but Aksel restrained me.

"Wait, please, my lady. Take a moment longer to recover."

I rose with Aksel's help and stood trembling beside him as I took in my surroundings: Beowulf's body lying on the ground, with gold and jewels heaped beside it, Wiglaf standing above him holding his helmet, and several athelings approaching. Beyond them I saw the yawning arch of a massive stone barrow. In its mouth lay great scaly coils and loops, the corpse of the fire-dragon. Blackened and scorched with many colors, the creature was clearly dead, bathed in its own hot blood.

As if from a distance I heard Wiglaf speaking.

"Often, when one man follows his own will, many are hurt. We all tried to stop him, but Beowulf would not listen; he would not consent to let the dragon lie unchallenged. Now its treasure hoard will be laid bare, but at a grave cost, a cruel fate for our king and our people."

Wiglaf paused and shook his head solemnly.

"While Beowulf still lived, he bade me gather up treasure to show him what he had won for his people, and so I did. Then Beowulf gave me his own gold collar, declaring that I should rule the Geats after him, as the last of our tribe. He also asked that we build a mound over his funeral pyre as a memorial, high enough to be seen as a landmark from the sea.

"For now," he concluded, looking sorrowfully down at Beowulf's body, "let us attend to him and then bring wagons to transport the treasure from the dragon's cave."

At Wiglaf's direction four of the stoutest athelings lifted Beowulf's body onto his shield and used it as a bier to carry him. Others stretched out the dragon to measure its full length — as long as ten men — before rolling it over the cliff edge, into the sea. I watched all this in numb disbelief.

This cannot be happening. This is not real. Beowulf cannot be dead!

Gently Aksel helped me climb back up the slope to level ground, where the ten so-called 'champions' stood huddled in a group, hanging their heads, eyes averted, steeped in their shame.

Ah, so young, all of them. They must have been utterly terrified to desert their lord as they did. Perhaps they could not have saved Beowulf any more than an earlier band of Beowulf's men could have withstood the Grendel monster.

Wiglaf sent Lars back to Eaglesgard to report Beowulf's death. He sent other athelings to seek out the major landowners and direct them to gather wood; a large quantity would be needed for Beowulf's funeral pyre. Then Wiglaf took seven thanes with him into the dragon's treasure hoard, returning with armfuls of booty — how dearly won! When they came near me, I put out a hand.

"Wiglaf? Let me touch that armor you carry."

Startled, he paused, but held out a rust-encrusted helmet. When my fingers touched it, I winced and drew back, appalled.

"What is it? What do you feel?" he asked, frowning.

"Someone . . . buried this hoard of treasure long before the dragon found it," I began slowly, ". . . the last survivors of an ancient race. To keep it safe, they've laid a curse upon it: whoever tries to take it will meet an evil end."

The thanes looked uneasily at each other. "Cursed?" said one. "Cursed indeed, for it has brought about the death of Beowulf, our king."

In the time that followed, willing hands appeared from every direction, each person eager to help and to honor their beloved king. By nightfall Inga and Runa had arrived on horseback, bringing a cart with food and provisions for several days. From the stores they brought I prepared an herbal wash to bathe Beowulf's body, mixing rosemary, lavender, and lemon thyme. Runa helped me strip his body, then respectfully moved away, leaving me alone with him.

Beowulf's hair and beard were badly singed by the dragon's fire. Taking out my knife, I cut off a lock of hair near the back of his head and slipped it into the pouch at my waist. In exchange I severed a curl from my own hair and folded it inside his palm.

Oh my love, my dearest—how cruel to have lost you so soon! Yet you died as you wanted: in battle, a warrior to the end.

Beowulf's swollen, purple face was almost unrecognizable. Not wanting to burn this image into my memory, I closed my eyes and pictured him as I'd first seen him at Heorot, years ago: a tall, handsome warrior with steely blue-gray eyes and a slow, questioning smile.

Two deep puncture marks on the side of his neck showed where the dragon had struck. His body was otherwise unmarked. As my hands moved gently over his once-powerful frame, I was almost blinded by my own tears.

When I finished bathing Beowulf's body, I draped him in a scarlet cloak brought out from Eaglesgard by Redbeard. Although far older than Beowulf, Redbeard still appeared hale and hearty.

"Oh my lady," he exclaimed, "that I should live to see my lord die before me!" Tears were flowing freely from his rheumy eyes. "We will never see his like again, my lady—never!"

Unable to speak, I bowed my head but took Redbeard's hand and squeezed it tightly.

Beowulf's funeral pyre was built in two days time, built solidly, foursquare and tall. His men hung it with helmets, heavy war-shields, and shining armor. Inside it they heaped gold and silver and precious jewels taken from the dragon's cave. Together they carried Beowulf's body to the pyre and placed it high in the center of the frame.

All of Eaglesgard trekked to the site to honor and bid farewell to their king, and to see the greatest of all funeral fires kindled on the height. As smoke rose, the fire roared, almost loud enough to drown out our weeping. Unable to contain my sorrow any longer, I lifted my voice in a keening wail, pouring out my grief and fear.

So many deaths, so many losses ... one upon another: faces came to me in a crescendo of pain: my dear nurse, Willa, and my old friend, Aeschere; Ingeld; Father, both of my brothers; Herdred and Hygd and her child; Saxe and Gorm; now ... my Beowulf. Caught up in a spasm of grief verging on madness, I foresaw sorrows to come: wars, slaughter, and captivity — a wild litany of nightmares. When I could cry out no longer, Inga, herself stricken with grief, helped Runa lead me away.

By nightfall Beowulf's body had been consumed, his bone-house burned to the core in the intense heat. A dark sky swallowed the billowing smoke as Beowulf flew to glory, flew to join Hygelac, feasting in Valhalla. Staggering between Inga and Runa, I headed back to our home — a home without Beowulf.

The next day the Geats began to build the monument Beowulf had requested. For ten long days they worked, sealing his ashes inside walls as straight and tall as willing hands could make them. With Beowulf's ashes they buried the rest of the treasure trove: torques and jewels and armor, returning to the earth that fatal treasure, declaring it as useless to men now as it had ever been. The Geats called his final tomb Beowulf's Barrow, a mound on the headland towering high enough for sailors to see from afar.

During the mound-building, Wiglaf came often to my longhouse. He came to see Inga and, at my invitation, to tell me more about Beowulf's death. Despite the pain I knew it would cause me, I wanted to know every detail of the encounter which had robbed me of my beloved. Wiglaf and I sat beside my hearth, accompanied by Inga, Ginnlaug, and Runa, who kept Wiglaf supplied with bread and ale. When he was ready to speak, we fell silent.

"Beowulf was fearless, my lady. He strode right up to the entrance to the dragon's barrow and shouted a challenge! We watchers heard a rumble from underground, then saw the creature glide forth, looping and unleashing itself, swathed in hot battle-fumes."

Inga shivered beside me and clutched my hand.

"Beowulf raised his sword and struck at the dragon's scaly hide, but could scarcely cut it. The dragon reared in anger, spewing billows of battle-fire. It was then that my comrades fled for their lives, running for the trees. I tried to stop them with commands and taunts, repeating their

Fanning the Flames

previous boasts and promises, but to no avail. I could not bear to see my lord so alone and beset — so I rushed to join him."

Wiglaf glanced down at his burned hand.

"My wooden shield was set aflame; I dropped it and sought shelter behind Beowulf's shield of iron. Beowulf raised his sword a second time, but the force of his blow shattered the blade, leaving Beowulf exposed to the dragon's wrath. The beast reared back, then rushed at Beowulf and drove its long, sharp fangs into Beowulf's neck. As my king and kinsman staggered back, bleeding, my own sword sought a place lower down in the dragon's belly. I must have punctured its gas sack, for the flames began to weaken."

Wiglaf wiped sweat from his forehead, caught up in the grip of his telling.

"Then Beowulf drew the knife at his belt and stabbed the dragon, cutting it through, slitting it completely apart, killing the beast at last. But as the dragon fell, so too did Beowulf. His neck wound began to scald and swell as the dragon's poison spread through his body."

Wiglaf paused to wipe his face again.

"Beowulf struggled to reach the rampart, where he sank down. I unbuckled his helmet and tried to clean the wound as best I could, while Beowulf recalled his many years as king of the Geats. Then he asked me to bring treasure from the barrow that he might see it before he died."

Wiglaf stopped speaking, choked with emotion. When he had recovered, he picked up the thread of his story.

"I hurried as fast as I could, returning to Beowulf with all I could carry: plates, flagons, a gold standard . . . Beowulf was bleeding badly and I tried again to swab his wound, but he stopped me. Removing his great gold collar, he handed it to me, asking me to take it, as well as his war shirt and gilded helmet, telling me that I must lead the Geats after his death."

I had been holding back my questions for much of Wiglaf's recital, but now I had to ask, "What were Beowulf's last words?"

Wiglaf frowned. "As I remember, he said 'Fate has swept our race away, taken warriors in their prime and led them to the death that was waiting. Now I must follow them.'"

Wiglaf bowed his head.

"Did he . . . did Beowulf speak of me?" I asked softly in the silence.

Wiglaf raised his eyes. "No, my lady, but . . . earlier at the forge I noticed something unusual on the inside of Beowulf's shield: the outline of a feather. I heard Beowulf tell Oskar that it was for you."

My eyes filled with tears. If only I *had* been able to shield him from the dragon's wrath.

On the day Beowulf's Barrow was completed, twelve champions — true champions this time, chieftains' sons, battle-hardened — rode slowly around the tomb chanting, mourning Beowulf's loss as a man and a king, giving thanks for his greatness, extolling his heroic deeds and virtues. As Olaf reported it to me — for I was too heartsick to attend — the Geats praised Beowulf, calling him "best of all the kings, kindest to his people, keenest to win fame, and most deserving of praise."

Such words gladdened my heart, but could not fill the emptiness there. In the days that followed I sank deeper into darkness, raising concern among my household.

"Mother, you must eat," insisted Inga, offering me a bowl of something she'd just prepared. When I pushed it away, she flared up.

"You are not the only one who loved Beowulf!" she blazed. "What would he think if he could see you wallowing like this?"

"He would understand," I groaned, then curled back into myself. Like a wound that would not heal, the loss of Beowulf had made me sick with grief.

The older women I had once looked to for comfort and guidance were all gone or far away: Signe was dead, Ana in her dotage, Mother . . . Mother . . . might she still be alive? Mother . . . alive. The possibility began to take hold of me, awakening a flicker of hope in my dark night.

Among the men there was much talk about defense and security. With Beowulf gone, they feared that old enemies might renew their attacks — particularly the Franks and Frisians. Some even worried that the ancient feud between Geats and Swedes would start up again. Wiglaf himself voiced such a concern, for his own father had killed the brother of Eadgils, the ruling Swedish king.

We had heard rumors over the years that Eadgils had become involved with sorcery, using dark magic to destroy any opposition. Beowulf, while he lived, had been our buffer, our defense. Now Beowulf was dead. What might news of his death set in motion? With winter approaching, there was less likelihood of any imminent attack, but the possibility remained.

Of more immediate concern was the question of leadership. Wiglaf, with the full consent of the council, was declared king of the Geats. He lost no time taking charge. Construction began immediately on a new mead hall for Eaglesgard. In advance of winter, Wiglaf supervised an inventory of remaining livestock and food supplies — much reduced by the dragon's attack. He doubled the number of thralls sent to fish to build up our supply of dried cod.

We would not starve, but clearly we must be frugal with what we had. One day as Runa and I were making cheese — for I had gradually begun to take part in daily tasks — she spoke of her childhood days.

"I remember one bad year when the harvest failed. That winter we ate dried peas mixed with ground birch bark — normally fodder fed to cows!"

"Ugh!" I said. "How could you swallow it?"

"As you know, my lady, desperate times require desperate measures." She gave me a piercing look.

"What do you mean?" I asked, giving an extra squeeze to the bag of curds I held.

"Have you given thought to *our* future here, my lady? There are others beyond our household who are left adrift in a world without Beowulf."

"Of whom do you speak?"

"I'm speaking of those ten young men who fled from the dragon. Wiglaf has denounced them as cowards, branded them with disgrace. They've become outcasts."

She spoke with such vehemence I was taken aback.

"Why, Runa, do you mean they deserve pity? They had no pity for Beowulf in his time of need!"

"No, my lady, but I think they deserve another chance. Right now they are miserable and desperate, with no place to go and no one to turn to. You told me that long ago you were chosen to be a peace-weaver, to bring peace between tribes. Your skills could be put to good use here in Eaglesgard — helping these men be accepted again in the community."

I was silent, pondering her words.

Later that day when he came to visit Inga, I sounded Wiglaf on the issue, taking him aside momentarily into my chamber.

"What will become of the ten young thanes who failed Beowulf?" I asked.

Wiglaf frowned. "They must leave Eaglesgard. I've told them they can stay through the winter, but they must be gone come spring." He looked at me suspiciously. "Why do you ask?"

"Oh, I've been wondering why Beowulf chose to honor them in the first place. Perhaps they have more backbone than they've shown thus far? Beowulf was a good judge of a man's mettle. He chose you, for example, to succeed him."

Wiglaf stared at me. "What are you saying, my lady?"

"I'm saying they might yet prove to be valiant warriors — if given another chance."

"Hmmph! Perhaps, but I would not trust my life to any one of them!" Wiglaf snorted, then looked embarrassed. "Beg pardon, my lady, if I seem to dismiss your words, but you'd best leave men's business to men."

He bowed stiffly and left the chamber.

That winter I made it my business to learn more about each of the ten thanes. Half of them had grown up in Eaglesgard and lived with their families, but the others had come to Beowulf's court from other lands. Vigo and Tor were northmen, members of the Bronding tribe; Bram was a Wylfing, from a tribe south of the Baltic; Knud was a Dane, though not from Heorot, and Alf called himself an Angle.

Runa was a good source of information, as she frequently mingled with other servants listening to their gossip. She told me that the five local men — Sigrod, Gunnulf, Eskil, Grim and Anton — were being shunned by their families, given food and sleeping space but nothing more. Not one of the ten dared to show his face in the newly-completed mead hall.

Among the older thanes and athelings, only Olaf and Redbeard showed any sympathy for the plight of those disgraced. Olaf confided to me that many young men experienced fear before battle, but were swept up with the rest when a charge carried them forward. I thought of berserkers, who worked themselves into a frenzy before battle in order to fight without fear.

Redbeard had helped train many of the young men, and knew they had the skills to be successful — if they could summon the courage.

"If Eaglesgard is attacked this winter, my lady, those lads may yet have a chance to prove themselves," he muttered to me over a cup of ale.

I shivered at the possibility. There must be a better way.

Fanning the Flames

That year's Yule was celebrated with more good cheer than I could have expected. The cook house had not been replaced, but our new mead hall stood tall and well-timbered, larger than the old one and with a bigger hearth. On that hearth the Yule log lay smoldering, a sturdy length of oak; above it a thrall turned the spit on a fat roasting pig.

Despite our loss of Beowulf, there were reasons for celebration. There had been no attacks from any quarter, our food supplies were holding out well, and a vision of hope had come to me. It started with a rune reading.

On the night of the solstice, that longest and darkest of all nights, I decided to draw a single rune to foretell my fate in the coming year. After dressing for the evening's feast in my best gown and kirtle, I lingered in my chamber. Pulling out my rune bag, I breathed a prayer to Odin and Freyja, then let my fingers find the messenger. The rune was Raido — rune of journeys and reunions. It set me thinking.

That night when I entered the mead hall, I searched for Olaf and beckoned him to join me. He had been talking and laughing with the serving girls, but came instantly to my side.

"Let's sit down here in the back for moment, Olaf. I have something to ask you."

"Gladly, my lady."

Olaf seated himself beside me at an empty table and looked at me expectantly.

"Olaf, is our old cargo ship, the one we sailed to Geatland, still seaworthy?"

His eyes widened. "Why, yes, my lady. It's taken out occasionally on trading trips. Do you wish to use it?"

"Perhaps. I do not yet know the answer to that question, but here is another one: if I did undertake a sea journey, would you be willing to captain my ship?"

Olaf's eyes lighted and his face glowed. "It would be an honor, my lady, a great honor!"

I lifted a finger to my lips. "Do not speak of this to anyone, Olaf. I have much to consider before making a decision."

Olaf's face took on a quizzical expression. "And now may I ask you a question, my lady?"

"Of course you may! What is it?"

Olaf did not answer immediately.

"My lady, you are always first in my heart, but there is a woman I have grown to love over the years. I would ask her to marry me, but... there is a problem."

"Why, Olaf, that's wonderful—your love, I mean. What is the problem you speak of?"

He cleared his throat and spoke in a formal tone. "In the eyes of the court she is a thrall, but you and I both know her to be a woman of beauty and wisdom."

My mouth almost fell open.

"You can't mean... Runa?"

Olaf beamed and nodded.

"I do mean Runa. Were she a free woman, we would be free to marry."

"I see." Dumbfounded, I let Olaf's proposal sink in—for clearly he was making a proposal, asking me to give Runa her freedom.

"Olaf, I will... I will consider it."

"Thank you, my lady. That is all I ask."

He rose and did something he had never done before: he kissed my hand.

Later that night in my bedchamber, I pulled from my chests every object that had once been touched by my mother: my ironing whaleboard, the silver armbands she'd given me on my coming-of-age, embroidered apron trims, a woven tapestry....

Spreading them out on my bed, I ran my hands slowly over each, summoning up my mother's gentle touch. Next I crumbled dried lavender—mother's favorite herb—into a bowl and set it alight. As its sweetness filled the chamber, I closed my eyes and pictured myself with Mother in the herb garden, working side by side.

As I turned toward her, her face began to change, aging before my eyes, and her hair turned snowy-white, but her eyes—the same brown eyes I'd loved as a child—smiled back at me.

"Mother! I feel your presence! Do you live? Your Freaw calls to you!"

In agitation I rose, reaching out my arms, but the vision faded and disappeared.

Shortly after Yule, Inga came to me with a proposal of her own. Runa and Ginnlaug had gone out together to bring water from the well, bundled against the cold of midwinter. I was sitting by the hearth staring into the fire, my hands idle, when Inga left her work at the loom and approached me. She put both hands on my shoulders and cleared her throat.

"Mother, it is time you knew. Wiglaf and I wish to marry."

I had known this was coming. Wiglaf's intentions were clear, but I was less sure of my daughter's feelings. She had seemed to welcome Wiglaf's attentions, but showed little open affection for him.

"Inga, my dearest, come sit beside me."

She joined me on the worn wooden bench, stretching her fingers out to the fire.

"Do you love this man, my daughter?" I asked anxiously.

She stared into the fire as if looking for familiar faces.

"He can make me a queen, Mother, queen of the Geats. Wouldn't you like that?" She did not turn her head.

"Yes, but it does not answer my question. Do you love him?"

Now Inga gave me what could only be seen as a pitying glance.

"I love him enough, Mother. I do not want to be consumed with an emotion that brings such pain as you have known with Beowulf."

Aghast, I stared at this fierce young woman, the child of my womb. What had happened to my little girl?

"Inga! How can you speak so?"

She grimaced. "Loving too much brings misery. As I said before, I love Wiglaf... enough. We would marry in the spring. May we have your blessing, Mother?"

I hesitated, shaken by the judgment she had pronounced on me and Beowulf.

"Not worth the pain? Of course it was worth the pain! I do not regret a single moment I spent with Beowulf!"

Inga was silent: then she prompted me. "Well...?"

I stood up. "If you are determined to marry, I will support your decision — but I may not be here in the spring."

"What?!" Now it was Inga's turn to rise in agitation. "What do you mean? You're not ill, are you? Tell me..."

"Be at peace, my daughter. I am not ill, but I anticipate a journey — to seek my mother Wealtheow."

The words of my old rune-master came back to me: "Freawaru, you will live long and visit many lands."

"Yes, Inga, a journey — to distant lands. I have decided!"